In A

Mirror

Praise for In A Mirror

"Brittany and Charli are twins, but they are first and foremost human beings with real issues and problems, and they handle them differently. I love that!" Becca C. Smith, *Author of The Riser Saga.*

"When they laugh, I laugh. When their hearts hurt, my heart hurt. Their story kept me on edge, and I just had to keep reading until I reached the end." Jasmine, *Goodreads Reviewer*

"The best way to describe this book, is like looking into a mirror, and watching it SMASH everywhere and having to pick up the pieces in an emotional rollercoaster." Lauren, *Goodreads Reviewer*

"This book sucked me in from the beginning... The struggles they deal with, both in school and out, from cliques to dysfunctional parents, to dating... Bourne treats these with seriousness and complexity." Diane, *Amazon Reviewer.*

"Brittany and Charli may be fictional characters, but they are two halves of my being. They are funny, sweet, awkward, loving and appropriately aggressive, and their story makes me cry upon every reread!" Dahlia Burroughs, *Newspeak Press*

"This is a bang-on representation of high school... reading a coming of age story which depicts the pros and cons of both sides of high school life." Joel, *Goodreads Reviewer*

Secrets. Rumours. Lies.

In A Mirror

EMILY BOURNE

First Published by Halo & Claws Publishing 2019

IN A MIRROR

For information contact: https://www.emilybourne.net

Stock Images via Bigstock, Shutterstock
Copy Editor: Dahlia Burroughs, Newspeak Press

ISBN: 978-1-925990-01-0 (Paperback)
ISBN: 978-1-925990-00-3 (Ebook)

For my parents, who are thankfully nothing like Rob and Julie Matthews. Thanks for believing in me and creating a safe and loving home.

1

My sneakers squeak against the shiny oak floor. Sweat beads at my hairline. My breaths are quick. I tap out the beats and hit my next cue. My shoulders relax and I dip on bent knees.

My feet fan back and forth as I shuffle to the right. I grin and a giggle spills out as adrenaline runs high. My thoughts are three steps ahead. I need to ace the spin. I missed it in the last few run-throughs.

Five, six, nailed it. *Knee, kick, jump.* Every class I'm less of a newbie and belonging to the dance group more and more.

"Ok great, girls!" our instructor Tiffany calls from the wall of mirrors. "We'll learn the following sequence next class. Let's end tonight with some freestyle."

A few girls squeal *woo*'s, but goosebumps run up my arms. I cup my ponytail and the hair unsticks from my neck. I keep to the back row of the makeshift circle as Chloe emerges into the centre. She hollers like a flamenco dancer, whips her hair and swirls her hips in sexy circles.

Giggles, claps and cheers fill the studio. Two more girls enter the circle, and I creep backwards. When I was in ballet, everything was way strict. I changed forms because I was sick to death of the regimented structure. Maybe I haven't reprogrammed myself to loosen up. I don't want to suck. I don't wanna be laughed at. I don't want to be a kicked-out-poser.

The other reason for changing dance schools, is her. Chloe Benson. Chloe struts out of the circle, playing with her platinum hair which illuminates against her fake tan. I have the talent to be in this class, but not the popularity at school to be near her. This is my chance to get in. Or at least, for her to remember my name. Life is easier in Chloe Benson's corner. There's no worry of the rumour mill because you make it. You're at the top of the pyramid. I don't want to be constantly doubting myself. I want to be her.

The clock strikes seven-thirty and I'm at my gym bag before the music stops. By the time Tiffany calls end of class, I'm ready to slink out of the studio. I should have jumped in with freestyle.

Next class.

I promise.

Maybe.

I keep my head down as I edge around the girls talking, laughing and bopping to their own beat. I always listen for openings but can never get my mouth to repeat the lines in my head. I imagine them laughing at my jokes and inviting me out for coffee.

Maybe.

One day.

Mum said the Macleans are coming over for dinner tonight. I'm so sweaty and gross. I hope I'm home before they show up. I swing my gym bag across my body for a faster getaway.

"*Whoah*, watch out!" Chloe stumbles backwards when my bag

whacks her.

Through clasped hands, "I'm so, so sorry."

Chloe gains her footing and lets out a throaty laugh. "No biggie."

This is your chance. Say something. Say anything. "You did really good tonight." I'm going to slap myself in front of the mirror later.

"You too. You seem like you've been in the group for ages."

She's noticed me. What? Dammit Brittany, stop blushing. Oh *geez*, respond. Make words happen. "Thanks, that's so nice."

"You do all right; for a ballerina." Chloe tugs open the front door. With a giggle and a wave, she glides through the doorway. "Well, see ya round."

I'm frozen as she skips across the pavement.

Seriously, she's noticed me?

Try to calm down.

I'm not invisible?

Brittany, take a breath.

Thankfully, our housekeeper Sophia's car is parked outside. Wonder if Mum's home yet? Probably not. Sophia greets me with her trademark cheery smile, and we head home. She tells me I have ten minutes before the Macleans are due to arrive.

As we drive, I sneak peeks through the houses at the sun setting over the ocean. As the end of summer draws in, I'm less and less tempted to visit the beach. But the Australian, beach-bum guilt always pulls me down there.

When the car is in the garage, I race into the house, bound up the stairs and burst into the bathroom. I inspect the damage in the mirror. Combing through my hair, I won't have enough time to wash and blowdry before dinner. I throw a shower cap over my head. Dry shampoo and a once over with the flat iron will have to do it.

Once showered, I drape around a towel and hurry towards my bedroom. I hit shuffle on my party-bangers playlist and shimmy in front of the popstar-postered wardrobes. Thumbing through the overstuffed racks, I yank out a scoop-necked, crimson dress and fling it over my shoulder onto the pile of teddy bears on my bed.

I sit at my makeup-caked dresser and dust foundation, flick mascara and glide lipgloss. I fish between the jewellery cases and photo frames for my perfume bottle and spray all the essential areas. My hair falls below my shoulders and still has a hint of hair dye scent. Every time the light hits the golden blondes, I can't hide my smile.

The distinct sounds of Will Maclean echo up the stairs. You do not have to be in the same room as that boy to hear exactly what he's saying. I do another once over with the iron and check my face. Don't want Will reporting to Chloe & Co that I looked like a total freakazoid.

"Brit, go help Sophia bring food from the kitchen," I hear Mum order as I walk down the stairs, but she's nowhere in sight. No way can she prove I heard that. I b-line through the living room to the dining room and get a waft of roast dinner. Will, his younger sister Daisy, and their mum are seated at the table.

Charli pushes through the swing-door from the kitchen holding a baking tray. "Don't worry, we got it," she scowls at me.

I still say we need further proof that we are twins. She wears an oversized alt-band t-shirt, baggy shorts, and a mess of frizzy, uncombed curls. Seriously, girl, we are not related.

"Hiya Will," I say, sliding onto the seat beside him.

"Hey Matty," his voice booms as he slaps me on the back. He's so tall that he slightly hunches when he walks. His sun-bleached hair stands on end, only enhancing his height. "Wassup?"

"Not much. Just got back from dance class."

I try not to jump when Charli slams the tray down in front of me.

"How was class?" Mrs Maclean asks. Her silky blonde hair twirls down one side. The gold jewellery and sheer white blouse accent her milky skin. She was a model back in the day, then gave it up for a husband and kids. If I ever end up like that, I'd hope to be a hot mum like her.

"It was great."

Sophia walks in holding two trays and Charli enters behind her with the drinks. Charli still gives me dirty looks. Like, I'm not wrong, Sophia gets paid to help us.

"I'm glad you're enjoying it," Mrs Maclean says, playing with her pendant necklace. "I was worried when you made the switch from ballet." Charli sits by Daisy, drawing Mrs Maclean's attention. "Charli, you had no interest in taking up dance?"

A laugh spills out of me. I stop when Charli also laughs.

"C'mon, Mrs Maclean," Charli says, reclining in her seat, "d'you really see me in a tutu?"

Mrs Maclean grins and raises her palms to the ceiling. "Maybe a hip-hop dancer?"

"You have to listen to hip-hop first." All eyes turn on me and I immediately sink in my chair.

The pressure lifts when Charli points at me and says, "Totally. Definitely not my jam."

"My jam?" Daisy screws up her face. "Who even says that?"

I giggle under my breath.

"I do," Charli says, playfully poking her.

"Oh good, the food's out," Mum says, walking into the dining room, mobile phone clasped in hand. "Thanks girls."

Charli's eyebrows raise and I choose to ignore it.

"Thanks, Sophia, smells great."

Sophia nods, walking towards the kitchen. "My pleasure, Ms Matthews."

"How was work, Jules?" Mrs Maclean asks, scooping food onto Daisy's plate.

Mum huffs and hunches over bent elbows. Her hands run through her short, sandy bob. "Gruelling. This client is so uncooperative. I want to help him, yet we don't have the required level of trust. It's making my job hard."

Mrs Maclean scoffs, placing food on her own plate. "How can he not trust you? You were the best lawyer we ever had. We would have lost the house if it weren't for you."

I put some veggies on my plate. I love when the Macleans visit because Mum is *actually* home for dinner. Mum is the definition of a workaholic. She wasn't this bad when Dad lived with us, but since the divorce she's become increasingly worse. Now Will's dad is out of the picture, the Macleans visit more frequently.

I hand the tongs to Mum as she lets out a faint laugh.

"Thanks, Penny. Maybe this guy needs a pep talk from you. Have you heard from Brad lately?"

"We are visiting him this week. It's hard, you know. I have to take the kids out of school."

Will cheers, throwing a fist in the air. "Day off school."

"*William.*"

"Well, you know I'm your sounding board, Penny." Mum then sends her attention to Daisy. "So, Daisy, first year of high school. How are you finding it?"

This is my chance. Everyone's paying attention to the opposite side of the table. Heat pricks my cheeks.

"So, Will..."

He turns, waiting for me to add more.

I gulp.

Like, *really* loud.

Embarrassing.

"Has anyone said anything bout me and Meah sitting at your table in the mess hall?"

Will's brows furrow. "Have you?"

Everything drops to the pit of my stomach. Hashtag invisible. "Well, technically no, I guess. We are, like, at the next table."

"I dunno," he says, shovelling food into his mouth, "sit wherever ya want."

He's no help at all. I frown and stab at julienned carrots.

"Hey Chaz," Will shouts across to Charli. She's right there; seriously, no need to be that loud. No idea where he plucked those nicknames either. He's the only one to call us them. I kinda hate that he calls me by a shorter version of my last name but asking him to stop goes in one ear and out the other. "How are things going with you and Trav?"

I hack at the carrots. It's bad enough Travis is constantly at the house, I don't need it rubbed in my face. Charli's always had the friends and the boyfriends. This tomboy got BOTH. I found my best friend Meah, and that's the extent of my luck. I'm ignored in this house and at school. If I had a boyfriend maybe that would change. Maybe I'd feel valued. Or accepted. Or even loved.

Love.

That would be cool.

"We're ok," Charli says.

"Uh-oh, just ok?" Will teases.

Charli's eyes roll. "We're fine. We're good."

My tongue pushes against my teeth. I have to psych myself up to ask him one crappy question. Now the spotlight is on my sister. Again.

"So, where's Rob these days?" Mrs Maclean blurts out. The chatter stops; cutlery clangs on plates.

Charli's eyes bulge and her bottom lip quivers.

Mum raises her chin. "Not quite sure on that one, Pen. Just receive the alimony each month."

"Men. Why do we even bother with them?"

I look between Mum and Mrs Maclean. Another late night with a bottle of wine?

I tried talking to Will more before the Macleans left, but he was in a group chat with the boys. All he did was show me gross memes I had no interest in.

After the goodbyes, I dawdle up the stairs to bed. Some weird band is blasting through the speakers in Charli's bedroom. She escaped in there a half-hour before the Macleans went home. I bang on her door, "turn it down," and continue along the landing to my room.

I flop on my bed and check the new text from Meah. My phone syncs to my speakers and I turn up the music louder than Charli's.

(Meah) **So you reckon they been talking bout us in mess?**

(Me) **Dunno. Will didn't seem to care.**

(Meah) **I can't believe you got to talk to Chloe tonight.**

(Me) **I know! Seriously - how has she noticed me!**

(Meah) **You need to stay on that. We need that in.**

(Me) **I know...**

(Meah) **We'll be round to pick you up before school k**

(Me) **No probs! Thankies.**

(Meah) **xxx**

Ms Giles kept us late after textiles. Now I have to run to science class. I sneak into the lab so Mrs Fields doesn't call me out.

Only a few steps into Lab A, I sharply suck in air. I halt because I'm making eye contact with him. *Ohmigawd.* Bryce looks so friggin hot today. He sits at his bench, the second back on the right, fingers playing in his butterscotch hair. Damn, he can wear the heck out of that school blazer and navy tie.

Total sizzle.

His gaze in my direction was so brief I'm sure he didn't register my presence. But to look at those eyes again. I've only seen them up close once. First day of grade ten, this year. His first day at *John Thomas High* ever. I was at my locker and he asked me where his homeroom class was. Those eyes captured me and I couldn't get a sound to come out. They are the kind of blue that shows all the details. Crystal surrounding a pupil. They have darker ridges that glide through, making both eyes different. Thank goodness I broke the silence curse and managed to point out the way to 12C. Just thinking about the way his lips curved left after he thanked me is enough to make my knees crumple.

Did anyone notice that big sigh I made?

I hug my books and keep my head down as I press on. Since then we haven't spoken a word. Now I just sit behind him in science, two benches back, and keep eyes on the back of that beautiful head.

My eyes close tight.

C'mon, Brittany, try to look appealing.

I shake my hair over my shoulders and jut my hips in a wider swing. I don't dare look in his direction. But I hope... I hope he looks. The thought of him looking at me sends my palms into a raging sweat. Beads of sweat line my hairline and heat radiates from my face. I don't notice the books are falling until they slide down my hips. My clammy hands can't grip them, and *SLAM, SLAM*. I kick one notebook into a nearby bench and stumble over the open textbook.

It's hard to tune out the simmering laughter as I crouch to pick up my pens and books. I almost roll an ankle on the textbook when I reach for a sprawled notebook.

"You know, hands can hold books, Matty," Will calls out behind me. He laughs as he steps over me towards our bench. Some of the boys laugh louder at Will's commentary. I don't dare look if Bryce is one of them.

"Want some help?" Rikki Hernandez folds over bent knees with a factory-made smile.

I gather my stuff in a pile and stand up as casually as possible. "No thanks, I'm fine." I brush down my blazer and straighten the stupid, mandatory navy neckerchief.

"Ok everyone, pipe down," Mrs Fields says, clapping her hands together. "Everyone at benches please. Miss Matthews, Miss Hernandez."

"Sorry Miss," Rikki says and moves away from me.

"Let's pick up where we left off last lesson," Mrs Fields says as she writes on the blackboard.

I hurl my stuff onto the bench and plonk onto the stool. My neck is as loose as spaghetti. All I see is the navy and white tartan of my school skirt.

"You ok?" Will asks, finally in a reasonable tone.

I meant to say yes, but some kind of inaudible grizzle slid out through gritted teeth.

"Dude, you dropped some books. Not the end of the world."

My cheeks burn. "I know!"

Will throws his hands up in surrender.

I rub my hands against my skirt, willing the clamminess away. My eyes form slits with a view of Rikki. She's partnered with Bryce.

Gawd, I hate her.

Her sleek, chestnut hair glistens over her olive skin. I swear she's trying to hypnotise poor Bryce with it.

Give it up, lady.

...Please?

My cheek rests in my hand as I watch Bryce's profile. Sure he's talking to Rikki, but I can imagine it's me sitting there. Calmness washes over me. It doesn't last long when Rikki never shuts up. She's the only person Mrs Fields let's run her mouth. Easily the smartest person in our grade. Surely that's not something Bryce is looking for. Is it?

I'm pushed towards the bench when Will nudges me.

"What?"

He nods forward where Mrs Fields, and the kids in front, are staring at me.

"Miss Matthews?"

"Yes?"

"For the third time, can you list a body part in the endocrine system?"

Gulp. *Andocrime?* Am I supposed to know this?

"I take it by your stunned expression you didn't complete last night's homework." I don't appreciate the sarcasm, Mrs Fields. "Miss Hernandez, can you please enlighten Miss Matthews?"

Rikki's hair swings as she turns my direction. "Sure. Pancreas, ovaries, thyroid, any of these are acceptable."

"Thank you, Rikki." Mrs Fields claps as she makes her way to the board. "Now let's talk about each in more detail."

Rikki giggles, eyeing Bryce.

Like she is so superior.

I tug at my bracelet.

At the end of class, Will leaves at lightning speed. He didn't touch a pen or skim a page the entire forty minutes. I collect my gear and struggle through the surge of students towards the door. Will is on his way to the dining hall, which we all nickname *mess*. He's headed there with Bryce.

"I've got no idea what we are supposed to do for that assignment," Will's voice echoes in the corridor. He dumps his books into his locker and he and Bryce keep moving.

I smash into a few kids as I race to catch up. It's worth it when I'm only a few paces behind them.

"I think I lucked out," Bryce says. "My partner already seems to know all the answers."

"Yeah, well I got screwed."

My gut tears in two.

Will spins around and beams at me. "We both did, hey, Brit."

"What?" I choke.

Bryce looks over his shoulder at me and every ounce of air escapes me.

"Neither of us can take the lead," Will says. "I don't think either of us could give two shits about that class."

My jaw tightens. Don't say anything stupid. "Maybe we can get Rikki to do our homework too."

Both boys laugh. *Phew.*

"I can ask for you," Bryce says. "You never know. Maybe she'd like the idea of doing more work."

Will laughs, shoving Bryce. "See how far ya get with the nerdy babe."

The boys quicken their pace as we approach the dining hall. Shell-shocked from my micro-convo with him, a dawdle is all I can muster.

I follow them into mess as Will still raves about Rikki. Telling Bryce he hit the jackpot. Are you freakin kidding me?

Bryce and Will land at their table and I side-glance my old table. The girls sitting there shoot me filthy looks. Meah and I have kicked booty these first few weeks of school. We moved from the slums of the entrance tables all the way to prime seating near the food lines.

The boys take their seats and I walk to the adjacent table and snag the seat next to Meah.

"Mr Phelps is the worst!" Meah shrieks, pulling her mousy brown hair over her jawline.

"What happened?"

I bat her hands away from her face. She's super self-conscious about her strong jaw. All the Watkins have it. Looks great on the guys, not so much on a girl. Her hands are always fussing about her neck or waist. She's put on some weight and is pudgy around the mid-section.

She needs to lay off the snacking.

Meah's dependable. We were both kicked aside and then we found each other. Yeah, we've had a group of friends over the years, but it was the two of us in a sea of people. This made things easy when we planned to infiltrate the popular group. Our friends didn't want a bar of it, so we ditched them. Ditched them for a bigger and better horizon.

"Mr Phelps gave us a test. With no notice. That should be illegal in a maths class. What a friggin jerk."

"That sucks."

"Anyway, how was science? Do anything besides stalk Bryce Kerry?"

"*Shoosh.* I'd hardly call it stalking."

"Just constantly staring at him."

"Meah, shuddup."

We always sit so we are facing their table. Chloe and Kimberley rampage towards it.

Chloe slams her bag on the table in front of Bryce. "Mr Phelps is a massive douchebag!"

"What happened?" Bryce asks, creeping back in his chair.

"We had a test already," Kimberley says, sliding down beside Chloe.

"So Benny, who are you scaring into giving you the answers?" Will asks Chloe.

Chloe turns to Kimberley. "Who's smartest in our class?"

Kimberley tussles her dark hair, and replies, "Charlotte Matthews?"

I check my phone for notifications to disassociate from the new topic.

Kimberley cackles. "We can work that bitch."

My skin crawls from the hideous way Kimberley talks. She hasn't changed since we were ten-years-old. She is skilled in backhanded compliments, spinning rumours and listing your faults in front of a room of people. And for some reason I desperately wanted to be friends with her. She's been on auto-attack since the day Greg Francis called her a dirty Abo in grade five. Her skin colour has never mattered to me. It's like honey-drizzled espresso. If anything, I'm jealous. It's inside where the horror show is at.

I was glad when she stopped coming over to our house. Unfortunately, that marked the turning point where she became Chloe's best friend.

I want in on Chloe's group.

Again, I need to be around Kimmy Jones.

"We should get food." Will scrapes back his chair. "Unlike you ladies, we don't have boyfriends to fetch our lunches."

As Will and Bryce get up from the table, I clutch Meah's wrist and we fly from our seats. The boys head for the food line, and we b-line around tables trying to keep up. We squeal as we run. The boys line up and we skid behind them. Still holding hands, we hunch in fits of giggles. I hate that I can't stop. Every time I look at Meah it makes it worse. My stomach cramps and my breathing is weird as I try to mute myself.

"What's happening, ladies?"

I turn around to Naveen Singh cocking an eyebrow and smirking at us. I take in the oaky, amber cologne lingering on his caramel skin. He's a boy worthy of a GQ cover.

"Nothin," Meah says, fidgety with giggles.

"Can't I know the joke?" Naveen leans over to meet Meah's eyes.

Will and Bryce turn around and red coats my face.

"What's happening?" Will asks.

I tug at my hair and shift my weight as Bryce stands so close to me. My heart thunders in my ears.

Ba-boom. Ba-boom. Ba-boom.

"Nothing's happening." Meah sashays her hips. "We're just gonna order food."

"Yeah." Will faces front and cups his hands around his mouth. "IF THIS FRIGGIN LINE WOULD MOVE."

Bryce faces me. "What should I get?"

"Eh, me? You're asking me?"

"Yeah. I can't decide. You decide for me."

"Then who will decide for me?" I literally have no idea what I'm saying.

"I will. I think it's easier to decide for other people. Less pressure."

"Are you kidding? It's way more pressure choosing for someone else."

He laughs which sets butterflies loose in my stomach. My knees beg for mercy.

"Oh no. Have I put too much pressure on you?"

My mouth opens to speak, but only a weird *gah* noise comes out.

"Dude, it's easy," Will says, spinning Bryce around. "Just get a burger. No-brainer."

All the air I was holding onto rushes out like a violent wind. My legs untense and my torso wants to wobble like jelly.

Naveen pushes past us and joins the boys as the line moves. I fixate on the flex between Bryce's shoulder blades and run my gaze below his blazer.

Best.

Wednesday.

Ever.

2

Charli

The sun shines today,
But the light has set,
I lay, weary and morose,
Turned away from warmth.

Unable to see ahead,
Clarity lost in the void,
Summer cannot embrace,
This lonesome fragile shell.

Coldness takes over,
Numb, blue to the core,
Trembling until fracture,
Forgotten in broken pieces.

I drop the pen when thoughts of my phone blanket my mind. Why won't he reply? His last text was five days ago.

What did I do wrong?

Where is he?

"What are you doing in here?" My boyfriend Travis leans against the door of the classroom. His shoulders broad and arms folded, his chocolatey hair a mess. How many teachers have gotten on his back today about improper uniform? His tie is unravelled, shirt untucked, and blazer sleeves rolled up.

My eyes pan over the empty desks around me, to the blackboard with scrawled notes, and down to the phone in my hands. I drop the phone and slide a hand under my cheek to rest.

"It's lunch time." Travis walks between desks. "Why are you still in the classroom? No way you got detention."

Guilt swells as I smooth over the open page of my textbook. Most of geography I texted Dad or wrote poetry. "Just catching up on work."

Travis pulls out the chair in front of me and sits backwards on it. "School started a month ago. There isn't anything to catch up on."

"I mean, get ahead."

Travis takes my hand. "Don't put so much pressure on yourself."

I sneak a peek at my phone and Travis notices.

"Your dad? Still not heard back?"

I shake my head, frowning at the phone.

"Hey, what's this?" he says and tugs at the notebook underneath my elbow. I lift my arm so he can spin the book and read the poem. Sometimes I don't understand my emotions and poetry helps. It's always super private, but Travis is my rock and I know my words are safe with him.

"I hate that he's making you so sad."

I take the book back. "Maybe we should go to lunch."

Travis helps me pack up my stuff and suggests, "Wanna hang out at the mess?"

I close a book and purse my lips. "You want me to sit with your friends?"

"They're getting shitty that I don't hang out in there that much."

"So, you shudda gone there instead of coming to find me."

"As if I'm not gonna see you. It's bad enough I don't get to see you during class because we're in different grades." He walks around the desk until we are face-to-face and adds a fake whimper to his voice, "I need as much Charli-Wharli time as I can get."

I push his stomach as a disgusted laugh pours out of me. "*Eww.* Shuddup."

Travis finds his footing, laughing, and hangs an arm over my shoulder, hitching my stuff under his other arm. He kisses my forehead and we make our way out of the classroom.

The corridors are almost empty. *Whoops.* Didn't mean to stay behind this long. We dump my stuff in my locker and head to the mess hall.

I shudder as we enter a barrage of noise. The dining hall is cavernous. The ceilings arch to a high mid-point with an echoing effect. Stained glass windows depicting John Thomas, Phillip Sanford and other Sanford settlers, run the length of the outside wall.

Aesthetically, the mess hall is beautiful. Unlike the cringe-worthy social politics. It's all about where you sit and who with. The Powers That Be want me sitting near the entrance doors; AKA bottom of the pyramid. Travis and his friends are A-List twelfth graders, they have the same table every day up near the food line. Everyone is nuts for these food line tables, like the freakin King and Queen dine there. Trav explains the benefit is being able to see gaps in the line to save on wait times. I still don't get the value.

I try to avoid the social experiment. My friends and I opt for fresh air and sunshine; more importantly the silence. A non-existent thing as we approach Travis' friends. They call out and wave like they haven't seen him in months. I pick out the grimaces aimed at me, while we get our food and join the table.

"*Ohmigawd* Maggie, seriously," GiGi Larkin shrieks, flicking her brunette waves away from her heavily painted face. "You're actually going to your dad's office party instead of coming to my house on Friday night?"

A groan reverberates from the back of Maggie Lee's throat. "It's not an office party. He's performing at the naval base. Like, it's a big deal, or whatever."

GiGi pushes her palm in front of Maggie. "You're a sucky friend."

Maggie rolls her eyes and scrolls through her phone. "I'll, like, try to stop by after."

"As if you're not gonna be there," Ray Martinez chimes in, pointing his thumbs towards himself, "when this stud is gonna be there."

Maggie's shoulders jiggle with a silent laugh. She falls onto his chest and continues to text.

While Travis talks with Lucas about a game that was on TV (sport, I'm guessing) my eyes wander the mess hall. My throat constricts at sight of my sister. Brittany's hair is now the fake blonde from a bottle and constantly scorched by a flat iron. She sits with her cohort Meah, giggling and gossiping behind cupped hands. Her eyes lock on Chloe Benson's table. She's relentless. It's been non-stop since summer break when she changed dance schools. All I heard was, *Chloe this* and *Chloe that*. It takes all my strength to not get up and slap sense across her face. What is the appeal? Especially when she knows first-hand what Kimmy is like. Well... second-hand, I guess.

I said no to popularity. Why can't she?

"Travy will be there though. Won't you?" My attention is snatched from Brittany by GiGi's baby voice. My hand slips onto Travis' thigh as GiGi flutters eyelashes at him.

Travis clears his throat. "Well, *ah*," under the table his fingers interlace with mine. "I'll probably be hanging with Charli."

Tension camps between my shoulders as GiGi's cheeks suck in and her nostrils flare. "Of course, your little girlfriend is invited."

Little?

Travis looks at me and pauses.

Lucas slaps him on the back, and slurs, "C'mon mate, don't be a pussy. We're all gonna be there. Just come hang out. Won't kill ya."

I rub my lips together and shrug a shoulder.

Lucas is a dick.

Travis squeezes my hand and says to his friends, "Yeah, maybe."

GiGi grins like the star of a dental commercial. "*Sweet.* You won't regret it. Gonna be epic."

"If I'm gonna come to this thing," Maggie begins, "don't invite that scumbag Jason Halberg."

"Oh fuck," Ray says. "Did ya hear that guy in maths? What a friggin turd."

"What did he say?" Travis asks, head tilted.

I tap between Travis' knuckles as the ugly words against Jason Halberg intensify. Jason. Someone who once helped me in the library find killer info for a Julius Caesar essay. A nice guy.

"As if I'd ever let that loser into my house," GiGi says and starts gagging.

I kick my feet against the chair legs.

"Maybe you should so we have home-court advantage," Lucas smirks.

Travis laughs and replies, "I swear I didn't hear any of this. Was I even in maths today?"

Ray winks at me. "You're getting all kinds of distracted, aren't ya, Trav."

Lucas cheers, "*Whoop, whoop.* Yeah, boy."

Before I hear another word, I'm standing.

Travis tugs on my hand. "What are you doing?"

"I'm sorry, I need to go."

"I'll go with you," Travis says, standing.

"You don't have to."

"I want to."

I smile and so does he.

"What, you're leaving Trav?" Ray asks.

More grimaces in my direction.

"I'll be right back," Travis tells his friends and he leads me away.

In the corridor he asks, "You ok?"

"I'm fine."

"Is it your dad?"

I bite the inside of my cheek. It wasn't, but it's now in the mix. I sigh, leaning against a locker and say to his shoes, "I'm sorry I made you leave your friends."

"You didn't make me do anything." His hands slide along my shoulders.

I hug my waist and whisper, "I just felt weird."

"Probably because you were near that pack of weirdos."

I push for a smile, but the welling is already in my throat. I swallow hard. It's scary when Travis is around his friends. I hate hearing anything from his lips that sounds like a version of them.

My hands fish inside Travis' blazer and run up his sides. He hooks a finger under my chin and lifts my head up. Air drains out of me as he edges closer. Our lips press together and linger. His kiss is soft and sends a tingle down my spine.

I smile and clasp his hand as we move along the corridor.

Halfway across the quad, he asks, "So, what did you think about going to GiGi's on Friday night?"

My fingers run through my curls and snag on a knot. "I don't mind if you go without me."

"Going without you would be no fun."

"As if. You know I'm not a partier."

"Me either."

"Whatever. I heard the wild party stories involving you before we started dating."

"I thought you didn't listen to rumours," he teases.

We leave the quad and I spy Kellie and Reece under our usual tree. Reece lies on his back, knees bent to the sky with a book held over his head.

Kellie, slumped against the tree, waves madly at us. She pushes her oversized, black-rimmed glasses up the bridge of her nose and leaps to hug me. It's not a Kellie-hug if your bones don't crack.

Kellie's bushy, copper hair attacks my face. I brush it back and she asks, "Where you been? We thought you ditched us."

"She wouldn't leave the classroom." Travis smirks as Kellie unleashes me.

"For twenty minutes? Like, most of lunch is over."

I fling a thumb at Travis. "He wanted to hang out in mess."

"Sounds bout right," Reece mumbles at his book.

"What's your problem?" Travis says, diving to tackle Reece.

"*Gah!* Dude, get off me." Reece whacks Travis with his novel.

Kellie yanks Travis' blazer. "Oi, get away from him."

Travis laughs, sitting on the grass. "Shudda known better than to go near my cousin when his bodyguard is around."

Kellie plonks next to Reece. "Damn straight."

I crouch and place a hand on Reece's book. "What ya reading?"

He lifts the cover. "'*Nineteen Eighty-Four*.' George Orwell."

"Any good?"

"Yes. You should read it when I'm done."

I never have the worry of what to read next. Reece is always adding to my TBR pile.

Reece sits up and shakes grass out of his side-swept hair. Side-by-side, it's clear Reece and Travis are cousins by the classic Watkins features: dark eyes, and heavy lower lips framed by strong jaws.

I run a hand over my skirt pocket and trace the outline of my phone. I want to check it. I want to check it. I REALLY WANT TO CHECK IT.

Kellie reclines against the bluegum. Her glasses slide down her button nose. Seriously, she needs a new pair. They've been broken for months.

"Reece and I were talking about Friday night," she says. "Both our parents are going to a banquet on base, and we don't have to go."

"Oh yeah?" Kellie's dad is a lieutenant or commander or something in the navy, and Reece's dad is something higher than that. "What ya thinkin?"

"Party at mine."

"With Bailey there?" Not ideal having her eight-year-old brother hanging around.

"Nah, he's sleeping over at a mate's house. It's perfect."

"We were thinking games like we played at Henry's the other weekend," Reece adds, re-opening his book.

"Cool, that sounds fun."

Crap. Travis.

"Travis, you're welcome to come," Kellie chimes in.

"Kel, no," Reece hisses.

Travis snorts. "Well, thanks, cuz."

"I just mean it won't be your scene."

"My scene is wherever Charli is."

I blurt out, "Travis was invited to something with his friends."

"Oh." Kellie waves her hands. "Don't worry bout it then."

"Well, I can go to yours instead."

I eye him. "Your friends are already pissed at you."

"Maybe I can do both?"

Travis rubs circles on my back and I force a smile. My attention falls to my phone. I can't take it anymore.

I slip it out of my pocket.

The screen illuminates.

Nothing.

I grunt and shove it back in my pocket.

"You ok?" the three ask at once.

"I'm fine."

No one comments but it lingers in the air. They know the text I'm waiting on. They're probably sick of it. Me too. Dad should just come home and give us all a break.

Kellie fills the silence with, "Well Travis, the offer is there."

"Thanks, Kel."

Neither Kellie nor Reece were jazzed when Travis and I became a thing. They didn't understand it. When it was clear he was not going anywhere, they came around. Well, they're trying.

The bell sounds for fifth period. Travis plants a kiss on my cheek and we agree to meet at his car after school. As he leaves for the gym, he tussles Reece's hair.

Reece hunches, combing his hair to its original position. I don't know much about Reece's condition, but I know one rule is not to touch. It's a massive deal when you get eye contact out of him.

"What games are you thinking for Friday?"

"You were getting a handle of Crown Slayer," Kellie suggests.

"I can bring that," Reece says as we walk toward the school building.

On the way Kellie gives me the run down on the invitees. I don't dislike anyone on the list, but honestly, I prefer when it's just us.

We stop by our lockers and I draw in a deep breath. "Thanks for inviting Travis."

She winks. "No probs."

"I'm so glad for the *get-out-of-jail-free* card from GiGi Larkin's party."

"*Eww*. That's whose party it is? Why is he friends with these people?"

I don't respond. Kellie one-arm hugs me and leaves for her history class.

I wait for Reece to find his books and we head to English. If you want the definition of comfortable silence, it's me and Reece.

Reece takes his seat in the middle of the centre row. Mr Palmer assigned me a desk in the back row, because, and I quote, he 'doesn't have to worry about me.' It's the worst. A view of everyone slacking off.

I open my copy of '*To Kill a Mockingbird*' at the bookmark. I've already read through the discussion questions so I'm ready if Mr Palmer calls on me.

"You enjoying it?"

On my right, the new guy, Bryce Kerry, points at my book with eyebrows raised in interest.

"Yeah, so far. How about you?"

He thumbs through his novel. "Not started yet."

He's textbook-classic handsome. Crooked smile, high cheekbones and a pair of mesmerising eyes. Ok, he's attractive, but is there anything underneath worth value?

"We've had the book for three weeks."

"Yeah, but we've got all term, right?"

"But we're discussing it every class."

"Maybe you could give me the highlight reel? You know, enough to get me by for the essay."

Unintentionally, I blow a raspberry. "I don't think it's gonna happen."

He leans in. "But you don't know for sure?"

"You know, if you really wanted to cheat, there is a movie."

"There is?"

"Yeah. With Gregory Peck."

A deadpan stare.

"Gregory Peck." The volume of my voice increases to shock level. "You don't know who Gregory Peck is?"

His eyebrows push together and his nose crinkles.

"Miss Matthews, Mr Kerry," Mr Palmer strides up the aisle to our desks, "having your own discussion group, are you?"

I gulp and wriggle in my seat as Mr Palmer makes eye contact.

Bryce slides down his seat and waves a hand. "Sorry, Sir. I didn't understand the discussion being held. And..." he turns to me, mouth ajar.

"Charli."

"Yeah, when Charli—" he stops and looks back like he heard it wrong. "Charli?"

"Yes."

"Like Charles?"

I snort. "Like Charlotte."

"Yes, when Miss Charlotte Matthews was kind enough to explain it to me. She is, like, *number one* in this class."

A giggle escapes me, and I clasp a hand over my mouth. He's slick, I'll give him that.

Mr Palmer applauds Bryce and walks to the front of class. Bryce pushes back on his seat and past him I see my sister. She's frowning at me with a clenched jaw. Is it about Dad?

I pull out my phone.

Nope, still nothing.

"Thank you, Mrs Watkins," I say, taking a piece of blueberry cheesecake from the platter Travis' mum holds out.

It's enjoyable going to Travis' house for dinner. His mum is a great cook. We've demolished a meal of oven-baked salmon with greens and béarnaise sauce. I can't recall the last time my mum made toast.

"Meah's probably gonna get shitty now that she can't get her double serving of cake," Travis teases, pulling faces at his younger sister.

"Oh piss off, Travis." Meah puffs out her plump cheeks and shoves her plate away.

The baked-ricotta-blueberry sours in my mouth.

"Meah," Mrs Watkins hisses.

Meah's face scrunches as her arms flap about. "What? He started it!"

Mr Watkins slams his fist on the table. "Well I'm ending it!"

Quiet sweeps the table like the gust off an evening wave. The tension makes eating uncomfortable, but I plough through the cake as an excuse not to talk.

I glance at Meah. She shifts in her chair, hands smoothing under her chin. Meah rarely says a nice word to me, but it's painful to hear anyone get picked on.

After an awkward end to dinner, Travis snags us the living room. Thankful, I snuggle with him on the couch.

"So, what's our next movie going to be?" Travis asks, stroking my hair.

I settle into the warmth of his chest and squeeze my arms around him. "Didn't we talk about starting the Hitchcock's? We could start with '*Rear Window.*'"

"Followed by '*Dial M for Murder*'?"

"Any excuse for you to watch more Grace Kelly."

"I've seen enough Cary Grant movies for you. You owe me."

I spring to sitting. "I had to teach someone who Gregory Peck was today."

"*Ehck.* You're friggin kidding me." He pulls me to his chest. "When my class studied '*To Kill a Mockingbird*' we watched the movie and I had to pretend to not like it because my friends were making this big deal about how lame it was."

I run my hand through his soft curls and close my eyes. I've started biting my tongue when he talks about pretending around his friends. Now I need to learn to deal with the stabbing against my heart.

"Remember what you told me at the old cinema when we watched '*Rebel Without A Cause*'?" I reminisce. "While they are in that empty mansion and Plato is holding that candelabra. You explained how they made the candelabra light up through wires in his jacket."

"Oh yeah. Smart, hey. Would be shitty to have to re-shoot because some candles blew out." Light dazzles in his eyes as his mind wanders. "The night they shot at the planetarium, people in the area called the fire departments saying there were forest fires." A hint of laughter escapes him. "The production lights were so bright, freaked em all out."

"Have you been working on anything lately?"

He glances at his laptop on the coffee table. "Not really. School's kinda getting in the way."

"You're actually studying?"

"Just friends and stuff."

Choosing to ignore. "When's the last time you filmed something?"

"Filming is easy enough. If I want, I can do it with my phone. It's the cutting and editing I miss. I really should finish a project."

I bounce to my knees. "You should! You should!"

Travis sits up and hugs me. "Ok! Ok!" His hand runs down my cheek. "I love you so much, you know?"

"I know," I reply with a cheeky smile. "I love you too."

He kisses me softly, pushing his tongue against mine. His hands slide inside my t-shirt and explore my torso. My elbows lock, stiff against my ribs. His hands move up until they can't move further. They find the clasp of my bra. I let out a weird *gah* noise, which makes us both freeze.

"Maybe you should drive me home. It's getting late."

Travis drives me home and I kiss him goodnight. I leave his car and walk the path to my house.

Summer is ending, yet there is still a touch of light to the night sky. The crash of waves echoes as I walk along the side of the house. I plant my feet at the edge of the back deck and draw in the salty air. The ocean never fails to be calming. It's getting late, so I go inside to view the waves from my bedroom balcony.

"Good evening, Charli." Sophia beams when I walk into the kitchen. "Have a nice night?"

"Yeah I did, thanks."

"I'm glad, gorgeous one." Sophia's smile could melt the coldest heart. When she's happy, her eyes round like an anime character. Her Filipino complexion is highlighted from the summer sun and her long, black hair is tied high with her trademark frangipani.

"Do we have any iced tea left?" I ask, opening the fridge.

"Should do."

Sophia takes the jug of green tea and ginger from the fridge and prepares it in a glass with ice. When she returns the jug to the fridge, she kisses her palm and plants it on the photo of her kids.

She hands me the drink and kisses my cheek. "Do you need anything else? I'm about done in here and I was going to call my sister to check in on the family back home."

"No, please, go."

Sophia tidies the kitchen sink and then leaves for her bedroom by the laundry room. I wish her a good night and walk to the stairs.

On the second-floor landing, Brittany walks out of the bathroom and turns toward her bedroom.

"Brit!" I'll admit it was way too loud.

"Yeah?"

I shift my weight between feet. "What you doing?"

"Going to bed. What do you want?"

"Oh, um. Just thought we could, um, catch up on what's been going on... at school?"

"What do you mean? We go to the same school."

"Yeah. But I hardly see you."

"*Ugh*, whatever. Seriously, I have to go to bed, ok? Night."

She slams the door behind her. I suck in air and fight the throbbing in my throat. I close my eyes as they become wet. I shake it off and head into my bedroom.

I let myself smile. Sophia has been in here. I'm trying to convince her she doesn't have to tidy my bedroom. Organised chaos lets my mind work. My 'mess' as she calls it, is her idea of hell. My wad of flannel shirts, jeans and books have shrunk. Smuggled to the laundry or neatly stacked.

I pass my wardrobe and show a peace sign to the jumbo John Lennon poster. As I walk toward my balcony door, my laptop pings with three notifications: missed video chats with Kellie. I circle back and click *return call*.

Four seconds later, Kellie appears on screen. "Sorry, man. I remembered you were at Trav's after the third call."

"That's ok. What's up?"

"Oh nothing. Just trying to ignore my ignoramus of a mother."

"Everything ok?"

"Yeah, you know how she is. Trying to push me to do things when she won't do a thing for herself." Kellie shrugs onscreen. "How was it at Travis'?"

I smile at the webcam, leaning into the subject change. Kellie's the kinda girl to do everything for herself. Her mother's expectant hand out towards her father exasperates Kellie to the point she now hates talking about it.

"Yeah, good. Meah was less of a pain. That was a plus."

Kellie's head bops with a silent laugh. "How unlike her."

"Tried talking to Brittany when I got home."

"Get anything out of her?"

I bite inside my cheek. Not worth answering. I scan between study notes. "Kel, which should I chose: history or geography?"

"You were talking to Brit about history and geography?"

I wave my hands at the screen. "No. Which should I study tonight?"

"You have a test coming up?"

"No, just making it a habit to study every night."

"Part of your *I'm-going-to-be-best-at-everything* scheme?"

"I'm not scheming."

Weighing up the pile of papers, I feel crappy about flaking on work in geography class. But I love history. Ending the day with history would make me happy.

"I really should catch up on geography."

"Need a study buddy?"

"I'm good. Thanks, Kel."

"See you tomorrow then."

"Catch ya."

I sign off and hit the books. Dad could be back in Sanford any day now. My grades need to be ace so I can make him proud. Make him so happy, he moves back into our family home.

3

Brittany

Last night's dance class was a disaster. If my footing was right, my arms were in the wrong spot. Total dork. I'm streaming the song from class to get practice in before school. Of course, I'm on point when no one's watching.

Meah flings my bedroom door open. "*Woo.* Slick moves, Brit."

Her entrance freaks me out and I trip over my foot.

"Or maybe not." She smirks and flops on my bed. "How was class last night? Talk to Chloe?"

I shake my head and turn off the music. "Nah. I wasn't really near her."

"Can't you get closer?"

"Maybe," I say while examining my makeup in the mirror. I coat my lips with another layer of dewy, strawberry lipgloss.

"Well, you better. You're the only in we've got."

A knot tightens in my chest. Thanks for the added pressure, Meah. I suggest we head downstairs to leave. Big mistake. Every step down the staircase creates a more perfect view of Charli and Travis making out in the foyer. Ok, it's only a small kiss. But does she have to flaunt it in my face?

Charli pulls away from Travis, rubbing her lips together and eyeing me like she's embarrassed.

Really? Are you really?

I roll my eyes and round the stairs towards the kitchen.

"Morning, gorgeous," Sophia greets with a larger-than-life smile, offering a mug of coffee.

I take it and thank her. Hazelnut latte with a dusting of cinnamon. Heaven.

"Meah, would you like something to drink? Or some breakfast?" Sophia asks as we slide into the breakfast nook.

"I ate, but coffee sounds *ah-may-zing*."

"Brittany, darling, you have to eat breakfast," Sophia says while grabbing a coffee cup from the cabinet. "What can I make you?"

I take a whiff of cinnamon-hazelnut goodness. "I'm not really hungry."

"Then I'm making you toast."

She always knows what I mean.

"Mum already gone to work?"

Sophia gives the answer I expected. An hour ago.

"You guys ready to go?" Travis asks, entering the kitchen hand-in-hand with Charli.

"Travis, let me make you something to eat," Sophia interrupts, head in the pantry.

Travis grins. "You know I'd eat anything if you made it, Sophia."

Charli and Travis walk further into the kitchen.

My insides clench.

Not in here. Not in here. DO NOT SIT IN HERE.

My heart slows its pace as they wander into the dining room.

Meah's cousin Reece lives three doors down. After breakfast Travis stops by his house when he drives us to school. I make Meah sit in the middle. That kid barely speaks, like, it's weird. When he comes over to our house to hang with Charli his head is always in a book. The entire car ride he reads from his phone, hair falling over his forehead and covering his eyes.

I guess I can't talk. I'm scrolling through *Instagram*.

My last class before lunch is science. Major bummer. Will is away visiting his dad, so I'll be alone at my bench. My books smack against my thighs as I trudge into the lab.

"Miss Matthews." I'm almost at my bench when Mrs Fields calls my name. I stop as she continues, "Sit at this station with Mr Kerry." I follow her pointed finger to the empty space next to Bryce. "With Mr Maclean and Miss Hernandez away, you two can partner up."

"Oh ok," I squeak. My shoulders bunch up to my ears and I shuffle to his bench.

I place my books on the benchtop and climb atop the stool. From the corner of my eye I see him open his books.

Say hi, Brittany, just say hi.

My mouth must be sealed shut.

Bryce shifts on his stool and I flinch. I look over and he gives me a small closed-mouth smile. I meant to smile back.

I face front.

Did I smile?

Ugh, moron.

Mrs Fields starts class and I take the opportunity to open my books and find the best pens in my case. Anything to seem busy. I weirdly need to clear my throat. It's so dry. How do I do it without being loud? I swallow a few times to see if it helps. Dammit. It's worse. I start coughing. Dry, loud coughs.

"You ok?"

I nod and clear my throat like originally intended. Mortifying.

I stare at the words on the open page. Head low. Breaths shallow. Pulse racing. He is so close. So DAMN close.

Bryce Kerry.

Right there.

DAMN.

"I'm so glad your partner ditched too," Bryce says. His fingers comb through his hair. Oh boy. "I'm no good in this class alone."

I take in a sharp breath and search my textbook. "I don't know how much help I will be. I'm not great at this subject."

"I have something that might help," he says and slides papers over my textbook. "Rikki left her notes."

I skim over the handwritten notes. "She gave you these? She's not usually that helpful."

"I don't know what to tell you." He slides a palm under his cheek and continues, "She said she wouldn't be in class because of a school council thing, and that I could have her notes to keep on track."

"Yeah, she's never that nice." Seriously? She wants him *bad*. "She's ruthless. Always looking for top spot in the class. Never helps anyone study."

"She seems nice to me."

I bite my lip. "Maybe she's turning a new leaf."

He lets out a breathy laugh. Cheeky. Handsome.

"Why is Will away?"

"He didn't tell you?"

He shakes his head.

Should I tell? "You haven't heard about his dad?"

"There is a lot to learn at this school. Maybe I have, but I'm getting everyone mixed up."

"I don't know if I should say."

"Why? It's bad?"

"I'm surprised he hasn't told you. You two seem close."

"We are. He talks a lot, but it's hard to actually listen to it all."

It's huge telling someone the story of how Brad Maclean went to prison. I open my mouth, but he stops me. "Don't tell me. If he wanted me to know, he would have said."

"Wow. You don't want gossip?"

"I hate being gossip. I don't want to do that to someone else."

"Being the new guy isn't fun?"

I steal a glimpse of his crystal eyes. For a moment they're sad. "Plenty of things aren't fun." A smile changes his expression and he taps Rikki's notes. "You can copy these too. Maybe we can help each other understand them."

I skim the first two bullet points. "It's like deciphering code."

He laughs like I'm funny. I look at him. He smiles at me like I'm funny. I'm smiling. No, I'm grinning. My hands shake. I grip a pen and focus on copying the code.

We are silent for most of class. Bryce comments on the paragraph entitled *'what is the difference between prokaryotic and eukaryotic cells'* asking if we were mistakenly in Greek class. He is so cute. His lips are a soft rose colour. I imagine kissing them and get woozy.

The bell sounds for lunch and I begin to pack up my stuff. I expect him to grab his gear and make a speedy getaway to mess like Will does. When I hop off my stool he is still by the bench.

He's waiting for me?

I walk beside him out of the classroom. He smells so good. Like cinnamon and sandalwood. Throughout class I became addicted to that cologne.

"So, you've always lived in Sanford?" he asks as we walk through the bustle of the east wing corridor.

"All my life."

"I was wondering if you were new. You seem different to your friends."

My forehead bunches. I guess Meah and I are different.

"I don't mean it in a bad way or anything." He shifts to make eye contact and my heart thumps. "Just that Chloe and the other girls are really in-ya-face, and loud, and gossipy. You just seem less judgey, that's all."

I don't mean to, but I laugh.

"What? Am I wrong?"

"I've never really been compared to Chloe before."

He stops by his locker and dumps his books. He offers to take mine and in a panic move, I hug them tight and tell him no.

"I didn't mean to offend you or anything."

I've trashed this opportunity. "No way, you haven't offended me. To be honest, I'm not really that close with Chloe." Did I just say that? "Yet, anyways."

"Oh ok, that makes sense. Just make sure she doesn't change you."

We walk into the mess and I find myself falling behind him. I've already changed my hairstyle, dance school, and ditched my old friends for a better table. What is left to change? No doubt he wouldn't be talking to the last-year-version of me.

I find a seat at my usual table, when Bryce stops me and asks, "Are you getting food?"

I'll go anywhere you go, blue eyes. "Yeah, sure."

I line up behind him and he turns to face me. Goosebumps race down my limbs.

"You're cold?"

My cheeks burn. His stare is intense. He'll see something wrong with me in seconds. Mascara dots under my eyes? Uneven layer of lipgloss? "No, just a weird shiver."

I breathe in his cologne again and my knees weaken. I should say something. I should ask him about his old school. I open my mouth but am overshadowed by...

"Hi guys!" Chloe jumps between Bryce and me. Kimberley squeezes beside Chloe.

"Hey, what's going on?" Bryce asks the girls.

"So glad to be out of class," Kimberley says. "Dying for a cheeseburger."

"How was class?" Chloe asks Bryce, running her hand down the length of his arm. My stomach swirls.

"Well," Bryce says, glancing in my direction, but Chloe cuts him off.

"You were probably just as bored as us."

Bryce smiles at Chloe. "Biology isn't very thrilling."

"Well, maybe you're doing it wrong," Chloe says, adding a cheeky giggle.

Kimberley steps back enough times that I have to take a wide step back. Just like that, I'm far away. Basically in another galaxy.

Fidgeting, awkward and alone, I scan the mess hall for Meah.

"No, it was kinda fun. Brittany and I spent class trying to work out what Rikki's notes were on about," Bryce tells the girls and I spin to face them.

"Oh, hey Brittany," Chloe says, smiling like she didn't see me before. Kimberley glares at me like it's the part of the movie when they throw dog food on me.

"Hi."

We work our way through the line of cold food to hot food and take our trays to the table.

Chloe walks beside me and asks, "So, you trying out for cheerleading?"

Colour drains from my face. "Who, me?"

Chloe puffs out a laugh. "I'm lookin at ya, aren't I?"

I put the tray down on her table because my hands are shaking. "No, right, yeah. Um, hadn't really thought about it."

"Well, you should."

"Really?" I grip the seat beside her with fear I might faint.

"What's this?" Naveen asks from across the table.

Chloe points at me and tells Naveen and Sean, "You have to see this girl dance. She's freaking amazing."

I bite my lip, blushing.

Naveen nods, eyeing me. "If you move like Chloe, you have to be on our cheer squad. Plus, we need more pretty things to stare at from the field."

Naveen and Sean laugh together and now I'm sure I will faint. I can't tell where Bryce is and I'm not sure whether I want him in on this.

Chloe pats the seat beside her. *Ohmigawd.* I've never sat faster.

"Try-outs are real soon," Chloe continues. "You should try to work in a routine from dance class."

"Yeah, I'll try that."

Someone taps my shoulder. Meah stands over me with an ear-to-ear grin.

"Meah." There's a sly smile on Chloe's face. "You should try out for the cheer squad too."

"I should?"

"Why not?" Chloe says and laughs. "The chubby girls never get in. It'd be fun to see how far you get."

My jaw drops and I swiftly turn to Meah. Meah's face sours and she hunches like she was punched in the gut.

Kimberley rocks on her chair and sets sights on Meah with a wicked grin. "Hey Chubba. Finished my math homework yet?"

Meah opens her mouth to respond, but she's pushed backwards

when Jace Wilson targets Chloe. They attack each other, all hands and lips. I avert my eyes, but not all the way. I've never been so close to Jace before. He's an Adonis. He has this silky, toffee skin, and sexy big build, courtesy of his Fijian heritage.

"Hey, you guys get the party invite?" Madison calls out, waving her phone as she and Fiona approach the table.

Everyone starts picking up their phones, saying, "Got it."

A phone slides in front of me. Chloe's. And she's smiling at me.

I check the details of the text message. "Sweet, I'll be there."

When Chloe sends her attention back to Jace, Meah crouches beside me to escape the firing line and for an explanation on my seating arrangement. All I can give her is a shrug and my best *no-flipping-clue* expression. I can't wait until the end of school so I can gush about science. I was one-on-one with Bryce Gorgeous Kerry.

My mind floods with 'where is Bryce.' One giant inhale, and I search the table. He sits next to Naveen who is whispering something. Bryce nods and looks in my direction.

My eyes plummet to my food. All bravery tapped out.

Chloe's arm brushes against me and my head spins. Am I really sitting at this table?

After school, Meah and I race to her house to find her the perfect party outfit. It didn't take her long to fall into crisis mode. All her clothes are out of the wardrobe and in a nest on the floor.

"I have nothing to wear," she yelps, pulling her stash from under her bed.

"Meah. Seriously?"

"What?" She pulls out the largest chocolate bar and begins unwrapping.

"Do you really need to go on a binge right now?"

"Nothing will fit, so why not?"

I reef out a black sequinned, spaghetti-strapped dress. "Wear this. This one's cute."

"*Pa-ha.*" She snatches the dress and tosses it across the room. "I look like a fat cow in it."

"You're not fat!"

She blows a raspberry and throws herself backwards.

"Would ya stop?" I pull her up. "You're gonna wrinkle all your dresses."

Meah breaks apart the candy bar. "No boys gonna get with me."

"Sure they will."

Meah laughs into her chocolate.

I sigh. "Give me one then, would ya."

She tosses me something filled with caramel.

Meah shrugs. "At least we are getting invited to parties."

I whack her arm. "Exactly."

She stands up with a dress pressed against her in front of the mirror.

"Go with that one," I say, nodding at the dress. "The magenta really suits you."

She takes another bite of chocolate. "Holy crap. You gotta help me with my makeup and hair."

I rub my temples. The chocolate high is really not helping with her freak out.

4

Charli

"Ok!" Kellie plants her hands on the dining table, glasses sliding down her nose. "Henry is ten points off conquering the castle. Anyone got high spell cards? Use em now."

She's way over excited. I pull her down to sitting and stroke her mess of copper hair. Kellie cuddles me and in unison we let Simon know he's up.

Simon ponders his remaining three cards. "Hell, I dunno." He tosses a card onto the centre of the game board.

Reece slaps his forehead. "Dude. You just screwed me." He throws a card on top of Simon's. "Henry, you should just take the win now."

"Hell no!" Kellie wriggles out of my arms. "I'm sick of him winning every game. Veronica, give us something good."

Veronica ponders her cards under her jet-black hair. "Let's end this game already. I gotta go out for another smoke." Her baggy, black clothing makes her pale, hunched frame look sickly. She drops a card on the board.

"Hells yes," Lenny cheers, placing a matching card and three tokens on his sector.

It's up to Tayla, whose face is a smear of confusion. "Ok, so I know we are, like, almost finished... but I still don't get this game."

Lenny leans over Tayla's cards. "Baby, if you don't have a spell card just use an animal card."

Rikki taps one of Tayla's card. "Cuz, use this one."

Tayla shrugs and does as instructed.

Rikki's shiny hair flicks over her shoulder as she elegantly places a card on the board.

Everyone erupts in cheers.

"What the hell?" Henry yells and throws his cards on the table. He stands and his chair slams to the ground.

"*Finally*." Kellie throws her fists in the air. "Finally, Henry is taken down."

Henry's scrawny frame heaves over the board. Steam sizzles out his ears.

Tayla high fives her cousin. "Good job, Rik. Now aren't you glad you came, instead of keeping your head in books?"

Tayla jumps on Lenny's lap for her usual routine of making the rest of us disappear.

Rikki gathers up the cards with a devious grin. "Another round, everyone?"

As Reece helps Rikki reset the board, Kellie says, "Did you get the info on the Ferguson Award?"

"*Pfft*. Please," Rikki replies, shuffling cards. "I've been ready for it since last year."

"The Ferguson Award?" I ask.

Kellie's eyes bulge in her frames. "It's a science program. You work on your hypothesis all year and submit your experiment. It's a cash prize and also extra credit towards your class marks."

"You can keep that to yourself," I say. "You know that science stuff goes over my head."

"Have fun coming second, Kellie." Rikki smiles at herself while collecting more cards.

"Dream on."

Rikki reaches to grab cards from Reece, but he drops them on the board and recoils his hand. Rikki's brow creases as she collects the cards. Kellie applies pressure to Reece's shoulder until he sits. Kellie is always so quick to act for Reece. It's like they have their own language. Man, sometimes she acts that way with me.

My jeans pocket vibrates. I slip my phone out. **New Text - Travis.** A shiver tickles my spine as I read he's parked outside.

Making way for the front door, I slip past Veronica and Henry but crash into someone in my blind spot. I moan, rubbing my neck.

"Shit, you right, Charli?" Simon says, massaging his shoulder.

He reaches to touch me, and I sidestep. "Yeah, yeah. I'm cool."

Head down, I hurry to the foyer. Yeah, it's been a while since Simon and I dated, but there's still this aura of awkward hovering over us. Now Trav will be hurled into the mix.

At the front porch I watch Travis exit his car. The butterflies swarm yet my temples twinge. I'm glad he's here, but is it a massive mistake? This is the first time he's mixing with this group. Will he think its super lame?

"Hey, beautiful."

He lands on the bottom step and my body lunges forward. My arms drape over him and I whisper, "Hi."

"You ok?" His breath tickles the curve of my neck.

"Yeah, fine."

"Should we go in?"

"If you're up for it." I brace through a smile. My hand clasps his and I lead him inside. "They're setting up another game."

He tugs my hand and I catch his eyebrow raise. "One of those fantasy board games?"

I nod, chewing the inside of my cheek.

We pass the kitchen as Kellie exits it.

"Hey Kellie, thanks for inviting me."

Kellie hugs a large bowl of chips. "Hey Travis. Glad you could make it."

We follow Kellie into the dining room. Travis lands behind Reece, who's hunched over fixing the castle prop, and slaps him on the back. "Wassup?"

Reece flinches, knocking over the castle and a stack of tokens. He turns and sighs at Travis.

"Another Watkins." Veronica cackles, rocking her chair. "Are you as fun as Reece?"

Travis puffs out a laugh. "No one is as fun as Reece."

Veronica giggles to herself and Travis takes the seat next to his cousin.

Kellie shuffles towards me, eyes wide and unblinking. I get the hint and walk backwards.

"All good?"

I nod like I haven't a clue what she's on about. "Yeah course."

"Worlds are colliding."

A retch flies from the back of my throat. "I know."

Her lips pout while she rubs my arm. My chest eases as her glasses slide glacially down her nose.

She finally blinks.

I let loose a short, loud laugh.

"So, Travis," Kellie says, sitting next to him. "Rikki just kicked Henry's butt, and we gotta make sure he don't win again."

"*Oi.*" Henry sulks, elbows hitting the table.

Travis' arm slings over the back of the chair. "Why is he picked on?”

“Cause he always wins.”

I slide between Travis and Kellie and comb my fingers through his hair. One fleeting moment it’s only us.

“Oh, sorry Charli,” Kellie says, standing up.

“No, it’s ok,” I push on her shoulder, “I’ll stand.” I scan the table and stop at Tayla on Lenny’s lap. “Maybe Travis and I can team up? Seeing as he’s new to the game.”

Henry blurts out the rules and Travis’ eyes glaze over. Should I feel guilty for smirking? My body leans into his as the cards are dealt.

The house floods with the boom of a car stereo. The board quakes like the car’s parked in the living room.

“Expecting more people?” Travis asks.

“No.” Kellie shakes her head. “Must be a party down the road.”

Travis pulls me onto his lap. My torso tenses as a gang of voices erupt outside.

“Who even is that?” Veronica asks, hugging a bent knee.

The voices close in towards the house. Kellie’s eyes narrow and ears prick. She jumps when a succession of knocks thunder on the front door. She grumbles and pushes her chair backwards.

I follow her up the hall. “Who would that be?”

From the foyer I watch the front doorknob turning.

My heart stops.

The door flings open and ten kids rampage the house.

“What the hell?” Kellie shrieks.

They push past us with loud and obnoxious laughter.

“Wh-what?” Kellie stammers. “You can’t just... Wha—”

More kids storm through the front door. Heart pounding, I race to the dining room. Further ahead, kids swarm through the back doors of the living room.

“Who did you tell?” Reece yells at Travis.

Travis points to his chest. "You think I did this?"

"Who did you tell?" Reece slams the table and looms over his cousin.

"Yo, Travis," an uninvited boy swaggers over to Travis. Reece and Travis roll their eyes at him.

"Not now, Flint," Travis says to the boy. Reece storms off, while Travis moves towards me, and asks, "What's going on?"

"Like I know?" I reply.

"You're not blaming me, too?"

"No... no."

"Babe?" He smooths my arm. His eyes find mine and gravity pulls me with double strength.

"What the fuck?" Kellie stops next to me. "Why are these people in my house?"

"Yo, Party Queen," Will says, throwing an arm around Kellie's shoulders.

"Will?" I say, squinting at him. "What are you doing here?"

Will squeezes Kellie in a one-armed hug. "Heard our girl is throwing a rager."

Kellie throws her arms up in the air, her face screwing up. "Where on Earth did you hear that?"

Will lets her go and takes his phone out. "I don't even know anymore. I got like three or four texts about it. It's spreading like wildfire."

"Show me those messages," Travis says.

Will smirks and puts his phone in his pocket. "What does it matter? We're all here now."

"Are you really this dumb?" I say to Will. "Kellie didn't set this up."

"So, there's going to be a ton of people at my party," Kellie says, her mind wandering.

Rikki runs to Kellie, puffing. "I didn't sign up for a rager."

"Kel, I thought tonight was gonna be chill," Veronica says.

Kellie cranes her neck and scans the room. "Where's Reece?"

I look around. "I don't know."

"I need to find him and send him home," Kellie says. She looks between me and Travis. "You two can take him home."

"What about you?" I ask. "Don't you want us to stay and get these people out of here?"

"Charli, I never go to parties," Kellie says. "Yeah, I can host game nights, but now there's a major party brought to me."

"You don't like big parties."

"No, I make sure you and Reece are happy so that usually means not going to them."

I bite inside my cheek as I try to work out who has possessed my best friend.

"If there's going to be a big party here," Veronica says, tugging on Kellie's arm. "You need to come with me first. You know, for what we talked about earlier."

"No, Kel," I say, trying to pull her back.

As Kellie lets Veronica lead her away, she calls out, "Find Reece. I'll be right back."

My insides slingshot. I face Travis but glance at the guys still around the table, standing and unsettled.

A scan of the uninvited guests.

Back to Travis.

"Why are you looking at me like that?"

I point to Lenny, Simon and the others. "None of them would have invited any of these people."

"I came here to spend time with you. Why would I invite people?"

I squirm in my sneakers and focus on shadows on the wall.

He groans and pulls his phone from his pocket. "I told Ray." He starts texting. "He asked why I wasn't going to GiGi's. He's my best mate, though."

My fingers dig at my waist. More random kids file into the house. My teeth grit and my eyes sting.

He's the only variance.

"Charli?"

His hands interlock with mine. My eyes are wet. He's always been honest with me. Hasn't he?

"We need to find Reece," I say.

Travis pushes through the crowd to find Reece, while I follow. I blink hard as my sister walks towards me. "What are you doing here?"

"Hey, I can't believe Kellie's throwing such a huge party," she gushes, dumbstruck. Her shiny, straight hair flows over her tight, red dress. I smooth over my big curls, noting my ripped jeans and old t-shirt. It's like looking into an overdone mirror.

"She isn't."

Brittany's head tilts like a confused puppy. Meah's glued to her hip.

My eyes roll. "Kellie didn't invite any of these people. Someone spread a rumour. Who told you about this?"

Brittany plays with her hair as she confers with Meah. "We got it from Chloe."

"What? She just decided to make it up?"

"No, there was a text," Meah chimes in. "Who was it from again? GiGi Larkin?"

A lump clogs my throat.

Brittany nods. "Yeah, that's right."

"Just go home," I tell the girls. "Everyone is going to be kicked out. Save yourself some embarrassment."

Meah nudges my arm. "Whatever. We didn't get all dressed up to not party."

I lock eyes with Brittany, tilting my head, waiting for her to take my advice.

Nothing.

Strained for air, I push Meah out of the way and move towards the back deck. I hug my waist and bounce off party people like a wayward beach ball.

I crane my neck. With Travis still on the hunt for Reece, perhaps I can find Kellie and convince her to stop this overgrown party.

I sidle down the side of the house and squeeze through bushes. A dank, earthy odour wafts closer and my nose scrunches. It grows more pungent and I hear Kellie and Veronica giggling. I push through two bushes and find the pair on the grass, leaning against the house.

Is Kellie holding a cigarette?

"Charli!" Kellie throws arms in the air like a cheerleader. "Charli's here!"

Veronica takes the cigarette from Kellie's hand. It's crudely rolled. The smell makes my mouth water in a bad way.

It's a joint.

"Kel, what are you doing?"

Kellie's arms, still in the air, beckon me over. "Come ere, come ere."

My hands slide into my pockets and I edge towards her.

She tugs at my t-shirt and I crouch next to her. Her eyes glaze as she giggles.

"Man, Kel, I only left you for ten minutes."

"Just the mention of weed got her excited," Veronica smirks.

I jerk my head away. "When you said you smoked, I didn't know this is what you meant."

With wide eyes and a goofy smile, Kellie whispers, "All these people came to my party."

"How is that a good thing?"

Veronica points the joint at me. "Mellow out."

I bat her hand away. I hold Kellie and try to maintain eye contact.
Kellie grins. "We should go party."

"We should call the cops and get these people kicked out."

Kellie stands and slips past me. I swallow whatever leapt in my mouth and tail her. Kellie swaggers up the deck and glides through the hordes of people and into the house.

I shove my way through in time to see Will holding a plastic cup in the air making a toast. "Kellie Saunders, the ultimate party queen."

Kellie cheers a cup towards the ceiling. Her head tilts back and she sculls the contents. She stumbles and I make it in time to catch her.

"Watch out, Kel." I prop her up but am unsuccessful at taking the cup away.

"Oh hi, Brittany." Bryce Kerry waves at me.

My posture droops.

Will smirks. "Nah, man. That's Chaz."

Bryce sucks in air. "Shit sorry. Yeah, Brittany's the pretty one."

What?

Will and Bryce wear matching freaked expressions.

"No, no. I mean, I just, I saw her before... and her dress was pretty. That's all. Not that you're not—"

Will bursts into a fit of laughter. "*Geez*, dig your own grave, why don't ya?"

Kellie loops arms around my neck and strokes my hair. "My Charli is beautiful."

I wince, trying to get some distance between our faces.

"Kellie," Reece calls, marching toward us.

"*Reece*." Kellie unlatches me and hurls herself towards him. "Oh Reece. I love you. You're my favourite."

Reece's body is rigid. "What the hell?"

Kellie swings her body and trips. Reece shuffles to catch her. As Kellie giggles, Reece's eyes widen, searching for an explanation.

I make fists in the pockets of my jeans. I can't announce she's high in front of everyone.

Kellie pulls her drink from behind Reece and gulps down the contents.

Reece arches a brow. "Whaddaya drinkin?"

"Want one?" Will holds a drink in front of Reece.

Reece frowns and says 'no.' Will shrugs and offers it to me. I wave it away.

I help Reece with the overly handsy Kellie. We pull her towards the kitchen and Reece gets water, which I order her to drink.

"Why are there so many people here?" Reece says to the benchtop.

"Dirty rumour," I say.

His body jolts in random shakes.

"Reece? Are you ok?"

"*Reece.*" Kellie flicks her arms out and spills the glass of water over the island bench. "Reece, there's so many people here."

"Why is she being weird?"

"She's high."

Reece grabs Kellie's wrist. "You're high?"

"As a cucumber!" she cheers.

"How is she high?"

"Veronica."

"Reece, Reece," Kellie says, "are you ok with all these people? We need to get you an escape."

"What about you?" he replies.

Her eyes become round as she giggles. "I'm ready to have some fun."

My hands run over my face. "Ah, Kel."

Is she serious right now? She wants some epic party? I've already gone through the drama of losing one friend to parties and popularity. Not to mention how dumb my sister is currently being. My body tenses with the thought I could lose Kellie too.

Kellie grabs my wrists. "You should take him home."

I shake her off, but her grip is strong. "We aren't leaving you."

"He doesn't even like school because of all the people."

Will saunters into the kitchen. "Where my party people at?"

Kellie flails her arms about. "Right ere."

Reece slides his elbows on the benchtop and cups his hands over his ears.

There's a tap on my shoulder and I turn to Travis. He tilts his head for me to follow him.

Kellie and Will talk over each other and I think Reece will be ok, so long as no more people file in. I tell them I'll return.

"You ok?" he asks when we move into the hall. He brushes my cheek, but I don't have a smile for him. "You're shitty with me?"

An unpleasant welling borders my eyes. I blink hard and involuntarily sniff.

He plays with my hair, waiting for an answer.

"So, Ray was the only person you told?"

He shuffles his weight and *humphs* a 'yes.'

"Brittany said she heard about this from GiGi."

"GiGi?"

He's silent. I keep swallowing so my voice doesn't crack.

"I didn't tell her. I don't know why she'd tell people to come over here."

My eyes sting. "She's obviously pissed you came here instead of going to her house."

"Why would I pick her over my girlfriend?" He scoops me into a hug. "I don't think she would have done this."

"Are you freaking kidding me?"

He lets go of me and takes a step back.

My chest tightens.

He pulls out his phone.

> *(Travis)* **Hey mate, did you tell GiGi there was a big party at Kellie Saunders tonight?**
>
> *(Ray)* **No why?**
>
> *(Travis)* **Cos the house is packed and rumour is she told everyone to come here.**
>
> *(Ray)* **Shit really? She asked me where you going tonight and I said cos I knew. But I didn't tell her it was a big party. Dunno where she got that from??**

I rub my temples. "Can we sit somewhere?"

Travis takes my hand and leads me to the living room. I'm grateful for his popularity when he easily gets kids to vacate a couch. I cuddle him as people Kellie and I don't associate with roam her house.

I'm not like Reece, I can stand crowds. I can talk in front of big groups and not lose my cool. But people are idiots. The more people you pile in a room, the more shenanigans occur. The conversations dumb down and make me want to rip my ears off.

I wish I were more introverted. Like, I'd be so internal I wouldn't notice everyone around me. It's exhausting seeing everything but not picking up on the details. Listening to crap. Watching idiotic antics. Like that guy over there, balancing one-legged on a tipping chair while sculling a beer.

As I lay my head on Travis' chest and listen to the rhythms of his heart, I'm glad for the privacy of romantic relationships. When it's just us, it's magic. But every time his friends, or anyone at school for that matter, try to intervene our connection fractures.

I love being with him. But I loved *us* before school started. All this crap is making it harder and harder to sustain my love for him.

Over the noise I just make out Travis' ringtone. He picks up his phone. **Incoming call: GiGi.**

"Don't answer it."

"I'll see what she has to say."   He hits answer.

Stab. Picking her over me. I move and leave a gap between us, knees to my chest. With only half the conversation, I can tell he'll forgive her.

She's such a piece of work.

I wish I'd never gone to the mess hall and sat with his friends. If I had insisted he go to GiGi's party, we'd still be around the table playing boardgames instead of being stuck in this noise.

But then she would have won in a completely different way. At least Travis is with me right now.

I slide back to hear GiGi. "Travy, you know I would never want to hurt you. I thought I was doing something good for Charli. I thought she would want some more friends. She always seems so alone and sad."

Oh, cram it.

When Travis ends the phone call, I recoil from his touch.

"She apologised," he says.

I look away from him and cross my arms.

"Charli."

I purse my lips refusing to break.

"I didn't have anything to do with this."

"I know," I say.

I eye Reece and have an urge to hide away in comfortable silence with him. I leap off the couch and tell Travis I'll be right back.

5

Brittany

At the bathroom mirror, I coat another layer of red lipstick. I smooth my hair and run my hands over my strapless, lipstick-matching dress. My heart and breathing are in a running race.

Brittany, stop freaking out.

Please?

I unlock the door and exit to the hall. Meah grabs my arm and we join Chloe's group.

"We needs drinks," Chloe says.

Meah and I follow the girls into the kitchen. I double-take as Will and Kellie Saunders shout and laugh at each other across the island bench.

"Are you lost?" Kimberley says to Will, side-glancing Kellie.

"*Pfft*, get outta ere, Harley Quinn." Will bats a hand at Kimberley, eyes all over Kellie.

"You can't say the third movie is better than the first," Kellie continues like we're not even here. "That's blasphemy."

"But the special effects got so much better. And Cody comes into the story. How can you not say it gets better with Cody?"

Kellie's nose wrinkles. "Ok, I will give you that one."

Madison pokes around the fridge. "*Oi*, where's the booze?"

"On a table out there somewhere." Will points down the hall, eyes still on Kellie.

"Will," Chloe begins, sliding a hand along the island bench. "How did the trip to see Daddy Dearest go?"

Will rolls his eyes. "Fine."

"Did he like the gift from my daddy?"

"I guess."

"Daddy just wants to make sure he's happy. He's got a new lawyer working on the case."

"*Ohmigawd*," Will groans. "Just shuddup, Benny. I don't care."

"Well, fuck you." Chloe slaps the bench. "I'm glad it was your dad and not mine."

Meah and I slide out of the doorway as Chloe storms out of the kitchen. We let Kimberley, Madison and Fiona follow before we do.

Before continuing, I hear Kellie ask, "Do you want to talk about it?"

Will's reply is hushed as his hands run over his face. I rush to keep up with Chloe & Co.

I've obsessively reminisced about my science class pair up with Bryce. As I follow Chloe, I wonder if I'd even be here if that didn't happen. Did she only talk to me because I was standing near Bryce in mess? If I wasn't near him, would I have sat at her table? Would she have shown me the invite?

Damn, it's been a monumental day.

Chloe orders the nearest boy to pour our drinks. Unimpressed, she says to us, "There's no dancefloor yet."

"Booze first, then dancing," Madison says, taking the first filled cup.

"*Gawd*, you're such a booze-hound, Madi," Kimberley says.

"Like you're any better." Chloe taps her cup against Kimberley's.

Fiona takes a whiff from Madison's cup and winces. "What is that?"

"Rum, I think."

Fiona's face stays screwed up and she refuses to take a cup. Fiona is like a porcelain doll with her pale complexion and naturally white-blonde hair. Her doll persona is enhanced every time she acts childish.

"Stop being such a baby," Chloe says.

Meah and I quickly grab a cup. Chloe shoves a cup into Fiona's hand, and we follow her to the centre of the living room.

"Sean, turn up the music," Kimberley calls across the room. Sean spins a knob on the stereo and makes his way over to dance with Kimberley.

Chloe marches towards me as I teeter on heels. "I wanna dance with you before Jace gets here."

I swear my heart has left an imprint on my dress. I casually wipe my hands along my hips and smile my best smile. Crap, hope there's no lipstick on my teeth. I sip from the plastic cup, hoping to wash anything away. My eyes squint and lips pucker. Whatever this drink is it burns all the way down.

Chloe takes my hand and swings me in front of her. My head bops to the music and hair swings wherever it wants. Chloe smiles and twirls me under her arm. I have the dopiest grin. *Geez*, I can't get rid of it.

I trip into nearby kids when I'm shoved from the side; the side where Kimberley is dancing. I don't look, I don't give her the satisfaction.

Chloe twists her body, fists pumping in the air. A quick exhale and I two-step, with Kimberley in my sideline. Impossible to ignore. She leads Sean in my direction. Their combined body weight smashes into me.

I reach for Fiona, so I don't faceplant the floor.

Fiona pushes me off and I stumble for my footing. I stay on red alert for Kimberley and Sean. Each time she comes at me, I bop out of the way.

She kicks at my heels.

GIVE IT A REST.

Chloe sips her drink, frowns and shakes her head. "Sean," she says, tapping his shoulder. "Are there better drinks anywhere? This rum is shit."

"I think Nav has something. Maybe vodka?"

Chloe grabs my wrist. "That sounds way better. Come with me."

Seriously? Of course. I'd let you drag me anywhere.

I can't hide the smile. Kimberley would hate that Chloe's leaving with me. She was always trying to exclude me when we were kids. It won't happen again.

We wall-hug until we get to Naveen. Chloe waves her cup at him. "Heard you've got the good stuff."

Naveen laughs. He leans down and plucks two bottles of hot pink liquid out of a box. He hands one to me. *Raspberry vodka.* Maybe that'll burn less?

I try to open the bottle but lose my footing when someone pushes me.

SERIOUSLY. GET LOST KIMBERLEY.

"Oh crap, I'm so sorry."

Someone takes my hand and helps me stand. I spin around and face Bryce.

"Are you ok?" he asks.

I bite my bottom lip and nod.

He smiles like he's about to ask me something.

Goosebumps swarm my arms. To dance? To dance?

"*Geez*, Bryce. How could you?" Chloe pushes in front of me and playfully hits Bryce's bicep. "You totally ran into me. You owe me big time."

"Oh, ah. Sorry, are you ok?"

Chloe flicks her hair and hangs an arm around his neck. "Nothing a dance with you won't fix."

"Um, yeah, ok."

I grip the bottle as Bryce and Chloe move towards the makeshift dancefloor. I close my mouth once I realise it's hanging open.

"Need a hand opening that?" Naveen asks, hand out for the bottle.

I hand it to him with little interest. He gives it back, opened, but I can't stop staring at Chloe.

She wasn't hit.

I put the bottle to my lips and guzzle.

Oh, it's sweet.

Oh, bummer, after taste.

Bryce's hands are on the small of Chloe's back.

One more large guzzle should do it.

I ask Naveen for another drink and find Meah.

"*Whoah*, you right?" Meah asks when I shove the bottle into her chest.

"Sorry. Preoccupied."

"What happened? You left with Chloe. Why aren't you still with her?"

My tongue pushes against my teeth as I point out Chloe, draping herself over Bryce.

"Chloe and Bryce? How did that happen?"

"I... I, I can't even tell you."

"Did he ask her to dance? What about Jace?"

I turn to Meah with direct eye contact. "Meah, I swear he was about to ask me to dance."

She squeals and almost drops her vodka bottle. "Are you serious?"

"He was smiling at me and then Chloe barged between us."

"He was smiling? Did he actually ask you?"

"*Ugh.* It's a feeling, Meah."

I sneak another peek at the dancefloor. Kimberley leans on Chloe, giggling and whispering.

Blood boils in my veins, pumping in my ears. The bottle returns to my lips and only lowers once completely drained.

"Wow... That was quick."

"I need another."

I trail back to Naveen, who is now popping and locking in front of Madison, who is paying more attention to her drink. I crouch by the box and pull out two bottles. Yellow this time. *Pineapple.* As I back away, Madison winks at me.

"You're only halfway through?" I say, handing the new bottle to Meah.

"Hold up, I did drink the rum as well."

I drink the neck of the bottle in one gulp.

"I wanna find someone to dance with." Meah giggles, a bottle in each hand.

"I just want to dance with him." On the dancefloor Jace has his paws all over Chloe. "Hey, where is he?"

As I tiptoe in heels, Meah whacks my arm. "There he is."

WHAT? He's sitting on a couch. He's sitting on a couch next to Rikki Hernandez. Bryce is sitting with Rikki. WHY? Rikki... WHY?

I pull at my hair. "What d'you think is going on over there? Does it look serious?"

"Hardly. They both look bored."

"Should I go over there?" I take another sip.

"Maybe. Think you have enough liquid courage."

Meah's voice garbles. I wobble on my heels. People near me move with a faint squiggle around them.

I nod and decide on another sip. As the bottle hits my lips, it's flung away.

"What the hell are you doing?" Charli screeches in my ear.

"Hey, give it back." I swipe for the drink but my vision blurs and Charli breaks in two.

"You're drinking? Really. You're being that dumb."

"Piss off, Charli!" Meah shoves Charli.

I rush a hand to my mouth as a hiccup-burp flies up my throat. My head is as light as a balloon. I *not-on-purpose* sway.

"Gimme back the drink."

"Brit, you've obviously had enough."

Meah pushes between us. "Just go back to the loser corner, Charli."

I clap my hands together, vision clearing, setting targets on the bottle.

"I'm not leaving you like this," Charli says.

My eyes roll. "Fine." I take Meah's full bottle and spin on my heels. I push through the crowd in any direction that is away from my sister.

I'm sick of being a total nobody. I need to push myself into the party scene. Social suicide is not an option anymore. Every day I brand myself a loser. I don't want the rest of school doing that. That's a level of torment I just can't take.

There's a signal in my brain telling me I should be mad, but I fixate on how numb my lips are. I drink more, then choke at what's in front of me.

A couple making out.

I blink hard.

Will Maclean and Kellie Saunders. Making out. In front of everyone. Phones take pictures, people cheer. I drown it out by gulping another mouthful.

I push through the crowd and Meah grabs me.

"Who should I dance with?"

I shake my head, *dunno*. I rub my temples as the light starts making shapes in the room. I squint as Bryce starts leaving the living room. I frown as Rikki follows him to the deck.

Meah takes me to Madison and Fiona, blurting out names of possible dance partners. I smooth over the dress I wore to grab Bryce's attention. Epic Fail.

"You guys are drinkin, right?" Madison holds her cup up.

I tap my bottle against it. "Everything."

BLACK.

My eyes spring open and I gasp. The room is pitch black. Where is everyone?

Panting, I grip the sides of the couch. I sit, and then immediately lie down. My entire head is in searing pain.

Wasn't I just with Meah? Did she ditch me?

I try to throw my feet off the couch, but they're stuck. I kick and kick. They're caught on something. I curl up to reach and find my feet are twisted in a blanket. I stamp until they're free.

Maybe I'm home?

I roll off the couch and land on my stilettos. *Ouch.*

I need my bed.

I crawl around the couch and pull myself up with the armrest. I trudge out of the living room.

I run into walls.

My temples pulsate.

Finally, I find stairs.

The climb is exhausting. On the landing I feel along the wall. With relief, I'm at my door. I clutch the doorknob but pause at a sound inside.

Grunting.

Am I at Charli's door?

Two people grunting.

I stumble back. Hands muffle my shriek. I am not home.

Something jumps from my stomach and hits the roof of my mouth. I swallow, cupping my mouth. My stomach continues to flip, and I hunch over.

I fly down the stairs and keep running until I find a bathroom. The oven clock lights up the kitchen and I know I can't wait any longer. I race to the sink where it all comes out. It's gross and loud. I wipe my mouth and run the water until everything is down the drain.

Maybe I'm still at Kellie's? I leave the kitchen and collapse on the couch. My body aches. My eyes are already closed.

A door closes and a lock clicks. Wearily, my eyes open to the sunlight filtering through the venetian blinds.

This is not my house. This is not Kellie's house.

Footsteps close in.

"Oh, good, you're awake." Chloe appears, smiling over the couch.

"Chloe?" my voice croaks.

Chloe giggles as she curls up on the armrest. "Lemme guess, you don't member anythin."

I rub my head. There's a gross taste in my mouth. I remember the kitchen sink and shudder.

"You were so wasted you couldn't even walk straight. You kept freakin out that ya mum was gonna kill ya. So we brought you here."

I hug my knees and sink into the couch.

"Jace had to carry ya. It was too funny. He just left."

"Crap. I don't remember any of that."

"Perfect. Means ya had a good time if you don't member it." She tosses my phone onto my lap. "I texted ya mum to say you were staying over here.”

“How did you do that?”

“Just stuck your thumb over it. Your phone is way boring. Except the cute mirror selfies you take. I posted a few to ya *Instagram*. Enjoy the likes.”

My stomach flips for a whole new reason. She went through my phone?

Something scampers down the hallway. Two puppies speed into the living room. One black and one white, toy poodles. They leap onto the couch and climb all over me.

“Oh, hey puppies, not my stomach.”

“These are my puppies,” Chloe says, scooping up the white one. “This one is Chanel, and that one is Coco.”

“They’re so cute.”

“They’re not so cute in the middle of the night,” Chloe’s mother says, clicking her heels into the room. Mrs Benson is elegant. Her bright blonde hair pinned high and her body is hugged by a black dress.

Mrs Benson stops by Chloe and points at Chanel. “This one was the worst. She barked all night. Seriously, they are little terrors when you’re not around.”

Chloe cuddles Chanel. “That’s just cause they know who their master is.”

Mrs Benson laughs and then looks at me. I suck in so much air I cough.

“You right, hun? I’m Cheryl.”

“Mum, this is Brittany. Member? She’s the one who shows us up at dance class.”

I fall back on the couch. She talks about me?

“Oh, the star performer.” Mrs Benson winks. She clicks towards the kitchen. “Anyone in need of coffee?”

“Yes,” I answer before thinking.

"Mum, will you take us to *The Pancake Parlour*?"

"Oh, yum, pancakes sound so good right now."

Chloe rolls her eyes. "No, not for you to come. Just drop me and Brit off."

Mrs Benson laughs. "Fine. That'll be ok."

"Morning girls," Mr Benson strides through the room, wearing a tailored three-piece suit. Two housekeepers hurry to follow him. He looks like grandpa age. Like, way older than Chloe's mum. Makes sense after hearing Chloe's two oldest brothers are nearing forty.

"Hi Daddy," Chloe beams, as her dad and the housekeepers leave for the kitchen.

I take in last night's outfit. "I must look like crap."

Chloe drops Chanel and bounces off the couch. "Come with me."

No matter how big the headache, I'll still follow her anywhere. I jump up with only medium-level regret.

She takes me upstairs to her bedroom. I grin like an idiot. I'm in Chloe Benson's bedroom. My head fills with squeals. It's styled with French provincial furniture. Lilac satin sheets are a mess on the white four-poster bed.

Chloe opens her walk-in wardrobe. "What d'you wanna wear?"

"I can wear something of yours?" I'm pretty sure I'm floating towards the wardrobe.

"Unless you really want to go out in that?"

I shake my head and giggle.

She lets me touch everything. This is better than going to a boutique with Mum's credit card.

The sunlight is harsh. Way harsh. I cup my eyes as I exit Mrs Benson's Mercedes. My walk is shaky as I dawdle behind Chloe. Feeling better, though, in her purple halter and black vinyl skirt.

We're seated at a booth and Chloe orders us two lattes. "And I always get the mixed berry stack, so can I just order that now?"

"I don't think I can eat anything." My stomach is so fragile.

"No, get something with bacon. That'll help." Chloe leans over the menu in front of me and taps a picture. "Can you get her that one?"

The waitress walks away, and Chloe asks, "Was last night the first time you drank alcohol?"

I bite my bottom lip and nod.

Chloe giggles. "You just went for it, hey?"

I bunch my hair in my hands. It's probably frizzing like crazy. Chloe opens her clutch and hands me a hair-tie. I grin and loop my hair into a bun.

"My hair is nowhere near as curly as yours, but I know what it's like to leave the house without blowdrying."

"I hate having curly hair. I have to straighten it every day."

"Yeah, I can't believe your twin leaves her hair curly all the time."

Our lattes arrive and my phone buzzes on the table. Irritating. I shut my eyes and rub my forehead.

"You gonna look at that?"

"Meah keeps texting. I'm not ready to look at em yet."

"Ah, she's so annoying." Chloe lunges for the phone. "Want me to tell her to piss off?"

"No, no." I grab the phone back. "I've just got a headache and can't read the screen, that's all."

When the food arrives, I take one whiff and my stomach churns. I tell Chloe I'm going to the bathroom and take off.

In the bathroom I rest behind the cubicle door. In the quiet, the need to puke subsides. I open the door and scuff towards the basins to splash water on my face.

I pull up and swallow. Ok. I'm ok.

Naveen and Madison have joined Chloe in the booth.

"Wow, you look better than I would have thought," Madison says.

"I do?"

"You were a friggin goner," Naveen says.

I frown and sink into the booth.

"Leave her alone," Chloe snaps at Naveen. "We are in the presence of Brittany's first hangover."

Madison snorts. "No way. That was the first time you drank?"

"We're not all alcos like you, Madi."

"Piss off, Nav."

"So, what am I looking at here." Chloe squints. "You two actually together now, or not?"

"Not," Madison replies.

"Well, that's up for debate," Naveen smirks, sliding an arm around Madison.

Madison retches and rolls her eyes. "We are not together."

"Nav, can you get lost then?" Chloe blurts out.

"*Pa-ha.* What?"

"I want girl-talk. And if you're not Madi's squeeze, then I want you gone."

"Piss off. I'm eating pancakes."

"Just go to the bathroom or somethin."

"Damn, girls are bitches," Naveen says and swaggers away from the booth.

Chloe leans over the table. "Why is he here with you then?"

Madison tightens her high brunette ponytail. Her oval eyes dynamic with smokey eyeshadows which contrasts her warm skin tone. "He stayed over. I cuddle up with him, but I never let him do anything."

"Why not?"

Madison covers her face with a menu. "Because I don't want to."

"He's cute, do somethin bout it. Speaking of cute boys, how freakin cute is that Bryce Kerry."

All air is gone. Seriously, I can't breathe.

"What about Jace?" Madison says, dropping the menu.

"Can't last forever. Every girl needs a backup, right?"

"A backup?" it tumbles out of my mouth.

"Sure. I'm not like you girls. I could never be single."

Not like I'm trying to be single.

"You would eat him alive, Chloe," Madison says.

"PS, he's a good dancer."

What was that look she just gave me?

"Am I allowed back?" Naveen asks, sliding into the booth.

"Only if you wanna gossip bout Bryce Kerry," Madison says, picking bacon off my plate.

"Oh, you know who he left with, don't ya?" Naveen replies.

"He left with someone?" Chloe's eyes narrow.

"You'll never guess. Rikki Hernandez."

"What?" Chloe and Madison shriek.

My heart leaps to my throat. He left with Rikki?

"Yep. The smart girls must have it goin on."

Madison smacks his arm. "Yeah, like Will and Kellie Saunders."

"They hooked up?" Chloe asks.

"You didn't see?" Naveen says. "They made out in front of everyone. Maybe you were too busy sucking Jace's face off."

"Amongst other things," Madison teases.

"So I didn't hallucinate," I smirk.

"Nope, Big Willy macked on the Mad Scientist Chick."

"She was drunk off her arse," Madison adds.

"She smelled a bit," Naveen puts his pointer and middle finger to his lips, "but I'm not sure if that was just from freakshow Veronica *Wassername*."

"*Eww*, really," Madison replies.

Chloe retches. "Stoners are disgustin. I can't believe we were actually in their presence."

"I doubt Kellie would do that," I say. "She's not the type."

"That Veronica was gross," Naveen says. "If she lingered near you, you had to burn your clothes. That smell was not coming out."

"They're weirdos, but at least we had a venue," Madison says, taking more of my bacon.

"Heck yeah," Chloe says. "Who cares whose house it is, as long as we can trash it?"

6

Charli

This morning I wanted to defend Kellie against her parents, but they wouldn't let me in the house. Kellie is grounded for a month. The house was gate-crashed, so she could have gotten out of it.

But she was wasted. There's no coming back from that.

I wanted to stay at the party and make sure she was safe. Also, to clean up. (Probably wouldn't have happened because her parents came home to a house full of kids.) But she kept pushing me away. Even in her far-out state, she kept insisting Reece and I had to leave. Some part of her really wanted a massive party, yet the normal part of her remembered we weren't into it.

And then I find out through *Instagram* she made out with Will Maclean.

Kellie and Will?

It's still not computing.

I'm sad I couldn't help Kellie, and more so I couldn't help my sister.

Brittany; downing all those drinks, staggering on heels, partying wild. She's literally becoming the idiot I despise. I don't want to lose my sister. I really don't want her to go down the path of talking like a ditz and showing off her legs and cleavage for boys.

Mum said she texted that she was at a friend's house. I don't know who, because she's not with Meah. I know that because of Travis' non-stop texts.

Fucking GiGi. HE FORGAVE HER. Beyond mad.

He wanted to protect me, but he picked her. He picked her when he didn't spray her with abuse. I don't like the distance the party put between us. It's that fear I have every time I see Travis with his friends. Even when they're not around they still get in the way.

My phone is set to flight mode. I can't deal with any more excuses. I need space. I need my bike.

The wind plays at my skin as I take up speed on my way to West Sanford. A twenty-minute cycle, and worth it. People from school are rarely that side of the train tracks. The houses are older and smaller in West Sanford. It's far from the beach, with no boutique shops. I pull up at a line of storefronts, untie my satchel bag and enter *Gina's Coffee House*. Mad craving for a gunpowder green tea.

The cafe is dark and cramped. I order my tea and wait by the counter. Posters line the walls. The cafe is hosting open mic nights, live bands, spoken word, and fundraising events. The waitress calls my name and I take my paper cup. I go next door to *Tabitha's Tales*. So many awesome reads found in this bookstore. The perfume of books wafts through the aisles. Calvin Klein needs to bottle that ASAP.

I round a display of crime novels, tapping at the spines. GiGi's voice from last night's phone call plays in my mind. My grip around my green tea constricts.

How could he not tell her off?

He should have stood up for me.

A book is presented on an easel. The cover is smeared with orange, reds and blacks. I pick it up and skim the back cover.

"Have you read any in the series?" a voice asks from behind.

Must be a salesperson. I turn around to a boy about a foot taller than me, smiling.

I put the book down. "Nah, I don't even read crime. Don't know why I picked it up."

"Marketing?"

I play with the strap of my bag, step backwards and turn away from him.

"The Hobbit?"

I turn as he's pointing to my bag. My ancient copy of 'The Hobbit' pokes out the satchel.

"Yeah. It's my favourite."

"Nice." His hazel eyes are bright against his dark mocha skin. Smile lines crease his face.

"If you like fantasy, you should check out this series." He takes a book from the shelf. 'The Firelake Five.' "I'm like their unofficial sponsor. I try to get everyone hooked on this series."

I take the book. "I haven't heard of it."

"It's a bit obscure. They have just released book three. There will be five in total."

I skim page one. "Maybe I'll give it a read."

"*Yes*. Converted another one."

I fixate on his smile.

"I'm Preston." His hand reaches out. My toes curl in my canvas shoes. I clutch his hand and say my name. "Glad to meet you, Charli."

I walk to the counter with my recommended purchase.

"Hope you like it," he says, following me.

"I'll hold you responsible if it's a dud."

"*Ha*. Fair enough."

"There you are," a girl says, walking up to us.

"Shae, this is Charli," Preston says to the girl. "I got her onto '*Firelake Five*.'"

Shae *tsks*, smiling. "Watch out, now he's gonna wanna have endless plot discussions with you too." She rubs Preston's arm and says, "Sorry, I can't hang at *Gina's*. I've gotta go. Mum wants help before her boyfriend comes over."

"Ok, no problem," he says.

"It was nice to meet you, Charli," Shae says, backing towards the door. "See ya, Pres."

We say goodbye and then Preston says to me, "Do you have time for a coffee?"

I waggle my cup. "I'm good."

"You know they let you take them back in right?"

I let a small laugh escape me. "Sorry, I really should be getting home."

"I haven't seen you at school. Do you go to *John Thomas*?"

"Yes."

"Don't think less of me because I go to *West Sanford High*. Ok?"

I shake my head. "I wouldn't."

"I'm almost out of there anyway. I'm in my last year."

"Oh, so is my boyfriend."

Preston recoils then lets out an easy laugh. "Shudda known. The pretty ones are already taken."

"What? Isn't..." Is he not with Shae?

"In any event," he says, taking a bookmark off the counter. "I'd really like to know what you think of the book." He writes on the bookmark and hands it to me. "That's my number. Just in case you ever want to gush over the amazing characters you'll read about."

I take it, staring hard at it. What am I supposed to do with this?

"No pressure," he adds.

I slip the bookmark into the book to skip through the awkwardness. "I should get going."

"Ok. It was lovely meeting you, Charli."

I nod in response and leave the bookstore.

I put my newly acquired book in my bag. The premise: *a group of camping teens are dragged into another world when mistaken for a galactic enemy.*

I'll start reading it tonight.

"Charli?" Travis says from the front porch of my house.

"Hey," I say, walking my bike up the path.

"Where you been? I've been textin you."

I park my bike in the garage and walk up to the porch. "Just out."

"I've been waiting for ages. You cudda replied."

"I was at a bookstore. Chill out."

"I could have met up with you."

I face the sky as my eyes roll. I sidestep him and march toward the house.

"Charli. Seriously?"

I stop. "What?"

"What is up?"

"Why are you so grumpy with me?"

"Me? You're the one that keeps ignoring me."

I continue to the house.

"Are you serious?"

"You don't have to be here right now."

"You're still pissed about last night?"

"Of course I'm pissed."

"How are you still blaming me for that?"

BECAUSE YOU FUCKING FORGAVE HER.

I don't say it. "I know. I'm just tired."

I let him put his arms around me. "I'm sorry for being such a dickhead."

"You promised you'd study with me, right?"

"Let's hit the books."

I know he only agreed to it to get in my good graces. When we talked about a study date at school he was disinterested. I tell him we need separate couches because of the amount of books I'm using. All I want is space. I should tell him how I feel. I'm being like my parents when they were together. Sweeping everything under the rug until the rug goes nuclear.

A metal band plays from Travis' laptop and I swear I've read the same line thirty times. He leaves for the bathroom and it's my time to strike. I pounce on his couch and seize his laptop. The screen is littered with his film projects.

My gut quivers.

A project is named '*Charli.*'

With a shaky hand, I hit play.

My favourite song, '*Here Comes the Sun*' by The Beatles, plays. The video fades in and out with photos of Trav and me. A short snippet of me typing filters in and fades into a shot of me laughing and telling him to stop filming.

My hand covers my mouth.

I remember that day.

A shot of me walking along the beach fills the screen, and words scroll down the side.

Coming out of darkness,
Lighting up my life,
Forgetting the pain and finding joy,

In troubles or adventure,
With you I share it all,
My heart, My trust, My best.

"Uh-oh," Travis mutters from the doorway.

My heart leaps into my throat.

He shuffles closer. "Sorry, you weren't meant to find that."

I push the laptop away. "I swear I wasn't snooping."

"You think I'm a total creep now?"

"What?"

"Cause I made that video."

"It wasn't creepy."

"It was ok?"

"I loved it."

"So, why do you sound so rattled?"

My chest heaves. "That poem."

"Sorry." He tugs at his hair. "You said you wrote it for me, so I thought I could use it."

"It's ok. It was just a shock to read it. I've never read any of my poems outside of my notebook."

He takes my hands. "Sorry."

"Don't be."

He eyes his laptop. "So what were you looking for?"

"I just wanted to change the music."

His body eases with relief.

I run my hands up his arms. A giggle squeaks out of me as he lifts me into a bear hug. I nestle in his warmth and close my eyes.

"I love you," he whispers.

My jaw tenses, and then eases. "I love you too."

Travis is my everything. He holds me and listens to my problems. All this stuff with my parents would be torturous without him.

Memories of summer break fill my mind. Dad was gone a few months. He left as soon as the divorce was finalised. It was hard to cope without him around.

In the school holidays Dad and I would cycle into town and watch movies at the old cinema. The old cinema is literally old and only plays classic films from the 1920s through to the 1960s. I didn't have Dad, but I did have my bike and the old cinema.

No one from school was ever at the old cinema, so it was weird seeing Travis, who I had only known as Meah's older brother, there. During '*Some Like It Hot*' he tried to talk to me at the concession stand. I replied with cold silence.

At '*Casablanca*' he sat in the row behind me, repeating lines word-for-word. '*An Affair to Remember*' he kept interrupting by spouting bits of trivia. *"Did you know Cary Grant was only fifteen years younger than Cathleen Nesbitt who plays his grandmother?"*

During '*Rebel Without A Cause*' I let him sit next to me. I noticed how light flickered in his dark eyes. His intoxicating scent of mint and vanilla. How much I wanted to play with the soft waves of his hair.

He slid down in his seat and told me how he'd always wanted someone to join him there, that his friends didn't know he went to the old cinema because they'd pay him out for it, that sometimes he felt like an outsider around them. He went to parties and played football because everyone else did. His dad was on his case about football and university. Travis' face drooped with disdain when he told me of his dad's plan for him to work in the family business.

His obsession with classic films was obvious as we discussed his dream to become a filmmaker. Then he fidgeted in his seat. His cheeks flushed. We held each other's gaze as he confessed that I was the first person he'd told that to.

He asked if I'd like to see something he'd made, and I was touched.

After '*It's a Wonderful Life*' he asked if I wanted to get pizza.

I said no.

He asked if I hated pizza, and I laughed. I laughed for the first time in a long time.

I was still wondering whether he was pranking me, but I left with him to *Sal's Pizzeria*.

Two slices in, I was telling him about my dad.

7

Brittany

"I'm still mad that you didn't text me to join you guys at *The Pancake Parlour*."

"I know, Meah, I'm sorry," I say as we head to the gym changerooms. "My head was killing. I wasn't thinking."

"If you weren't my best friend, I'd murder you."

"I'm so lucky to have you in my corner."

"We did it, though. Since the party we're allowed at her table. *We're in.*"

"I know. It's crazy."

My insides jumped rope all last night. As we walk into the gym I'm just as green. Its cheer try-outs.

"*Maclean,*" Chloe calls as Will rushes out of the male changeroom. "A four-day hangover? You really let loose on Friday night."

Will hunches, head hanging loose. "She hexed me. Swear. She's an evil witch who sucked the life outta me."

Fiona waggles her phone in front of him. "Yeah, looks like ya was havin a real bad time."

"*Ugh.*" Will smacks Fiona's phone away. "Don't worry; I've seen that pic all over *Instagram*."

Chloe elbows Will's ribs. "You loved it. Were you home all week so you could keep reliving it?"

"Shuddup. Seriously. She took control over me. I had no choice. She's evil. Like, possessed or somethin."

Chloe's eyebrow arches and a wicked grin appears. "All right, Willy. I gotchu."

I grab Meah's hand and we hurry to the changeroom to get into our PE uniforms.

Chloe is the first to try-out. She's already cemented herself a place, this is merely a formality. She was the only grade nine in the junior squad last year.

She's fast. She's loud. She's on point.

We erupt in applause.

Meah is painful to watch. She can cheer. Well, she can yell. But she's slow. She stumbles on her footing and is two beats out on her moves.

I smile so she doesn't know.

My name is called last. I'm jittery, waiting for the music to start. Once the beat hits, my eyes close and my feet do the talking. I'm afraid of messing up, so I don't stop moving. At the end, I yell, "*Go Sharks,*" so technically I'm cheering.

The music stops and is replaced by silence.

My breaths are heavy.

A clap breaks in the corner and waves through the group as the rest applaud.

I grin, panting and blushing, and run from the spotlight.

#

I spend English class slumped in my chair. We don't hear if we get into the squad until sometime later in the week. How am I supposed to wait? If I get in, Chloe will definitely want to keep me around.

My sister is giving a long-winded explanation about this bird book. Or whatever it's about. I've read three chapters and still don't know what I'm reading. Can't we read a book from this century?

If I glare at her will she stop talking?

Eep. Locked eyes with Bryce instead. He smiles. I face the front.

That smile couldn't have been for me. Could it?

The bell sounds and relief loosens my body. I stack my books and slide my chair back.

"Brittany."

Bryce walks toward me and I point to myself. "Me?"

His eyes grow wide. He turns between me and Charli. "I didn't get you two mixed up again, did I?"

Again?

I shake my head. "No, I'm Brittany."

He smiles. "*Phew.*"

My arms lock round the books. My weight shifts on knees two seconds off buckling.

"How you going with class?"

"Ah, all right, I guess."

"So, you're not struggling as much as me?"

I bite my lip and grin. "I haven't read very much of the book. I've got no clue what Mr Palmer is on about in class discussions."

"You know there's a movie?"

"There is?"

"I downloaded it the other night, but it's so boring. I only got fifteen minutes in."

I giggle. "Well, that's not helpful."

"You have a cute laugh."

Someone call the fire department, I'm burning up. I cradle my books as we walk out of the classroom. My cheeks have to be Ferrari red.

"Your sister won't give up any answers," he says as we walk the corridor, "no matter how many times I ask."

"Oh yeah, she never does that."

"Not even for her sister?"

I shake my head, pouting. Shudda known. People always use me to access Charli's homework.

"You wanna help each other out?"

"Whaddaya mean?"

He shrugs. Lips crooked left. Eyes kind. "Maybe we could meet up after school. Go to *Shakes* and try this study thing?"

My heart bashes my ribs. *Shakes*... with me? *Ohmigawd.*

He tilts his head. "You don't have to if you don't want to."

"No!" I blurt out. "I'm in. Definitely in."

"Awesome. I'll meet you on the front lawns after school."

I nod.

He gives me a short wave and walks into another classroom.

I'm panting.

There has to be more people out here than usual. On the front lawns after school, I crane my neck to find Bryce. Seriously everyone, get outta the way.

I fidget awkwardly for ten minutes, deciding he's changed his mind. I'm so dumb. As if he really wanted to hang with me. Just go home, Brittany.

I stop mid-step when I see him. He leaves the school building with Will and Naveen, taking the steps two at a time.

He jogs up to me. "Hey."

Body temperature skyrocketing. "Hi."

"BK, you coming?" Naveen calls out as he and Will veer in another direction.

"Nah, you guys go. I'm hanging with Brittany."

"Matty," Will shouts, throwing his arms in the air. "Where we going, guys?"

Bryce pushes Will away. "You're going to Nav's."

"Hmm." Will swivels on his heels. "Ok then, I see what's going on."

Steam rises from my collar.

Bryce smirks. "He's such a crack up."

"*Heh-heh.* Yeah, he can be."

"Ready to go?"

I nod because words are stuck in my throat.

We walk out of school in silence. Cars whiz by as I play with my hair, the straps of my backpack, my blazer, my neckerchief.

"So happy to be out of school," he says, breaking the silence. "How was your last class?"

"Chill. Textiles. Easy blow-off class."

"I need more blow-off classes in my life."

"It's my only one. My mum was pretty strict about what classes I had to take."

"My mum's the same. I had geography last. Snooze fest."

"Oh, I hate that subject."

My attention turns to my feet. Am I walking weird? My pace slows. Every step I concentrate hard. Should I walk closer to him? No, that'd be weird. *Gawd,* you're a loser.

We reach the boardwalk and fall into silence again. I gulp and force out words. "So, you moved here from Sydney, right?"

I sneak a peek at his eyes. Sunlight flickers against the layers of blues. A warmth cloaks me. I look away and touch my forehead. Dammit. Definitely sweating.

"Yeah. This is the first time I'm not living in an apartment. It's weird that we own grass."

"You must miss it, though. Sanford's gotta be way more boring than the city."

"Nah, it's ok. Everyone here is super cool. I didn't expect to make friends this quick."

Um, you're gorgeous.

"It's cool being able to walk everywhere."

I snort and instantly hate myself. "You're excited to walk?"

"Beats constantly checking train timetables."

As the crash of waves calms my running pulse, I fight against the salty air to keep smelling his cologne.

"So you live along the beach?"

I clear my dry throat. "Uhm, yep."

"That'd be nice. My parents almost bought there but decided on the view from The Heights."

"The view would be nice, but nothing beats the convenience of the beach as your backyard."

"My parents probably didn't think it was worth it. They would never go down to the beach."

I look over at him and he smiles. I bite my lip and face front.

Brittany, he SMILED at you.

I shake my head and laugh. I turn to him and smile.

At *Shakes*, Bryce holds the door open for me. My shoulders bunch and I squeak a thank you. We find a table and dump our books. Bryce takes off his blazer and hangs it over his chair. I check him out and notice how lean his frame is.

Bryce opens '*To Kill a Mockingbird*' and says, "Why do we need English as a subject? We can already speak it, right?"

I pull out my class notes and add, "One more way for them to torture us."

"You're funny," he says, smiling. He leans over my notes. "What did you write down?"

I spin the notebook. "Whatever Mr Palmer wrote on the board. Feel free to decode it for me."

He laughs and reads them over. I rub my clammy hands along my skirt.

"So, you and Charli are twins?"

I smirk, "What gave it away?"

He smiles and lets out a breathy laugh. "I just mean you're so different."

"Yeah, we are a bit."

"You're so nice, and she's... she's a bit mean."

"*Ha.* You think Charli's mean?"

He wriggles in his seat. "Well, you're here helping me study. She pretty much snapped at me. She's harsh."

"Yeah, she can be. I mean, we're sisters, so we're always mean to each other. Didn't realise other people would think that about her."

"I don't think everyone thinks that," he says waving his hands. "Hope I didn't offend you."

I shake my head. "Course not."

"I shouldn't have said anything about your sister. That's not cool."

"Don't worry about it. She's a pain in the butt."

He grins. "Really?"

"She's a mopey sook. Our parents separated almost a year ago, got divorced end of last year, and she can't get over it. It's tiring." I huff. "Part of me hopes he doesn't come home."

"Huh?"

"My dad. He left town after the divorce went through and hasn't come back."

"What? Why?"

My jaw clenches. "His words were, *'I need to find myself.'*"

"That's heavy. I'm sorry about your parents."

"It's ok. It's peaceful at home without them yelling."

He nods, frowning. "Families can be tough." He pauses, then adds, "What part do you want to work on?"

Happy for the opportunity to sideline the family talk, I point out a question. "I have no idea about this one."

Bryce flips through his novel. "I think I know that one."

He holds his book in front of me, explaining his answer. I barely hear him. My focus is on his hands. My lips rub together. I want to toss the book and intertwine my fingers with his.

"Hi guys, can we join?" Chloe plants her hands on the table, making me jump.

Jace drags a chair from a nearby table and sits backwards on it. Chloe finds a seat and nestles between Bryce and me. Her elbows rest on the table. "So, what we up to?"

Bryce flips the book in front of her. "Studying for English."

"*Pfft,*" Chloe splutters, rolling her eyes. She grabs the book and tosses a thumb at me, "Just steal the answers from her sister."

Bryce grins at Chloe. "Already tried that."

My heart plummets from the way Chloe and Bryce look at each other.

"School's boring enough when we're stuck there," Jace groans. "Why you doin school work now?"

"Sorry for trying to not get an F," Bryce jokes.

I push far back on my seat, feeling crowded.

"So, what did you think of Winters' pass in the *Nets* game?" Jace says to Bryce. "Rookie move or what?"

"Totally. He can do a lot better than pulling an amateur stunt like that."

"*Ohmigawd*," Chloe groans. "Can you guys talk about anything other than sport?"

"I'm sick of talking about reality TV with you," Jace says, throwing a palm at Chloe.

Bryce fishes around in his pocket and pulls out a buzzing phone. He reads the screen and says, "Oh man. Sorry, I gotta go."

"*Naw*, so soon?" Chloe whimpers.

"Yeah sorry," Bryce says, meeting my eyes.

I stare into flecks of navy against topaz. "I'll go too."

He smiles. "Walk you out?"

"You're leaving together?" Chloe asks as Bryce and I pack our books.

"My mum's office is close by," I reply.

"Bye guys," Bryce says to Chloe and Jace and I follow him out.

He holds open the door for me, again, and says, "Thanks for hanging out with me."

I blush. "Thanks for asking me."

"Sorry I have to cut out early. See you at school tomorrow?"

"Yes. See you then."

His lips crook and we hold the gaze.

As he walks to the parking lot, all the air pours out of me.

It's like I'm walking on clouds when I get home. Charli and Kellie are in the kitchen's breakfast nook and my high disappears.

"He's telling everyone I'm stalking him," Kellie says. "Like I went after him. I barely spoke two words to him before Friday night."

"I can't believe he's being such a dick."

"Is this about Will?" I ask, opening the fridge.

"Yeah, your new besties are spreading rumours about Kellie," Charli says. "You wouldn't know anything about that, would you?"

I slam the fridge door. "Why are you attacking me?"

"Girls," Sophia hushes.

"He's telling people I forced him into it," Kellie whines. "He made all the moves. Can't you tell them that?"

"Tell who?"

Charli groans. "Why are you being a bitch? You know who we're talking about. Chloe and her posse."

"What makes you think I have any pull?" I stomp out of the kitchen.

Trust Charli to ruin my good mood.

The next morning in English I sit in silent giggles. The question Bryce and I discussed came up. He was only half wrong. He turns to me with the cheekiest of grins and I melt.

When the bell rings I get up slowly as he moves my way.

My sister storms past him. "Can you get out of dance tonight? Dad wants to *Skype* us."

I put her on mute as Bryce hovers behind her. He gives me a closed-mouth smile and leaves the classroom.

"*Ugh*. I hate you," I say, locking eyes with my sister.

"What the fuck? How can you say that to me?"

"Don't swear at me!" I push past her. "Forget it. Like you'd even care."

"*Whoah*. What's up?" she says, tugging on my shoulder.

"*Leave me alone*."

"Brit, you didn't answer my question."

"What?"

"Dad. Tonight. *Skype*?"

"*Ohmigawd*, no. You know I have dance class."

I bolt out of the classroom and tear through the corridor. With distance between us, Charli should get the message to get lost.

"When's the best time to weigh yourself?" Meah asks, joining me in the corridor on the way to textiles.

"What, like daily?"

"Yeah morning or night? I'm doing both and I even weigh myself right after school. I am such a freaking heffer. People at this school must think I am such a fat cow."

"You're not fat," I say as we sit at our sewing machines. "And stop weighing yourself right after school. You've eaten lunch and stuff."

"I barely eat lunch anymore."

"Just promise me you'll only weigh yourself once a day. Morning. Before you shower."

"Stop acting like I'm the only obsessive one. How many times a day do you check your pores?"

"I wash my face twice a day," I say, threading the bobbin, "it's the perfect time to be staring at your face."

"Hey, Madi and Naveen aren't together, right?"

"She said they're not. Why?"

"Because he's dreamy and he's talked to me a few times."

"You wanna hook up with Naveen?"

"Like it's impossible? What about you and Bryce?"

"Oh, and about that..."

Meah is the best of best friends. After hearing me go on and on about my one-on-one with Bryce, she agreed to help me get more face time with him. We sit at the table in mess with an empty chair between us. The plan is for me to slide over so they are either side of me. It's the only way to save a seat without being super obvious about it.

When all the girls are at the table, and not a single guy, I have to ask, "Where are the boys?" My neck is sore from all the *trying-to-be-subtle* turning.

"Footy try-outs," Fiona replies.

Meah slides across to the closer seat. That stings.

Chloe tosses her hair and adds, "And we know they're all going to get in."

"Who can say the same for all of us?" Kimberley says and throws a chip across the table at me.

It hits my cheek and I wipe the salt dust off with disgust.

"You didn't even cheer," Kimberley smirks.

YES I DID. I want to say it out loud, but my body closes in and my throat slams shut.

Madison throws a chip at Kimberley. "We can't all be loud mouths like you, Kimmy."

"You're one to talk." Kimberley throws another at Madison.

Fiona and Chloe shriek.

"Stop!" Chloe snaps. "Don't you dare start a food fight. We don't have Kellie Saunders here to aim at."

"You're humanising her, Chloe," Fiona giggles. "She's the witch remember."

"Dirty demon dog," Chloe replies, laughing.

I try to mimic their laughter. Meah does it well. A little too well.

I get that Will wanted the heat off him, but he really did a number on Kellie. Chloe owes him big time over what went down with their dad's, but he shouldn't have given her ammunition against Kellie.

All I can say is, thank goodness I'm sitting at this table, where it's safe.

I have one small victory when I get to my last class of the day: Science. With Bryce. Well, two benches behind. I still love staring at the back of his head.

His fingers run through his hair and down to his neck.

I bite my bottom lip.

His shoulders pivot.

He turns and our eyes meet.

My breathing stops.

He faces front.

I take a large inhale.

Rikki taps his textbook and I notice how Bryce doesn't pay attention. He slides back on his stool and turns to my bench. Back at me.

"*Oi*, BK," Will shouts through cupped hands. "Send us the answers."

A scowl tightens Rikki's face. She clicks her fingers at Bryce and he swivels toward his bench.

I click my pen and busy myself with copying notes.

Will pokes my arm and repeats, "Whadda we doin? Whadda we doin?"

"I dunno. Just write somethin down."

"Write what?"

"I dunno. Anything."

"You think Kellie has heard all the stuff people are saying about her."

I drop my pen and glare at him. "What do you think?"

"I think there's a lot of people saying stuff."

"Yeah, what did you think was going to happen? You know how the rumour mill works here."

"I thought Chloe would stop people talking shit about me."

"You made it about Kellie."

"Yeah... Think she's mad?"

"I don't think she's happy. Why did you get with her, anyway?"

"You've met alcohol, right?"

I roll my eyes. "*Ugh*." Will is so careful to not be a target since his dad's trial. Kids pummelled him with abuse, making out his dad was worse than just a white-collar criminal. Because his dad worked for Chloe's dad, there was this rumour Mr Benson made Mr Maclean take the fall for some shady financial stuff and he'd work on getting him out. Chloe squashed that one quickly and now seems to always have Will's back.

I face front and my cheeks flush when Bryce is already looking at me. I find all my courage and smile at him.

"Oi!" Will shouts at Bryce. "What we doin after school?"

"Mr Maclean. Mr Kerry," Mrs Fields calls out. "You two buckle down and get your work done, or you'll be hanging back with me in detention."

Bryce swivels to the front and I pick up my pen. How can I stab Will and make it look like an accident?

When the bell rings, Will speeds out of the room. I don't have the energy to chase. I could not catch a break today. I sit as the rest of the class leaves.

I trudge towards the door. The wind is knocked out of me when Bryce runs back into the classroom.

Forget something? Is what I want to say, but I'm busy trying not to pant.

"I'm sick of this," he says, smiling. "Every time I want to talk to you, someone gets in the way."

I hug my books to my chest. I haven't got the bravery to meet those eyes.

"The only time we got to talk was at *Shakes*," he says, "and that still got ruined. You doing anything on Sunday?"

I manage a quick shake of the head.

"You been to that arcade in Tully?"

I tilt my head, taken aback. "Not for ages."

"I've heard good things. You wanna go with me?"

Me and him?

Like... a date?

His brow furrows from my long pause. "You don't have to, like, if it sounds dumb or something."

"No, no. I'd love to."

"Awesome." He pulls out his phone. "Can I get your number to organise a time."

The screen illuminates. Holding these books is barely covering the fact that my hands are shaking. I hold them tighter and suggest, "How about I tell you the number and you type it in?"

# #

At dance class I'm on a total high. My head bops side-to-side. There's bounce to my steps. A smile cracks my face. I whoop as I spin circles and I clap where a clap is not choreographed.

The music stops.

"Brittany," Tiffany calls out.

Crap. Did I majorly stuff up?

Tiffany points in front of her. "Move front and centre."

I suck in air and run to the spot. I try to block out the muttering behind me.

"Let's start over." Tiffany bounces, hitting play on the music.

It takes a moment to settle into my new position, my energy level is still on overdrive. Bryce clouds my mind. My number saved in his phone. I grin and power through my steps.

Tiffany claps us off for the end of class. "Well done, girls. Just one announcement before you go. Congratulations to Brittany. She gets the solo for this routine."

My hand hovers over my heart. "*Whoah*, seriously?"

"What?" Chloe snaps.

Tiffany walks up and pats my arm. "Keep smashing it out like today and you'll be golden."

"Thanks, Tiff."

"We'll work on the solo next week."

I involuntarily skip to my gym bag.
Chloe swishes her hips towards me. "Congrats, Brit."
"Thanks."
"You picked up some extra spunk since last class."
"Guess I've been saving it up."

8

Charli

I need a good luck kiss. It's my first debate match today and soon we will leave for *West Sanford High*.

Travis texted that he was down at the footy fields with his mates. I can't control the shudders as the girls recline on the grass, checking their nails and taking selfies, and the boys let insults fly and tackle each other to the ground. Travis blending in with them is the worst part.

"Hey girls, we got babysitting duty. Little Charli is here." GiGi cackles from the grass.

"Hey," Travis says, jogging towards me, "when do you leave?"

"Pretty soon."

He kisses my cheek. "Good luck, Baby."

"Aw, is wittle Charwi gonna go win a pwize?" GiGi mocks, cackling so much she falls backwards onto the grass.

Blood pulsates in my veins.

"She's just playing," Travis says, twirling my hair. "When's the next debate? I hope it's here so I can cheer you on."

"Um," I stammer, eyeing GiGi. "I'm not sure yet."

Travis' hands slide up either side of my face. "I have no doubt you'll be textin me that you won."

My big smile mimics his and our lips press together. Not that I'm a fan of PDAs, but they need to know he's mine. I won't lose him to this pack of fools.

I give his hand a squeeze and say, "I'm going to head to my locker and get ready to go."

"I'll see you tonight then."

I nod and turn to walk towards the school building. Behind me GiGi adds, "Oh no, is the little virgin leaving?"

For a moment I stop. My nails dig into my palms.

I keep walking.

My fists curl. What else could spit out of her mouth?

Lucas adds, "Nah, Trav, you guys have to have done it by now."

"Guys, can you quit it?" Travis says.

My walk morphs into a run.

At my locker, some kids whoosh past me. Kellie's name is repeated, followed by witch, psycho, stalker, and demon.

My skin crawls.

This junk is still headline news?

I grab my notebooks and tablet and walk toward the arts department.

Greg Francis from my maths class points at me. "Watch out! She's friends with the witch. She'll get us, too."

My eyes narrow. "Excuse me?"

I shake it off and keep walking. Greg's group snickers behind me.

I stop by the arts bulletin board. I find the sign-up sheet for the winter formal committee and sign my name. I figure it's an easy add to my extra-curriculars.

Mrs Vandergarten walks out of her office and pins a poster to the bulletin board. '*Your Year Abroad!*'

"What is that?"

Mrs Vandergarten hands me a pamphlet. "Applications will be opening for students to spend a year at our sister school in Madrid. It'd be an eye-opening experience." She puts the rest of the pamphlets in a stand and walks into her office.

I slip the pamphlet into my notebook. Behind me more comments about The Witch cursing Will, the hex forcing him to jam his tongue down her throat. New part of the rumour; it was a satanic ritual.

This snowball is on crack.

I dial Kellie's number.

"Hey," she answers.

"Just checking you're ok. Dickheads around me are opening their flaps with F-grade comedy."

"Man, I'm barely listening. Wanna meet at the mess?"

"Sure, I'll head right over."

"I'm dying for a milkshake," Kellie says at the entrance of mess.

"Chocolate sounds awesome."

We meander through the tables towards the food line. Chloe Benson's table closes in. Acid lines my throat and I order it back down.

"Uh-oh, Will, man," Jace Wilson calls out, "your stalker is on her way over."

"Keep away from me, psycho," Will shouts across the table. He turns to laugh with his mates.

I cuff my hand around Kellie's wrist.

Kellie rolls her eyes. "Just keep walking."

I eye the table. Chloe Benson arches her back, standing from her seat. I glimpse my sister and want to scream at her to get from that table.

Chloe plants a hand on hip and juts her head towards Kellie. "Like, just move on, freak."

Mean-streaked laughter reverberates from the table. My neck twinges. Sean Hastings moves forward. My nerves scatter. He picks up a large paper cup, tosses the plastic lid and hurls the contents towards Kellie. In a matter of seconds, red soda bubbles coat her glasses and soak her white blouse.

Kellie is frozen and wide-eyed.

What do I do?

I turn to the cackling table.

To my best friend.

What do I do?

Before I can formulate a plan, Kellie takes off.

"Suits her," Kimberley smirks beside Sean.

"I can't believe this is how you turned out," I say, glaring at Kimberley.

Kimberley screws her face up at me, but I don't have time for her. I spin and chase after Kellie. She's running fast. Barrelling with her head down, she collides with someone.

"What the hell?" Bryce grimaces, wiping soda off his shirt. He clutches Kellie's arm, finding her eyes. "Are you ok?"

Kellie knocks his hand away and pushes past him.

"Oh no, she got BK," Sean shouts. "Watch out, you're next!"

I follow Kellie into a bathroom where she hunches over a basin.

"You ok?"

She furiously turns the taps. "They were at my house."

"I know."

She tears away paper towel and dampens it under the water. "They weren't invited. They trashed it. And I'm the freak?"

"Forget em."

She mashes the paper towel into her blouse. Her fogged up glasses fall down her nose and she sniffs. "I didn't initiate anything. He kissed me. How am I the bad guy? He fucking is."

My eyes sting as hers well. I rub circles on her back.

Kellie drops the wadded-up paper and looks at her shirt. "This ain't coming out."

"You got a PE shirt or somethin? I could run to your locker for you."

Her eyes are red-rimmed. "He was so sweet to me. He was funny. We share the same views on DC versus Marvel. We opened up about how damaging our mothers are. How could he be so mean?"

"I don't know. It's not fair."

Kellie takes a long exhale and rests on a closed toilet seat.

The bathroom door swings open and Kellie slams her cubicle door shut.

It's Brittany. "I was just checking she's ok."

I spit the words, "You're seriously becoming friends with these people?"

"What?" She pivots to the door.

"I'm so sick of everyone acting like morons to be popular. You want to make people feel like shit? Well, congratulations. You found the right people."

Brittany is out in a flash.

Kellie unlatches the door. "You ok?"

I tumble forward and rush out a massive moan.

"At least she came to check in. That's a good sign."

I straighten up and wipe my eyes dry. "That's true."

My thoughts don't stray from Kellie during debate prep. My heart is shattered from seeing her so upset. Someone that upset, who still checks that I'm ok is the kind of person who does not deserve to be harassed.

My brain is fried. Mr Palmer rapid-fired questions at us for twenty minutes of prep. I need air before the actual debate begins.

I leave the library with Henry Davenport on my tail. His lanky frame hunching over me as he jabbers incessantly. "Hey, where you going?", "Can I come?", "Wanna hang out after school?", "I just got a new video game. You should come over and play it with me."

I stop dead and shove a palm in his face. "Henry, you're quantifying my headache. Can I please have five minutes alone to recharge?"

Henry shrinks. "Ok then."

I stretch my arms and gaze at the open corridors of *West Sanford High*. A shabby metal awning covers the corridors. The classrooms are lined with orange bricks, which are tagged. It's not fresh. What school doesn't wash off graffiti?

A few *West Sanford* students pass me, giving me the once over. I'm ridiculous in all these layers. *West Sanford's* uniform is grey pants and a lemon polo shirt. That's it. I guess there's a lot of differences between public and private schools.

"Oh hey," a girl says, waving at me. "Charli, isn't it?"

I recognise her from the bookstore the other weekend. The girl with Preston. Damn, what was her name?

She smiles, pointing to herself. "It's Shae."

"Hi. How are you?"

She shrugs with a cheeky smile. "Yeah, you know, waiting for the bell to ring. What are you doing here?"

I bop my head towards the library. "Here for a debate match."

"Ah, thrilling," she teases.

"Yeah, shouldn't be too bad. So, how was the rest of your weekend?"

She tired sighs. "It was good. Just long. I chauffeured my siblings around. Man, they have way better social lives than I do. Got any siblings?"

"One sister."

"You two close?"

"Not as much as I would like. We kinda drifted apart when we started high school."

"Aw, that sucks. Sometimes I think I'm too close with my siblings."

"That sounds really nice."

"Our mum works super hard because she's a single parent, so a lot of the time it's just the three of us at home."

"I only have my mum around too. I wish that made us closer."

"I mean, don't get me wrong," Shae says. "We still see Mum a lot. It helps having her new boyfriend around which makes her constantly fuss that everything at home is *perfect*."

"Wow. I couldn't imagine my mum dating someone new."

"It's very strange at first, but he's a good guy. Mum just needs to take a chill pill. I get the vibe she think she's not good enough for him. She was the reason I had to ditch Pres at the bookstore. She was freaking out about him coming for dinner."

"*Heh-heh.* She sounds very stressed."

We walk into a courtyard of steel benches and cracked cement. Preston sits at a bench, scrolling through his phone. I clutch my hands as a strange heat lines my collar. He looks up and surprise coats his face. "Charli? What are you doing here?"

"She's here to kick our school's butt at debate," Shae says, plonking down on the bench.

Preston smirks. "Look at the monkey suit they've got you in."

"I know. I'm overdressed for this place."

Shae's hand runs over her neck, and she winces. "I couldn't imagine wearing that thing around my neck all day. Isn't it annoying?"

I touch my neckerchief. "It is, but I've never known any different. Just happy to jump into a t-shirt and jeans when I get home."

Preston taps the space beside him. "You can sit down."

I shake my head. "I should be getting back."

"How long are you here for?" he asks.

"Maybe an hour and a half? We go back to *John Thomas* straight after the match."

"Maybe we should watch," Shae jitters with excitement. "We will have to appear like we are supporting our school, but secretly we will be the Charli cheer squad."

Nervous laughter seeps out. "No, you don't have to watch."

"I only have modern history next," Preston says, nodding. "I can blow that off."

I smile at him. "Ok, if you want to watch I can't stop you."

Preston and Shae were so cute during the match. After each point I made they would slyly throw their hands up and clap. The charade of supporting their school was given up quickly and they soon began cheering my name. They were embarrassing but loosened me up after the rough start at my school.

We won the debate.

That night after dinner, Travis and I snuggle on the couch watching 'The Birds.' Our fifth Alfred Hitchcock movie together.

My head rests on his bicep and I'm thankful it's the weekend. Just the two of us with no bystanders commenting.

On the side table my laptop buzzes with the *Skype* ringtone.

I launch off the couch. "Brittany! Brittany, get in here!"

"*Ohmigawd*, stop shouting," Brittany says, walking into the living room.

Brittany and I take a seat at the table by the bookshelf and I place the laptop in front of us and hit answer.

Dad fills the screen. "Hi girls."

"Dad! Hi!" I wave frantically at the screen.

"Hey Dad," Brittany replies in a flat tone.

"Where have you been?" I ask in a mild pant as my heart ping-pongs in my chest.

"Are you both well?" Dad asks with a big smile.

My chest rises high as I wonder whether he heard me. "Very."

"Yeah. We're good," Brittany says.

"That's great. Well, I'm calling because I've got an announcement."

I hold my breath and my body tenses. Travis hovers behind the laptop and I cross all my fingers and toes.

"I'm moving back into the apartment. I'm back in Sanford."

My mouth falls open as air rushes in and out. Out of webcam view Travis slides by the table and takes my hand, which helps slow my pulse.

"Dad, I'm so happy." I gush.

"Yeah, great," Brittany's tone barely rises an octave.

"Be ready at seven tomorrow night," Dad says, smiling. "I'll be over to pick you girls up."

"Ok," I say as Brittany gets up from her seat. She walks away from the table. "Brit?"

"Brittany?" Dad says, his face pivoting to get a glimpse of her on the screen.

"Sorry, I got homework," she says, leaving the living room.

She pounds up the stairs and I bite inside my cheek as Dad and I stare at each other.

"Where have you been travelling?"

"Down the coast," Dad replies. "I'll always love the beach, and none will ever compare to Sanford. Glad to be back."

Dad's eyes light up as he talks and it's like he's back home. I glance at the living room. But it's not like that. He's not home.

I slip my hand away from Travis' and purse my lips. "Why did you stop texting me?"

Dad shifts in place and an ugly, twisting stab hits my abdomen. His silence is scarier than words and my eyes prickle with tears.

"Dad?"

"It wasn't on purpose."

My forehead crinkles. What does that mean?

Dad tilts his head and smiles at me the way he did the last time I saw him in this house. "Pumpkin, I'm sorry I've been off the radar. There was a lot to organise with coming home. Now is the time to make up for that."

I press my hands into my frail stomach and smile. "I can't wait to see you."

"We have so much to catch up on," Dad says. "I have to get going. Have a great night, see you tomorrow."

"Bye Dad."

The video chat ends and Travis rushes to throw his arms around me. This has to be an *out-of-body* experience. My body is rigid and I'm looking down on everything like in a dream.

I hold onto Travis and bury my face in his chest.

Travis brushes back my hair. "You ok?"

There's a pang in my heart, but I smile. "Yeah, I'm fine. I get to see my dad tomorrow."

He places his hand over my heart. "You sound outta breath."

I clutch his hand. "I am."

"I hope it goes well."

"Of course it will."

"I just don't want you to get hurt."

I pull away from him. "Hurt?"

"What if he's not back for good?"

I frown and my eyes fog. "He just said he is."

Travis pulls me into another hug. "I know. I'm sorry. I didn't mean to make you upset. It's just that you've been doing so well."

"I want him home. Then I'll be doing well."

"You know I want it to go perfect for you, right?"

I run my hands from his shoulders into his hair. I swallow the lump tickling my throat and nod. "I'm so glad you're here. I love you so much."

He slides me off the chair and onto his lap. I straddle his hips and we kiss long and slow. Our lips part and his tongue slides into my mouth. His hands play at my waist and I pull him in close. As his lips move below my ear, my eyes close in the comfort of his warmth.

"Charli?" my mum calls, leaving her study, and we instantly break apart.

My heart pounds and I wipe my lips with the back of my hand. We exchange goofy grins and stand up, making our way to the couch.

"Your dad call?" Mum asks, passing the living room entrance.

"Yes, he's taking us to dinner tomorrow night," I say and run to hug her.

She pats me on the back. "Good, I'm glad."

Mum almost pushes me off as she leaves to go upstairs. She's not happy Dad's back? I bite the inside of my cheek and walk back to Travis.

"Should we finish this movie?" he asks.

I stare off to the side and nod.

"Is this your mum's new book?" Kellie asks, picking up a children's book in Reece's living room the next day.

"Yep," he says, eyes glued to the TV as he and I battle it out with our controllers.

Kellie bounces on the couch, grinning as she flips through the illustrated book. "Man, I love your mum so much."

Kellie always says she wants to be adopted into the Watkins family. She aspires to be like Reece's mum. Not in a writer way, but a powerful way. Like Kellie's mum, Mrs Watkins is a navy wife. Kellie is embarrassed by her mother who sits at home and doesn't make something of herself. Once Mrs Watkins had kids she wanted to stay home to raise them, but she also needed a creative outlet. She started writing children's books and never looked back.

"Oh, shit guys!" I yelp, tossing the controller.

"*Whoah.* You blew our high score," Reece whines.

"Sorry, not sorry," I say, chucking on my sneakers.

"What up?" Kellie asks.

"Um, hello?" I flash the time on my phone. "Dinner with my dad. I gotta go." I curl up next to her and cuddle. "Sorry I have to leave you."

"Don't worry about it. I'll be fine. So, what are you going to say when you see him?"

I side-glance her. "Probably start with hi."

She snorts. "No, I mean like, what will you ask him? Are you gonna grill him about where he's been?"

My shoulders bunch towards my ears. "I'm not going to badger him the first time I see him."

"I would," she says.

"Ok, whatever. You sure you're ok?"

"There's no Will Maclean, Chloe Benson or Sean Hastings in sight," Kellie says, forcing a smile. "Gotta love the weekend. Never throwing a party again in my life."

"Don't say that," I reply, holding her hand. "We still need to have actual games nights."

"Yeah, we can still have them," she smirks, "just at your house instead."

"Holy crap. I can't even imagine what GiGi Larkin could concoct for a party at my house," I say, tucking my latest borrowed book from Reece under my arm.

"Now go, go. Your dad is coming. Video call me directly after."

"Goodbye," Reece says, swivelling back to his TV.

I wave goodbyes and dash for the door, almost tripping on Reece's golden retriever Sammy, who's sprawled across a rug. Thankfully Kellie prefers being at Reece's than her own house. I run past two houses and land at mine. Hopefully her parents don't catch her out whilst grounded. I don't need her grounded for another month. Perhaps they'd lay off because she escaped to Reece's? She has to check in on him every so often anyways.

I jog upstairs with not much time to get ready. In my bedroom I search my wardrobe. Nothing feels appropriate. A little voice tells me to wear a dress. I haven't worn one since I was twelve, but dresses mark special occasions. Right?

I swallow my pride and knock on the neighbouring bedroom door where music blares inside. I knock again.

The door swings open. Brittany rolls her eyes. *"Ohmigawd*, what?"

I slouch. "Can I borrow a dress?"

Brittany snorts. "Sorry, what?"

"Brit, I'm serious. Dad's gonna be here any second. I wanna look good."

"You really think I should help you after how you've been speaking to me lately?" She looks me up and down. "Fine. C'mon then."

"How are you not psyched that we get to see Dad?"

"Just not."

"Serious? He's been gone so long."

"And what?" Brittany says. "We're just supposed to come running?"

I bite my tongue. The words 'why are you being such cow?' want to fly out of my mouth, but this time better judgement stops me. I need to stop fighting with her. It's the last thing I want to do, but always seems to be my first response.

Following Brittany into her bedroom, I wince at her lacey, pale pink dress. "No offence, but I want nothing like what you're wearing."

Brittany laughs, opening her wardrobe. "As if I'd let you touch anything this nice."

Her wardrobe is an array of bright colours, unlike the neutrals and grey-scale that cover my hangers.

I fidget with my curls.

Maybe this was a mistake?

Brittany eyes me. "Are you going to do something with your hair?"

"Like what?"

Brittany rolls her eyes and pulls out a mid-length navy dress. "Why do I even own this?"

The neckline is high and the sleeves are long. "I actually don't hate it."

Brittany tosses it at me. "Keep it."

I race into my room, change into the dress and make an impromptu decision to toss my hair in a high bun. Sophia calls from the bottom of the stairs and I squeal.

My dad is here.

My feet wriggle into black flats and I break for the staircase. I squeal all the way down. I jump at the end of the stairs. My dad catches me.

He smells the same. His hug is the same. His laugh is the same. I squeal again.

"Wow, Charli. Is this really you?"

I giggle. "It's certainly not Brittany."

"Nope. She's right here," Brittany says, dawdling down the stairs.

"Wow, both my girls are beautiful young women." Dad opens his arms to welcome Brittany in. Brittany wrinkles her nose, smiling, and joins the hug. "Brittany, you look so different."

Brittany huffs a response.

Dad strokes her hair. "It's a different colour and you've lost your gorgeous curls."

She side-glances me and by the tension in her jaw, I can tell she's holding back a catty remark.

The waiter takes our orders and I continue to gush. I've regurgitated the last few weeks of my life from car ride to restaurant. I can't sit still. I need to tell him everything. He needs to know everything.

"I've been working really hard since you've been gone, Dad. I'm ahead in my classes and I'm beefing up my transcript by joining school committees."

"That's excellent, Pumpkin," he grins and pats my hand.

My jaw rocks. Not a big enough reaction. "I had a debate match yesterday. We won."

His eyes soften and his hands sit over his heart. "Ah, captaining the debate team in high school is one of my best memories. It stirred a passion in me that helped set my sights on working in law."

My heart warms. Yes, I've heard the story a million times, but having it compared to me is the cherry on top.

He squeezes my hand and kisses the top of my head. "Proud of you, kid."

Eep. "Thanks, Dad."

Dad turns to Brittany. "Sweetheart, how are you going with school?"

Brittany taps the side of her water glass. "Fine."

"What's your favourite class?"

She shrugs her answer. Body falling in a heap.

Dad's face goes stony. "Have you been slacking off?"

"Fine. Textiles."

"What about something more academic?"

"You asked me a question, and I answered it. Ok?"

"I talked with your mother before I started travelling. Did she not look over your timetable?"

Her eyes roll. "Yes. She chose my classes."

"Yeah, she signed off on both our classes," I reassure, nodding. Pleading. "I have an art subject too. It's photography."

"Language?"

"Spanish," I buzz.

Brittany taps her glass. "French."

Dad breaks into his apology smile. "What about ballet, Sweetheart? What performance are you doing this year?"

"I quit."

"What? Your mother just let you quit?"

"*Ohmigawd.* Would you stop trying to blame Mum for everything?" Brittany shouts, looking Dad in the eye for the first time. "At least she's been here for us. Where have you been?"

I suck in air as my eyes grow wide. My fingers jam into fists as my eyes dart between my dad and sister. My mouth grows dry and a lump pulsates in my throat. It grows bigger with every moment no one talks. I swallow hard but it doesn't budge.

My vision clouds. I didn't want to bring it up again, but I'd really like to know his answer.

Dad fidgets in his chair and plays with his linen napkin. "I've told you girls about that," he begins in a low tone, "when I've called you. You know I've been moving around. Trying to gain perspective."

My lip quivers. "You stopped calling."

"I know. I'm sorry. I needed space."

Space? "You didn't want to talk to us?" Tears surge my eyes. "Your daughters?"

"Of course I did. You two mean the world to me."

"It was summer holidays," Brittany says. "Why didn't you take us with you?"

"I didn't mean for the timing to line up like that," Dad says to his place-setting. "I knew I'd be gone longer than your time off school. I just had to leave."

A wimpy sob squeaks out of me as I fight back tears. Brittany slams her elbows on the table; her head rests in her hands. I squeeze my eyes shut, hoping to avoid a public scene.

"Girls," he whispers, "I've missed you too."

I hiccup and swipe at tears. "You shouldn't have left."

His hand rests on my back. "I had to."

"No, you didn't."

He pulls away. "I'd lost who I was. There was no way I could be a proper father with where my head was at. I'm sorry for cutting you girls out... I had to."

The waiter brings around our meals and we eat in thorny quiet. Fumes billow off Brittany. My eyes are puffy, my throat inflamed. I tear at the pasta on my plate.

A phone that doesn't ring,
A heart that doesn't sing.

How could he leave for so long?

Vanishing from sight,
And taking all the light.

Is he even sorry? Does he care about our side in this?

Happiness was promised on your return,
Not more questions left to burn.

My eyes well and I shake off the train of thought. Brittany's attention is on another table, and my dad overtwirls his pasta.

He drops his fork and sighs.

"I've had great success," my dad says in a perfect Jerry Lewis imitation, "being a total idiot."

My hands shake as I wipe my eyes. A familiar light shines in his eyes and I regain hope. A goofy grin pushes at my cheeks, and I curve forward, laughing.

He may have left.

But he's back.

My dad is back in Sanford, one step away from moving back into our home.

9

Brittany

"He was such a dickhead." I kick a foot on the dashboard of my mum's car.

Mum whacks my foot down while driving. "You need to spend quality time with him."

"How is it quality when all he can do is rag," I pause before slipping out 'on you', "on me."

"I'm sorry, Sweetheart." Her lips purse as she turns the steering wheel. "I know what he can be like."

I slouch in my seat and stare out the window. "Don't know how you can defend him."

She puffs out a laugh. "I'm not defending him. We're both your parents and we need to work together to look after you and Charli."

"It's been fine with just you around."

"Well, you'll have to get used to seeing him more."

I slap my thighs. "Why?"

"He's your dad," Mum answers like what I said was hilarious.

"You're going to have to go to his place half the time. He came to my office before taking you girls to dinner. We're going back to arbitration to work out a visitation schedule."

"No. Really?"

"A weekend here and there. It won't kill you."

"We don't know that for sure."

"Stop being so dramatic. So, where am I dropping you?"

"Just at the boardwalk. And remember, you're just dropping me off. No waiting around."

"Why, am I going to embarrass you?" she teases. "Who are you meeting? Obviously not Meah then. It's not a date, is it?"

"*Ohmigawd* Mum, stop it."

"Brit? Is it?"

"Mum, no! I'm just meeting up with some friends. And yes, you're embarrassing."

My mum is a ball of giggles when she parks the car. I thank her as I get out so she will leave quickly. She blows kisses as I walk away. I was seriously adopted into this family.

I lean my elbows on the railing of the boardwalk. The afternoon rays warm my bare shoulders. It's mid-autumn and soon it'll to be too cold to wear a sundress.

I check my phone. 12:51pm. I open my phone to messages from Bryce.

> *(Bryce)* I have a family thing on in the morning. Meet at the boardwalk at 1pm?
>
> *(Me)* Yeah, sounds great!
>
> *(Bryce)* Awesome. I'm so glad we're friends.

That last message tossed me about all last night and this morning. This isn't a date. It made dressing so hard. The line between *non-date* and *I-wanna-turn-this-into-a-date* outfits.

The crashing waves howl below as I rest against the railing. The salt air dances around my nose and the sunlight reflects off the water like a jewellery store display.

I check the time again. 12:53pm. I fidget in my wedge sandals and swivel towards the road. I snap my head left and right.

Is he walking here? Coming by car? *Ohmigawd*, he's not going to show up. I'm such an idiot. Why would I think this was real?

My knees knock and I turn to the ocean. I focus on the waves and time my breathing with the whoosh of the tide.

"Hey Brittany." I jump away from the railing, surprised by Bryce's voice.

"Oh hey." My phone lights up. 12:58pm. Early. "How are you?"

"Yeah, I'm good. How was your Saturday?"

I twist my lips. "Let's just say I'm sure my Sunday will be loads better."

"I'm sure we can make that happen," he says, smiling. "Ready to go?"

"Sure."

I walk beside him, noting the beats of his walk so I stay in time as he leads. We stop by the bus stop. "You wanna take the bus?"

He puffs out a laugh. "No need for the screwed-up face. Did you expect to walk there?"

"No. I assumed someone would be driving us."

"Yeah, the bus driver."

"Ha, ha," I say with a smile. I have the urge to playfully nudge him but resist.

"The guys at school have a problem with public transport too," Bryce says, shaking his head. "I'm so use to it. I had to take the train every day when I lived in the city. Plus, this way you can go somewhere without the parentals knowing about it."

My shoulders relax. "That's a good point."

The bus arrives and Bryce insists I board first. I take an empty seat at the back and slide close to the wall, unsure whether he will want his own seat. He approaches my seat and I jitter as he sits beside me.

The bus pulls onto the road for the fifteen-minute journey to Tully Beach. I stare out at the trees that line the road and clasp my hands together. All the good lines I had rehearsed for today have gone out the window. I'm too nervous to turn his direction.

I purse my lips and feel a need for lipgloss. Would coating my lips send a weird message? I smile. Maybe it's the message I NEED to send out.

I open my clutch and clasp my lipgloss. My hand is shaking in the bag. To save embarrassment I drop the lipgloss and shut the bag. My cheeks grow warm.

Bryce clears his throat and asks, "So what's your favourite arcade game?"

I bite my lip thinking of a type of game. It's been years since I played a video game.

"If you say Pac-Man I'm going to have to ask the bus driver to turn around."

I laugh and ease into my seat. "What about Ms Pac-Man?"

He slaps his hand over his heart. "Uh, Brittany, no."

I smile. "I don't really know if I have a favourite. What about you?"

"I wanna say Street Fighter, but I think I'm better at hunting games."

"You like to shoot things?"

"Not really, just good aim."

I go to respond but I have no words. An awkwardness lingers in the air, so I return to the safety of gazing out the window. Through the trees I spy yellow sand and waves of turquoise and cerulean. As the bus rounds a corner, I latch onto the seat in front of me and focus on the calm of the beach.

The bus jerks on the brakes and hurls us forward. Bryce's hand covers mine as he clutches the seat ahead.

His hand is warm.

His hand is on top of mine.

We're basically holding hands.

It lasts only a few seconds. Bryce pulls his hand away and there is a shift in weight as he slides away from me.

I smooth over my dress and pull my hair behind my ears. His warmth lingers on my hand. I replay the moment so it never leaves my memory.

We exit the bus and it's only a short walk into the mall.

"You gotta be my tour guide," Bryce says. "I've never been here before."

"I may not have gone to the arcade in a while, but luckily Tully Mall has great shopping, so I more than know my way around."

I lead him to the arcade, but once inside I'm half a step behind. We round a few machines and I point out a Deer Hunter game.

It's a relief to watch the screen. From the neck up I am flushed with a rising temperature. I rest my hands on the edge of the machine to ease my fidgeting.

His arm brushes against me when he hits the button to start the machine. My breaths are slow as his arms position the rifle. He stays in my side view as I fixate on lowering my body heat.

Bryce was right about his aim. He soars through the levels and a bundle of tickets spurt out of the machine.

"Oh, we have to try this one," he says, beckoning me to follow him.

We land at a superhero themed game. He barely needs to persuade me to battle against him. I'm so tongue-tied I can't respond.

My Wonder Woman tries her hardest to beat his Superman. The toggles, buttons and sound effects were enough to get used to. Add the back of our hands knocking together, his breathy laugh, the scent of sandalwood, and the noise of people around us... oh boy, there is a lot going on.

I lost easily. I'm not sad about it.

"Hey, you didn't do too badly," he says, looking at the scores.

I grab my bag and step away from the machine. "Stop lying."

He laughs and follows me. "Ok, let's find something more your speed."

"I think spectator is more my speed."

"*Nah-uh*. You gotta play."

He stops by a *Whac-A-Mole* and my first reaction is to laugh.

"C'mon, even my little sister can play this game," he says, lifting the mallet.

I hesitantly take the mallet. I find my groove after the first few swings. I focus on all the holes and start whacking moles left and right.

After my victory against the moles, I succeed in playing spectator as Bryce plays three more games. The endorphins have kicked in and booted my shaky fidgetiness. I can even look him in the eyes when we comment on the games.

We verse each other in a race car simulator. It's bad. Bryce has obviously done this bunches of times. I don't do so well. For a majority of the race, I'm in bushes, stuck at the side of tunnels, or going the wrong way and working out how to turn around. We are both in stitches by the time the race ends.

A big WINNER banner fills Bryce's screen.

"Well, that's just mean," I say, laughing and pointing at my LOSER banner.

"Yeah, technically you came second. That's worth a medal."

I blow a raspberry, but I'm laughing so much I don't care. "No, I didn't. All the computer cars kept lapping me." I curl into a ball and turn towards him with my head resting in the curve of the seat.

He turns to me, his elbow resting on the seat with his head against his palm. "Well, we can just forget that part."

I smile as he smiles at me.

"You tired already?" he teases.

I bite my bottom lip. "Beaten."

"You don't play many video games?"

"Only the occasional game on my phone. Basically, any version of *Tetris*."

He laughs. "I call those the *better-than-studying* games."

My clutch buzzes beside me and I fish inside for my phone. **New Text - Dad.**

> **(Dad)** Any meal requests for when you come over for dinner?

I roll my eyes and toss my phone into my bag.

"Bad text?"

Annoyance coats my exhale. "My dad. He's already at me about going over for dinner."

"He's back?" Bryce asks, sitting up.

I nod. "I saw him last night."

"You don't look happy."

"Wasn't the best reunion," I mutter, looking at my knees.

"Was Charli happy to see him?"

My eyes roll again. "Way over excited. Either word-vomiting or a blubbering mess."

"He'd have to be happy to see you guys. Did he spoil you?"

I run my hands through my hair and scrunch it together. "He's exactly the frickin same. Overbearing, judgemental, hovering over my shoulder. Nothing I do is right in his books."

The back of Bryce's hand rubs against my forearm. It's gentle and my tension eases. I let go of my hair and drop my arms. As my hair falls by my face, I stare into his kind eyes. His eyes frame my reflection and a shiver runs down my spine.

A wet sting creeps across my eyes. I blink hard and swallow the catch in my throat. "I just don't want him around. I never feel good when he's here. I have to constantly tailor my words to what he wants to hear."

Bryce takes a lock of my hair and twirls it between his fingers.

My chest eases and I'm happy in the silence. It's like he knows to not push the subject.

"I never talk about this stuff," I whisper. "Please don't tell anyone."

He leans in close. His hand glides onto my cheek and he whispers, "I would never tell anyone."

He stays close. My eyes stay locked on his. We smile at the same time. As he leans in, my eyes close with instinct. A soft, warm sensation covers my lips. I pout and push my lips against his. Our mouths stay closed with perfect pressure. My nose rubs beside his and I can't help smiling while kissing him.

He pulls back and my lips tingle, wanting more.

I open my eyes as my heart throbs.

He smiles nervously. "Ah, hope that was ok?"

YES. A million times yes. I can't get the word out as my mind is overcome with visions of giant cartoon love hearts.

He rubs the back of his neck and looks over my shoulder. "Um, wanna get some food?"

I manage a nod and we leave the arcade for the food court. With every step there is only one thought.

Step. Did that really happen?

Step. Did that just happen?

Step. That happened!

We wait in a line at the food court and Bryce begins to laugh.

My shoulders bunch and I side-glance him. "What?"

"I really should tell you something."

My body closes in as I'm sure it will be, 'Brittany, you're a terrible kisser.'

He smiles and says, "Today's my birthday."

My jaw drops. "What? Today?"

He laughs again, nodding.

"What? Why didn't you say anything?"

His palms turn upwards. "Didn't want to make a big deal about it?"

"*Ohmigawd*, I can't believe it's your birthday."

"Well, I wasn't going to say anything," he confesses, "then we kissed, so I thought I should own up."

I shiver in the best way from the words *'we kissed.'*

"I just wanted to say, that I'm glad you trusted me with the stuff about your dad."

I fixate on those kissable lips. I smile and nod. "I trust you."

We get a large serve of hot chips smothered in chicken salt and move to a table.

"So, I guess I should say thanks for celebrating my birthday with me," he says, holding back a laugh.

I pick out a chip. "Now I can say I let you win all those games as a birthday present."

He nods. "Of course, that's totally believable."

"If it is your birthday," I say, taking another three chips.

"You say that like it's up for debate."

"Well who knows with you," I tease. "Why didn't you invite the guys here?"

"Why? You want out?"

"You know what I mean."

Bryce exhales and slides his forearms along the table. "If the guys at school knew it would have been a whole big deal. I didn't want everyone pushing me to have a big house party."

"You don't have to have a party."

"C'mon. Everyone expects a party."

"I spose."

"Besides my house isn't really ideal for a party."

"Why is that?"

"My mum," he begins slowly. "She's really sick."

My hands gently raise to my mouth in time with the slow beat of my heart. "That's awful. I'm so sorry."

"We moved because her doctors said the change of pace would be good for her health. She used to have this hectic job as a CFO. Now she's mostly stuck in a wheelchair. She felt trapped in our apartment so we moved to Sanford and got the big house in The Heights," he says. "It's been a really weird adjustment. I guess it's kinda getting better at home, but I'm worried something will go wrong. I always want to be there."

I place my hands over his with a gentle squeeze. "Can I ask what she has?"

"It's MS. She was diagnosed after my sister was born. For a long time she could still work like normal. Last year she got really bad."

"I'm sorry."

He smiles. "Thanks for letting me vent. Rikki knows there's stuff going on at home and that's why she helps me with homework. I haven't told her everything. I didn't trust her with that."

"I won't tell anyone." I interlace my fingers with his.

"I feel like I dumped a heap of stuff on you."

"I did the same with the stuff about my parents."

"Thanks, Britty," he says and squeezes my hand. "You're a good friend."

We go to the bus stop shortly after eating. I think I ate most of the chips. I guess the talk of his mum's health ruined Bryce's appetite.

As we wait for the bus he tells me about spending the morning with his family for his birthday. "And they wouldn't let up all week that I had to spend the day with friends. In the end, I thought of you."

Full.

Blown.

Butterflies.

I swear every fibre of my being is about to explode.

"I am glad to be heading home," he continues. "I do want to be there this evening."

"Your mum's health is always on your mind, huh?"

He nods. "Pretty much."

As we board the bus, Bryce follows me with his hand nestled on the small of my back. It's hard to walk up the aisle when you're melting inside.

Our trip to Sanford was mostly silent. We sat with only a centimetre of space between us. It was the most fulfilling bus trip of my life.

That night, in my bedroom, I open the school portal on my laptop. Junior cheerleading results are posted. Tingles run from my toes to the top of my head. *I got in.* Whoah.

Seriously, can this day get any better?

My phone buzzes beside the laptop. **New text - Bryce.**

(Bryce) Thanks for today.

I fall onto my bed. I should go to sleep right now so that nothing can ruin this.

10

"Ah shit! They're letting the demon near the chemicals!"

"*Whoah*, watch her over that Bunsen burner! She's gonna kill us with a potion!"

"Damn! We better run for our lives!"

Kellie's hand shakes, attempting to pour yellow liquid into a beaker. She stops, pushes the measuring cup aside, lifts her glasses and pinches the bridge of her nose. "I can't even enjoy my favourite fucking class."

All class, the jerks at the back benches hurl abuse Kellie's way. I am going to murder Will Maclean. It still hurts my brain that he would ever start such hurtful, idiotic rumours about my best friend.

I pick up the measuring cup and hold it over the beaker. "Just tell me when."

She slips her hand out from under her glasses and frowns at my hand. "Weren't you listening? It's the whole thing. That's why I measured it."

"Sorry," I say as I tip the contents into the beaker. "You know I'm no good at this class."

Kellie slams her elbows on the bench and rests her head in her hands. I rub circles on her back.

"It's been over a week," Kellie quietens. "Shouldn't they have a new target by now?"

I frown as my stomach cramps. I wish I had comforting words for her.

When the bell rings, Kellie jumps off her stool and flies out of the lab. I dart past the other kids to keep up with her.

"*Kel*." I grab her hand and slow her pace. We pull off to the side and I keep a lookout for potential bullies.

Kellie hunches and blows out laboured breaths.

I spy Travis strolling down the corridor with his mates. "Hey Kel, why don't we hang with Travis? He could help—"

"No!" she cuts me off. "I don't want your boyfriend's help. He's one of them. I don't trust being around any of those people."

"But—"

"No, Charli!" Kellie pushes me away and runs up the corridor.

My mouth hangs open as I rub where she jabbed. Travis hasn't noticed me and walks towards mess. I could go sit with him, the hell with Kellie.

"It was the craziest place Maggie and I have done it so far," Ray brags and high fives Lucas.

Lucas slaps Travis on the back. "When are you going to start spilling about your escapades with Charli?"

My stomach swirls and an angry pain seers my forehead. I hightail it through the corridor towards the quad.

"Kellie! Kellie!"

Kellie stops in the middle of the quad and turns around. I catch up to her and her red-rimmed eyes are brimming with tears.

"I'm sorry," she whispers.

"Sorry?"

"I'm such a fucking bitch," she cries, tumbling to her knees.

"What? Kellie. No, no you're not."

Kellie doubles over and howls gut-wrenching sobs. I drop to my knees and cradle her in my arms.

"I... don't... like..." she gasps sobs between each word, "this... spotlight."

Kellie wipes her face with the sleeve of her blazer. I'm gonna hurl. Our strong Kellie, the Kellie that fights our battles, is broken. My jaw juts as I try to find words.

Kellie takes my hand and whispers, "Let's hide with the smoker kids. I need to escape."

I'm still in shock that Kellie bought the bag of weed. Its allure makes me curious. I mean, if Kellie does it, it can't be that bad... right?

When Travis came over tonight, I was weighing up whether to ask him if he's tried it before and if he'd want to try it with me. Before I could ask, the real problem walked in. Will Maclean has some nerve coming to my house for dinner. I need to convince my mum to stop being friends with his mum.

I sit across from my sister as she makes small talk with Will. *Earth to Brittany. He's a douche, stop talking to him.*

I ask Travis about his football team. My desperation level for a distraction is off the charts.

"I got on our team," Will chimes in. "I so know they want me to be captain. They're scared *big-islander-dude* Jace will pummel them into the ground if they don't call him captain."

I gnaw the inside of my cheek as I make fists. My body temperature rises, my chest tightens. I will snap if I hear his voice again.

"Whatever ya reckon, Willy," Travis says.

I slide my chair back with an ear-piercing screech. "Mum, can I be excused?"

"You've hardly touched your food."

"Sorry, I have to go." I leave the dining room before she can convince me to stay.

I storm into the living room and pace back and forth with a heaving chest.

"Charli? You ok?" Travis pulls me into his arms. My palms press into my face and I huff into his t-shirt. "Will is still in your bad books?"

"Bad books?" I break out of his arms. "Kellie is miserable because of him."

"I know. What can I do to help?"

Kellie's reaction plays in my mind. "You can't do anything."

"I can go in there and punch his nose in. Will that help?"

I pull him further into the living room. "How in the world would that help?"

"I'm just making suggestions," he says, cracking a smile.

My chest eases and I smile back. "Will you come with me to my dad's tomorrow?"

He winces. "Think he'll be ok with that?"

"Yeah. I want you there with me. And I want him to meet you. It'd mean a lot."

"Well, of course. If you want me there, I'll be there."

I kiss his cheek. "Thank you."

Travis pulls me to the floor and tickles my waist. Laughter spills out of me as I tumble backwards and bat his hands away. My legs kick as the laugh hurts my gut in the best way. Travis holds me at the waist as I try to squirm out of his grip. I grin and play wrestle against him.

"Oh well, well, well," Will says, leaning against the doorframe. "What's goin on ere."

Travis lets me go and I slide away. Will saunters into the room and plonks on a couch. I sit with my back turned to him.

"Hey, don't stop on my account," Will jokes.

Travis' hand slides along my spine and I flinch, knowing Will's eyes are on us.

"So, Charli," Will begins and my jaw clenches. "Is Kellie going to the formal?"

My forehead scrunches. "What, so you can turn her into another practical joke?"

"I just want to talk to her again."

"Why?"

"Because she's really cool. It was the first time I had talked to a girl and felt like she was a real person."

I keep my back to him. "You've been such a pig."

"I know. Last year sucked balls so I didn't want any heat on me again." Will slides off the couch and thumps to the floor. "It was a dumb thing to do. What should I say to her?"

"*Whoah*," Travis says, sliding behind me to keep distance between me and Will. My knuckles crack at the idea Will would get that close to me.

"What?" Will says.

"Give her some space, man. You royally screwed up."

"I know but—"

"No, you don't," Travis argues. "Kellie is a target now, and it's all your fault. You're going to have to come up with something major if you want to apologise to her."

Brittany scuffs up the hall and I call out to her.

She stops by the door. "What's going on?"

"Can you please come in here and distract Will with something shiny," I reply. "He's being a twat."

She takes a few steps forward, eyes darting between all three of us.

"He wants to win Kellie over," Travis explains.

Brittany crosses her arms and stops dead. "You called her a demon."

"Yeah but—"

Travis shoves Will. "But what?"

"C'mon Travis," I say, getting up.

Will grabs my hand. "Please, Charli. Help me out. I didn't mean for it to play out like this."

"First of all, let go of my hand." I yank my hand out of his grip. "Second of all, I don't owe you anything. Kellie told me you two hit it off and you had a lot in common. Maybe you can use that peanut you call a brain and come up with something." I walk towards the doorway. "Don't ask me for any more help because you certainly don't deserve it."

"So, how long have you two been dating?" Dad asks when Travis and I sit down at the dining table in his apartment.

"Since January," I answer for us.

"Swooped in while her father's out of town?" Dad eyes Travis.

"You being out of the picture has nothing to with me and Charli," Travis replies.

"The timing is peculiar, though," Dad continues, "don't you agree?"

"No. I'm always here for her. Unlike some people."

"Trav," I squeak.

Dad folds his arms across his chest. "You can understand how I'm worried about my daughter dating an older boy."

"It's only two years," I reply.

The buzzer sounds and our Chinese takeaway is on its way up. Dad moves to the front door and across the table Brittany is glued to her phone.

"Do you need to be on your phone right now?"

Brittany grizzles a reply and drops her phone to the table. The screen is bright, and a text chain appears labelled 'Bryce.'

I point at the screen. "Are you two together?"

Brittany huffs and locks the screen of her phone. "Shuddup."

I swallow the bad taste in my mouth and focus on Travis' hand on my thigh. I cup his hand and smile at him.

We spread the takeaway containers across the dining table and have at it. Between bites, Dad asks Travis if he's still into football. At least he's trying to get to know him. Right?

Travis hurries to swallow his mouthful. "Yeah, Mr Matthews, I represent the school and town teams."

"Any idea of what you want to study at uni?" Dad asks. "You are planning to go to university?"

Travis nods and drags his fork along his plate. "Yeah, my dad wants me to study business so I can work with him."

Dad beams. "I'm sure he'd appreciate your help."

I spot Travis' fake smile a mile off. He eats to avoid the topic.

Dad's head tilts pensively at a food container, and I ask, "You ok, Dad?"

Dad clears his throat and straightens. He looks to Brittany and then to me. "I do have something to tell you girls. It really should be just the three of us."

I shake my head. "Dad, you can say anything in front of Travis."

Dad rocks his jaw and his shoulders droop. "Girls, I've been seeing someone." My heart pounds. "Her name is Tara and I would like you to meet her."

"You're dating?" Brittany eyes him, leaning forward.

Blood pumps in my ears. "How is that possible? You just got back."

"Unless you've brought someone back from your trip?" Brittany adds.

The room is spinning. Travis squeezes my hand.

Dad is still talking yet I can't make out his words, so I blurt out, "I thought you were going to move home."

The silence is raw. All eyes are on me. Dad looks at me like I'm strange. "Moving home? Pumpkin, your mum and I are divorced. I'm not moving into the house."

I fling Travis' hand away and cover my face. "Don't talk to me like I'm an idiot."

A chair slides back. Dad moves in close and places his hand on my shoulder. "Charli, you're not an idiot. I didn't mean for you to feel bad."

I suck in my lip as my throat quivers and tears threaten to fall. I push off my chair and dart to the bathroom.

Dad calls after me, but I slam the door. I perch on the edge of the bathtub and sobs spurt out. My hand trembles over my mouth as my thoughts jumble together.

There's a soft knock on the door. "Baby, you ok?"

I squeeze my eyes shut. I want to let him in, but I'm a mess.

"Charli?" his voice wavers with worry.

As my hand rests over my heart, my pulse slows. Coughing a final sob, I splash cold water on my face and clear my throat.

I open the door and tug Travis inside. My face buries in his chest. He anchors an arm behind me and strokes my hair. He hushes me softly, swaying our bodies. I swallow and exhale slowly.

"I don't know what I'd do without you," I whisper.

Even though I'd rather stay in the bathroom alone with him, I hold Travis' hand and walk into the open-plan living area.

"Pumpkin, you ok?" Dad asks like I'm a child with a busted knee.

Brittany stands off to the side, clutching her elbows.

"Are you ok, Brit?" I ask.

She chews her lip.

I ask Dad, "You're dating?"

"Yes."

My heart thumps to a broken beat. "How is this possible?"

"Come to the table," Dad beckons us over. "Let's talk about this. Travis, maybe it's best you go home."

I latch onto Travis' arm. "No."

Dad's face tightens. "Charli?"

"Travis, can you just drive us home?" Brittany says, walking over to us.

"No, girls. You'll stay and we'll talk about this," Dad insists.

Travis squeezes my hand and Brittany stomps her frustration.

My legs shake as I look directly into Dad's eyes. "You had time to start dating, but not to keep in contact with us?"

Dad's chin drops and he doesn't say anything.

I shake my head. "Forget this. Travis, take us home."

"Stay overnight," Dad suggests as we move towards the door.

"Dad, no," Brittany snaps. "Let us go."

Pain radiates up my back. "Bye, Dad."

Dad's eyes show the hurt, but he nods. I hug him goodbye and don't latch on like usual.

Brittany is silent the whole trip home. I'm lost for words. Travis looks over to me but never says anything.

Man, what do we tell Mum?

The next day at school I stared at the pages of my Spanish textbook, and the words may as well be squiggles. Señora Flores asked the class questions and handpicked students to answer.

Dad's news has thrown me so off my game. I sat in class repeating in my head: *please, please, please don't pick me.*

Rikki answered a question with flawless pronunciation. "*Tengo dos hermanos y tres hermanas.*"

At the skatepark. after school, I'm still not over it.

"Seriously, Hispanic people shouldn't be allowed in the same classes as us."

Reece whacks my arm. "Holy crap, shuddup." He points across the rink at Tayla. "Even I know you sound crazy."

"*Ugh*, I wasn't generalising." I meander behind him as we pass Lenny and Simon. "You get my point, right? If you have family who speak the language you have an advantage and should be in a different class to those who don't."

Reece keeps his back to me. "If it ends the topic then yes."

"Why are you grumpy at me?"

Reece slides on his noise-cancelling headphones, drops his board and skates down the rink.

Are you kidding? He's avoiding me? I drop my board and skate after him.

"What the hell, man?" I call out as I gain on him.

Reece brakes and flicks up his board. He pulls off his headphones with a huff. "You've been avoiding what's bothering you all day."

"Whaddaya mean?"

"You're complaining about Rikki instead of your dad."

I rock a foot on my board. "My dad's got nothin to do with this."

"You told Kellie and me what happened but brushed it off. Like you're not mad at him."

"Well, I'm sorry if I'm scared he'll leave again."

Reece's eyes twitch. His mouth opens but no words follow.

"Don't worry about it," I mumble.

"Sorry. We need Kellie out of lockdown. She's the one you need right now."

"It's ok. I've just got to meet this woman at some point and it's all a bit much. Dad doesn't like Travis and he's back in that apartment. Mum said Dad filled her in on the new girlfriend drama when they met at her office, but left it to him to fill us in. A heads up would have been nice. There's so much to deal with."

"Don't tell me you need a hug."

It could be the one thing I need right now, but his fidgety body language makes me snort a laugh. "No. I'm good."

11

Brittany

Things would be different at school after Bryce and I kissed. I didn't expect it to mean he'd be ignoring me.

I had jitters to the point of almost puking on Monday morning. It was a mixture of relief and disappointment when I discovered the reason I couldn't find him was that he didn't go to school that day.

All my free time is spent staring at the last text message he sent on Sunday night. No new texts have come through since. Meah's theory is that because we kissed I'm now his girlfriend. I don't know the rules of dating, but the fact he keeps referring to me as his *friend* doesn't help me believe her.

The next two days were a slap across the face when he kept his head down in science and didn't turn around once. Was it really that bad a kiss? He regrets it so much that I am now invisible?

"I'm so nervous," Meah whispers as we walk to the gym.

"Me too."

It's our first practice in the cheer squad. I'm so happy to have Meah by my side, I was so scared she wouldn't get in.

"*Woohoo.*" Tayla Martinez skips ahead of us. "How exciting we already got our uniforms. See ya in the gym."

"Woohoo?" Chloe repeats. Her nose wrinkles like she smelled something foul.

"Can't believe they let her in," Kimberley says. "Bad enough I get stuck with her in gymnastics."

We walk into the changerooms. We are supposed to practice in our PE uniforms, but Chloe protested for Ms Harvey to let us wear our cheer uniforms for the first practice.

Once changed, I stop in front of the mirror and reapply my lipgloss. Meah stands behind my reflection, tugging the clingy fabric at her mid-section.

"*Whoah* Chubba, looks like you gotta lose some of em kilos," Chloe says, leaving her cubicle.

My body tenses as the room fills with giggles and hushed comments. Meah trudges to the bench beside me and I whisper, "You ok?"

She nods, smoothing her uniform. "At least I'm in it, right?" She tosses her mousy brown hair. "You think I gotta tie it up?"

Meah pulls her hair around her jaw and I bat her hands away. "Leave it out and see how you go."

We enter the gym and with no surprise, Chloe was appointed captain. Ms Harvey asks her to teach us a routine from last year's squad.

A wolf whistle echoes in the gym. Will and Naveen stand by the entrance.

"Looking good ladies," Will calls out.

"No way will we be able to concentrate on the game," Naveen adds.

"Mr Maclean, Mr Singh," Ms Harvey shouts at them. "Move along, please."

The boys leave the gym laughing and Chloe pushes us into three lines. I'm in the centre row to the right and Meah is behind me. Chloe shouts steps while demonstrating them. Meah has nervousness written all over her face. I give her an encouraging smile and shrug my shoulder to give the impression I'm lost too.

The steps are simple. Tiffany gives us harder stuff to learn. During the first run-through I easily keep up with Chloe.

"Are you getting this?" Madison asks beside me.

I nod.

"I'm totally lost," Fiona whispers from the first row. She tugs on my arm. "You should swap with me so I can follow along."

"Yeah go," Madison says, shoving me in front.

I slide to a stop as Fiona darts behind me.

"What is up?" Chloe asks, hands on hips.

"I want to watch her," Fiona says, cowering behind me.

"I put you in the front for a reason, Fi," Chloe replies with a huff.

As I return to my original position Kimberley remarks, "Like Brittany would have a clue what to do. Her moves are totally awkward and her timing is way off."

My jaw drops. We've only had one run-through and Kimberley is already on my case?

As we do a few more run-throughs Chloe paces glaring hawk-like at us. "*Gawd* Meah, could ya be any sloppier? Like, damn. And Tayla try to do the actual moves not whatever the hell that was. Madison, your turns are two beats too long."

After practice I overhear Kimberley talking to Chloe. "Brittany is such a poser. I don't know why you let her hang around you."

Before I can process the remark, Meah screeches, "I freakin suck!"

"It was only one practice. You'll get better. We'll practice more after school."

We change into our regular uniform and head to lunch. At the table

I notice Bryce approaching with his food tray. Butterflies go berserk in my stomach. Even though I haven't spoken to him since Sunday he still turns my body into a bundle of nerves. I purse my lips to hide the big goofy smile.

I eye him, hoping he will make eye contact or crack a smile in my direction. He doesn't notice me. He sits at the other end of the table and pushes his food tray away.

Beside him Madison grabs chips from his plate. "You look tired."

Bryce rubs the sides of his face. "I am tired."

Madison continues to take food from Bryce's tray. He slides it in front of her telling her to take it. His colour is a little off. He's been away sick?

"Madi, you are such a pig," Fiona frowns. "You can't eat two lunches."

"Watch me," Madison mumbles with a mouth full of potato.

Fiona covers her mouth, giggling in a doll-like pose.

My eyes dart between Madison and Bryce. What is going on here? Is that why nothing happened with her and Naveen? Is something going on between Madison and Bryce? Is that why he's avoiding me?

I'm deflated as Meah and I leave the mess to go to textiles. I dawdle into the corridor contemplating just how slow I can walk.

There's a tap on my shoulder. It's Bryce. Meah eyes him with a cheeky grin.

"Can I talk to you?" he asks me.

My legs are jelly. "Sure." I say to Meah, "Give us a minute?"

She frowns, but nods and leaves.

"How have you been?" he says, looking beside me not at me.

My lips part for words to come out, but I can't function.

"Look, I'm sorry," he fidgets in place, "I'm sorry we haven't talked. Life's been a bit crazy and I've been dealing with stuff. I forget I have someone to talk to.”

I take a breath, hoping it will help get the words out.

“It’s cool if you don’t want to hang out,” he says to the ceiling. “I know I dropped a lot on your plate.”

“No!” is all I could get out, and way too loud. He blinks at me. “No, it’s ok.”

“I’m glad. I do really want to be friends with you.”

That F-word is like a stab in the gut. “Me too.”

“You free this afternoon?” he asks, finally meeting my eyes. “Wanna try studying again?”

I put all my might into not letting the frown show. “Sure. I have dance class tonight so I can’t stick around for too long.”

“Are you ok? You seem really down.”

I bite down on my tongue so I don’t blurt out IT’S BECAUSE YOU’RE IGNORING ME. I blame something else. “Just drama with my dad. He wants me to meet his girlfriend. Kinda came outta nowhere.”

“Oh shit, Brit.” He pulls me into a hug. My eyes bulge as my face rests against his collarbone. “I am such a shit friend. I haven’t even checked in on you.”

“It’s ok,” I say, building the courage to put my hands on his back. Am I seriously in his arms right now?

He pulls away and shakes his head. “No, I’ve been the worst. Meet up after school and talk?”

I nod, smiling, but the smile fades when I notice the way his cheeks are sunken. “Are you feeling ok?”

He scratches the side of his head. “Yeah, I’m good. Why?”

“Oh, um, nothing.”

I got a text from Bryce, but it wasn’t good. He rescheduled *Shakes* for tomorrow afternoon.

"*Ohmigawd*, whatever," I whine in Meah's bedroom. "I don't know what the deal is with this boy."

"What am I supposed to do?" Meah squawks, unpacking a box. "Chloe never stops telling everyone how fat I am. I'm only drinking these from now on."

She pulls sachets from the box. I walk over and take one, *The Shake Diet*. "You're only going to drink shakes?"

"What choice do I have? She's never going to stop."

I plonk down beside her on the bed. "I can't believe I'm friend-zoned."

"At least he quit ignoring you. Now I need any nickname except Chubba. I'm seriously going to jam a pen in her neck the next time I hear it."

I side-glance her. "Why a pen?"

"It's school... I'll probably have one handy."

"Please don't turn to a life of crime. I need you around." I cuddle her. "*Geez*, I don't wanna go to dance class now."

"Stay here and play hooky."

"And give Kimberley more ammo against me? No way."

Meah sighs at her box of sachets. "Maybe if I drop some weight I'll land a boyfriend."

"You really want a guy who just wants you for your body?"

She deadpans. "Yes."

I squeeze a hug out of her and leave for dance class.

I can't get Kimberley's stupid voice out of my head. I'm working on the solo Tiffany gave me and I keep messing up.

"*She's got no idea what she's doing*," plays over and over. "*She's a complete poser.*" I can't believe she's getting between Chloe and me. Although I guess I shouldn't be surprised. It's the same game she played in primary school.

"Brit, what's going on?" Tiffany gives me the concerned-mum-look.

"Nothing."

"You're missing your cues."

"I'm fine. I'll get it."

She steps to me and whispers, "If you can't do it, I can give it to Chloe."

I groan and take a step back. "No, I can do it."

I start over. My mind drifts to that kiss. My body eases and a hint of a smile tingles my lips. *He regrets kissing you.* My back knots. I scrunch my eyes closed. I want to scream. I lose balance and fall to the floor.

Gasps fill the air and I pull myself up.

Chloe smirks at me. Can I curl up and die now?

"Take five," Tiffany tells me.

I slink to my gym bag. My face radiates the heat of embarrassment. What am I even doing?

TGIF. I didn't have science or English today to stare at him, but he found me by my locker and asked if I was still good for this afternoon. Between the smile lines and the brightness of his eyes, the word 'yes' has never been spoken sooner.

We order choc-shakes and sit on the decking overlooking the sandy bay.

"I'm sorry I ditched yesterday," he says, twirling his straw.

"It's ok." I don't mean it.

"No, it isn't. I got really caught up in wanting to see you again; I forgot I had to be at an appointment yesterday."

I shrug. "It's fine. Is everything ok with you?"

"Um..." he begins. "Yeah, everything is ok. I just want to apologise for ignoring you.”

The fact he admits it kinda stings. I was happy having it in my imagination instead of it seeping into reality.

“I got freaked out.”

“By what?”

“I was paranoid you would tell people what we talked about.”

I push back on my seat. “You didn’t trust me?”

“No, no, I do,” he rushes, clamping his hand on mine. “When you told me stuff about your family and asked me to keep it between us, it made me feel like I could really trust you. I liked it and that’s why I told you the stuff with my family.” He pauses for a moment. “I was scared because when people at my old school found out it was tough to escape the rumours. I just didn’t want it to happen again.”

My heart pangs. “I told you I wouldn’t say anything.”

He rubs his temples, frowning. “I know. I know and you haven’t. I’m such a jerk.”

“Bryce, don’t worry about it,” I say. “We’ve all got stuff going on that we’re scared people will find out about.”

Bryce drops his hands and meets my gaze. “You doing ok? What’s happening with your dad?”

I throw my hands up. “All of a sudden he has a girlfriend. He just gets back and next minute he’s telling us about her like it’s no big deal. My head is seconds from exploding.”

“I can’t imagine one of my parents dating someone else.”

“Well, yours are together, right?”

“Yeah. Still.”

I nod. “I know.”

“I’m sorry I didn’t take your trust seriously.”

“I guess we still don’t know each other that well.”

“Well, I’d like to,” his words are shaky. “I kinda think we could be each other’s rock.”

Bolts of goosebumps send me into the biggest, weirdest shiver of my life. "What are you saying?"

He takes my hands. "I really like you, Britty. I'd really like to date you."

I try to rush out a reply and instead choke on air. I steal my hands back and cup my mouth as I dry cough.

He touches my knee. "Hey, are you ok?"

I stop coughing and nod, lowering my hands. He smiles at me and I smile back.

"You're one of the best people I've met, Brittany Matthews," he whispers. "Will you be my girlfriend?"

I nod and whisper, "Yes."

His smile gets bigger and he leans closer to me. My eyes fall shut and my lips tingle as they meet his. My arms wrap him as our lips gently part. I play with his hair as I apply more pressure to the kiss.

His arms pull me closer.

Is this really happening?

12

Charli

I spent most of Saturday with Reece at the skatepark. He doesn't ask questions, which is perfect because I don't have any answers.

Tonight, I meet the girlfriend: Tara.

Dad just came back into my life. I want to be around him as much as possible. I don't want to be angry at him. If meeting this woman guarantees an hour or two with Dad, then so be it.

At the restaurant, the maître d' checks my board and looks down his nose at my attire; ripped jeans and a fading Nirvana t-shirt. I refuse to dress up for this meeting.

I'm late and Dad and Brittany are already seated at a table. A tall, skinny brunette laughs next to my dad.

I hate her already.

"Charli," Dad stands up, arms wide. "How was your day?"

I hug him. "It was good."

Dad pulls out of the hug, an arm extended to acknowledge the woman to his right. "Charli, this is Tara."

"Hi hunny." Tara's thin lips spread into an exaggerated smile. She stands up in a puke-worthy peach sequinned dress. "I'm so glad I got to meet you two individually. I've been so nervous. I always mess up people's names, and I expect to be worse with twins."

I give her a fake smile and slink around to sit next to Brittany who is picking the polish off her nails.

Tara continues in her cheery tone, "Just lemme apologise right now for getting your names mixed up in the future."

"Tara's a legal secretary," Dad adds.

My chin drops. I want to say it, but Brit gets there before me, "Did you two work together?"

"No," Dad and Tara say at the same time.

"I work down at *Clarkson & Garricks*," Tara explains. "We met through work. It's unavoidable in our field."

My back stiffens. "You know our mum, too?"

Tara shakes her head, smile fading. "Not personally. Know her reputation though. Your mother is a powerhouse. She's an amazing woman."

"We know," Brittany replies.

Dad shifts in his seat. "So, Brittany, how's dance going?"

Brittany arches an eyebrow at him. "You want to talk about it now?"

"Oh wow, you're a dancer?" Tara claps her hands. "Are you performing anywhere soon?"

Brittany nods. "Somewhere soon."

"She got a solo. Isn't that right, Sweetheart," Dad urges.

Brittany slouches in her chair, nodding.

"And Charli's following in my footsteps," Dad beams at me. Goosebumps. "She's killing it in debate. When's the next match? We'd love to come."

I cough. "We?"

Tara leans forward. "I'd love to watch a young lawyer in the making."

The room spins. I clutch my forehead and close my eyes. "It's at King's Cliff."

"Oh, it's lovely there," Tara squeals, clapping again. "We could make a day of it. Have lunch in the mountains overlooking the water. Maybe we could take Brittany out of school to join us?"

"Our school generally doesn't like us going out on long lunches," I reply, flicking the prongs of my fork.

Tara's freckled cheeks grow rosy and an awkwardness hushes the table.

"So, do you have kids?" Brittany pipes up.

"Three. Two girls and a boy."

My mind clicks and I ask Dad, "Have you met them already?"

He clears his throat. "Yes. Yes, I have."

When did you have time to do that?

"I'd love to have you all meet," Tara continues.

"When you girls are ready," Dad adds.

Ready? Ready for what? To wake up from this nightmare?

Throughout dinner I pulled a Brittany and made my replies a series of grunts and mumbles. My desperation to get away was so high I actually texted 'yes' when Travis asked me to go to a party with him.

Travis drives us to a house in West Sanford. The host is a guy named Mackellar, who throws senior-only parties where the booze is always overflowing. A party is the only exception to the rule that West Sanford sucks. It's further away from parents and decreases risk of being caught doing something you shouldn't be.

The house is loud and overcrowded. I squeeze Travis' hand. All I want is to be around him, but it means being around all these meatheads? Being mad at my dad gave me a serious lapse in judgement.

"Charli!" Maggie Lee swooshes a drink at me. "You need a drink."

"Oh no, I'm ok."

"Just freakin take it," Maggie scowls. "I made it. It's called a French Kiss."

I take the drink to stop the girls' death stares.

Lucas pulls Travis away and he laughs and drinks with the boys. I fidget in place with a deep inhale, not ready to follow.

"Hey, what are you doing here?" someone asks, clutching my shoulder.

It's Preston. "Hey. Oh, you know, being a party animal."

He lets out a throaty laugh.

"Are you at a lot of these parties?"

He shakes his head. "Nah, few of the guys like to go. Got pestered and gave in."

"Yeah, I followed Travis here. Not usually my thing. This week was crazy, so what the hell."

Preston looks around. "Is that your boyfriend? Where is he?"

My chest heaves and I point over to the table by the wall. "Over with that lot." I flinch as he does a shot.

"You going over to join him?"

I take my eyes away from Travis and his over-the-top friends. "Maybe I'll step outside for a minute."

"My friends are out on the deck. You can hang with us," Preston says, and I follow him outside.

On the deck Shae swings on a hammock with another girl. "It's good to get a night away from the house. Mum's gone bonkers lately." She sees me and smiles. "Charli? What you doing here? Pres, did you invite her?"

I shake my head. "Random coincidence."

"You're drinking?" Shae points to the French Kiss in my hand.

I offer the cup to her. "No, you want it?"

She takes it from me and takes a sip. She coughs as she swallows. "Hot mumma, that's strong. You are definitely not allowed to drink that."

"Shae's gonna mother hen you now," Preston smirks as we sit on a bench.

"She's fifteen," Shae protests.

I raise my hands in defence. "I wasn't gonna drink it. It was just for show."

A boy joins us with a six pack of beers. He hands them out, and comments on Shae's new drink, "You going with that instead?"

Shae sets the drink down. "You know I don't really drink."

"Miss Holier-Than-Thou," the girl by Shae jokes.

The boy offers Shae's beer to me which I kindly decline.

"So, what are you doing here?" Shae asks.

"She's here with her boyfriend," Preston says.

"Who's your boyfriend?" Shae asks.

"His name is Travis."

"You have to point him out to us."

"Yeah, maybe," I say.

I recline on my seat and let Preston and his friends continue with a conversation that doesn't include me. Sitting out here in the crisp night air is relaxing. Most people are inside, so I let myself become mesmerized by the night sky.

A while later I tag along with Shae who goes inside the house in search of bottled water. I figure I should let Travis know where I am. As we cross the living room, I find Travis where I left him.

"Hey, where have you been?" Travis shouts over the music, pushing past his friends to get to me.

"Outside," I say, focusing on his cup filled with brown liquor.

"Outside? I was looking for you." He's still so loud even though I'm right next to him.

"You were looking for me? From here?"

"Charli, where the fuck you been?" Ray slurs, draping an arm around Travis' neck.

"Aw, the little one came," GiGi smirks, stopping beside me and tussling my hair. "Thanks for putting in some effort, Charli. T-shirt, jeans and messy hair. You stylin."

I sidestep away from her and dive my hands into pockets to avoid smacking her in the face.

Travis finishes his drink and a glaze coats his eyes. My heart sinks. Is he going to pay more attention to alcohol than me tonight?

"Charli, you going to introduce me?" Shae asks.

Travis chucks his empty cup. "Who's this?"

"I'm Charli's friend, Shae. Are you the boyfriend?"

He blinks hard. "Friend?"

He's having difficulty making eye contact and I have to look away. "Yeah, this is Travis."

"Travis, we're hanging outside," Shae continues. "Why don't you join us? Fresh air might do you good."

Travis squints at me. "Wait? Who are you with?"

I pinch the bridge of my nose. "Travis, slow down a bit. Come outside and be with me."

Lucas hangs himself off Travis' shoulder. "*Whoop, whoop.* Time to get busy out in the backyard is it?"

I bite my tongue so hard the pain radiates through my temples. I storm towards the deck with Shae on my tail.

Behind me, the morons cheer, "Someone's gettin lucky tonight!"

"Charli." Shae grabs my arm when we hit the deck. "Are you ok?"

I shake my head quick. "Can we just forget it? Can I just sit out here and ignore what's going on in there?"

Shae lets me go. "Sure. Talk to me if you need to."

I give a small smile. "Thanks."

It's easy being around Preston and Shae with their friends. I like that they have heated discussions and they don't push me to weigh in.

I relax to the point I don't realise an hour has passed.

An hour.

A WHOLE FUCKING HOUR?

How has he still not come outside?

I tell the gang I'm going inside to find him. The living room is jam-packed. I duck between groups to spy the table Travis was at, but a new group is there.

I scan the room and double-take on bright white hair. Chloe Benson. A hand combs her hair, belonging to Lucas Rivers. She pulls him closer. They lock lips until she pulls away, biting his lower lip.

I gasp and spin a one-eighty. I did not want to see that.

The difficulty of moving through the crowd increases. People bump into me, crushing my toes and spilling beers on my arm. Near the kitchen, I see Travis. My jaw clenches. GiGi Larkin is hugging him from behind and playing with his hair. My insides vortex. I hold my stomach and look for a bathroom.

In the solitude of the bathroom, I cool off and take my time steadying my hands. I came here to be with him and we separated immediately. This is bullshit. I rest against the tiled wall and huff.

It's my cue to leave when someone bangs on the door. Dawdling into the living room, I take in the crowd. Before I can think of my next move, I'm grabbed and spun around. Wrapped in Travis' arms.

His lips attack mine with a bitter taste of alcohol. He stumbles, leaning on me. I put my hands on his chest to push him back.

"Trav, slow down."

"Let's find a room," he whispers.

My heart pitter-patters at the thought of escaping with him.

He takes my hand and leads me down the hall of bedroom doors. He finds a vacant room and tugs me inside. The party noise muffles behind the door. I exhale and relax my shoulders.

Travis scoops me in his arms. His kisses burn with passion. I'm weightless. Then the alcoholic fumes bring me back to reality.

His hands move down my body and slip inside my t-shirt. I grab onto his wrists. I try to tell him to slow up, but my voice is a grunt against his lips. He kisses my neck and the warmth weakens my knees. My eyes close as I rub my lips together.

"You're so beautiful," he whispers, fumbling with my bra clasp.

I push down on his forearms. He presses me back on the bed and the sides of my bra fling against my ribs. I cup my chest as he lies on top of me. Travis' kisses are soft and sink me into the bed. His fingers dance along the top of my denim shorts and his thumb flicks at the top button.

"Trav," I whisper.

I study his dark yet vacant eyes. My throat tenses and I tremble beneath him.

One of his hands slips into my pants.

Shock jolts my body. "Travis. Stop. Please."

He kisses me again and I pull away. I bend my body but he's heavy on top of me.

"I just want to be with you," he whispers with a hoarse voice.

My fly unzips.

"Stop. That's enough."

He grinds between my thighs and I grow rigid. His fingers explore my midriff and my heart thumps. Travis lifts himself up and pulls off his shirt. He's wonky as he sits up. I lunge forward, shaking, and shove both hands into his stomach.

He hunches and falls backwards. I scamper away and crawl across the bed to barrel to door. He follows me and my skin prickles. I spin and soar my knee into his groin.

He moans and collapses.

I pull up my shorts and fling open the door. I race down the halls clasping my bra hooks. Tears stream my cheeks as I dart through the drunken crowd.

"*Whoah.*" An arm barricades me. Preston holds my arms, but I push him away.

A sob splutters out as I try to get past.

"Hey, hey. What's happened?"

"Let me go," my voice garbles. "I need to get out of here."

He pushes people out of the way. "I'll take you wherever you need to go."

I run ahead of Preston and out of the house. The cool night air smacks my face. I shake uncontrollably.

Preston points to his car. "C'mon, I'll drive you."

I hug myself all the way to his car.

"What happened?" he whispers, unlocking the passenger door.

I lean against the car, unable to make eye contact. He wipes a thumb over my wet cheek and I flinch.

His eyes narrow. "Did he hurt you?"

A sob coughs out of me. I wipe my flooding eyes. With a wavery voice I say I don't want him to find me and give Preston my address.

Preston opens the door and I slip into the car. My fingernails pierce my bottom lip the entire trip home. Preston glances at me periodically. I count the seconds between breaths. Before I can think *one*, the next breath hiccups.

Preston parks at my house. Before he speaks, I leap out of the car and sprint to the house. In the foyer I pant so hard it hurts my throat. An avalanche of sobs rush from me.

"Charli?" Through the appliance glow of the kitchen, my sister walks towards me.

I lower my head and hide my face.

"You're crying?" she asks, edging closer. "Is this still about Dad? Didn't Travis make you feel better?"

I choke on sobs.

"*Whoah*. Charli?"

I latch onto my sister and soak her pyjama shirt with tears.

"Holy crap," she gasps, hugging me tight. "Tell me what happened."

"I don't know," I sob. "I don't know." My mind whirs too fast. "I don't know."

"Yes, you do," she says firm and clear. "Something is wrong. You need to tell me. Do you want me to get Mum?"

I shake my head violently against the nape of her neck.

"Well, c'mon," she whispers, pulling out of the hug. "Come upstairs with me. Lie down and just breathe."

My feet scrape across the carpet of my bedroom and I escape under the covers. Brittany sits a glass of water on my bedside table and sits on the edge of the bed, waiting for me to explain.

"Did Travis bring you home?" she starts.

My face is smooshed against the mattress as I answer, "No, I think he's still at the party."

"Did you guys have a fight?"

Every muscle in my face tightens. I start babbling into the mattress when Brittany stops me. She reefs the bedding off me and uses her firm voice again, "Charli, are you ok or not? You walked into the house looking hellish. Do you need me or not?"

My silent cries and streaming tears cause my head to ache. I sit up and wipe my face. "Travis tried to force me."

Brittany tenses. "Force you?"

I claw the sheets and nod.

"Wh-what? You mean, like, sex?"

I wipe my face, too exhausted to nod again. "He tried to take my clothes off."

"You told him no?"

"Yes."

Brittany kneels in front of me. "I don't understand. Have you guys talked about sex?"

"He was so drunk," I sob. "I said no but he kept going."

"Charli!" Brittany squeaks, pulling me close. "Did he hurt you?"

I shiver, unable to answer.

"I am going to murder him. Being drunk is not an excuse."

My hands slide along Brittany's back. Her soft, pomegranate scented hair calms me down. "Would you stay with me, Brit?"

"Of course."

Brittany held me the entire night. It was hard to close my eyes because I'd get flashes of Travis on top of me. I'd shudder or jolt and Brittany would groan or shove me. She would then pull me close again and drift back to sleep. The sounds of her sleeping and her warmth was comforting.

The exhaustion won because I woke up this morning as Brittany left my bed.

I squint at her blurry figure and she says, "You sleep ok?"

"Yes," I lie.

"You want coffee?"

"You know I don't drink coffee."

She *humphs* and opens the bedroom door. "Thought you might wanna start."

"Brit."

She stops and looks back at me.

"Thanks for last night."

"No problem," she replies with a small smile. "You want me to call Kellie or something?"

I pull myself up to sitting. "Nah, I'll text her later."

Brittany goes downstairs and I take a notebook from the bedside table. Kellie is on her last grounded weekend. I don't want to text her because she'll be over within seconds. I can't stand another month of her on lockdown if she got caught.

Kellie was amazing during my parents' separation. Half the time we spent watching anime, other times she asked the most random questions to get my mind off things. Somehow, she always circled back to the heart of the issue. I know I need that help. Just not yet.

I can't look at my phone. I don't want to see any texts from him.

I'm not ready.

I focus on the notebook and work out the mess in my head.

My head is a jigsaw,
With half the pieces missing.
My heart is a Swarovski,
That you smashed into shards.

We were padlocks,
Gripped around each other.
Strength and security,
Promises to be kept.

When I say something,
You used to hear it,
You felt it,
You loved me?

13

Brittany

(Charli) Tell Mum or Sophia I'm sick and not going to school and not to come in here.

Mum? Like she'd still be home.

I'd already organised Sophia to drive us to school today. I don't want Travis anywhere near my sister.

"We can still take you to school even if they break up," Meah says when we meet by her locker.

"I know. It's just too soon right now."

"Are you sure Charli wasn't exaggerating?" she asks, rummaging in her locker. "Travis is being Travis and not telling me anything. I don't have his side of the story and don't want to rely on the rumour mill."

"Are you seriously defending him?"

"I'm just saying, I can't believe he would do something like that." Her eyes wet. "He's my brother, you know... I'm hoping it's not true."

"You know I call out Charli's BS," I say low and firm. "Seeing her like that, it's one hundred percent true."

Meah exhales and looks to the floor. "Sorry, Brit. This is all really uncomfortable to talk about. Let's promise not to let it come between us."

"Agreed." I pull her into a hug. "Promise to give him the message to stay away from her."

"Fine by me. I never liked them together anyway."

We pull out of the hug and tingles run down my spine as I spy Bryce over Meah's shoulder. His cheeky smile grows bigger as we lock eyes. Between dinner with Dad and Tara and being exhausted on Sunday from Charli's fidgeting, I've only talked to him via a text chain since *Shakes* on Friday.

And now we're dating.

Apparently.

Weird.

Amazing.

Freaky.

Ohmigawd.

"Hey," he says as he stops by us.

"Hi," I unintentionally whisper.

Meah stares back and forth at us, eyes wide and mouth open. Bryce fidgets with the straps of his bag and I stand on the sides of my feet, to the balls of my feet, to rocking on to my heels.

Do I hug him? Am I supposed to kiss him now?

Do we kiss whenever? Only at certain times?

I take in all the kids walking up and down the corridor and a clamminess coats my forehead and hands. I don't want to kiss him in front of everyone.

"How was your weekend?" Bryce asks. "Besides meeting your dad's girlfriend."

"Yeah, that kinda sucked. How was your weekend?"

"Our nanny had the weekend off so I had to babysit my sister. Living the dream."

"Yeah, your texts made her sound super bratty."

He laughs. "She is a brat."

"I went to the day spa with my mum and my aunt," Meah pipes up. "Ok, so not the greatest company in the world. I got a mango and coconut scrub and did you check out this *fab-u-lo-so* manicure."

As Meah waggles her pearly fingernails, my guilt swells. I wish she would get lost. My first-ever-boyfriend is standing right there and she's getting in the way.

"Yeah, they're beautiful, Meah," I reply. I turn to Bryce, eager to talk him about anything and everything.

"*Oi*, BK," Sean calls from behind Bryce.

Bryce turns around and high fives Sean and Naveen's hands that are hanging in the air.

"You coming, bro?" Naveen says, looping an arm around Bryce's neck.

"Yeah," Bryce replies, ducking out from Naveen. The boys keep walking and Bryce takes my hand and asks, "I'll see ya later?"

I nod. "Yes."

He smiles and squeezes my hand then follows the boys further down the hall.

I sigh like a princess in a Disney movie.

Meah steps up close and whispers, "Did you see how Naveen just looked at me?"

Three, two, one. It begins.

"Think you can ask Bryce if he likes me? Like, maybe Bryce can put in a good word for me. Say I'm great and he should ask me to the formal."

"*Ohmigawd* Meah," I groan.

"What?"

"I told you I won't use him like that."

"Excuse me, Brittany, we always said we would help each other get boyfriends. I helped set up things between you two."

I roll my eyes. "Ok, fine. I'll talk to Bryce."

Meah hugs her books and skips up the hall. "Thanks, Babe."

After a bunch of classes with no Bryce to stare at I race to mess. The *ba-booming* of my heart crowds out all other noise as I approach the seat next to him.

"We gotta go," Chloe says, sliding in front of me and blocking the view of my boyfriend.

Boyfriend.

It's still sinking in.

"Go? Where?"

"Our first game is coming up fast," she says, hands slamming on hips. "We have to practice our arses off."

"Oh, c'mon, really?"

"Yes," Chloe huffs and spins me toward the exit. "Everyone is headed to the gym."

She pushes me forward and I stumble on my first few steps. Chloe rushes past me, catching up with Kimberley and Fiona.

"Hey, Brit," Bryce calls out. My epic grin resurfaces. I turn around and he stands in front of me. "We never get any time to hang out here. Wanna meet up after school?"

"For sure."

"Seeing as winter will be here soon wanna go to the beach?"

"We can meet at the stretch by my house."

He takes my hands. "Awesome. I'll head to my place to dump my stuff and then swing by."

I squeeze his hands. "Can't wait."

"BRITTANY," Chloe thunders my name from the entrance of mess.

"Gotta go. See you soon."

He kisses my cheek. "See you soon."

"So, howzit going with Bryce?" Kimberley asks as we walk towards the gym.

Chloe looms on my other side. "Yeah. We are, like, totally surprised you are a couple."

I shrink. "Um, yeah, it's going good."

"You gotta be careful, ya know," Kimberley says, scrolling through her phone.

"Careful?"

Chloe grabs my wrist. "Cause you're, like, punching above your weight."

I gulp and blink at my shoes.

"You just started hanging with us," Kimberley states, eyeing me.

"You can tell Bryce has always been popular," Chloe adds. "It's weird you two even talk."

I squirm. "We look weird together?"

Chloe flicks her hair and laughs. "Maybe it'll work out? You obviously did something to get his attention."

"Yeah. Maybe we're wrong." Kimberley nods, smirking. "Maybe you two won't crash and burn."

I push into my stomach and swallow hard. Please. Nothing come up.

"Hey." Chloe tilts her head and touches my shoulder. "We just lookin out for ya. Member we're friends, right?"

I nod slowly. "Right."

"So, you have to tell us things." Chloe moves her head until I meet her eyes. "Every detail."

"Ok."

She smiles the same way she did at her puppies. "Good girl."

#

My gut was a swirling mess of yuck once home. After my struggles with eleven outfit choices, I paced my bedroom balcony to spy the sand beyond our backyard. Not knowing how quickly he'd be over had me beyond flustered.

The nerves disappear when I see him. We meet on the beach, a few houses away from mine. His eyes are an extension of the tide behind him and his soft rosy lips crook in a gentle smile.

His arms wrap around me in a warm hug. "You look really nice. I'm so glad to see you."

"Thank you. Me too."

"You wanna go for a walk?"

"Sounds perfect."

Electric currents pulse under my skin and zip through my veins when he holds my hand. We move where the tide has hit the sand; where it is easier to walk. The foamy white remains of a wave rushes over our feet.

Bryce squeezes my hand and stamps his foot. "*Geez*, that is so cold."

I bite my lip and giggle at him. "The water is getting so cold in the mornings," I tell him. "This time of day is when the water has soaked up all the sun. Best time of day to swim is midday."

"Do you swim a lot?"

I laugh and shake my head. "I'm all about summer swims. I'm bad at coming down here the rest of the year."

He laughs as we continue to walk. "Well, I'm still getting used to beach life. I get up early to run; maybe I should try to come down here to do that."

I can't help running my eyes up and down him. "Is that why you're so lean?"

He smiles and looks away.

Did I just make him blush?

The tide surges towards us again. Bryce lets out a gasp like you would when the shower runs out of hot water.

"Maybe we should move towards a dryer part of the beach?" he suggests.

Giggles burst out and force me to lean forward.

"Didn't realise I was so funny, Brittany," he jokes, tugging my arm.

My laughter subsides and I apologise. We move farther up the beach and I point out my house. "We can sit up on the deck. This wind is not helping my hair out anyways."

Bryce accepts quickly.

We share a sun lounge on the deck. He caresses my cheek and leaves behind a thousand tiny tingles. His hands fit snuggly above my hips and I fold my arms loosely around his neck. He smiles and leans forward with a kiss that is soft and wonderful. His hands press into the small of my back as I add pressure to his lips and slide a hand down his chest.

I feel his heartbeat.

Can he feel mine?

The door clicks and slides.

"Oh, um, hello," my mum says, stunned.

Bryce and I break apart as my mum fidgets and stares in our direction.

"Mum," I say, looking down as I wipe under my bottom lip. "What are you doing home already?"

Bryce wipes his mouth with the back of his hand. His shoulders hunch and his cheeks flash red.

"*Ahh*," my mum, who is usually full of words, begins. "I came home to grab something to take to the office." She glances at Bryce. "Who's your...*friend?*"

I eye Bryce and my chest thumps. "This is Bryce." I pause, debating whether to say the next part. "My boyfriend."

Bryce's eyes shine from the title, yet his body closes in, ready to run if Mum flips out.

"Really, Brittany?" Mum asks.

I gulp and nod.

Bryce squirms in his seat. "Should I go?"

Mum places a hand over her heart. "No, not at all. Brit, I need to run to the office, but I'll come home for dinner. Bryce, can you stay for dinner?"

My jaw drops.

Bryce eyes me and his shoulders rise in a slow shrug. "Yeah?"

"Mum? You'll be here for dinner?"

Mum checks her watch. "Yes, I'm going to have to fly so I can wrap a few things up. I'll be back."

I leap off the sun lounge and toss my arms around her. She pats my back and then repeats that she has to go. When she leaves, I say to Bryce, "I can't believe she'll be here for dinner."

"She's not here much?"

I sit next to Bryce. "No. She's always having dinner at the office or with clients. I can't believe it."

Bryce slides an arm around my shoulders. "You look really happy."

"I am." I touch his cheek. "I'm really happy you're here."

"Me too," he replies and kisses me.

Bryce and I spent the rest of the afternoon in that exact spot until Sophia announced dinner was ready.

I lead Bryce into the dining room, and we take seats next to each other at the table. I frown at Mum's empty chair. It was a long shot.

As Sophia places food in front of us she smiles at Bryce and introduces herself.

"Sophia is basically the full-time parent around here," I half-joke.

Sophia pinches my cheek. "Anything for my angels." I wince and she lets go of me. "Have you seen your sister? She has been very quiet all day."

"Nope."

Sophia leaves towards the staircase to wrangle Charli.

"Oh good, you stayed for dinner," Mum says, walking into the dining room.

I spin towards her. "I didn't know you were home."

"Yeah, I went straight into the study to finish a few things up before dinner," Mum replies, sitting down.

Sophia returns with Mum and Charli's plates. Charli shuffles into the dining room. Her frizzy hair hangs over her face and she scratches her nose with a crumpled tissue. When she sits, she pushes back her hair revealing reddened eyes.

"*Whoah.* Are you ok?" Bryce asks.

Charli looks up, not realising he was there. She looks at Bryce and me through shiny tears. She cups her mouth, moving towards the archway.

"Charli?" Mum calls, reaching out to grab her.

Charli tremors, and then walks back to the table. "I'm ok. No, I'm ok."

"You're still sick?" Mum asks, planting a hand on Charli's forehead.

Charli frowns and pushes her head away.

"I'm booking you in with Dr Bourke tomorrow," Mum tells her.

"I'm fine," Charli grumbles, scraping her fork through her food.

"So, Bryce," Mum turns her attention to our side of the table, "are you and Brittany in the same grade?"

"Yes, we are. I moved to Sanford this year."

Mum smiles. "Oh, that's why I can't place you. How are you finding it?"

"Yeah, it's good. It's cool being so close to the beach." He notices the floor-to-ceiling window showcasing our backyard. "Well, not as close as some."

Mum smiles. "Yes, we are very lucky."

It is hard to compute that Mum and my first-ever-boyfriend are chatting so normally. Mum and Dad were never this welcoming to one of Charli's boyfriends. She must hate this. I steal a look in her direction. Charli looks ready to faceplant her dinner. Her overgrown hair dances around her food. Girl, you're such a grot.

I shovel food in to avoid Mum's annoying questions. However, Bryce draws circles around his food with his fork. He asks my mum, "Have you guys always lived here?"

"No, we had to work for this place," Mum replies. "We had this shoebox at the back of The Heights first. By the time the girls were toddlers we were moving in here."

"That's a long time in one place though."

"Yes, that's true." Mum notices Bryce's plate. "Not hungry?"

"Oh," he whispers at his plate. "I must have forgotten to eat."

Charli disappears after a poor attempt to clear her plate. Mum made Bryce super nervous because he barely ate anything. I look like a total overeater next to those two.

We sit on a couch after dinner and Bryce texts his Dad to pick him up.

Bryce interlaces his fingers with mine and says, "Thanks for having me over."

"Thanks for being here."

We nuzzle our faces together and I'm giddy.

"Your house is so calming."

I squeeze his hand. "You think?"

"Compared to mine. Yeah."

"A year ago it was far from it," I whisper. "There was so much yelling and slamming of doors. I forget it's good now."

"Is that why you were sad that your dad came back? You were scared it'd get chaotic again?"

"Maybe. I know he's not coming back to this house. I guess the feeling never really goes away."

He kisses my cheek and whispers, "I know what you mean."

14

Charli

Two days off school and I still feel like shit. A ghoul stared back at me in the mirror this morning. I pulled my hair into a bun and, in a moment of weakness, slapped on some concealer. Those bags under my eyes are outta control.

Sophia drove Brittany and me to school. I checked my phone out of habit. It's much quieter since I blocked Travis' number. I'm not ready to see an excuse, apology or compliment from him.

I don't know what I'll do when I see him. I hope I don't. I wish we could go back to how it was before.

It's so confusing.

Most of the day I went incognito. It's easy when your boyfriend... ex-boyfriend... I dunno. When *he* isn't in your grade and you can hide in classes. Now it's lunch and I need a better way to hide. He knows our spot outside, and I don't want the crowded noise of mess. Kellie texted, suggesting we meet in a science lab. He knows I hate that subject so it's a perfect cover.

I sneak towards my locker, knowing it's a bad idea, but I need my stuff.

"Charli."

My stomach flips. Deep down, not even that deep down, I knew he'd be waiting for me here. I turn to find his dark eyes gleamed with sadness. A sharp pain jabs at my heart. It hurts because he looks the same. He looks like my Travis. It hurts because for four nights visions of whoever that was in that room have taken residence in my mind.

"Are you ok? I've been worried about you," he begins, hushed. "You've been ignoring my texts?"

I shake my head and lie, "I haven't had my phone on."

"Oh, ok." His voice is small, his posture broken. "You've been away. You been sick?"

My eyes well and sting. "Travis, I can't do this."

"What?" He takes a step forward.

I step away. "Don't."

"Don't?"

"Travis, I need space. I can't be around you."

"Charli, I'm sorry," he says, rushing towards me. "I don't know exactly what happened that night. It's a blur and I have blacked out memories. But I know I did something wrong." He rubs my shoulders. "Super wrong. And I'm sorry. I didn't mean for it to happen. Can you forgive me?"

I blink back the tears and my words catch in my throat. His grip on me increases and my body shrinks.

"Get away from her!" my sister yells, storming towards us. She yanks Travis' hands off me and pulls me towards her.

"Brittany, can you just leave us—"

"Alone?" Brittany interrupts Travis. "As if! I don't ever want to see you around my sister again."

Brittany is like a vice grip around my arm. She races us through the corridor and my breathing is so shallow it's hard to keep up with her.

She pulls me into an alcove, and I wipe my eyes dry. "Brit, thanks for—"

She pushes my chest. "You're an idiot if you go back to him."

I whimper and rub my chest.

"I don't want to see you come home like that again." Melancholy droops her face as she returns to the corridor, leaving in the sea of students.

The lump in my throat breaks. I hunch over and wail with a twisting in my gut. I cup my hands over my mouth and run to the nearest bathroom.

I hold onto the bench as the water streams and swirls down the drain. My body shakes and I sniff runny mucus. A toilet flushes and I hurry to splash the water over my face.

Footsteps click towards the basins.

I tear at the paper towel and brush it across my face.

"Hey, you ok?"

I eye Tayla Martinez in the mirror and clear my throat. "Hi."

"You look upset," she says, washing her hands. "Wanna talk about it?"

I take a long exhale and my tears dry up.

"No judgement," she persists.

I turn to the tiled wall. "Honestly, I wouldn't know where to start."

"Heavy. I didn't mean to get in your business."

I hug myself, close my eyes and rest against the wall. "I think I have to break up with my boyfriend."

"Shit. Really?"

"Or we already are... I don't know."

"You don't know if you've called it quits?"

My eyes bulge. "Don't say anything."

Tayla mutes and draws a cross over her heart.

"It's just that I haven't told Reece anything. I don't want him to overhear something."

She shakes her head. "I won't say anything."

"I mean it, not even Lenny."

"I got it."

I wipe my face with paper towel one more time and move for the door.

"Hey, you signed up for the formal committee, right?"

I face her, not seeing the connection.

"We have a meeting. Did they tell you about it?"

"I've been away."

"C'mon, it's in the library." She gets to the door before me. "I think we're assigning job roles."

The walk to the library is rough.

"Isn't that the girl who cock teased her boyfriend then refused to do it?"

"No, she's the one who had that threesome at Mackellar's party."

"That's the girl that bashed one guy and went home with another."

I always preach to not listen to losers, but it is so hard when all the lies are aimed and fired at you.

Throughout the committee meeting I beg my stomach to be still. My head grows woozy and I haven't heard a word Heather is saying.

Until, "All in favour?"

I jump as everyone around me answers, "Yes."

Heather grins and boasts, "Great, with a unanimous decision I'll head the committee."

What? Unanimous? I didn't vote. I didn't even get to put my hand up.

I have rehearsed the moment I tell Dad I'm chairing a committee so many times. Now it's taken away from me?

"I'm sorry," I pipe up. "We just voted?"

Heather groans and rolls her eyes. "Well, maybe if you weren't such a space cadet, Charlotte, you could pay attention."

"She's been off sick for two days," Tayla says. "Give her a break."

"Who did we vote on?" I ask, frazzled I missed an important part of the meeting.

"I ran unopposed," Heather says, hands on hips.

"Can I contest?"

"That part is over," Heather huffs "We don't want a chairperson who considers everything an afterthought."

I slump in my chair. Heather assigns miscellaneous tasks to everyone and at this point I couldn't care less.

School ends and I wait by the front steps to meet up with Kellie. I have some time to kill because she's stopped by Mr Pieterson's office to discuss her theory for the Ferguson Award.

I open my copy of '*Firelake Five*' to the dog-eared page and skim a paragraph. No words are sinking in, so I drop it into my bag. I curl up on a step and pull out a notebook.

My prince of light,
Of kind and pure heart,
Crushing dreams with might,
Tearing love apart.

The prince of darkness,
Cloaked and deeply unknown,
Devilish black eyes, Starless,
Leaving your love deeply alone.

I scrawl the last line, distracted by someone racing past me. Reece leaps down the steps and I go to call out to him until I look ahead. Travis is in his firing line. My toes curl and I grip my book so tightly it may break in two.

Reece drags a skateboard behind him.

Travis puts his hands up like stop signs. "Reece. Look man, it's not like it sounds."

Reece swings the board like a baseball bat, and it thwacks into Travis' stomach.

Travis doubles over with a horrendous moan.

I lunge forward. Hands clasped over my mouth, too shocked to shriek.

Reece tosses the skateboard aside and leans over his cousin. "Don't you dare touch her again!"

I stand, trembling.

"*No, no, no, no, no.*" Kellie rushes past me towards Reece.

Reece walks away from his cousin as kids chant, "*Fight! Fight!*"

He jogs up the steps and takes my wrist. "C'mon. Let's get outta here."

A sob thunders out of me. "I'm so, so sorry."

He drops my hand. "Why are you apologising?"

"He's your family. I've screwed things up between you two."

"You're blaming yourself?" He steps in close. "That creep did it to himself. Charli, why didn't you tell me what happened?"

I scrunch my nose and blink back tears.

"Reece, what was that?" Kellie asks, breathlessly.

He replies with, "Let's get her out of here."

Kellie takes charge and decides we need our bikes and we head towards the forest.

It's too long since I've spent time up here. It was home during my parents' separation. Kellie and Reece became my new family and we would collectively bask in the silence and beauty of majestic tall trees and the natural paths that formed around them.

We find flat ground and form a triangle.

"Let's make things more green," Kellie says and puts a joint between her lips, flicking a lighter.

She takes a puff and then hands it towards me. I reach out, tempted. What would Dad say if he found out? I recoil my hand and tell her no.

"Can I smell it?" Reece asks, leaning toward Kellie.

I throw my hands up. "Why would you want to smell it?"

"Charli, it would help you," Kellie says, pushing Reece away.

"Whaddaya mean?"

"You can mellow out and work on hashing out what happened between you and Travis."

I hug my drooping body.

"You can't do this again," Kellie insists. "What are you going to do? Are you breaking up with him?"

"Yes," Reece answers for me, staring at his shoes.

"No, stop. I don't know, ok."

"It's fine to not have an answer right now," Kellie replies. "Don't bottle it up. You're a hard nut to crack. You gotta help me out."

At that, my lips curl. "Oh, this is hard on you, is it Kel?"

She laughs and takes another puff.

"Why are you keeping that up?" I ask, pointing to the joint.

"It's zen," she replies in a hippy state. "It's crazy how clear my mind becomes. I've never felt freer."

"Freer?"

She holds the joint out to me again. "Dude, it'd probably do you some good."

"Nah. Um, I'm good."

"So much hesitation in your voice," Kellie says and takes another drag.

I say to Reece, "I'm sorry I didn't tell you."

He nods, eyes off at the trees beside me. "Don't do it again."

In my gut I want to ask him who told him, but my heart won't let me.

"You still love him?" Kellie asks.

I think so..? *Gah!* I don't know.

"Do you hate him?" she asks.

No. I can't hate him.

15

Brittany

There are so many people here.

SO MANY.

When I was on the verge of puking this morning, I calmed myself down by repeating, '*no one ever comes to this festival any more.*' Turns out I was wrong.

Our dance group takes to the stage at *Horton Park* to perform as part of the annual Cultural Festival. I think it marks the date John Thomas and Phillip Sanford founded the town. Now it's a way for people to show off talent or sell something.

Jitters overtake me as a crowd forms before the stage. This routine I'm ok with. I blend in. I hit my steps and stay in sync with the other girls. While the crowd applauds, beads of sweat frame my face. The next routine revolves around my solo.

My heart pounds a mile a minute. I flex my fingers to distract my mind. The song intro blares through the speakers, and I can still hear Jace hooting affections for Chloe. I scan the crowd and find the group.

Kimberley cheers amongst the other girls and I catch her nudging Meah aside. Bryce lingers behind them and smiles at me. It both eases and panics me.

The dance begins and I try not to acknowledge Dad with his arm around Tara. By the other side of the stage, Mum's *go-get-em* grin is embarrassing in the best way. Sickness swirls inside me as I'm centre stage. The stage smile that was drilled into me from age six at ballet masks my face. Remembering ballet performances releases the pressure. I'm no longer strictly controlled and stressed out. I lift my chin higher and my smile becomes genuine. I glide through the solo and the applause coats me in chills.

Tiffany cheers us off stage, giving individual praise.

Chloe darts towards Jace, and before I can follow, Dad and Tara block my path.

"Sweetheart, you were magnificent," Dad cheers, with arms out wide.

I lean in for a two-second hug.

"I'm so impressed," Tara chimes in. "I could never move like that. You are very talented."

"Thanks," I reply and eye Mum in the background. "Thanks for coming, and bye."

I jog towards Mum, hugging her before speaking.

"I'm so proud of you," Mum whispers. "You looked incredibly happy. I'm so glad."

"Thanks, Mum."

"You did really well, Brit," Charli says. She stands close by with Kellie, who is holding her brother's hand.

"Thanks." I turn to Mum, "I'm going to meet up with my friends, ok?"

"Sure, we'll catch you at home."

I approach the group, flattening out my costume and feeling like a spectacle.

"Well done, Brit," Fiona cheers.

"Thanks."

"You're so freakin fast," Madison adds.

Bryce rounds them and I quicken my steps to meet him. He takes my hands and pulls me in for a kiss.

"I couldn't keep my eyes off you," he whispers. So thankful right now for the stage makeup hiding my tomato-red face. "You are so beautiful and talented."

I bite my bottom lip. "Oh, thanks. I have to go get changed."

"I'll meet you here."

When I leave the changeroom he's right outside. He takes my bag and hoists it over his shoulder. We hold hands and join the moving crowd towards the sideshow games.

Bryce stops by a Shoot-the-Ducks game. He slides his arms around my waist and says, "This reminds me of the best day of my life."

I giggle. "What day is that?"

"The day I kissed you for the first time."

He applies perfect pressure against my lips. My eyes fall shut and I drape my arms around his neck. His tongue teases mine.

He pulls back with a cheeky grin.

Damn, he's cute.

Our hands link magnetically, and we continue through the festival.

"*JT Sharks* gonna tear it up!" Jace bellows, pumping his fist in the air.

I hold Bryce's hand and slink behind him. We stop at the group who are mid-conversation about our first football game happening this week.

"Brit," Madison calls to me. "Make sure you get the night before free. You're coming over to mine so we can prep."

"Cool, definitely."

I lose grip of Bryce as he joins in with the boys. Talk of football plays glaze over me, so I head towards the girls. Meah hugs me as Chloe and Kimberley rag on Tully Beach cheerleaders. "Pack of skanks and slags."

Fiona huffs. "I'm sick of talking about it. Can't we shop instead?"

Meah and I follow Fiona and Madison along the line of stalls. Chloe and Kimmy hang back to bat lashes at the boys.

"You and Bryce look super cute together," Meah says as we stop at a handmade jewellery stand.

I bite my lip. "He's so cute."

"You're so lucky."

"It'll happen for you too," I say, picking up a purple beaded necklace.

"Nav doesn't even know I exist."

"Sure he does. Maybe he doesn't know you're interested?"

"Whatever," she groans, stepping away from the stall. I put down the necklace and chase after her.

"So, you're going to Madi's?"

She nods, frowning. "Of course, why wouldn't I?"

Ouch. Bad mood, much? "You ok?"

"Well, like, you've kinda been ditching me since you got a boyfriend."

"I'm sorry. It's still so new."

She rolls her eyes.

"Meah, as if you wouldn't do the exact same thing."

"You're calling me jealous?"

"Aren't you?"

"I don't want Bryce."

"You want anyone." I regret it immediately.

"You bitch!" She shoves me.

"*Whoah!*" Madison rushes between us.

Meah takes off and I'm left speechless.

"What was that?" Madison asks as Meah runs toward the carpark.

I shrug. "Hates that I have a boyfriend?"

Madison scoffs, "Bitch needs to grow up."

I walk further with Madison and Fiona until I feel a tap on my shoulder.

I turn around to Bryce, smiling. "Can I steal her, girls?"

"Sure," they reply in unison.

Bryce pulls me aside and says, "Close your eyes."

My chest tightens and I suck in air. "What? Why?"

"Just do it."

"No."

"C'mon, close your eyes."

I reluctantly close my eyes. Bryce's arms seem to be around me and then something lands on my chest. I open my eyes to see purple beads sitting on my chest.

"Hey, you peeked," he says, clipping the latch behind my neck.

"Is this the one from...?"

"I told you I can't keep my eyes off you."

I place a hand over the beads and rush my lips to his.

He bought me something.

He was with all of them and he was still thinking of me.

"Thank you. I love it."

"You're welcome."

My goofy grin won't go away. We continue and he asks me what I want to do next. As I think on it, a man calls out Bryce's name.

Bryce turns. "Dad?"

Dad? His dad? *Ohmigawd*, I'm so not ready to meet his parents.

His dad smiles and waves at me. "Hi there."

"Dad, this is Brittany," he hesitates, holding back a laugh, "my girlfriend."

"Hi, Mr Kerry," I say, just audible.

"So glad to meet you, Brittany," Mr Kerry says, his smile kind and welcoming. He says to the girl beside him, "Say hi to Brittany, Caitlyn."

Caitlyn scowls and pokes her tongue out. Bryce had told me she's eight-years-old, but he didn't say she was this unfriendly. I wave to her anyway.

"We are about to drive home," Mr Kerry says to Bryce. "You can call me when you're ready to come home."

"Is Mum ok?"

"Yeah, she's fine. We are just going to keep her company."

"Oh, ok," Bryce says flatly.

His forehead scrunches like he's thinking. Home is always on his mind. The rest of the group are laughing and shouting. It'd be much better alone with Bryce rather than them all gawking at us.

"I wouldn't mind hanging out with you at your place," I offer.

His eyes light up. "Really?"

"If that's ok."

Mr Kerry answers, "Brittany, if you would like to come over to our house, you're more than welcome."

I smile and nod.

Happiness floods Bryce's face and he takes my hand towards his dad's car.

"So, Brittany, has your family always lived in Sanford?" Mr Kerry asks as he drives us to their house.

"Yeah, my sister and I were born here. My dad grew up here, and when he met my mum at university he convinced her to move here with him."

"Seems like a really nice place to grow up," Mr Kerry continues. "I grew up in a small town myself. It was in the sticks, though, nowhere near the beach."

The small talk is nerve wracking. I'm thankful when the car pulls into the driveway. Bryce's house is at the top of The Heights. It's a massive, modern house with sharp angles yet only one storey unlike the multi-storey homes surrounding it.

Bryce takes my hand when we leave the car. I bite my lip and hope he doesn't notice the clamminess. We follow his dad and sister into the house. My muscles tense as I walk through the hall. The house is shadowy for the middle of the day and railings line the walls. We stop in an expansive living area and a woman in light blue scrubs walks across the room away from a woman in a wheelchair.

A shudder takes over my body as I focus on the wheelchair.

Bryce's mum.

"Hi guys," the woman in scrubs says, waving. She's peppy with a bounce to her steps.

"Hi Gwen, everything all good?" Mr Kerry asks, walking towards his wife.

Gwen-in-scrubs nods with a thumbs up.

"Have a nice time?" Mrs Kerry asks her husband.

"Yeah, it was a great festival. This town does all right," Mr Kerry replies jovially, sitting by the wheelchair.

Mrs Kerry sees me and frowns. "Who's this?" Her steely eyes cut right through me.

"Bryce's girlfriend Brittany," Mr Kerry introduces me, same happy smile.

Mrs Kerry's frown spawns into a grimace. I glance at Bryce as his jaw stiffens.

"You always wear that much makeup?" Mrs Kerry grumbles at me.

I panic and touch my face. "Oh, no. I'm a dancer."

Mrs Kerry arches an eyebrow. "A dancer? And that forces you to over paint your face?"

A rapid flush of heat rampages my body. "No, I mean, it's stage makeup. I was performing on stage... at the festival."

Bryce squeezes my hand and then lets it go. He walks towards his mother and drops before her chair. "Can I get you anything, Mum?"

"No." She sighs, looking across the room. "Peter, I'm tired."

"Ok, hun," Mr Kerry says, getting up from his chair.

Bryce backs away as Gwen unlocks the wheelchair and she and Mr Kerry guide Mrs Kerry out of the room.

"Hey Bryce, how was the festival?" asks a girl of about twenty with pigtails in her hair, holding Caitlyn's hand.

Bryce plonks on a sofa and rubs his temples. "Yeah, it was really good."

The girl turns to me with an ear-to-ear grin. "Hey, I'm Amy. How you going?"

"Good," I manage, still working out who everyone is and what is going on.

"You sticking around for an hour or so?" Amy asks. "Cause Cait and I are making choc-fudge cupcakes if ya keen."

"Yum," I squeak.

"C'mon Cait," Amy says and the two leave for the kitchen.

I edge my way to Bryce and sit beside him. His thumb and forefinger still massaging his forehead.

"You ok?"

He drops his hands and forces a smile. "Yeah."

"You don't look it."

He lets out a weighted exhale and takes my hand. His eyes are tired, but his smile softens. "Thanks for coming over."

"I'm happy to."

He interlaces his fingers with mine and whispers, "I don't get to see that much of her. I just feel better being here."

"I understand." I don't really. "The house was a bit crowded just then."

He tilts his head, furrowing his brow.

"Amy, Gwen."

"Oh. Gwen is Mum's nurse and Amy is Caitlyn's nanny." He slides down the sofa. "Or maybe mine, too. She does the most stuff for me."

"Yeah, that's how I grew up too. We used to have a nanny and a housekeeper. After they left we found Sophia, who basically runs our house."

"It feels normal having extra people in the house because my parents always worked round the clock. Now my mum is home, I still feel like I never see her. I just want to help, but I don't think I ever do."

I squeeze his hand. "I'm sure you help. You come home so often."

"Her mood swings are really rapid which is normal for someone with MS," he whispers. "Everything can change in an instant. Like, some days she's even up and walking."

"Those days have to be good, right?"

"Her work meant everything to her. Besides the disease making her mad, I think not being able to work is causing her downward spiral. I wish I could do something to make it easier for her."

I bite my lip and face the wall-length window behind the couch. My eyes wander over the cliff's edge and down to the tossing cobalt waves of the ocean, thrashing against the rocks, trying to find something encouraging to say.

He pulls me close and I hug his waist. "I'm glad you're here."

I lay my head on his chest and listen to the beats of his heart.

Caitlyn and Amy make a racket of clanging and giggling in the kitchen, so Bryce shows me to his bedroom where it is quiet. I walk into the scent of his cologne and it is instantly my favourite room in the house. The walls are grey-blue, and the furniture is a mix of charcoal and oak. On the wall opposite his bed hangs a calendar, a poster of a football team and a framed collage of photos.

"That's some friends from my old school," he says as I examine the faces.

"It'd suck to change schools. Do you miss them?"

"I guess. It was getting hard to stay in touch when I was still there. They didn't understand why I stopped hanging out after school. They kept saying that I'd changed."

I sit next to him on the bed, tucking my hands under my thighs.

"I was kinda glad for the fresh start," he says, nudging me and smiling.

"I'm really glad you moved to Sanford."

His hand slides down my back and I press my lips onto his. Our lips part on cue and my hand runs down his t-shirt. I play with the material and trace his ribs.

He shudders and pulls away.

"Are you ok?" I ask.

He coughs and nods. "Yeah, I'm fine. I'm kinda tired, you wanna watch a movie or something?"

"Yeah, that sounds great."

I do not care what movie he picks. It is a guaranteed ninety minutes alone with him. We cuddle on the bed and I take in his warmth. His head nuzzles against mine, and his arms fit snuggly against my body. I play with the purple beads around my neck and remind myself just how freakin lucky I am.

I'm lying on a bed with Bryce Gorgeous Kerry.

16

Charli

"And how many tickets would you like?" I ask, sitting in a classroom and marking Kathy Reeson's name off the ledger.

"Just one," Kathy chirps and hands her cash over.

"Thanks." I hand her one ticket.

"Two tickets," a boy barks, pushing past Kathy.

I push back on my chair. He's in the grade above me, but I don't recall his name. "What names?"

"What does that matter?"

"They just need to know who's going."

"Why? It's just a stupid dance."

I let out a groan. "Just tell me who to mark off."

The boy flares his nostrils. "Fine. Jim Withers."

"And the other ticket?"

"She doesn't go to this school."

"That's fine; I just have to write her name down."

"Louise."

"Last name?"

"No friggin idea."

My scowl intensifies. It's not hard to follow a rule. *Name, cash, ticket, done.*

He rolls his eyes. "Louise Marsh. *St Marks High.*"

I write down her name and school on the guest list and take Jim's money without making eye contact. He snatches the tickets from my hand.

I lean over the desk and rub my temples. It's too hard being around people.

"Hey hun," a voice sings.

I look up and fire burns inside of me. GiGi Larkin shines her pearly whites. Seriously? Five other kids are selling tickets in here and you have to stand in my line?

"Hi." I scan the ledger for her name. Larkin, Georgia. I need this interaction over ASAP.

I hold out a ticket when GiGi taps the ledger and says, "Two, hun." I pick up my pen and ask for the second name and she answers, "Travis Watkins."

My hands tremor.

"You gonna mark it off... or what?"

I uncomfortably clear my throat and strike through my ex-boyfriend's name.

GiGi waggles cash in front of me and I exchange it for tickets. My body grows limp as I blink over my sandpaper eyes. GiGi smirks and saunters away. I slide away from the ledger as the next student approaches. This committee thing officially became not worth it.

Kellie joins me at my house after school and we walk into the kitchen where Brittany sits with Bryce. Still weirds me out she has a boyfriend. She seems happy, but I'm still worried about her making all these changes. She quit ballet, changed her hairstyle, and follows Chloe around like a lost puppy. It's terrifying to think she'd do anything to be like Chloe. Where does it end?

I go to the fridge for drinks and when I close the door Will Maclean enters the kitchen.

Crap.

My eyes dart to Kellie. Her chest heaves, arms rigid with her hands balled into fists.

"Hey Kellie, wassup?" Will pats Kellie on the arm.

Kellie flinches and backs away from him. "Wassup?"

"Hey what's wrong? You didn't mistakenly see the new DC movie? That's bad enough to put anyone in a sour mood."

Kellie's jaw swings from side to side.

Will puts his hands on his hips. "C'mon, Kelarino."

"Kelarino? Don't do your cutesy nickname thing with me."

"Don't be like that," Will says. "You're usually a crack up."

"A crack up?" Kellie hisses. "I thought I was a witch. Or was it a demon?"

Will scratches his head. "*Geez*. That was a joke."

"I didn't think it was funny."

"Kellie, I'm sorry," Will says, holding onto her arm. "You're a strong woman, unlike the airhead banking on her looks that parades around my house. I liked all the things we shared. It's nice talking to you."

I push Will away from her as Kellie says to him, "You're such a fool."

I pull Kellie out of the kitchen and whisk her to the sanctuary of my bedroom.

She flops onto my bed. "What is he doing here?"

"Hanging with Brittany and Bryce." I look to the giant John Lennon on my wall and search for calm in his eyes.

Kellie punches my pillow.

"Hey, my pillow didn't do anything wrong," I protest, tossing my Spanish textbook onto my desk.

Kellie stiffens. "He won't try to come up here will he?"

"*Pfft*. He'd better not."

Kellie scampers off the bed and leaps towards the door. "I'm not sticking around to find out. Let's go."

"Go? You promised to help me study."

"We can do it later." Kellie pulls out her phone and starts texting. "Maybe we can go to Watkins' instead."

"I guess. But I'm really behind in Spanish. You have to help quiz me."

"Yeah sure, whatever," Kellie mumbles, typing on her phone. "He's at the comic book store. Let's go."

"That's not studying."

"Just bring your stuff. We can go to mine afterwards."

I clench my jaw and draw in a long breath. I hurl my stuff in my bag and swing it onto my back. As Kellie hurries me out of the house I long for a distraction to blur out the images I continually concoct of Travis and GiGi together.

We find Reece and Lenny in the centre aisle of the comic book store.

"Wow, Tayla's not tied to your hip," Kellie jokes, tapping Lenny on the arm. "What happened?"

Lenny folds his arms over his puffed chest. "She's at gymnastic practice."

"She hasn't been around much," Kellie ribs him, "now that she's a cheerleader."

"Yeah, what is up with that?" I ask. "I never pegged you to be with a cheerleader."

"She's an ace gymnast," Lenny says. "She'll wipe the floor with those bitches."

Reece asks me, "Weren't you guys studying?"

"Will was at my house."

"He wanted to pal around with me," Kellie says. "Can you believe it?"

"You ok?" Lenny asks her.

Kellie shakes her head and moves down the aisle. "Yeah, I'm fine. I can't think about the dickhead right now."

I skim through the manga section and find a copy of '*Angel Heart*' I don't have. Kellie picks up another '*Fullmetal Alchemist*' and we make our way to the register.

The boys suggest heading to the skatepark. I am a firm no, as my Spanish textbook screams out to me, but Kellie answers yes, telling me I can't ditch her.

The afternoon sun is blinding compared to the dank comic book store. I pinch the bridge of my nose, trying to adjust.

"Charli?"

I drop my hand and flick open my eyes. "Dad?"

Dad walks down the footpath with a happy grin.

"Hi, Mr Matthews," Kellie says, waving.

"Hi Kellie," Dad replies. "And Reece, and..."

"Lenny," Lenny pipes up.

I leap in front of Dad and link my arms around his neck. Dad pats my back and says, "I'm glad I ran into you. I wanted to see you and your sister."

"Really?" I say, lowering my heels to the ground.

"*Robbie*. You need to come in and help me decide which rug to buy," a woman calls, exiting a nearby boutique.

Tara.

Something sour leaps from my gut.

"Tara and I are wandering through homeware stores," Dad says, beckoning Tara over.

I take a step back from Dad. *Homewares?* Pretty things for your home? Together?

Kellie stops by my side. "That's her?"

"Hi hunny. How are you?" Tara beams at me.

By the pet name I can tell she doesn't know which one I am.

I ignore her and lock eyes with Dad. *You wanted to see me. Ditch her. Ditch her now.*

Dad fidgets with his shirt collar. "You're with your friends. Go have fun, we won't bother you now."

"It's not a bother."

"What night are you free this week?" Tara blurts out.

I eye her. "Huh?"

"You and your sister," she continues, "to come to my house for dinner."

Kellie spurts out, "*Pa-ha.*"

My head pivots between Dad and Tara. Dad takes Tara's hand and gives her an apprehensive look. He says to me, "We were hoping you and Brit could come over and meet Tara's family."

I swear I've stepped out of my body. Everything is a hazy blur and my dad's voice grows distorted.

"Come over tomorrow," Dad says. "You and Brit, and we'll discuss."

"Yeah, Charli," Tara over-pronounces my name. "It'd be great to have you guys over."

Dad and Tara leave hand-in-hand, and my friends rush around me.

"What the fuck was that?" Kellie says.

"That was weird, right?" Reece adds.

"Mega weird vibes," Lenny agrees.

My head spins. "I need to sit down."

Dad convinces people for a living. He took his work home with him when he got Brittany and me to agree to get in a car to West Sanford and meet Tara's family. I'm sick to my stomach the entire trip. Matchbox houses pass the window and I wonder how many times Dad ventures over here.

My air cuts off as the car stops at a small, yellow weatherboard home. I rub a hand over my chest. Good, it's still pumping.

"All righty, here we are," Dad announces, unbuckling and hopping out of the driver's seat.

I look behind to Brittany who gives me a shrug. With every ounce of courage, I force myself out of the car. Dad gives us an impatient look from the garden path and I ensure Brit is following as I catch up.

My knees wobble as Dad knocks on the front door. The door swings open and Tara greets us with an exaggerated smile. "Hello, hello."

Dad leans in and gives her a quick peck on the lips.

My stomach somersaults.

Tara moves to the side of the doorframe. "Come on in."

We enter the dimly lit foyer and a girl, about six-years-old, stares at us. My eyes narrow. Is that one of Tara's kids? I assumed they would be our age.

"Why do they look the same?" she blurts out.

"This is Brittany and Charli. They're twins, Alyssa," Tara says. "I told you that. Girls, this is my youngest daughter Alyssa."

We give Alyssa mediocre waves.

"Hi," a boy says as he pops out of a room to the right.

"And this is my son Nicky," Tara introduces. "He's the same age as you girls."

He walks towards us shaking his head. "Just Nick is fine." Nick is clean-cut with his thick brown hair swept up and back. He has a welcoming smile and I don't want to like him.

"Hi Nick," Brittany waves.

I eye the floor. If I ignore them they might go away.

"Let's not hang in the hallway," Tara suggests. "Follow me into the living room."

We follow her into the room Nick came from. It's dark and cramped with bulky curtains framing the windows. Floral sofas centre the room and face a scratched coffee table and small TV. Overstuffed bookshelves line the walls and one corner hosts a mahogany piano.

I wait as everyone sits first. Dad sits next to Tara while Nick sits on the armrest next to her. I take a seat next to Brittany on the adjacent couch.

Tara pats her thighs. "So, how was school?"

I hold my elbows and gaze at a run in the carpet. Alyssa plays with toys on the floor and I want to ask her if we can switch places.

Brittany whacks my knee with the back of her hand and answers, "Yeah, it was fine."

"Any cheerleading practice or debate practice?" Tara eagerly shows off her memory skills.

"I had cheer practice during lunch. We have our first game this week, which should be fun."

"Charli, how's it going with debate?" Dad pipes up.

"Good thanks, Dad."

Tara nudges Nick's side. "You need to get into team-oriented things."

Nick rolls his eyes, smiling.

Tara laughs at him and asks, "What's keeping your sister?"

Nick shrugs and looks at his phone.

Tara announces she will get some food ready and Dad leaves to help her in the kitchen. I sink into the sofa. It's lumpy. I take out my phone. The screen fills with new texts. Kellie, Reece, Tayla. Who gave Tayla my number?

"Oh hey, Shae," Nick says.

I drop the phone.

I turn to the doorway.

Shae stares at me.

My hands tremble mid-air. I utter sounds, but no words. I blink hard. My brain whirs into overdrive.

"Hi Charli," she stammers, waving.

"You two know each other?" Brittany and Nick say at the same time.

"How... How..." I stammer. "How long have you known my dad?"

She smooths down her dress and her eyes dart around the room. "Rob's your dad?"

"Oh shit," I gasp, planting my hands over my face.

"I'm sorry, Charli. I honestly had no idea."

"What is going on?" Brittany questions.

A stabbing pain hits my abdomen. I hunch over and let out an ugly moan.

"Are you ok?" Brittany stands and leans over me.

"Charli?" Shae moves toward me.

They loom over me. I swallow the bile that lines my throat. I want so badly to crawl into a ball with this pain.

I push through and stand up. "I need to go."

"We can talk," Shae suggests.

I march into the hallway with Brittany on my heels.

"You've said so many times you hang out with your mum's boyfriend," I wail at Shae. "He saw you guys when he didn't see us!"

"What's going on?" Dad races to us as Brittany opens the front door.

"I can't," I shake my head, "I can't"

"We're leaving," Brittany says.

My breathing shortens and I choke on coughs. My body sways and everything blurs.

Dad's arms are around me. "Charli? Are you ok?"

"Dad, take us home," Brittany demands.

Dad makes Brittany hold me while he apologises to Tara for our abrupt leaving. Out of the house I still can't see clearly. The rise of my chest softens on the drive home and I'm less shaky on the path to our house. Brittany orders Dad not to come inside, telling him we need space.

I cough inside the house, scratching my throat. I slam a hand against my chest and begin to steady. I follow Brittany into the kitchen where Mum types on her laptop.

She lifts her head. "You two are home earlier than I expected."

Does she have any idea how long this was going on? A giant lump fills my throat. Was Dad cheating on her? I swallow, and the lump bursts. My eyes fill and stream. My face collapses in my hands and I croak loud sobs.

Brittany groans, "I'm out."

"What?" Mum rushes by my side.

"I can't deal with this mess. I'm going to for a walk," Brittany's voice trails towards the front door.

Mum briskly rubs my arms. "What did your father do?"

I fling her off me. "Stop trying to put me between you two."

"Charli, I'm not."

My eyes sting. I rub them dry and run towards the door. I escape to the sunlit deck and fall to my knees.

"What happened?" Mum asks, crouching behind me and wrapping me in her arms.

"Leave me alone," I sob.

"I know it's an adjustment, your dad dating someone new," Mum replies. "It's weird for me too. You know we're not getting back—"

"Stop, Mum!" I yell. "Leave me alone!"

She backs off. "Ok, I'll give you some space. But I'll be right inside when you need me."

She goes into the house and I crawl in a ball and squeeze my knees, rocking softly. I exhale and wince at the broken glass in my throat. I kick off my shoes and walk barefoot across the timber deck. Pinks and orange streak the setting sky. Maybe a walk along the beach will ease this pain.

Footsteps sound from the far end of the deck.

Dad?

I turn and almost fall backwards. "Travis?"

He stands on the deck, hair a wavy mess, and chest heaving like he's run a mile.

"What are you doing here?"

"I just drove past Brittany," he says, puffing. "She was frantic because of something about your dad. I had to check that you were ok."

My eyes pool and my wavering chin dimples. All I want is to be in his arms. Like before. Like when he made everything better.

I give in.

I run to him.

I leap into his arms, secure in his strength. He strokes my hair as my cheek rests against his and I pant into his neck.

"It's ok," he whispers. "It's ok."

I manage a garbled, "He's a liar."

He holds me close. My fingers curl around the fabric of his t-shirt and my heart punches its way towards him.

Travis lowers me to the ground and asks, "What happened?"

"We met Dad's girlfriend's family," I say breathlessly. "I knew one of her kids. I know she's known Dad for a long time."

"How? She's talked about him?"

"She mentioned her mum's boyfriend a lot." I stumble woozily as I talk.

He takes my hand. "You should sit down." He leads me to a sun lounge where we sit.

He squeezes my hand and a smile lifts my face. I find his dark, almond eyes and drift towards his body, nestling my head on his shoulder.

"I hate seeing you sad," he whispers.

I wipe under my eyes and feel the puffiness.

"I was worried coming over here," he continues. "How you would react. But I had to see you."

My heart pangs yet I resist moving my head.

"Charli, I'm sorry about what happened." His hand moves down my back and I stiffen. "I hate what happened and I'm sorry. I miss you."

I lift my head and run my hands over my face. "Stop."

"I started drinking because everyone was on my case. I was trying to block them out. But I got drunk and they got in my head."

"I can't hear the excuses."

"Charli."

I slide away from him. "No, stop."

"Charli, I love you," he says, leaning toward me. "I don't want to lose you. We can't be over."

I stand up and take a few steps of distance between us. "You stopped listening to me."

He shrinks. "What?"

"I told you no so many times and you didn't hear it." Visions of him lying on top of me flood my mind. My eyes fog with tears and a sob breaks free.

He stands. "But, Charli."

"But nothing," I say clearly through sobs. "We're nothing."

He rushes towards me. "No, we're not."

"How can you say that when she bought you your ticket?"

"What?" he asks, taken aback. "Who? What ticket?"

"She was draped all over you. Is that what every party I'm not at is like? You two cosied up? Replacing me?"

"Replacing you? You're the only girl I want. You are the only person in the world that matters to me."

"It doesn't matter. You don't listen and I can't trust you. Go away and stay away from me."

Red lines and tears pool in his eyes. "Charli, I'm sorry. I promise not to drink like that again. It was everyone getting in my head. That wasn't me. I didn't mean to."

"You're right," I say, nodding. "That wasn't the Travis I love. But it was you."

Tears streak his cheeks. I bite the inside of my cheek and my eyes dry up.

"Travis, you need to believe me. We are through."

He wipes his face and shakes his head. "It's not done."

"Go home," I order, and without hesitation, I walk into the house and click the lock behind me.

Lies,
Strangling, controlling, contorting.
Trust,
Shattered, vanished, pretend.

A man returned,
Long awaited and jubilant,
Secret pasts washed in light,
Shadows confounding reality.

A boy with love,
Manipulations from a beast,
Lusting over whispered words,
Carved a heart irreplaceable.

That night while studying at my desk, I pick up my copy of 'Firelake Five' and slip out the bookmark. I run my finger over *Preston* and the number beneath it. My neck twinges as I type the number into my phone.

I miss Travis. But I can't be with him.

But I miss him.

I want that special person. The connection. The privacy. The understanding.

Travis and I have lost that.

Maybe someone can fill that void.

I text Preston.

(Me) Hey

There's a knock at the door. "Yeah?"

It opens and Brittany steps into the room. "All right if I come in?"

I drop my phone. "Yeah, of course."

Brittany's forehead scrunches and she hugs her waist. "You ok?"

I force a limp smile. "I guess. Are you?"

Brittany nods and moves over to the bed. She sits and holds her thighs. "Did Travis come round?"

"Yes."

Brittany slaps her thigh. "I told him not to come over. I yelled at him to stay away from you. I swear."

I wave my hands out in front of me. "It's ok. It's ok. Maybe, in a way, it was good to see him."

She frowns with disappointment. "You're not getting back with him?"

"No. I just think, maybe, it was closure. To be done with him."

"I'm glad to hear it. Was he a total dick?"

No.

She doesn't want to hear that.

Brittany curls her legs up on the bed. "He's not allowed to hurt you again."

I lean over the back of my chair. "He'd be pretty dumb to come back over here."

"How did you know that girl?"

I frown. "I met her a few weeks ago."

"And she said she knew Dad?"

"She talked about her mum's boyfriend. I had no idea it was Dad, but now I know he visited them before telling us he'd moved back to Sanford."

"That's so crazy."

I stand up and move over to the bed, flop backwards and let my body melt into the covers.

Brittany snuggles beside me. "Think he'll make us go back there?"

"He'll want to. I don't want to."

"Me either," she whispers and holds my hand.

"I just want to see him. I miss him like crazy."

"Don't bother."

I jerk up. "How can you say that?"

"Do you not hear what you just told me?" She tosses my hand away. "He left town. Or didn't?"

"So? He's still our dad."

Brittany shrugs and shifts further down the bed.

Shit. It's so rare to get a one-on-one with her. I shouldn't ruin it. "How's things with Bryce going?"

She nods and relaxes. "Really good. Mum seems to like him. Never letting Dad near him though."

A *tsk* rushes out of me and I cover with, "You met his family?"

"Yes. He has a really complicated setup over there. But we've done the family thing already, so maybe we will be an *it couple.* You know, like Chloe and Jace."

A belly laugh vibrates out of me I can't hold back.

"What's funny?"

"She cheats on him."

Brittany whacks me across the arm. "What are you talking about?"

"With Lucas Rivers. I saw them at the party... I saw them together."

Brittany hovers a hand over her mouth. "You're kidding."

"You seriously need to stop idolising her."

"I'm not."

"You're amazing on your own, Brit. You don't need to be her clone."

Brittany giggles, "Says my twin."

I beg my lips not to part, but sure enough, I'm grinning like an idiot. My cheeks burn and I laugh, rolling on the bed with my sister.

17

Brittany

"Haven't you left yet?" Madison groans as she lets me into the house.

"You could have put yourself together if you are having people over," her mother replies, strutting down the hall in a glitzy, floor-length gown.

I panic over the t-shirt and sweatpants I'm wearing.

Madison slouches in her sweats. "*Gawd*, whatever."

Mrs Lee is an elegant, older version of Madison. Same angular face and striking oval eyes, yet Mrs Lee is amid a regal air.

I peek into the family room adjacent to the hall where violin music filters in from. Madison's older sister Maggie stands by a music stand, gliding her bow over the strings of her violin.

"You should be practicing for your cello recital," Mr Lee says to Madison, tightening the cufflinks of his tuxedo.

My eyes bug. Is this really Madi's dad? He's white?

"*Mum*," Madison's younger sister Marissa screeches from the living room. "Will you make Madi run lines with me?"

"Help your sister," Mrs Lee says, securing her crystal earrings.

"Maggie can do it," Madison protests.

"She's practicing," her Dad replies.

"Bye Mum," Marissa calls out, "bye Dad."

"Bye Missy," their parents call back.

Mrs Lee walks up to Madison and brushes her cheek. "Try to do something productive with your time. Don't slack off."

Mr Lee adds, "I want to hear your entire piece perfect in the morning."

When her parents leave, Madison lets out a frustrated groan and beckons me to follow her up the hall. As we pass the family room, Maggie stops playing and spies through the curtains at her parents. She swiftly packs up her violin.

Marissa runs towards Madison, waving a book. "You have to run lines with me!"

"Piss off I do," Madison hisses.

"Mum said!"

"Maggie will do it."

"I'm leaving with Ray," Maggie calls out. "Cover for me and I'll owe you."

"You two suck," Marissa pouts as Maggie leaves out the front door.

"Whatever. C'mon, Brit." Madison giggles and adds, "Marissa thinks she's going to be an actress."

"I am an actress!" Marissa yells, storming the hall.

I picture Madison's Dad's face next to hers. "Did your dad take your mum's last name?"

"Huh?"

"Isn't Lee Chinese?"

Madison bursts into laughter. Belly laughter. Collapsing forward, gasping for air with a jiggling mid-section.

"You racist bitch," Madison splutters, still laughing.

My hand races over my heart.

Oh no! Oh no!

Racist?

Where is the nearest exit?

"Chinese?" Madison straightens, eyeing me. "You think I'm Chinese?"

"Um?"

"Oh, this is too good," she says and jogs up the hall.

Oh crap.

I chase as she barrels into her bedroom giggling.

"What's going on?" Kimberley asks, sitting on the bed with Fiona.

Meah jumps up from the desk chair to hug me hello. I'm stiff as a board.

Fiona bounces on the bed. "Madi, what's so funny?"

Madison grins ear-to-ear. "Brittany just asked me why my dad's not Asian."

Kimberley and Fiona collapse on the bed in a fit of giggles.

"What? No! No, I didn't say that," I protest, waving my arms like a crazy person.

Madison slides on the vacant desk chair. "Brit, I'm playing with you. Stop freaking out."

My heart jackhammers my ribs. How quickly can I run and jump out the window?

"Lee isn't an Asian name," Madison smirks.

My panting is so loud I'm sure everyone can hear it.

"Maybe you confused it with Li, spelt L-I?" Madison continues. "Yeah, my Asian genes are more dominant, but my mum is Vietnamese. Her maiden name was Giang."

I don't know what's faster, my heart or my breathing.

"Lee is a plain ol' English name. I'm just a mixed-race person."

I exhale, clutching at my battered heart. "I feel so bad."

"You called me Chinese. I had to make you pay." Madison points to the bed. "Now sit down and shut up."

"Damn, Brit," Fiona smirks as Meah and I flop onto the bed.

"Well, racism aside," Kimberley says, pulling her sleeves down and over her dark skin. "We were deciding on hairstyles for tomorrow. Fi wants pigtails which make me instantly want to vomit."

"What? It's classic cheerleader," Fiona protests.

Madison pulls a half-empty vodka bottle out of her bottom desk drawer. "Who wants one?"

"You freakin alco," Kimberley snaps. "Can you pay attention?"

"*Ohmigawd*, it's hair," Madison says, opening the bottle. "What does it matter?"

"Fine, pour me one," Kimberley replies, smiling.

Madison hands out cups and the smell burns my nostrils. "It's straight?"

"Yeah. You chicken?" Madison replies.

I twist my lips with the thought of drinking it. The mixed drinks are fiery enough.

"Fine," Madison sighs. "There's lemonade in the fridge."

Meah grabs my hand. "We'll go get it."

Meah and I rush out of the room and down the hall to the kitchen.

"I'm glad you're here," Meah says. "I feel outnumbered without you."

"I thought you were enjoying being around them without me."

"I'm tolerated."

"Well, if you want me around more stop getting mad at me for having a boyfriend."

"*Gawd*," Meah groans. "I told you I was sorry about that."

"Whatever, I don't want to fight with you."

We grab the drinks and walk up the hall as Chloe enters the house.

"Ladies," Chloe says as she joins us.

"Hey Chloe!"

"I brought all the proper sleepover essentials," Chloe says, emptying her bag onto Madi's bedroom floor. "Gummy bears, chocolate, pretzels, wine coolers, nail polish and face masks."

"Toss me chocolate," Kimberley says, clapping.

Meah pours lemonade into our drinks, avoiding the snacks that everyone is chowing.

"I'm offended, Meah," Chloe begins. "I thought this junk would be right up your alley."

"Oh, no. I'm ok."

"Just spit in my face why don't ya," Chloe scowls.

"C'mon, Chubba," Kimberley smirks.

Meah freezes. She looks at me, at the chocolate, to Chloe, to me, and then grabs a bar. She sits beside me with the snack she doesn't want while I hold the drink I don't want. Appearances are everything.

Chloe takes a cup of pure vodka and starts coughing. "*Oop*, nope." She winces, shaking her head. "Remember Lucas' party last year when I tried shots? I've never puked so hard. What can I mix this with?"

Meah takes the lemonade over to her.

"So, Brittany, what's goin on with you and Bryce?" Chloe asks.

My heart pounds as Fiona and Kimmy lean forward and Madison swivels on her chair. My hands shake around my cup. I need a diversion.

"You watched a movie together, right?" Meah says.

"*Oooh*, a romantic one?" Fiona asks, laying her chin in her hands.

I bite my lip. "I didn't really pay attention."

Madison whacks my knee. "*Damn*. You two got busy, didn't you?"

Kimberley's eyes narrow. "Living room or bedroom?"

I clear my throat and fidget in place. "Bedroom."

Madison and Fiona squeal while Chloe and Kimmy deadpan.

"So, how far did ya go?" Chloe asks, taking her cup to Madison to refill.

"Whaddaya mean?"

"Over the shirt or under?" Chloe elaborates.

Kimberley giggles. "Over the pants or under?"

"Uhh... Err..."

"Give her a break," Madison says, pushing Chloe away with her refill.

"Touchy Madi?" Chloe says, sliding on the bed. "Don't take your frustrations out on us. You know where Nav is."

"*Ohmigawd.* Would you give it a rest, Chloe?"

"Yeah Chloe," Kimmy whines. "You know Madi's sensitive."

Madison reefs a book from the desk and hurls it at Kimberley. "*Bitch.*"

"*Ohmigawd!*" Fiona shrieks, jumping off the bed. "Can the violence please stop?"

Madison beckons Fiona over, who sits on her lap for a cuddle. Madison always gives into Fiona's childish ways.

"What about Chubba?" Chloe asks, head resting on Kimberley's shoulder. "Who do you have ya eye on?"

Meah wriggles beside me.

"You have a crush?" Fiona says, clutching Meah's forearm.

Meah shakes her head. "No. No I don't."

"Spit it out," Kimberley urges.

Meah side-glances Madi and gulps.

Chloe gasps and starts laughing. "Holy shit! You like Nav!"

Kimberley and Chloe roll around in laughter.

Meah squeaks and drops her face in her hands.

"I don't think you and Nav are suited," Madison says.

Fiona cuddles Madison. "Jealous much?"

Madison rolls her eyes. "Not jealous, just know them both."

Meah uncovers her face. "Why?"

Madison shrugs. "A feeling?"

"Madi, don't be a bitch," Chloe says, scampering forward on the bed. "If Meah wants Nav, we should help her."

Meah gasps. "You'll help me?"

"Sure. The winter formal is coming up soon."

As Meah can't control her excitement, I catch the glances between Chloe and Kimberley.

"C'mon, Kimmy," Madison says, getting up from under Fiona. "You're beefy and strong. Help me get the mattresses on the floor."

"*Eh-squeez-me?*" Kimberley spits, getting up. "Beefy?"

"Those gymnastic muscles," Madison giggles, squeezing Kimberley's bicep.

Chloe groans. "Speaking of gymnastics. How do we get freakin Tayla Martinez off the squad? She's annoyin the shit outta me."

"Do you really want to deal with the wrath of her older brother?" Kimberley asks.

"Or the rest of family," Fiona adds. "There's millions of those Hernandez. They'll go all mafia on you."

Chloe rolls her eyes. "Oh, *pah*-lease. The Hernandez aren't mafia."

"They stick by each other though," Madison says. "I've heard enough stories from Ray."

"Well, if someone can come up with a bulletproof plan to wipe her out they can skip the registry for my sweet sixteen and I'll consider it my birthday present," Chloe says.

Once the mattresses are on the floor, we cover them with a mass of pillows and blankets. Chloe and Kimberley stay on the bed whispering and texting, while the rest of us collapse on the floor.

Madison and I pick from the same packet of lollies and I whisper, "Are you cool with Meah going after Naveen?"

"Yeah, we've fooled around, but we're just friends. Like, I don't think I actually want a boyfriend."

"Why not?"

"I can't even figure myself out." She takes another swig of vodka. "My parents are way harsh. Mum was a champion ballroom dancer and Dad travelled the world as a violinist in the symphony. They want us all to do something amazing and artistic. I don't think I even like the cello."

"Then quit."

"Yeah, right."

"I quit ballet after I started hating it."

"My parents would murder me."

"They get over it."

"Your parents are lawyers. They care about different shit."

I shrug and dip a gummy snake into my mouth.

"You going to put the moves on Bryce?"

I choke on the snake.

"According to them," she nods at the two on the bed, "he'll dump you if you don't do the nasty."

I eye Chloe and Kimmy.

"Sounds like he likes you."

"I really like him." I pick up my phone. There's a text I didn't notice. **New Text - Bryce.**

(Bryce) I miss you.

My body shakes in the best way and my goofy grin comes out to play.

"What is it?" Madison leans over my phone. "Aw, cute."

Fiona and Meah crowd me with *awes* and Chloe and Kimberley call out to be in the loop.

"Bryce texted Brittany, he misses her," Fiona tells.

"Tell him to come over," Chloe says.

I push the phone to my chest. Seeing him right now would make everything better. But seeing him around these vultures would be the worst.

"Horny, Chloe?" Kimberley teases. "You've got Jace's number."

While Chloe and Kimberley tease each other I take the opportunity to text back.

> *(Me)* I miss you too.

> *(Bryce)* My bed is not the same without you on it. I want to cuddle you more.

> *(Me)* You're good at that.

> *(Bryce)* How's the sleepover?

Awful.

> *(Me)* Good. Just talking bout the game tomorrow.

> *(Bryce)* Oh yeah. Bit nervous bout that.

> *(Me)* You'll do fine. You're awesome.

> *(Bryce)* Can't wait to see you in your cheer uniform.

"What are you texting him?" Fiona asks, grabbing for my phone.

"*No*," I squeal, wrestling it off her.

"*Ohmigawd*," Kimberley cheers. "Get it! Get it!"

Chloe dives onto Fiona and snatches my phone. My skin prickles. Chloe could text my boyfriend anything and everything.

"Oh dammit, Fi," Chloe shouts. "You hit the friggin lock button."

Chloe tosses the phone at me and my body shakes with tremendous relief.

The next morning Madison ties my hair in a high ponytail to match hers and douses me in hairspray.

"*Chubba*," Chloe hisses. "Pigtails? Really? Fiona, fix her hair."

Fiona, wide-eyed, giggles as she undoes her handiwork.

We are all dressed in our cheer uniforms with matching scarlet lips. We cover up with JT windbreakers. Now that it's winter, the sea breeze is growing ferocious.

I sit by Madison. "How's your head?"

"What?" she asks.

"From the vodka."

"Oh," Madison giggles. "That was nothing."

As we get ready to leave Meah pulls me aside, looking green. "I'm gonna be a clumsy shit."

I cuddle her. "You'll be fine."

"I still can't believe we're in."

"I know. But we are. We are so in."

The boys warm up on the field and my heart flutters as Bryce jogs by.

"I'm glad I get a front row view for this."

"*Ohmigawd.*" Meah nudges me in the ribs. "You're all over him. Are the girls right? Did something go down between you two?"

I nudge her back. "Shuddup. You know you'd be first to know."

"I oughtta be. I've been here since the beginning of your obsession."

Ms Harvey calls us in for a huddle when Bryce notices me from the field. Butterflies intersperse when he waves at me. I wave back and play with my hair as I follow the other girls.

Ms Harvey attempts a pep talk and we half listen. We check out the Tully team on the field and the squad on the sidelines.

"Those bitches are no match for us," Kimberley says.

A crowd forms on the stands and the boys run off the field, waiting for the game to begin.

"Hey, I wanted to see you before the game starts," Bryce says, jogging up to me.

"I had the same thought."

He brushes my cheeks and kisses me.

"You look so pretty," he whispers. He notices my neck. "Aw, you're still wearing it."

My hand traces the necklace he bought me. I bite my lip and nod.

He pecks my cheek and whispers, "I gotta get back. Cheer for me?"

"Only you." I can't erase my smile.

Until I turn around and catch Chloe staring at me.

When the buzzer signals the beginning of the game, we cheer in formation and wave pompoms. Bryce is a halfback with Naveen so luckily he spends most time down our end of the field. Sometimes I watch the player with the ball, but let's be real, I'm ogling my man.

I search the stands and don't see my mum. I didn't expect her to make it. I spot Mr Kerry in the stands and I'm warm with happiness for Bryce.

We grab the crowd's attention with our cheers. Kimberley and Tayla kill it with flips and twists. Tully squad ain't got nothin.

Midway through the first half Bryce is subbed off the field. The urge to go over is outta control. I drop my pompoms and slink away.

Someone grabs my arm and jerks me back.

"Where do you think you're going?" Chloe asks.

"*Erhh*. Just over..."

"You're not going anywhere. Get into your position."

I pick up my pompoms and frown at the back of Chloe's head. I curve back to check out the bench. Bryce hunches over holding a drink bottle. Mr Kerry approaches the bench and taps Bryce's shoulder. His dad talks and gestures with his phone. Bryce replies with nods and Mr Kerry walks away towards the parking lot.

He's leaving already?

After the half-time buzzer, we cheer the boys off the field. Their coach, Mr Felding, pulls them in for a pep talk and I wait to grab Bryce.

"Hey," Bryce says leaving the huddle. He pulls at his t-shirt. "I'd hug you, but I'm sweaty."

I wrap my arms around his waist. "See me caring?"

His breathy laugh plays like music.

"You've been playing really well," I say.

"Really? Thought I was shit because you've been distracting me."

"You're trying to blame me?"

"So you do think I was crap?"

I shove his chest, fighting giggles. "Stop it."

"BK," Naveen calls out. "We gotta go."

"All right," Bryce replies. He runs his hands down my back and kisses me goodbye.

"Hey Abo!" a Tully cheerleader calls out.

The whole squad snaps to face the cheerleader. Kimberley throws her pompoms to the ground and marches towards the girl. "What did you just say?"

The Tully squad surrounds the cheerleader. "We heard the shit you've been talking," the girl says. "Slags and sluts, are we? Why don't you go and climb down the dirty hole you crawled out of?"

Chloe and Madison lunge at the Tully cheerleader.

"What the fuck did you just say?" Madison shouts.

"Get the hell away from our end of the field before I beat you with your ratty Kmart extensions," Chloe fights back.

As Ms Harvey and the Tully coach run between our squads, Sean breaks away from the team huddle eyes sharp with purpose.

"*Hastings*. Get back here," Mr Felding calls out.

The Tully teachers push their girls away and Sean heads straight for Kimberley. He pulls her into his arms and her head nuzzles against his shoulder. He whispers in her ear and strokes her back. I've never seen Sean act so caring. The guy whose noteworthy achievements include throwing a soda all over Kellie.

I stand by Meah, both of us unsure how caring we should act towards Kimberley. We turn away and start talking about getting ready for the next half of the game.

We won our first game of the season.

"Everyone meet at Mermaid Cove," Jace shouts through cupped hands.

Mermaid Cove is on the opposite side of Sanford Beach to my house, so I persuade Sophia to drive me and we pick Bryce up on the way. We get to the Cove and everyone strips off layers and heads into the water. Sean runs past us and hoists Kimberley over his shoulder. She squeals as he barrels into the waves.

I tug the strap of my cover up and ask Bryce, "Ready to go in?"

He leans against the rocks. "Um, not yet."

"You're such a fraidy-cat with the ocean."

He pokes under my ribs. "Don't tease me."

I giggle, batting his hands away.

"You guys going in?" Meah asks, dumping her stuff by us.

"It's too cold for Bryce," I tease.

Meah smiles. "You are so not a beach baby."

"I'm not stopping you guys," he says pointing to the water.

I sit up on the rocks. "I'm fine staying with you instead."

Bryce sits by me and I'm kinda disappointed when Meah sits next to him.

"Bryce," she begins.

"Yeah?"

"What can you tell me about Naveen?"

Oh gosh, Meah.

"Whaddaya mean?"

"She likes him."

"I just wanna find a common ground with him."

"Do you ever actually talk to him," Bryce asks.

Meah shrinks. "Not much."

"Do you even try to hang out with him?" Bryce pushes.

"Not alone..."

Bryce's grin is adorable. I clutch his hand as he says, "Well, how'd you expect to get to know him if you don't hang out?"

"I was waiting for him to ask me out so we can."

Bryce laughs and squeezes my hand.

The clouds above grow grey yet the water morphs into dark indigo. The waves crash and the wind howls and Meah's yammering continues. Bryce forces her off the rock and in Naveen's direction. She stands by the group staring at him, muted. Bryce laughs at her again.

"She's trying," I say.

Bryce shakes his head. He kisses my forehead and says, "Not my problem."

I tug at his hoody. "I'm so lucky to have you."

"Not as lucky as me."

"What are you two doing?" Will asks, stopping by us.

"Chillin," Bryce answers.

Will shakes his head and winks. "Sorry dude."

Before I can ask what he's sorry for he hoists me off the rock and carries me towards the water. I shriek in his arms until he tosses me into the surf. The water crashes over my head and I am drowned head-to-toe. I sit up and spit out salty water. I push back the drenched hair suctioned to my face as others laugh and splash around me.

Bryce walks up to the water holding a towel and smiling. He holds out a hand for me and I can't resist. I pull him in. He laughs next to me, pulling at his soaked hoody.

"You cold?" I tease.

He eyes me and moves out of the water. I follow him on the sand, and we cuddle up.

He looks down to his clothes and doesn't take anything off. "When it's just you and me, I think I have something to tell you."

"Ok, sure."

He touches my hair. "Wow, it's curly."

"Oh, dammit, I'm gonna kill Will."

"It's pretty. I like it."

"Really?"

"You should wear it curly for school."

"I don't think so."

"Oh, c'mon, just once?"

I giggle at how cute he is and lean my head on his shoulder. Everyone parties around us, yet it feels like it's only the two of us on the beach.

18

Charli

I spent Sunday morning kneeling on the grass, peering through the viewfinder of my camera. *Snap.* All my photos were crap. So bad that I wanted to peg the camera across the backyard. All I needed was one stupid macro shot for photography class, but the lens never focused right.

My grip on the camera was so intense I built up sweat. Dozens of shots, all unusable. I forced myself to take a break and dumped the camera on a sun lounge by Brittany, who was painting her toenails. I asked her how many assignments she was blowing off and went inside the house without an answer.

Turns out I had no interest in returning to photography. The camera stayed outside until the evening. Seriously, Brit, you could have brought it in with you.

Now I'm in photography class uploading the horrible images. Scrolling through the images is confirmation they suck. Dammit.

Wait.

I click back on an image. It's not bad, but I don't remember taking it. Three images at the end of the upload are in focus and look promising.

"Oh Charli," Mrs Vandergarten says behind me. "That image is perfect. Exactly what we are looking for."

"You think?"

"Absolutely," she replies. "Work on editing this one and you will be a real contender for the Whitby Prize."

My eyes light up. The Whitby Prize is an award given to four finalists and an overall winner during a photography exhibition open to the public. Mrs Vandergarten spruiks about it in class and wants to enter up to five students. Man, I really want to be one of them.

When the bell rings, I'm still trying to wrap my head around these miraculous photos. I head to lunch and behind me Tayla shouts my name up the corridor. I frown and roll my eyes.

She catches up to me. "Hey Tayla."

"How you goin? I just had food tech. Naveen Singh left his station and smoked out the whole room. It smelled real bad. It was way funny. Do I still smell like smoke? I tried to cover with loads of perfume."

My head spins from her lack of breath and overload of perfume. "You're definitely covered."

"Are you heading into mess?"

"No, I'm going outside."

"Cool. That sounds way better. I have cheer practice later. It'd be good to get in a bit of sun."

"You're not going to find Lenny?" I ask as we cross the quad.

"Nah, I'll catch him later."

Relief skyrockets at the sight of Kellie and Reece.

"Hey Tay. Lenny said he was heading to the woodwork room to talk to Mr McNeil," Kellie says.

Tayla giggles. "*Geez*, I'm not always with him. I can have other friends ya know."

I grab a hold of Kellie's arm and drag her to the side. "This chick will not leave me alone. Everywhere I turn there she is. Checking in on me or talking my ear off.”

“Calm down, she’s not stalking you.”

“She’s smothering me.”

“Cut her some slack. She needs some female friends. All she’s done all year is hang with Lenny.”

“Shouldn’t someone consult with you if you are in the market for new friends?”

“Yet you let Preston in? Or is that more than a friend?”

I shove Kellie playfully. “Shuddup.”

“What’s going on?” Tayla asks, sitting on the grass next to Reece.

“Nothing,” I say shaking my head, sitting beside them.

“Just quizzing Charli on this guy she has the hots for,” Kellie smirks, sitting by Reece. She puts her hand over the open page of Reece’s book and says, “Can you stop reading and eat something.”

“I will,” he mutters.

“No, you won’t,” Kellie says. “You’ll be preoccupied reading and then I’ll be in the bad books with your mother.”

Reece huffs and places the book on the grass.

Tayla squeals and grabs my forearm. “You’ve got a new boyfriend?”

I fling her arm off. “No. No, I do not. Don’t you dare spread that around.”

Tayla shifts away. “Like I would do that.”

“Whatever. You told Reece about me and Travis.”

“What? No, I didn’t.”

“Then how did he find out that very same day?”

“Because I overheard Lucas and Ray,” Reece says.

I turn to him, mouth ajar.

“I told you I wouldn’t tell,” Tayla persists.

I shove my face in my hands. “Oh shit.” I lift my head and meet her eyes. "Tayla, I'm sorry."

She smiles and nods. "It's ok. You were dealing with something major. Your head was probably all over the place."

"It still is."

"Sorry to make you feel worse. I shouldn't have used you like this."

"Used me?"

Tayla smirks. "I have cheer practice and I didn't want to be in mess with those bitches hanging shit on me. I'm not dumb. I hear what they say. It's exhausting acting cutesy all the time."

"Then why do you do it?"

She shrugs. "I love gymnastics and the school doesn't support it enough."

"I'm sorry I demonised you," I apologise again.

"*Ugh*," Kellie groans. "Please do not utter the word demon in my presence."

"So, who is this guy?" Tayla asks.

I shrug. "Just someone I met at a bookstore."

"You don't see anything romantic happening?"

I pull my knees to my chest. "We just text."

"Ok," Kellie says, tapping Tayla's arm. "Cool it before Charli has a meltdown."

Tayla bites her lip. "Sorry, Charli."

I wave it off. "It's ok."

That night Sophia drives Brittany and me to Dad's apartment. It's the first time we're seeing him since the blowout at Tara's. We stop at the locked glass doors and I take a deep breath in.

"Hey Brit, did you take some pictures with my camera?"

"*Ohmigawd.* Like it matters."

"What? So, you did?"

"Does it matter? I just pointed and clicked. Is it really a big deal?"

I grit my teeth. "Just pointed and clicked?"

"*Geez*, Charli. Would you get over yourself? Sorry I touched your precious camera. I was bored, ok."

Brittany punches the buzzer and I want to punch it just as hard. She makes it sound so easy. Point and click? My insides boil.

Tara's voice sings through the intercom. "*Hi hello.*"

I grimace. "What? She's here?"

Brittany stares at me, wide-eyed, hand still on the buzzer.

"I don't care. I don't care that she heard me."

"Um," Tara's voice grows sheepish, "come on up, girls."

Upstairs Dad greets us with hugs and thankfully, Tara backs off.

"We need to talk about what happened at Tara's," Dad says.

I eye Tara behind him and frown. "Dad, I thought we were only seeing you tonight."

Dad tenses and his heads pivots between Brittany and me. "You two need to apologise to Tara."

"*What?*" Brittany and I shriek.

"Robbie, no," Tara says as she walks up to us. "They don't need to apologise. They are going through a big adjustment."

"That behaviour wasn't called for."

"You knew they were having difficulty handling things, or you wouldn't have taken them home."

My forehead scrunches as Tara goes into bat for us. She knows this is hard for us? That their relationship is wrong? My lips beg to smile. Maybe this is the big moment where she ends the relationship.

Tara takes Dad's hand and says, "C'mon, let's take a seat and discuss this."

I'm not discounting it yet.

"Shae explained what happened with you two," Tara says as we all sit at the dining table. "I'm sorry that made for such an awkward encounter."

"That's one word for it," I reply.

"Shae said she was developing a good friendship with you," Tara says. "She's upset about losing it."

Pain springs between my shoulder blades. "I don't know if it's lost."

"She really wants to talk to you again." Tara turns to Brittany and smiles. "You too, Brittany. You two barely got to introduce yourselves."

Brittany replies with stony silence.

Tara clears her throat and adds, "We all want to get to know each other better."

"Girls," Dad presses. "Any feelings you want to get off your chest?"

Brittany whips out her phone and begins scrolling.

"Brittany," Dad mutters. "Put the phone down."

Brittany tosses the phone on the table. "Fine, whatever."

"We don't mean to make you mad," Tara says.

Brittany shrugs. "I'm not mad."

"We want to try everyone meeting again," Dad says. "It doesn't have to be at Tara's. We can go to a restaurant."

I'm on the verge of imploding. Every fibre of my being rages inside and to avoid detonation I spit out, "No. I don't want to go."

Dad's chair screeches as he pushes it back and stands. "Charli, come with me."

His disappointment is unmistakable. I stand on jelly legs and follow him to the balcony. He closes the door behind us and exhales heavily. "What is your problem, Charli? You are continually rude to Tara. This is not how I raised you."

"My problem?" I slam a hand over my heart as my eyes fog. "I've been waiting for you for months."

His face softens and he shifts his weight.

"You come back and tell me I need to share you with another family? It's not fair." A loud sob croaks out of me. My eyelids crinkle as tears fall. "I wanted you home."

"Charli." He pulls me into his arms. "I'm sorry. I've been selfish. I was excited to see you girls and to see Tara. I wanted you to all instantly get along. I shouldn't have forced it on you."

I pat my face dry and hiccup one last cry.

"You girls should stay over tonight. We will do a movie night like we used to."

I bite inside my cheek. "With Tara?"

"No," Dad whispers. "Not with Tara."

Part of me feels awful, but the bigger part is cheering. We managed through an awkward dinner. Tara left the apartment, and Brittany instantly contacted Sophia to pick her up.

Just me and Dad.

Finally.

Dad microwaves popcorn and tells me to pick a movie. I jump on the couch, thumb through his tablet and cue up 'Roman Holiday.'

"How could I guess you'd pick this one?" Dad walks in with the popcorn, smirking at the TV.

I press play and when he sits next to me I say, "Did you know this was originally going to be shot in technicolour?"

"Is that so?"

"They were going to make sets to look like Italy, but the director insisted they had to go there instead. They had to lower the budget, so they opted for black-and-white."

"Going to Italy was a good choice."

"It's also why Audrey Hepburn was cast. She was an unknown at the time."

"Have you watched the behind-the-scenes or something?"

I shiver. "Just learnt a lot about films over the summer."

"You know," Dad says, pensively staring at the screen. "I heard they shot it in black-and-white so that Rome's beauty didn't outshine the actors."

I smirk, "C'mon Dad. It's all about the money."

Dad tilts his head back with a loud laugh and my body melts into the couch.

He wipes under his eye and smiles. "It's a shame Brittany never got into these old films."

"Oh well. It's our thing."

"I did love our bike rides into town. Do they still run the old cinema?"

My jaw clenches from all the new memories I made in the old cinema this summer. "Yeah they do. We should go back."

"Now, that's an idea."

My heart picks up speed. I bounce on the couch. "We should! We should! This weekend?"

Dad laughs, shaking his head. "Would love to, but I've just started up the firm."

I slide down on the couch.

"But I'll find us a date."

My eyes light up.

"I need to do more juggling with my schedule."

"Dad, I really want more time, just us."

"I know, Pumpkin. So do I."

I attack him with a hug. "I've missed you so much."

"You and Brittany need to be my top priority."

I hug him tighter.

"I'll be putting you kids first," he says. "Believe me."

Oh man.

Could this be it?

He'll break it off?

"So," he says cuddling me. "What other trivia facts do you have for me?"

Audrey glides across the screen and I recount, "Apparently, Audrey got the role because after her audition the camera was still rolling. Without playing a role she still gave off regal vibes."

"You know your stuff."

I laugh as I remember the best one Travis told me. "She was so overwhelmed when she won her Oscar; she left it behind in the bathroom."

As Dad laughs I rub the pain from my heart.

"How's school going?"

"To be honest, overwhelming. I have heaps of extra stuff going on after school, plus I'm working to keep the top marks in my classes. It really is work."

"Stick with it," he says and pats my arm. "You've made commitments. It is hard work to keep everything to a high standard. You're more than capable."

After the movie we say goodnight. I hug Dad and thank him.

It's nearing midnight, and I fire up my laptop. Dad is proud of me and I need to keep it that way. Every minute is valuable.

I open the photo Mrs Vandergarten deemed the best and begin editing.

Tonight is the winter formal and I'm meeting the committee to set up. On the way to the gym I see him by his locker. I remember his timetable and I'm usually careful to avoid this wing when he's between classes. There is a sadness to his profile. My hand slides over my heart. He feels what I feel?

"Trav," Ray calls out.

A smile brightens Travis' face and his hunched body grows tall and strong. My heart sinks as they high five. I run to the gym before they notice me.

Heather paces in front of the committee, tapping her clipboard. I hide at the back of the group. It's like I've forgotten how to stand straight. With everything going on with Dad, and constant reminders of Travis here at school, it is so hard.

Travis.

How genuine could he have been? He walks around here with his head held high. Like, he's over it? He's told me how well he plays fake at school. I don't know if that makes things better or worse.

And that bitch.

That bitch bought his ticket.

He's with her now? Already?

How often was he with her when we were together?

"Earth to Charli!"

I jolt and stumble backwards. "Huh?"

"We're putting you down for first shift at the confectionery stand," Heather says with an exaggerated huff.

"Ok, sure, whatever."

I sense eyes on me. To my left Tayla waves at me.

Ugh.

My attention falls on the men building the stage for the band. Heather reads from her list and I pick at a knot in my hair. Maintenance workers trolley in tables, banging and stomping, and we arrange chairs and decorations.

"Howzit goin?" Tayla says, following me around a table.

"Fine."

"Ya look a lil down."

"Holy crap. I'm fine."

Tayla steps back, hands up. "Ok, ok."

I lean on a chair and sigh. "Sorry."

She nods, smiling. "Excited for the dance?"

"Not really?"

"Got a dress?"

"My mum got me something. I wanted to come in jeans."

Tayla blows a massive raspberry. "I would love to see you rock jeans to a formal."

"I thought it would work."

"I'm glad you're coming. I kinda wish I wasn't on the committee though. Cuts it fine to go home and get ready."

"It doesn't take that long to get changed."

"Hair and makeup."

My body eases and I laugh. "I didn't even think about doing that."

Tayla throws her arms up. "How is that possible?"

"I've never done my makeup before. I've had it professionally done for events, but I never do any of that stuff."

"Brittany is good at it. Didn't you learn when she did?"

I shake my head. For a moment I'm worried I should have learnt.

Tayla shrugs. "Don't worry about it. You don't need makeup."

Should I ask Brittany to do mine?

"I'd help you get ready, but Lenny is picking me up and my mum wants to do the whole picture thing. And because of the committee we have to get here super early."

"No, that's cool."

Tayla leans in and whispers, "Between you and me, is this not as fun as you thought it'd be?"

"I dunno. It's not about fun. I just wanted to be on a committee."

"Nerd-alert," Tayla teases.

I laugh. "And proud."

Tayla and I continue setting up the decorations and I spot a figure by the entrance. I double-take as Preston walks into the gym.

"Hi," he says, waving.

I bunch my curls to the side and walk towards him. "Hey. What are you doing here?"

"I wanted to check on you. Your texts earlier weren't giving happy vibes."

I gnaw inside my cheek. "Not exactly looking forward to tonight."

"Wanna talk about it?"

I check over my shoulder for an eavesdropping Tayla and step outside the gym with Preston.

"I'm working the formal because I wanted to join clubs and committees, and now I have to stand around and watch my ex-boyfriend on a date."

"Aw, shit."

"This girl bought tickets for the two for them so soon after we broke up. I just can't believe he'd move on so quickly."

Preston finds my eyes. "You don't want him back, right? Cause after—"

"No, of course not," I say. "I made it clear it was over. But it still hurts."

"*Geez*, of course it does."

"I just don't wanna have to work this stupid thing and see them together."

"How about I help distract you?"

"Whaddaya mean?"

"I'll come to the dance and help you work. I'll make sure those two are the furthest thing from your mind."

I smile. "You don't want to do that."

"Why not? Your dances have to be way better than *West Sanford*'s. Plus, you're my friend. I hate the thought of you being here all miserable."

My heart warms. "That is really sweet, but honestly I'm just going to work my shift and get the hell outta there. Perhaps we can hang out over the weekend instead?"

"I'm down for that."

"So, I've almost finished the second book," I tell Preston. School takes up so much of my time, I haven't been able to speed through '*The Firelake Five*' series.

"*Ugh*. Isn't Franklin the worst?"

"No. I love Franklin."

Preston gasps and slaps a hand over his mouth.

"What? What?"

"Shit. You haven't gotten to that part, yet?"

"What part?" My eyes bulge. "What does Franklin do?"

"No. No, I can't. I can't ruin it for you."

I crack a smile. "You basically did ruin it for me."

Preston laughs. "Sorry."

"Preston?" Kimberley stops by us, gawking. "What are you doing here?"

"Oh hi, Kimmy," Preston replies.

"Seriously," she says, hunching. "What are you doing here?"

"Just came to see Charli."

Kimberley's nostrils flare. "Guess that fits. The two bookworms together."

"Don't be jealous just because you can't read, Kimmy," Preston teases.

A trickle of laughter seeps out of me.

Kimberley arches her back and composes a steely expression. "Oh c'mon, we all know it's you two who are jealous of me."

She sashays her hips away and I ask Preston, "What was that? How do you and Kimmy know each other?"

"She's my cousin."

"Get out."

"Seriously. We don't see her family that much. Her dad married a white woman, they had her, moved to Sanford Heights and think they're the shit."

I smirk. "Yeah but she's down the back end of The Heights."

Preston tilts his head. "What do you mean?"

"Oh man," I drop my face to my hands. "I just sounded like an *uber* snob."

"Well, it might all be different this side of the tracks, but in West Sanford all this side is rich... and a bit snobby." He gazes at everyone in the gym. "I had a feeling she'd be the only indigenous student at this school."

"She's not the *only* one."

He folds his arms. "It'd be safe to say there's a lot more of us at *West Sanford High*."

"You wouldn't believe that Kimmy and I used to be best friends."

"Really? When?"

"In primary school," I say. "We hung out all the time and went on adventures. Just before high school she was pushing for us to become super popular. I liked hanging out just the two of us and occasionally my sister would join us, but Kimmy got annoyed and ditched me."

"So, you started high school without your best friend?"

"Kinda. I started hanging with Chloe and the other girls for Kimmy's sake, but I couldn't stand the vapid conversation. Even at twelve-years-old," I say. "I started hanging out at my friend Reece's house. I didn't know him that well then; one of his older brothers was my babysitter. Reece's friend Kellie was always over there. She would wrestle with Reece's brothers, like, fighting Reece's battles for him. I found her so funny and soon the three of us clicked. Now those two are my best friends."

Preston taps his index finger to his lips. "You're a twin, right?"

I nod.

He laughs. "I remember you."

"What?"

"When we were younger, at Kimmy's house, I remember you," he says. "My family visited Kimmy's family and she had friends over. Twins with curly blonde hair. That was you!"

I giggle at the excitement in his voice.

His brow furrows. "Your sister's name is Brittany?"

My eyebrows lift. "Yes, it is."

"Yeah, I remember Kimmy leaving her out of a game, so I tried to be nice to her. She wouldn't speak to me, she just kept sobbing."

I hug my waist and frown. "Yeah, she was super sensitive when we were younger. I don't know why Kimmy didn't like Brit. I loved having Brit around, I still do, but Kimmy was so mean to her. I feel so bad about leaving her out. I shouldn't have let that happen. I think that's why things are so bad between us now."

"How is it bad?"

"We aren't close. We butt heads over the smallest things."

"Sounds like sisters."

"But we're twins. We were one being. As corny as it sounds, I can feel when she's happy or when she's hurt. I know she does the same with me. We shouldn't be at each other's throats. I hate how far apart we are."

"I'm sorry, that sucks."

"This thing with Dad has brought us closer, I guess. She stayed with me after the blowout at Tara's."

"Shae is gutted over that."

I meet his eyes. "Tara told me. I don't mean to take anything out on her, but she got time with my dad when I didn't."

"She asked me for your number."

My eyes bulge.

"I didn't give it to her," he's quick to add.

Phew.

"She really wants to talk this through with you."

I gather my hair to the side and sigh. "I dunno."

"I could take you to Tara's," Preston offers. "She's really nice. The whole family is. You should get to know them."

"You want to play buffer?"

"I want to see my friends happy and getting along."

"I'll think about it."

"I'm free for you any time this weekend."

"Thanks. I'll need a distraction after this struggle of a night."

19

Brittany

Three loud bangs rattled my bedroom door. "*Ohmigawd.* What?"

"Can I come in? I need your opinion," Charli says on the other side of the door.

My eyes roll back into my skull. "Seriously?" I ask, reefing the door open.

A shock-filled laugh puffs out of me as I take in my sister dressed in a fifties-style navy dress.

"You're laughing?" Charli asks, her voice small and eyes rounding.

"I'm just surprised."

Charli pulls out the sides of the dress. "Is it ok?"

"Yeah. You look really cute."

Her eyebrows rise at me.

"What are you doing with your hair?"

Charli huffs and her shoulders droop. "I was talking to Tayla and she suggested I had to do the whole hair and makeup thing. I'm only working at the formal and then leaving. Do you think I have to?"

"You never do. Why worry about starting now?"

She shrugs, glancing around my room.

I clap a hand over my mouth to muffle a giggle. "My, my, Charlotte Jane. Are you asking me to do your makeup?"

"Brit," Charli whines, stamping a foot. "Just, c'mon, ok?"

I take a few steps back, grinning at her. "Ok, but you have to actually sit still, and you can't argue with me."

"Well then don't stick mascara in my eyes."

"*Gawd*, are you never going to let that go? We were twelve."

I pat the stool in front of my dresser. Charli sits saying, "I can't forget because in all the photos at Aunt Stephanie's wedding I have red, puffy eyes."

"Stop being a baby."

As I blend the foundation on Charli's face, I say, "This is kinda nice. I usually do Meah's makeup. This is the first time we're not getting ready together."

"Why isn't she coming over?"

"Bryce is picking me up. I just thought it'd be easier."

"Is she ok with that?"

I toss the brush onto my dresser. A small plume of dust puffs into the air. "Either way I'll be in trouble."

"You two aren't fighting because of me and..."

"No," I cut her off. "It's fine. Kellie coming over?"

"Yeah, she's going over early with me."

"Do I have to do her makeup too?"

Charli laughs. "I don't know, but I'd love to see that."

I finish her eye makeup and twirl her freshly washed hair into a side braid, and then Kellie joins us upstairs.

"Holy shit, Charli," Kellie gushes. "You're Brittany's clone."

"I guess that means I've done a good job," I reply.

"Thanks, Brit," Charli says, slinking towards Kellie.

"And Brit, curly hair?" Kellie says. "Been a long time since I've seen that."

Kellie is in an emerald dress that compliments her copper hair gorgeously. "Kellie, I would have put money on you rocking up in a suit to be Charli's date."

"This dress is purely for solidarity," Kellie replies. She chucks an arm around Charli and says, "If my girl's in a dress best believe I'm gonna be too."

Sophia drives Charli and Kellie to the dance. I do the finishing touches on my face and then get to work on my hair. My dress is cream chiffon with white flowers across one shoulder, and I pin flower pieces between my curls.

Mum knocks on my doorframe and rests her hand over her heart. "Oh Sweetheart, you're breathtaking."

I stand up. "You think?"

She nods, grinning. "Someone else might think so too."

I don't catch on.

Mum's eyes widen. "Bryce is here."

Eep. "What? Really?"

"Easy down the stairs in your heels."

Every nerve in my body electrifies. I fan my face to combat overheating. I suck in air and swallow hard. I hate that Mum is following me down the stairs.

I spy him in the foyer. He turns around in a dapper charcoal suit. His crystal eyes glisten as he smiles at me. "Wow, Brittany, you look incredible."

"Thank you," I say, landing at the bottom of the stairs. "You look so handsome."

He spins in place. "You approve?"

I giggle and clutch his hand. "Very much so."

"Ok, you two," Mum says leaping in front of us. "I need a photo."

"Mum," I grumble for show, but secretly I'm so glad she whipped out her phone.

"Say cheese," she says like a dork and we cuddle up for the photo.

Mum smiles at the photo and Bryce takes his phone out of his pocket. "D'you mind taking a photo with mine, Ms Matthews?"

I'm blushing and I don't care. He is the sweetest. I love that he did that.

Amy waits in the car for us. I had assumed Bryce's dad was driving us, but I don't bring it up.

We walk hand-in-hand into the gym. It's *ah-may-zing*. Twinkle lights and glitter balloons are strewn across the rafters, while flower garlands and ivy decorate the trestle tables boarding the dancefloor. I spy my sister with Tayla working the candy bar and I lead Bryce in the opposite direction.

Bryce twirls one of my curls around his finger and I catch him smiling. "So glad you decided on curly hair."

I bite my lip and eye the timber floor. "Only because you asked me to."

"It's pretty."

I laugh. "Don't get too use to it."

"Brit," Meah calls, waving madly.

"If she starts on about Nav again," Bryce whispers, "I'm outta here."

I rub my lips together to hold back a laugh. "Good plan."

Meah and I embrace in a one-arm hug. She looks gorgeous. Her sunshine yellow dress flatters her body. Her hair is in beachy, boho waves that cascade down her left side. Getting ready without me did not hurt her.

It's hard to decide how happy I am about that...

"Just thought I'd say hi. You know, didn't wanna be labelled as rude or anything," Meah says, playfully tapping me on the shoulder. "I'm about to meet Madi at the photo booth. We scoped it out once we got here together. So, you know, gotta dash."

"Oh ok. Cool." You're not going to invite me?

I maintain eye contact until she turns away from me.

Seriously? I'm ditched?

"Wanna dance?" Bryce asks, tugging on my hand.

Tingles.

I nod because the word 'yes' is lodged in my throat.

I finally get to dance with him.

Bryce leads me into the centre of the dancefloor and his hands slide around my waist. I clasp my hands behind his neck and watch my smile reflected in the blue of his eyes. The song is fast, but our pace is slow. One of his hands moves up and glides through my hair. Our lips touch in a soft, sweet kiss. I lean into his warmth as we sway to the music.

"Hey lovebirds," Sean yells over the music.

Sean and Kimberley dance beside us. My arms tense as I brace from the fear that Kimmy will kick me.

"Hey. They did a pretty good job in here, didn't they," Bryce say, pointing out the decorations.

"They have a photo booth," Sean says. "We were just making out in there and someone ran off with the photos."

"What?" Bryce and I reply.

"I know," Kimberley says. "What freakin perve would go and do that?"

"That's really gross," I wince.

"I know, right?"

"I'd suggest we go," Bryce says to me, "but maybe we won't get the photos."

I take his hands. "I'm willing to give it a go."

As we walk towards the photo booth, Bryce steps away while

holding my hand. "I really wanna spin you in that dress."

I giggle and let him spin me. The skirt of my dress billows out and I squeal as he catches me. He dips me and pulls me up with a kiss.

"You are so beautiful, Britty," he says close to my ear.

I hold onto him, resting my cheek against his.

We wait in the line for the photo booth. It is a really long line, but we don't care. We bop to the music and chat about all the couples on the dancefloor. We start a weird game of trying to poke each other below the ribs without the other slapping our hands away. I'm bursting with giggles. I notice the laugh lines under his eyes and his big smile. I love being with him. I love everything about him.

I skip a heartbeat.

I love him?

His lips crook to the left as he looks at me like I'm the only girl in the world.

I love him.

I love him so much.

In the photo booth I am a mixture of nerves and confidence. It's an odd sensation, but all I know is that my heart and mind are screaming to never let him go.

Two of our photos are cutesy and the third is ridiculously silly. I'm in heaven.

The overhead lights shut off, and the twinkle lights play against the laser lighting of the stage. The band is finding their groove with a pop melody and old school rock beat. We pass the candy bar as Tayla hands Naveen a can of coke. My head cocks as someone marches towards Charli.

GiGi Larkin.

"Little service?" she snaps at Charli.

I don't hear Charli, but I imagine it is a grumbled, *whaddaya want*?

"Wow. Superb customer service," the sarcasm rolls out of GiGi and

I realise I'm walking towards them.

GiGi taps her manicure on the table, peering around the stand. "Hmm, which one was Travy's favourite, again? Hmm, Charli, you oughtta remember that?"

My skin prickles as I notice Charli shaking.

Tayla steps ahead of Charli. "Why don't you just tell me what you want?"

"It's ok, Ray's-Little-Sister, Charli's serving me."

"It's Tayla."

GiGi smirks. "Whatever."

I suck in a breath as Travis walks up to them.

"GiGi, what are you doing?" he asks.

"Hey, Baby, what can I get ya?" GiGi says, running a hand along Travis's shoulder.

Baby? Over the last few months, I'd heard Travis call Charli *Baby* countless times. Now he and GiGi are using it?

Charli's eyes shine and bulge.

I take a step forward and Bryce takes my wrist. "Hey, what's going on?" he whispers.

I shake my head. *Nothing good.*

Charli covers her face and runs to the back of the stall.

"Charli?" Travis calls, moving behind the stall. "Charli, are you ok?"

"No!" I storm towards Travis. "No! Leave her alone."

Charli cups her mouth to muffle her heavy breathing. Her eyes seal shut.

"Charli." Travis reaches to touch her, and she flinches.

"*Ohmigawd*, Travis," GiGi huffs. "Let's go."

"You don't have to be here," Travis whispers to Charli.

"Travis, leave her alone," I insist.

Charli's panting gets faster in her hands.

"I know you don't want to be here," Travis continues like we're all on mute. "I can take you home."

Charli pushes her palms over her eyes. She croaks, "Go away."

"I don't want to leave you."

Charli stays strong in silence.

"But I will show you that I listen," Travis replies and slowly walks away.

His path is nowhere near GiGi, but she frantically chases after him.

Charli drops her hands and frowns at me.

"Is he serious right now?" I say to her.

"This dance has got to be over already," she replies in a monotone. "Did you see where Kellie went?"

"No, last I saw she was still hanging around here."

"If you see her can you tell her to come over?"

"Sure."

"Thanks." She fakes a smile and walks into the booth.

I walk back to Bryce who has uneasiness and confusion written all over him.

"What was that about?" he asks.

"Travis has to get the message to stay away from her."

"Looked like that scary chick was the problem."

We meander along the outskirts of the dancefloor and Bryce asks, "So, why did they break up?"

"What?"

"Charli and Travis. I always saw them together and then suddenly they were over."

"Oh. Um, they had a fight."

Bryce whisks me in his arms. "Well, I'll never be so dumb to let anything get between us."

I touch his bottom lip. "You could never be as dumb as Travis."

"Is that?" Bryce says, squinting at the back corner. "Holy crap, it is."

"What?" I ask, trying to follow his line of sight.

He lowers his voice, "Back corner."

I squint at a couple huddled on the ground furiously making out. I spy her reddened hair and his long legs.

"What?"

"*Shoosh.*"

"What? Why? How?"

Bryce laughs. "They're really going for it." Bryce leads me away. "I hope no one sees them for Kellie's sake. Will might deserve it."

"I really don't get those two."

Escaping the up-and-down excitement of the gym we part for our respective bathrooms. I need air and a lipgloss re-apply.

Chloe stands at the basins touching up her makeup.

She winks into the mirror. "Howzit going?"

"Good. Chloe you look like a million bucks."

"Thanks, chick. You look super cute."

I stand beside her and check my reflection.

"So," Chloe says, "where are you and Bryce going after this?"

"Whaddaya mean?"

"Yours or his?"

I flinch. "After this?"

"You didn't tee up a story with the parentals?"

I shake my head slowly.

Chloe crosses her arms. "Brit, you'd better get on it. You wanna keep him, don't ya?"

I gulp at my worried reflection.

Chloe tussles her hair, smiling. "Don't worry, hun. You gotta second opportunity. My sweet sixteen is next weekend. I'll reserve a bedroom for ya."

"A bedroom?"

"And you've got your lingerie sorted, right?"

"Lingerie?"

"*Ohmigawd*, Brit. You're like a little kid. You and me are going shopping tomorrow. Meet me at the food court entrance tomorrow at one pm."

I nod, feeling like I'm in shackles.

Chloe kisses my cheek. "It'll be sweet. See ya out there."

When Chloe leaves the bathroom I exhale loudly. I exit the bathroom to find Bryce and suddenly it's weird walking up to him. It doesn't help that when I find him *his* posture is all weird.

"What's up?" I ask.

He gazes off to the side and his jaw tenses. "I want to go home."

I suck in air and my chest tightens. "With me?"

He looks at me with an eyebrow raised. "I didn't think you would want to go home yet. I've just been texting Amy about what's happening at home and, I dunno, I just want to go back there."

I take a step back. "Hold on, are you not having fun here?"

"No, no, it has been fun."

"But you want to leave?"

"I can't get it off my mind now."

"Have you tried? Seriously, it's our first formal together. Why don't you want to stay with me?"

"It's not you," he says, taking my hands.

I can't look at him.

"I'm sorry," he whispers. "We can hang out tomorrow. You wanna do something?"

I huff. "Chloe just invited me shopping. Maybe you can rescue me an hour into that."

"Deal," he says and kisses my forehead.

"Stay for one more dance," I whisper.

He wraps his arms around me. "Ok. I'll make it two more dances."

# #

"Chloe, I don't think I can wear this," I say, staring at myself in the dressing room mirror. Chloe made me try on black lace lingerie with red piping.

"Sure you can, you'll look *hawt*," Chloe says, reefing open the curtain. "Damn, you're smokin."

I hug my mid-section and can't stop slouching.

"Girl, at least act like you're hot," Chloe says, pulling me out of the dressing room.

"No," I squeal, trying to hide in the dressing room. I'm terrified my mum will find me in this boutique. Or, just as bad, someone will see me and report back to my mum.

"C'mon, Brit, you need to wear this. Black and red means sex."

I check myself out in the three-way mirror. "I dunno, it's just so different for me."

"So, like, you want the *baby-doll-pink-fluffy* thing in the window?"

"That is super cute, but I still don't know about lingerie. It's so... it's so..."

"Sexy?"

"Obvious."

"Well, *duh*. That's the point. Bryce is gonna be droolin over ya."

I slink into the dressing room and close the curtain.

"He will be begging to be in that bedroom with you. You can get all steamy on the dancefloor and then at the end of the night, *bam*. Or, should I say, *bang*."

"I dunno, he usually goes home early."

"What? Why would he leave early?"

I shrug, squirming inside.

"Seriously, you are so clueless," Chloe huffs. "You have no idea about relationships, and you will totally disappoint him. If he goes home early it's because you bored him to tears."

I unhook the clips and stare at myself in the mirror. I'm gonna need to buy this to keep him interested?

When I hand cash over at the register (no way was this purchase going on Mum's credit card) Chloe acts so pleased with herself. Like she's had to teach the helpless lamb how to survive.

It was an hour and a half into Chloe time when Bryce saved me. He found us window shopping at the jewellers and hugged me from behind, planting a kiss on my cheek. I could have melted into him.

I hug Chloe goodbye and she whispers in my ear, "You can so tell that he wants it."

Chloe took my shopping bag home with the plan that Bryce needs to be totally surprised at the party.

"Did you two shop up a storm?" Bryce asks when we are alone.

I bite my lip and then say, "Yeah, outfits for Chloe's party."

"Girls need a new outfit for every event."

"Something like that. Are you excited for Chloe's party?"

"Of course," Bryce replies. "Chloe was the first friend I made in Sanford. I wouldn't miss it."

"Chloe was your first friend?"

"Yeah. We met this summer before school started. My mum and her dad had met at conferences because they work in finance. So we ended up hanging out."

"Does Chloe know about your mum? You know... her being sick?"

Bryce eyes the ceiling to think. "I dunno. She's never said anything. I don't know if her dad would have told her."

"So you met everyone through Chloe?"

"Yeah, she made everything so much easier for me. I guess you could say she's my oldest friend," he laughs. "In Sanford that is."

Maybe Chloe is right? If she's known Bryce the longest, and she's stayed with Jace for so long... *Ohmigawd,* I'm so dumb. I totally have to listen to her.

Bryce checks his phone as we walk through the mall and then stops.

I turn to him. "What?"

He shows me a black screen. "It's dead."

"Oh."

"I have a plan," he says, propping a hand on each of my shoulders. "Wanna get a cab to mine so I can charge this and then spend the afternoon by the beach?"

"I'd love to."

We sat so close in the back of that cab that nothing mattered except being with him. When we walk up the path to his house, he pulls me in close. The giggles spill out of me as he nuzzles his nose against my cheek. His hands run through my hair and he kisses me, slow and sensual.

"Using your time productively, Bryce," a voice calls out.

We pull apart and turn to the house. Mrs Kerry paces the length of the veranda, no wheelchair in sight.

My jaw drops.

"Mum, you're up?" Bryce gasps.

"Yes, I was having one of the good days," she says, hands clasped behind. "But I feel I am getting weakened now that you've decided to parade this hussy around."

Me?

"What?" Bryce blurts out.

Mrs Kerry's lips purse between each sentence. "It's very disappointing, Bryce."

"You can't talk about Brittany like that," Bryce says, taking my hand.

"Bryce, I'm getting tired." Mrs Kerry dabs her forehead. "Come inside. Just you."

"No."

Mrs Kerry glares at her son.

I have an overwhelming urge to bolt.

"Brittany is not a hussy. She's my best friend. She's the one that's there for me."

Mrs Kerry scowls and walks inside the house.

I take a step back. "I can't believe you just said that."

"What?" He squeezes my hand.

"I should go."

He tugs on my arm. "No, come inside."

"She doesn't want me in there."

"So? I do."

The navy ridges in his eyes draw me in. I want to follow him everywhere, but his mum obviously hates me.

He leads me up the front steps. "We'll be like five minutes, and then we'll leave."

We flee to his bedroom before any family members see us. Bryce pushes me against his closed bedroom door and kisses me. I pull him in closer and wrap my leg around his.

"I'm sorry about last night," he whispers.

I shake my head. "It's ok."

"No, it's not. I should have stayed and taken you home at the end of the night. I just got in my head and started to make myself sick."

I touch his cheek. "Bryce, don't worry about it."

"So, you forgive me?"

"There was nothing to forgive. I know the deal here."

"You were mad."

"I was surprised."

"I wanted to wait till the beach for this, to have the perfect setting, but I can't hold it in."

"What?"

"I felt so stupid last night once I was back here. I left behind the prettiest girl in school." His eyes lock on mine and there's no doubt it's getting hot in here. He pushes back my hair and says, "I was an idiot because all I could think of was how much I love you."

My heart thunders in my chest. My mouth hangs open but I'm too motionless to close it.

His hand brushes under my chin, and he whispers, "I love you, Britty."

I throw my arms around him and say much too loud, "I LOVE YOU SO MUCH."

Bryce laughs as I wildly kiss and paw at him. We are a mess of hands and giggles and end up collapsing on the floor.

"You're my favourite person," he says.

I kiss his nose. "You're my prince."

20

Charli

"How on earth did Will Maclean convince you to make out with him again?" I ask, bouncing on the couch in Kellie's living room.

"What makes you think it was up to him?" Kellie says, turning the volume up on her cartoons.

I slap the remote out of her hand. "Kel!"

Kellie sinks further down the couch, cinching her dressing gown around her pyjamas.

"I thought you hated him."

"It's complicated, ok?"

"Complicated? He humiliated you at school."

Kellie strikes the volume button again. "I understand why he did it, ok?"

"Kellie Margaret Saunders, turn that TV down," Mrs Saunders yells from the hall.

Kellie groans and turns the volume down.

"Better yet turn it off and go and do something productive," Mrs

Saunders says as she stomps up the stairs.

"Like she's ever done anything productive," Kellie grumbles. "To her, productive means finding a rich husband *and then* laze around the house all day. How dare she say I'm not being productive when I'm the one staying up all night working on my experiment to get shortlisted for the Ferguson Award? That seemingly means jackshit to her."

"You should focus on science not that stupid boy."

"*Pah.*" Kellie boffs me with a pillow. "Like you're one to talk."

"Whaddaya mean?"

"If it's not Travis, it's your dad, or it's Brittany, or it's Preston."

"Preston?"

Kellie's eyes light up. "Preston?"

"Kel, whaddaya doing?"

"I just think it's interesting that that's the name you gravitated toward."

"Because it shouldn't be on the list."

"Why not?"

"He's basically an acquaintance."

"So, you didn't make a date with him this weekend?"

"Stop getting in my business. I can't believe you ditched me last night."

"I didn't ditch you."

I whack her with a pillow. "You said you'd be there the whole time. You disappeared right away."

"I'm sorry. You seemed fine when I left. I needed to hear what he had to say. He did try to make an effort that time in your kitchen."

"So, lay it on me. What did the boy-genius have to say for himself?"

"An apology."

"And what could he possibly say to wash away the weeks of harassment?"

"Look, I just get him, ok?"

I let out a frustrated groan. "No! No, it's not ok."

"Don't put what happened between you and Travis on me."

"I'm... I'm not."

"Will said something dumb that got outta hand. That night in my kitchen I got to know him. We get each other. We complain about our mothers the exact same way. It was nice to finally have someone to talk to about that stuff."

"You told me you don't like talking about your mum."

Kellie *tsks*. "It was easier."

"What? You're implying you can't talk to me."

"You do get wrapped up in your own stuff."

My jaw drops and I utter nonsensical sounds.

"All I'm saying is that I liked Will," Kellie says to her cartoons. "He said mean things because of the vultures at school. It was rough on him when the vicious stuff about his dad was in circulation. I want to teach him how to have a backbone."

"I can't hear you make excuses for him."

"Charli. I see how you look at Travis even though he's now with GiGi."

My gut swells and I sink into the couch.

Kellie takes my hand and says, "I'm sorry for what I said. And I'm sorry I didn't stick by you last night."

"Why is he with her?"

"She's a vulture."

I swallow uncomfortably and squeeze her hand. "I wasn't ready to break up with Travis."

"I know, man. But you had to." Kellie clears her throat and continues, "Really for *his* safety. If he hurts you again, he has me to contend with."

I smirk. "If you're not tied up with your loverboy."

The room sounds with the echo of the doorbell, followed by three bangs on the front door. A housekeeper answers the door and then heavy footsteps close in.

"Hello, hello," Will says with a gigantic smile.

My frown couldn't appear sooner.

As Kellie says hi, Will plonks between us and curves his arms around our shoulders. I reef myself away and my chest tightens as Kellie snuggles into him. Will runs a hand through her messy hair and comments on her PJs.

"Maybe I should go," I suggest, already standing up.

"You just got here," Kellie replies.

I grimace as she hugs Will. "I didn't know Will was coming over."

"I didn't ask," Will says. "Imma rock up kinda guy. Can't blame me for wanting more Kelarino time."

My head pivots between the two as my brain catches up. "Are you two *together*?"

They shrug with shy smiles.

I raise my hands up defensively and creep backwards. "Yeah, I'm leaving."

I pace toward the front door as Will calls out, "See ya, Chaz."

I get out of the house and shake off the weirdness. What the hell was that?

I pull my bike from the side of the house and don't want to go home. I unlock my phone and text Dad.

(Me) **Are you working?**

(Dad) **I'm at the apartment. What's up?**

(Me) **Feel like getting on your bike?**

I cycle down the back of The Heights and meet Dad.

"Good idea, Pumpkin," Dad says, patting his bike.

"It's been too long," I say as we cycle towards the forest.

"So, along the track and pull around towards the boardwalk?"

"Sounds like a plan."

We start on the dirt track which winds through the forest, when Dad remarks, "Could not have been better timing, Pumpkin."

"Yeah?"

"Had my face glued to case law for thirty-six hours. Well overdue for a break, and some sunlight."

"I'm glad I could rescue you."

"Tara will be happy. She's been on my case about getting out and being less work focused."

My jaw stiffens. "Tara's been at your apartment?"

"No. That's her complaint."

Phew. He's still on course to break it off. I don't know why he's still stringing her along.

"Still doing well at school?"

"Yes, I'm managing."

"The big dance was on last night, wasn't it? You girls get all gussied up?"

"Gussied up?" I smile as the bike shakes against the stony ground. "Actually, it was really nice getting ready with Brittany."

"Aw, you two are friends again?"

"I think I lucked out. Meah wasn't over because Brit's boyfriend was taking her to the formal."

As Dad's bike skids to a stop, I slap a hand over my mouth. *Crap.*

"Brittany has a boyfriend?"

"Oops." It's all I can say.

Dad passes me and asks, "Nice boy?"

"Really nice. They're really good together. Please don't tell her I told you."

"It's ok, Charli. I'll let her tell me on her own."

As we cycle through a clearing Dad's phone rings.

"You have reception?" I ask. "I never get anything out here."

Dad hops off his bike and pulls out his phone. "Must have gotten lucky." He puts the phone to his ear, "Hello?"

I lean my bike against a tree as the sunlight dances between the leaves and the smell of wet earth swirls around me.

"No, hunny, I'm out of the house. I'm cycling with Charli."

Tell me that's not Tara.

"Yes, my girl is a great influence on me."

I rock on the balls of my feet, boasting a big grin.

"Dinner tonight?" Dad says into the phone. "Might be pushing it."

YES. Keep rejecting her.

"I know, I know, I miss you too."

Sorry, what now?

"Ok, let's get a cheeky takeaway. Honestly, I'll only have an hour to spare."

Dad proceeds with schoolboy laughter and my grin does a one-eighty. Why is Dad bothering to spend time with her? It'll only make it harder when he dumps her.

"Ok, see you then. I love you too."

Love?

Dad slips his phone in his pocket and says, "Shall we continue?"

The L-word won't get out of my head. "Love?"

"Excuse me?"

"You love her?"

Dad looks confused. "Well yes, Charli. She's my partner."

"Partner?"

"We plan to make a life together."

I step out of my body and stare at the two of us. None of this makes sense.

"I thought you were breaking it off to spend time with Brittany and me."

Dad lets out an exhausted sigh. "Pumpkin. I said I was putting you first. It didn't mean things with Tara would end."

I snap out of my trance and jump on my bike. I pedal as fast as I can.

"Charli!"

"I'll race ya!"

As the wind hits my face, all I can think is how badly I don't want to be around my dad right now.

When we reached the boardwalk Dad used the excuse of his paperwork to head back to his apartment. The awkwardness was so heavy I couldn't bear to let him hug me. For who knows how long I stare at the blues and greens of the ocean crashing with rage.

I need someone who will just listen to me. Who will not throw their own crap at me. Someone to hold me and keep me safe.

I whip out my phone.

(Me) You busy?

(Preston) Where do I meet you?

When Preston finds me on the boardwalk I fly into his arms. I rest my head on his chest and he holds me.

"Was everything ok at the formal?" he asks.

"No, but I don't care about that anymore."

"What's wrong?"

"My dad," I sigh. "And Tara."

"Well, that's what I wanted to bring up too."

"What do you mean?"

"I was with Shae when you texted..."

"And?"

"I drove over here with her," he says, and I unravel myself from his arms. "She's at a café. She understands if you don't want to meet her, but I think it would do you both some good. And like I said I'll be there to buffer."

My heart is so battered that my whole body feels wounded.

I bite my lip and nod my head. "Ok. Let's go."

I'm woozy as we enter *Shakes*. I spot Shae who is fidgety with a brave smile.

We walk to her table and Preston sits, and I stand by my chair. A lump throbs in my throat.

"Charli, I'm sorry," Shae blurts out. "I had no idea Rob was your dad."

The throbbing worsens. "I don't think I can do this."

Shae walks around the table and takes my hand. "Charli, it's been a blast getting to know you. Now it seems our families will be getting closer. I really don't want a rift between us."

"Our families?" I choke.

"This wasn't our fault. And our parents haven't done anything wrong."

I pull my hand away from hers. "Easy to say when you were kept in the loop."

"Can we talk?" Shae urges.

I rub my temples and nod.

Preston orders me a green tea and Shae and I take our seats.

I swallow hard and ask Shae, "Can you start from the beginning?"

She leans in. "What do you mean?"

"When did you first meet my dad?"

She frowns. "Last year."

My heart jackhammers. What? Last year?

"Nick and I came home one day and he was in the driveway, giving my mum a ride home. Mum didn't want us to meet him yet, but he ended up staying for dinner. He seemed really nice, but we didn't get to know him that much. He was super nervous."

"When was this?"

"Around October or November, I guess?"

A tear drops to my cheek. "Before the divorce was finalised."

"I only saw him a few times throughout summer. It became more regular once he moved back to Sanford."

My eyes sting as I ask, "So, he hasn't been living with you?"

Shae crinkles her nose and puffs out a laugh. "Heck no!"

Relief pours out of me as my hand rests over my slowing heart.

"I don't know why he kept you guys in the dark," Shae says. "We didn't know what he was telling you guys, but we assumed you knew the same details as us. I knew he had twin girls, but I didn't know you were a twin."

A green tea is placed in front of me and I breathe in the calming aroma.

"Nick and I would love to get to know you and your sister. Brittany and I can have a do-over on first impressions. I'm willing to forget her yelling in our hallway."

I force a smile and say, "I'm sure she will be glad."

"My mum is gaga over your dad. I know we haven't spent that much time together, but it seems like our parents will create more opportunities for us to be at the same place."

I remember Dad's phone call in the forest. "I get that feeling too."

Shae shifts in her seat. "I just wanted to get any tension out of the way."

I take a large gulp of tea and set it down. "I appreciate that, but it doesn't make me hate the situation any less."

"You hate that our parents are together?" Her bottom lip quivers.

I find her eyes and quickly look away.

"They seem good together," Shae urges.

"I've never seen Tara happier," Preston adds.

I swivel away from him on the seat. I know I allowed him to be buffer, but I don't need him butting in right now.

"Sorry," Shae whispers, "I know this is all weird. Us randomly meeting and then finding out our parents are together."

"My dad was gone for ages." I pick at the slightly chipped wooden table top. "I was waiting for him to come home. He stopped responding to my texts, but apparently he had time to visit your family."

"I..." she stammers. "I don't know what to say."

My arms fold around my torso and I hunch forward. "There's nothing to say. It happened. He picked you over me."

"*Charli*," Shae says, leaning forward. "How could he say that? He loves you and your sister more than anything."

Preston rubs my shoulder, and I bump him off. I eye Shae. "No. He shouldn't have left us."

"I'm sorry," she says. "I know I haven't seen this from your perspective."

I groan and straighten up in my seat. "I'm not blaming you."

She raises an eyebrow. "You sure."

I frown and nod. "Truly. I know you're not the reason he left us. I'm just upset he did."

"I hope you and your dad can sort things out," Shae says. "And I hope things can be ok between our families."

Preston edges closer to me. "You all right?"

I push for a smile. "Thanks for bringing us together." I stand up. "I should be going."

Shae stands. "You don't have to go."

"It's not you," I say, stepping backwards. "It's been an exhausting day."

Shae steps in front of me. "I am glad we talked. I really hope to see you at dinner sometime."

I nod but don't give her an answer.

"Let me walk you out," Preston says.

Once we're on the sidewalk Preston says, "It had some rocky

moments, but I hope you're glad you talked things out."

"Yeah, I needed answers." I rub my heart. "And to get some things off my chest."

Preston takes my hand and I study the green in his eyes. The back of his hand strokes my cheek. It tingles and I shiver.

He whispers, "You know I'm always here for you."

I gulp and need his face not to be so close.

He continues with, "You are really special, and I want to be around you all the time."

His face edges closer and his lips graze mine.

I pull back. "*Arrh.*"

Preston's hands shoot up. "I'm sorry."

I smooth over my hair and shake my head. "It's ok. It just that... maybe I misunderstood—"

"*Shit.* No, sorry, I shouldn't have done that," he apologises. "Sorry. I don't know why I did that."

I shrink. "It's ok. We're friends, right?"

Preston smiles. "Friends."

"Travis and I," I awkwardly start, "we're still fresh, you know, and..."

"Charli, seriously, it's ok. You don't have to explain."

"Well..." I pivot away from him. "I'd better get home."

"Yeah. I'll be seeing ya," Preston stammers. "Ok."

"Ok," I say, walking away. "Bye."

"I love you too."

He loves her?

"We saw him a couple of times over the summer."

He never saw us.

I drop my pen when my grip is so fierce it burns. I plant my elbows on my desk and lower my head to my hands. It's two-thirty in the morning and sleep is the last thing on my mind. My laptop is a collage of Photoshop, Word docs, and Google searches. Busying myself by flipping between assignments isn't as successful as it normally is.

I don't know who my dad is. I don't know what he wants.

From me.

I don't know what he wants from me.

Inside his head,
Scramble of mistaken words,
Riddles unable to shed,
As cuckoo as the birds.

I return to my English assignment. I know good grades get his attention. That is never going to change. I know keeping at the top of my classes will distract him from the Tara Clan. I can't lose to them.

But it's getting so hard.

Preston pushes his way in my brain, and I need him out ASAP. Yeah, ok, maybe I used him... but I just wanted someone to listen. I rub my temples with ample pressure. Now I have that awkward mess added to my list of problems.

I click on the last tab of my browser, a link to 'focus pills.' The ingredient list is hard to understand, but the side effects of heightened mental clarity and staying alert for more hours in the day, make me *add to cart*. It has to help with the all-nighters I'm pulling. Without questioning it further, I finalise the purchase.

A dagger to the heart,
Unaware of grief you cause,
Keeping at an upstart,
Praying for your applause.

21

Brittany

"Mum, can you look at my math homework?" Charli asks, sitting across from me in the breakfast nook. "I can't work out what I'm doing wrong."

Mum leans over her, forehead creasing. "Don't know how much help I'll be, coffee hasn't kicked in yet."

Charli is working on an algebraic equation, like, the easiest part of maths. It's all patterns, and patterns are my thing. I peer over her book and tap the equation. "You haven't divided both sides. You need to divide by four on this side and then minus seven from nine times X, and then you can find X."

Mum and Charli stare at me like I'm a new-found discovery.

I pick up my coffee and hold it close to my chin. "What? It's not hard."

Mum laughs to herself as she walks away. "*Ha*, and she did it upside-down."

My phone buzzes on the table.

I down the rest of my coffee and bolt to the front door. I say goodbye to Sophia when I almost knock her over in the foyer.

Bryce waves at me by the car and Amy is in the driver's seat. I run and leap into his arms.

"Good morning, gorgeous," he says, nuzzling his face into my hair.

"Good morning."

I want so badly to kiss him, but Amy's eyes are burning holes in us. Just hold on, Brittany. Hold it until you're in the school gates.

At school Bryce holds me tight in the doorway of my homeroom until he's threatened with detention. Even though we will be together first period in Lab A, we still can't bear to be apart.

Love.

Love is powerful.

In the lab Bryce takes my hands as I sit on a stool at his bench. We joke about how much time has passed since we were last together. We're ridiculous. I ask Bryce which part of the class assignment he is up to when Rikki stands over me, grimacing.

"You're on my seat," she huffs.

"I was thinking you could sit with Will," I reply. "He could really use the extra help and you would enjoy how much smarter he makes you feel."

Rikki rolls her eyes. "Seriously, move."

"Miss Matthews," Mrs Fields calls from the front of the class. "Your station, please."

"But," Bryce starts, but the look Mrs Fields shoots back gets me right off my seat.

I squeeze Bryce's hand, kiss his cheek and whisper, "I'll find an excuse to come back."

His smile is so cheeky-cute that walking away is nearly impossible.

"Check it out," Will says excitedly as I sit next to him. He slides his workbook in front of me. "Kellie finished all my homework."

I squint at him. "What are you doing?"

"What?"

"With Kellie. What are you doing?"

Will smirks. "Want all the dirty details do ya, Matty?"

I gag, plant a hand in his face and shake my head furiously.

We've moved onto chemistry now, and Mrs Fields instructs us on setting up today's experiment. I hope Will's even half paying attention because Bryce is looking at me and all I can register is how much I want to taste those lips again. Since the lingerie store thoughts of Bryce and me taking the next step won't leave my head. We love each other so it makes sense, but it is so mega.

Do I have to do some kind of striptease to show him my lingerie? Do I have to find the right playlist? And, *ohmigawd*, is it gonna hurt? I've heard it hurts.

And there's blood?

"Ok everyone, please gather the equipment needed for today's lesson," Mrs Fields says.

Eep. I turn to Will. "What do we get?"

"Huh?"

"Seriously?"

Will laughs. "You don't know either."

I groan, sliding off my stool to dawdle to the cupboards where beakers, Bunsen burners, and other utensils are kept.

"Hey," Bryce says, pushing past people and wrapping his arms around me.

I giggle as I try to walk with him hugging me. He kisses behind my ear and immediately I want everyone to leave.

"*Naw*, aren't you two just the cutest," Will mocks us in a funny voice.

Bryce hugs me tighter and says to Will, "Yes, yes we are."

"Bryce?" Rikki grunts, passing us with a tray of equipment.

While I love the hint of jealousy in her eyes when Bryce doesn't pay her attention, it still kills me Rikki is partnered with my boyfriend. Bryce lets go of me and follows Rikki. I pout as I follow Will to gather our equipment.

As Will and I walk to our station, Rikki passes us to grab another item from the equipment cupboard.

I just can't help myself. I have to say it.

I sidle up to Rikki, place a hand on her shoulder, and whisper *kinda* loud, "Sorry you have to see Bryce and me together. It's gotta be rough."

Rikki recoils and screws up her face with disgust. "What are you on about?"

"I know you had a thing for Bryce."

Rikki bursts into laughter. "What? No, I didn't. Where did you get that from?"

I pull my hand away from her, pursing my lips.

"Oh, *pah*-lease," she mocks me. "Whatever you think is going on, it's all in that pretty head of yours. Bryce is an easy partner because he listens. That is all I want. Someone who listens to me and doesn't bring my grades down."

Rikki moves onto to the cupboard and I turn on my heels, exhaling. I creep to my station, shaking off the encounter.

We start the experiment and it's such a tease that Bryce is so close. I roll my eyes at Rikki beside him. I sneak down the aisle while Mrs Fields is at Simon and Heather's bench.

I slide behind Bryce and tap his shoulder. "Hey there."

He spins around and greets me with a smile. His hands cup my waist. "Hey, what you doin?"

"Can't a girl say hi?"

"Sure, she can," he says and brushes his nose against mine.

My hands nestle under his jaw and I kiss him slow. I open my mouth and push against him, and for a moment I forget we are in a classroom.

"Miss Matthews!" Mrs Fields snaps.

Bryce and I break apart and all my limbs begin to shake. Wolf whistles and laughter erupt from the benches.

"Back to your bench, Brittany," Mrs Fields orders. "One more second away from it, and its detention."

Bryce squeezes my hand and we separate. I walk back to a smirking Will doing a slow clap. Usually all this would make me die inside, yet I can't stop thinking just how much I want that boy.

#

"You two are actually going to have sex?" Meah deadpans, squeezing the life out of two of my teddy bears.

I slide across the bed to rescue them. "Mr Bear and Ginger didn't do anything wrong. Let the hostages go."

Meah lets go of the bears and crawls to sitting. "This is major, Brit."

I move to my open wardrobe. "I know." I pull out the bag from the lingerie store. "Do you want to see it?"

"Is this the one Chloe picked out?"

I nod and drape the lingerie over my body.

"Holy *ba-geezus*," Meah shrieks, bouncing on my bed. "That is so freakin *hawt*."

I bite my lip as my cheeks flush. "I also bought these." I pull out red slingback, peep toes with black lace overlay.

"Damn. They are gorgeous." Meah gets up and takes the shoes from me. "So, what, you're going to take these and wear them in the bedroom?"

"No, I'll have a dress to match the shoes and have the lingerie underneath. That's ok, right?"

Meah shrugs. "I guess?"

I picture Bryce's face and drop to the ground. "I can't wait."

"D'you think it hurts as bad as they say?"

I cross my legs instinctively. "Chloe didn't say."

"It can't hurt that bad..."

"Can it?"

We stare at each other and then whip out our phones for Dr Google to tell us more.

"Aw, Brit, you look super cute," Fiona says as Bryce and I walk into Chloe's house.

Cute wasn't exactly what I was going for, however I say, "Thanks, so do you."

Fiona drapes herself over Naveen and I'm caught between *I-shouldn't-look* and *I-can't-look-away*. Naveen tosses two cans at Bryce who catches them just in time. Bryce hands one to me. *Gin, lime and soda.* That'll do it.

As Bryce and I walk further into the party I smooth down my little black dress hoping to calm my nerves. All week I've tried telling myself it's not a big deal... but tonight is a massive deal.

Our.

First.

Time.

We put our assigned gifts on the large table with the rest and I notice Bryce go for his phone. My chest constricts. He told me his mum's mood has been up and down and for two days she didn't get out of bed. I know home plays on his mind, but I can't let it win. Not tonight.

When his phone slips out of his pocket, I lunge for it. I whack it out of his hand and lose grip on the icy can of gin. The phone and the gin somersaults in the air. The can smacks Lucas Rivers on the back and crashes onto the hardwood floor, liquid spilling and pooling on the floor.

Lucas picks up the can and yells over the music, "Someone get a mop or something. *Shit*."

"What was that?" Bryce asks me, picking up his phone.

I teeter on my heels as my mind whirs for an excuse. "Ah, um, I dunno... Guess I lost my balance."

Bryce eyes me like he half believes me and slips his phone in his pocket. I boast a proud yet small smile.

Cheers fill the room as heads whip towards the staircase. Chloe sashays down in a strapless, white cocktail dress and silver, snakeskin stilettos. Her hand fans over her heart while a mask of surprise illuminates her face. *Surprise?* You organised the party, Chloe.

She hugs and kisses Kimmy and Fiona at the bottom of the staircase and starts her rounds. As she gets closer my posture gets straighter and I tussle my hair.

Chloe's eyes focus on Bryce. She bounces on the balls of her feet, wraps her arms around his neck, nuzzling her face close to his. "Aw, Brycey, thanks for coming."

"Of course. Happy Birthday, Chloe."

I fixate on his hand pressed against the bare skin below her shoulder blades.

Chloe pulls out of the hug and smiles at me with oodles of surprise. "Hey Brit."

Why is she staring at me like she's shocked I'm here?

I embrace her with a kiss on the cheek. "Happy birthday. You look gorgeous."

"Thanks, hun."

She gives me a firm pat on the back and moves onto more guests.

That was weird.

"Brittany." Meah storms towards me. "We need to talk."

"Now?"

She grabs my arm and pulls me to the other side of the room.

"Have you seen what Fiona is doing?" she asks, puffing her reddening cheeks.

"What?"

"With Naveen!"

"What? What are they doing?"

"She's been on his lap all night when she knows I like him."

"C'mon, Meah, the night has only just begun."

"No, nah-uh, this means war."

"*Whoah.*" I tug her back. "Do not go crazy chick on me. I can't be wrangling you tonight."

"Oh, so it's all about you tonight, is it? You're the only one that matters?"

I roll my eyes and step away from her. "That's not what I meant."

Meah sidesteps past me. "Excuse me. I have a party to be getting to."

I shake it off and walk towards Bryce. He's with Will and Madison, and that damn phone is in his hand.

"Aw," Madi says, linking our arms together. "Have you seen what ya boy did? There's the cutest effing photo of the two of you as his phone's wallpaper."

I bite my lip and nod.

Bryce eyes me, his smile is embarrassed yet cheeky.

Will hovers over me and leans his body weight on my shoulder. "*Naw*, Matty, are you two in loveskis?"

I suck in air and feel this strange tension, like a big secret is being dug up.

Madison gasps and points at us. "Look at their faces! They are L-words for each other."

Bryce laughs and pulls me away from Will. "Would you two just leave us alone?"

Will slings an arm around Madi as they walk away. "Watson, my dear girl, what mystery shall we uncover next?"

Bryce kisses my forehead and lets out a whisper of a laugh. "Those two."

"So nosey."

"Wanna dance, Britty?"

I take his hands and nod like my head might pop off.

I'm really wishing my drink hadn't gone flying, I could use the liquid courage. With my back against him, I grind up and down. I pull his hands across my centre. His breath patters against my hair as his chin rests on my shoulder. It's happiness in his warmth, yet I feel on display in the middle of the living room. He spins me round and I'm met with his lips. Everything feels right when he holds me.

After a few songs I excuse myself for the bathroom. When I walk back into the living room Kimberley marches towards me and grabs my arm. "Come with me."

"Ok?" I say, already dragged away.

Kimberley leads me up the stairs and across the hall. She opens a bedroom door and says, "This is Chloe's parents' room. Its lux and perfect for first-timers. Chloe wanted me to make sure you and Bryce got it."

I gasp, hands over my heart. The bedroom is huge with chic, glitzy furniture. It's too much.

"Sean is getting Bryce," she says, shoving me in the room. "Get ready."

I sit on the edge of the bed, my nerves scattering.

"There are condoms in the top drawer."

She slides open the drawer and I see the wrappers arranged in a ceramic bowl. I scrunch the bedding. My heart beats with the thud of a basketball hitting the court.

Kimmy winks at me and leaves the room.

This is it. I stand up and hug my waist.

What do I do now?

Strip off my dress?

My stomach knots.

Lie on the bed? Strike a pose?

I'm so queasy.

Voices rampage up the hall and the door flings open. My heart hammers as Jace and Sean hurl Bryce into the room. I'm ready to puke as they laugh and high five each other and close the door on us.

Noises outside the room makes this all so wrong. I hate that everyone is expecting something to happen in here. I hate that this is an orchestrated plan by someone other than the two of us.

"What's going on?" Confusion wavers his voice as he takes a step towards me.

I bite my lip and sit on the bed. My body is rigid. I force a smile and pat the space beside me.

Bryce sits next to me and places a hand on my thigh. "You need to talk or something?"

I stare straight ahead.

Talk?

Deep breath.

No, I don't need to talk.

Just do it, Brittany.

I close my eyes.

DO IT.

My hands glide into his hair and my lips suction to his. He holds onto me without pulling me close. I paw at him and climb onto his lap without breaking our lips apart. He grabs onto my hips and I push him backwards.

I tease his bottom lip and move down his neck. He takes my wrist and says, "What are we doing?"

My hands run down his chest as I kiss his collarbone. I get woozy in the good way from his cologne.

My hands slide up his shirt and in an instant Bryce pulls us up to sitting. "Britty, hold up."

"What?"

"What are we rushing for?"

My thighs hug him as his body heat sends me into a shiver.

He rubs my arms. "Babe, you're shaking. We don't have to do this right now."

"What do you mean?"

"I love you, but we don't need to do anything we're not ready for."

I swallow hard. "You don't want to be with me?"

He holds me against his body. "Of course, I do. But we are already together."

"We could do..."

He pulls away slightly, pushes the hair away from my face, and says, "Not now."

We stare at each other for what feels like eternity, and then I slide off him. The gap between us is a galaxy.

He lays his hand over mine. "You wanna get outta here? Wouldn't you prefer to dance?"

My gut and my heart flip on opposite loops. I don't know what to say to him, so I say nothing. I force a smile and nod, and he leads me by the hand out of the bedroom. Adrenaline courses through my veins as I relive the moment I straddled him. It was all stopped in a matter of minutes.

What even happened?

The party is so jam-packed I barely recognise faces. The overhead lights are off and the disco lights spins. Voices warp with the undercurrent of the dub beat. Bryce slides his arms around me, and I lean into his chest, burying my face to hide my frown. He makes circles on my back as his heart races.

I'm glad it's so noisy. I have nothing to say to him.

The party is rowdy, and people bump into us left and right. A drink spills on my leg and someone elbows the back of my head.

Bryce checks his phone. He shows it to me and says, "I've got three missed calls from Dad. I'm gonna go outside and call him back."

I step back and huff. "Fine."

"I'll be right back."

As Bryce leaves, I find a space on the wall and slam myself against it.

I give up.

On tippy-toes, I scan the room for Meah. I spot her with Madison, laughing by a group of boys. Naveen being one. I'll never get her attention.

I spend five minutes picking at my nail polish until Bryce returns. He's frowning which can only be a bad sign.

"Sorry, I have to go."

"Why?"

"I need to be home."

I squeeze his hands. "Can't you stay with me?"

"Don't be mad at me. You know why I have to go. You'll have fun here anyways."

My eyes prick. "I don't want you to go."

"I don't want to go. Believe me."

"You said going home last time was a mistake."

"It's different this time."

I try to smile. It doesn't happen.

He kisses me gently. "I'll miss you."

I nod.

"I'll text you later," he says stepping back.

I don't look at him. "Bye."

I scrunch my eyes closed and hold my breath until the welling goes away. It works and I take in the crowd. I squint and rapidly grow wide-eyed. Meah and Fiona are clawing at each other. Their high-pitched squeals ring over the music. I bust through the crowd and try to break the two apart. Meah hurls herself at Fiona, who ducks out of the way, leaving me in the firing line. Meah tackles me to the ground.

Oof!

"Get a grip, girls," Jace says, pulling Meah off me.

Meah takes off into the crowd and Jace hovers over me with his hand out. He pulls me up and asks me if I'm ok. I tell him I need a drink, stat.

With drink in hand, I find a spot on the floor and don't intend to move until it's empty.

"What's a pretty girl doing sitting all alone?" a boy asks, sitting next to me when I'm on... I've lost count of what number drink this is.

I take another sip to ignore him.

"I'm Damien," he says. "Chloe's brother."

I lower the drink. "Oh. Hi."

"So, what's wrong?"

"Whaddaya mean?"

"Well, your outfit says, 'I came here to party,' yet you're sitting here on your own."

"Not in the mood, I guess."

"Anything I can do to help?" he asks, sliding closer.

I take another sip and the can is empty. I plonk it down as my head wobbles. All the lights are swishy.

"Need another drink?" he offers.

I rest my head against the wall and shut my eyes. My lips are numb and I'm floating.

"What's your name?"

I blink my eyes open and have trouble finding his face. "Brittany."

"Brittany, you wanna try walking and maybe drinking some water?"

I frown and shake my head. "I'm sleepy."

"Sleeping here would be a really bad decision." He pulls me up to standing. "C'mon, let's get outta this room."

He leads me out and I stumble like a baby giraffe. My eyes close as we walk and open wide when a rush of cold hits me.

We are outside and Damien cloaks his arms around me.

"Sorry, you needed sobering up," he says, smiling.

"It's so cold." My teeth chatter.

"You're lucky you're drunk. You're only feeling half of it."

I flop my thumping head onto his chest. He holds me up and I like how strong he is. He lifts my chin and he smiles.

"How you doing, Brittany?"

I nod. "Ok."

His smile is so friendly that I grin at him. His face moves closer until his lips are on mine. I don't kiss back and it takes too long for me to work out what to do.

He pulls back. "Was that ok?"

I blink at him, unable to form words.

He pulls me in close and kisses me again. My forehead scrunches and my brain still can't work. I open my mouth and kiss him back.

BLACK.

My eyes spring open. Sunlight strains into the room and I stretch out of the ball I was sleeping in. I pull myself up but fall back against the pillow as my head thumps. I rub my temples as I turn over.

I gasp at the shirtless male body lying beside me. His back is to me and I whisper, "Bryce?"

I creep next to him and peer over at his face. I scamper away, pulling the sheet around me.

I'm in Damien's bed.

With Damien.

I peer under the sheet and I'm only wearing my lacey black bra and panties. The ones for my special night with Bryce.

What am I doing here? What happened?

I spy my phone on the bedside table and open the camera. Mega panda eyes. I lick my finger and rub under each eye. Good enough.

I slip out of the bed and search the floor for my dress. Where the hell is it? My head pounds from last night's drinks. I creep around the room with no luck.

I need out of this room. Out of this house.

I pick up a hoody and put it on. It's oversized enough to cover my bum. I tiptoe to the door and open it gently. In the hall, I jump at Sean lying on the floor. He lazy smiles, and then closes his eyes. *Phew*. I don't want to get caught being in this room. *Geez*, why was I in this room? *Ouch*, my head. I make my way downstairs and out the front door.

It's a slow trudge to my house. A howling wind rages off the ocean. The cement path is rough under my bare feet and I shiver against the cold. My house is a few streets away and I take a short cut via the beach. The softness of the sand is a welcomed change.

My feet drag towards the water and I collapse. The tide rushes over me, soaking the hoody, and the sea salt calms my nerves. The coldness numbs my headache and I block out all of my hideous questioning thoughts.

22

Charli

"I'm so, so, so sorry about that awkward encounter last weekend," Preston babbles when we meet at the mall. "I wanted to make sure we're cool."

"Don't sweat it. I'm cool with forgetting it even happened."

"Good, because I didn't want to ruin the friendship we've started. Didn't mean to jump the gun on anything."

"Really, it's fine."

"Maybe I just think about you too much. In my head we were at a place where it was ok to kiss you."

My skin crawls. I clear my throat and hurry my walk. "I need some new stationery for school. Hope you don't mind following me on my errands."

"Sure. I'm the one who pestered you to hang out. I need to make amends for being a doofus."

He needs to stop talking about it already.

We wind through the Sunday morning crowd at a brisk pace before being halted by a pack of old ladies. They dawdle, taking up the walkway, so we are forced to zombie-march behind them.

"Did you hear GiGi and Travis at the party last night?" A girl by the coffee stand says.

"*Ohmigawd*, you could hear them?" another girl replies.

"That moaning and bed-rocking was so loud."

I don't want to listen. I don't want to keep my eyes on them. But I can't stop.

"Hey, isn't that the girl who he dumped to be with GiGi?"

I snap my gaze away, cheeks warming.

"I heard she was shit in bed."

"He really traded up."

My face overheats so much that I don't notice oncoming people. I trip as I try to get out of the way and crash land to the ground.

"Shit, Charli, you ok?" Preston asks as my satchel bag flies off my shoulder and spills on the ground.

I groan as people walk over my papers, books, and me. "I'm fine," I mumble as I scoot to grab my belongings.

Preston kneels beside me to help. As I stuff things into my bag, he says, "Hey, this is really good."

I look up as he flips through my notebook. "*Don't.*" I lunge and snatch the book.

He lifts his hands up in surrender.

I hug the book. "It's just... I don't share this with anyone."

Preston smiles. "I didn't know you were a poet."

"I dunno. I wouldn't say I am."

"You have a book full of poems. I think you're a poet."

"Can we drop it, please?"

"You should share your work. I think people would like it."

I shake my head violently. "It's just for me."

"Sorry. Just looks like you have a talent."

I grunt. "Forget you saw it, ok?"

"Ok, I will," he says, handing me another book.

I shove everything into the bag and stand up. "Thanks."

We walk in silence. Great, more awkwardness. I knew today would be awkward, but I didn't know we'd find another layer to add. I agreed to meet because I felt bad that I'd misled him, but maybe I should have just let it be.

Preston pulls out his phone and smirks at the screen. "Just Shae wanting to know what I'm up to." He replies to the text, and then says, "She says your dad is at her house."

I stop mid-step. "My dad?"

"She said you should stop by. I can drive you over if you want?"

I swallow the yuck creeping up my throat. "I dunno. I had a bad moment with my dad."

"You can make up."

I pull my curls to the side and purse my lips. He said he was working too much to leave the house. Why is he there? Why is he still with her?

He loves her...

Gah. He does not love her. I'll make him see.

"Ok. Can we get my stationery and then go?"

"Of course."

Preston pulls up at Tara's house behind my dad's car. As we walk up to the house Dad opens the front door. He smiles like he's been expecting us all day. A shyness takes over me as I smile back.

Dad leads us into the house which fills with piano music. He taps a finger to his lips and nods for us to follow him. We walk into the living room where Shae reads on the couch. She beams at us, leaping up. Dad nods to the back corner where Nick is playing the piano.

I don't know much about the piano, but the song he's playing sounds classical and professional.

"Hi Preston," Alyssa yells from the floor, waving.

The music stops and Nick swings around. "Oh hey, when'd you guys get here?"

"Just now," Dad says. "I knew you'd stop if you heard them and I wanted Charli to hear you play."

Nick smiles and says, "I can play something for you if you want."

"Oh, it's ok," I reply. "Whatever you were just playing sounded nice."

Nick swats a hand and says, "That was Mozart's sonata number ten. I have to practice for my next piano exam. I think everyone is getting sick of hearing it."

"Yes," Alyssa grumbles from the corner.

"So good to see you again, Charli," Shae says. "So soon."

"So soon?" Tara's singsong voice enters the room before she does.

"We had coffee together," Shae tells her mum. I'm thankful she doesn't elaborate further.

Dad slings an arm around me. "So good to see you kids getting along."

I clear my throat and whisper to him, "Dad, can I talk to you, um, in private?"

Dad looks at Preston and me. "Did you two meet through Shae?"

I raise an eyebrow. "You two know each other?"

"Preston practically lives here," Tara says. She looks into the hall and smiles. "Same as this guy. No one can visit our house without meeting Preston and Zach."

Zach steps into the living room. He stands tall with a flat-brimmed hat shadowing his face. He smiles and waves. "Hey."

There's a tug on my pants leg as Alyssa stands behind me. She holds up a colourful drawing. "I drew this."

I crouch to her level. "Oh wow. That's really good. Are you an artist?"

Alyssa pushes out her stomach and starts giggling.

"Charli's an artist too," Dad says to Alyssa. "We've been told her photograph is going to be on display at the art gallery."

Tara claps her hands. "Oh, Charli, that's wonderful."

"Wow, that's awesome," Preston says. "When is that?"

Zach walks past me and leans against Nick's piano, and I smile at him for a getaway from the attention. "Sorry, Zach was it?"

"Sup," he replies, grinning.

"Zach is the drummer in Nick's band," Shae explains.

I decide to be friendly to Nick. "How long have played piano for?"

"Long time. Like, eight or something years. Mum makes me keep it up," he says, tapping the keys. "I prefer guitar."

"That's what he plays in our band," Zach adds.

"This is Rob's daughter," Nick says to Zach.

"Charli," I add. "What sort of music does your band play?"

"Classic rock and alt rock," Zach replies.

"Sometimes I wish I had learnt to play an instrument," Shae says. "But the sheet music looked like gibberish to me."

"Lunch is almost ready," Tara says. "Charli, I hope you are up for roast beef and veggies."

"Tara always puts on the most amazing Sunday roasts," Preston says.

"Pres always talks up my cooking."   Tara squeezes him in a hug. "It's a tradition I took on from my mother to have a roast slow-cooking whilst we're at church."

I take in Shae and Nick's conservative clothing as they leave the room. Church? That's so weird. We've never had religion in our home, and now Dad is dating a religious woman?

As everyone follows Tara to the kitchen, I grab onto Dad's arm and motion to the side.

Dad's face falls and we move towards the bedrooms. "Pumpkin, I'm sorry for what happened at the forest. I left abruptly and I probably should have stayed and talked things through."

"No, but Dad—"

"I was putting work first again," Dad says, running his hands through his hair. "That's why I made time for lunch today. Tara was right. I need to think of others not just my paperwork."

"*Tara* was right?"

"Being a workaholic started the rift in my marriage, and I can't let that happen again."

"But—"

Dad wraps his arms around me. "Oh, kiddo. Sorry if you felt like you haven't seen enough of me. I liked cycling with you. We need to pencil that in more often."

He lets me go and all I can manage is, "Sure."

"How's debate going?" he asks as we walk into the kitchen.

"Good. Maybe next time I'm at your apartment we could go over some tactics?"

"I'd be delighted."

Preston pipes up, "You're good at public speaking aren't you, Tara?"

Tara cuts away at a hunk of beef. "When I have to."

"Maybe you could show Charli some of your moves," Preston says.

"You can win an argument," my dad jokes.

"I bet Charli and Tara have loads in common," Preston adds.

My eyes beg to roll. Seriously, dude?

"Well I hope so," Tara says, "with both of Rob's girls. Everyone hungry?"

Nick and Zach sit up on the kitchen bench and Tara says, "The rest of us can cosy in around the table."

Tara and Shae plate our food when a rapid succession of knocks rattle the kitchen door. The door swings open a man steps in from the backyard.

"Daddy!" Alyssa squeals, running towards the man.

The man scoops Alyssa up. "Hiya, squirt."

Nick slips off the kitchen bench, eyes wide and vying for attention.

"Mason, this isn't a great time," Tara says to the man. "We're about to sit down to lunch."

Mason huffs. "Settle down, Tara. I've just come over to give something to Alyssa."

He carries Alyssa out of the kitchen and Tara, now tense, returns to serving. Nick fidgets in place, head tilted towards the doorway.

Shae places two plates on the dining table and I ask her, "How often do you guys go to your dad's?"

Her nose wrinkles. "Mason? No, he's only Alyssa's dad."

"Oh," I say, trying to process that. "Sorry, what?"

"Mason lived with us for a long time, but mine and Nick's dad hasn't been around for years."

"Years?"

She nods, placing a finger to her lips. "We don't really talk about it in front of Nick."

"How could you let me go on and on about my dad when yours isn't even in the picture?"

"You seemed like you needed it."

I slump in the chair, rubbing my punched heart. I sigh and look at my dad. I shouldn't be mad at him. At least he's in Sanford with no signs of making a run for it. I don't like seeing him in this house, but I do like seeing him.

"Dad," I whisper. He eyes me. "Can I stay over at your place tonight?"

He brightens. "Of course. If it's ok with your mother."

I grin. It hurts my cheeks, but I'm happy.

"Do you cook with your mum, Charli?" Shae asks as we begin eating.

A laugh slips out of me before I can hold it back. "Ah, Mum doesn't cook."

Dad crosses his arms and chortles. "And if she did, I doubt you'd have been interested, Pumpkin."

"Maybe if you whipped out a frying pan I would have been interested," I say.

He smiles. "Good thing we had Sophia to save us from my bad cooking."

"Who's Sophia?" Shae asks.

"Our housekeeper," I say.

Silence sweeps the kitchen as everyone deadpans me. The silence breaks when Zach cracks up, slapping his thigh.

Tara shakes her head and giggles. "You guys sure do live differently on that side of town."

"It was a necessity," Dad says. "With Julie and me working around the clock, we needed someone to look after the girls and maintain the house."

"You could have worked around it though," Shae says, gesturing with her fork. "Mum worked and raised three kids by herself."

"Shae, please," Tara hisses. "And that's not fair. We had Granddad and Nan here for quite a few years."

Shae shrugs and goes back to eating.

Alyssa and her dad burst into the kitchen with arms spread and making aeroplane sounds.

"Mason," Tara huffs, "seriously, we are eating."

"Don't fret, Tara," Mason replies, "I'm on my way out."

"No, Daddy, don't go," Alyssa squeals, hugging Mason's leg.

"Squirt, let go," Mason says to his daughter.

Tara's posture stiffens. "*Alyssa*."

"I want to go with Dad!" Alyssa cries.

I frown, feeling for the little girl.

"It's no problem for me to take her," Mason says and Alyssa squeaks with joy, jumping into his arms.

"Not today," Tara argues, getting up.

Mason takes in the room. "This place is crowded enough. I'll bring her back in a couple of hours."

Tara grows cross but Nick cuts in, saying, "Let her go, Mum."

Tara's tension releases when she turns to her melancholy son. She gives in and the two leave through the back door.

We eat in silence until Preston says to Tara and Shae, "Well, maybe the two of you should invite Charli over to cook with you. Like, teach her."

"What a great idea," Tara beams, forgetting she was mad. "Bonding moment."

I eye Preston, willing him to shut his mouth.

"I'm sure we could make a cook outta you," Shae says, giving me a nudge. "And Brittany. Where is she?"

"Sick," I say quickly. I saw her come home this morning looking ghoulish and sopping wet. When I left the house she was puking in the toilet. I hate that she's partying so recklessly. I had hoped Bryce would be a *good* influence on her.

"Oh, I hope she's better soon," Tara says, pouting.

"Bug going around school?" Dad asks.

"Maybe?" I stay clear of the subject by asking Shae, "What are you planning to study at uni?"

"Social work," she says. "I want to help kids know that even if they have a crappy start in life things can get better."

Tara eyes Shae. "You always make it sound like you had the worst childhood."

Shae huffs. "I'm not saying that. To be honest, we had a very rough start, but we were lucky to have family take us in. A lot of kids don't have that support. That's where I want to help."

I know there's got to be more to the story, but I smile and say, "That sounds really nice, Shae."

She smiles back and then we shift our attention to our plates.

"I know how you can get help on your English assignment," Preston says to Shae. "I found out today that Charli is a genius with words. She could help you write something magical."

I slam my fork down and stare at him, dumbfounded. *You said you'd forget it.*

I scrape my chair backwards and stand up. "Preston, can I talk to you for a minute."

I'm shaking but stand as tall as possible. I walk out into the hall for him to follow. He meets me in the living room, where I hope we're out of earshot.

"What do you think you're doing?"

He shifts uneasily. "Whaddaya mean?"

"*You.* Trying to make me buddy-buddy with Tara. You're going too far."

"How am I? I think you're both wonderful people who would get along. You're not opening up to her, so I thought I'd help."

"You're not helping. You can't force people into liking each other."

"Then why do you keep wanting to see me?"

I blink at him.

He groans. "Why are you still hung up on Travis?"

"What?"

"I saw you listening to those girls. You blamed him for not being into my kiss. Why are you still holding a candle to him?"

"Why are you getting in my face? It's none of your business."

"In case you forgot, Charli, I was there that night. I'm the one that saved you. I saw the terror in your eyes."

My eyes sting. I wipe them clear and storm out of the living room. Dad walks towards me in the hall and I blurt out that I must have caught what Brittany has and that I need to go home. Dad's eyes go to slits as he finds Preston in the living room. He agrees to take me to his apartment.

Lying is all they seem to do,
When they get caught up with you,
First it's all smiles,
Kisses and hugs in stockpiles,
Romance and good wishes,
Until everything switches,
With grab and take,
All the wants for their sake,
Without care of my mind,
Their ego so strong they turn blind.

"Want to talk about what happened with Preston?" Dad asks, handing me a cup of tea.

I curl up on the couch, wrapped in a blanket. "Nothing to talk about."

"I heard Travis mentioned."

"Mhmm."

"You never told me what happened there."

"Yup."

"You seemed quite smitten with him."

"I was."

"Pumpkin, I'm here to talk."

I sigh and put the teacup down on the coffee table. "Sorry, Dad. Preston really got in my face. He was annoying me."

"Yeah, he can be a bit pushy at times I've noticed."

"Can we just forget him? I don't think I'm going to see him for a while."

Dad kisses my forehead and says, "Perhaps that is for the best. I'm glad you came to Tara's anyhow."

"I'm glad I got to see you." When Dad takes a seat and scrolls through his phone, I ask, "Does it bother you Tara has had kids with two different men?"

Dad lowers his phone to look at me.

"Doesn't it seem like she won't be able to make it work with you either?"

Dad sighs. "Tara and I are fine. We've discussed all these concerns. Don't worry, I'm well aware of the skeletons in her closet."

"So there's more?" I ask and quickly take a sip of tea.

Dad frowns and turns his attention back to his phone. "I thought we talked about being rude to Tara."

My teeth grit. Just break up with her already.

That night I didn't sleep a wink. Boys wrestle to take up space in my mind, and I don't want either of them in there. I busy myself with my essay on '*Taming of the Shrew*' for English class, while flipping through articles Dad recommended for my next debate match. I wriggle in my chair, swamped by the mounting work heaped on my plate.

"You've made commitments. Stick with them."

Dad wants to see good grades. To see that I can match what he did in school... or beat it. If he could prioritise schoolwork over everything else, so can I.

My stomach twists.

But this stuff is hard work.

I rummage through my bag for a notebook, to mark down a debate tactic that takes my fancy. As I pull the notebook out, a piece of paper falls to the carpet. I pick it up and read the heading, '*Your Year Abroad!*'

I flatten the piece of paper on my desk and skim the description of the exchange program in Spain. My heart flutters with excitement at all the possibilities, and then a small chuckle escapes me. Yeah, right. Like I'd be able to fly off to Spain for a semester.

With a crack of my knuckles, I remind myself that study is priority number one. I envision myself finishing a law degree and working under Dad at his law firm. I see the enlarged smile on his face and winning over every ounce of his pride.

I move the flyer to the side and slip another two focus pills out of the container. I can't disappoint him. I swig them back with water and stay planted at my desk until sunrise.

23

Brittany

That had to be the most alcohol anyone has ever had to drink. I barely remember anything from Chloe's party after Bryce left. I don't remember going home beside the freezing cold wave that jolted me awake. How could I fall asleep near the water? I am such a loser.

What do I tell Bryce?

Do I have to tell him anything?

There's no way I'd get that drunk if he'd stayed.

Why didn't he stay?

I shiver as I remember the cold wind and dark night sky... and another guy's lips on mine.

I was in his bed.

Half-naked.

Repulsive.

I don't know what happened before I went to sleep... If I don't remember, then there is nothing to tell. Nothing happened.

Right?

I hug my waist as I dawdle up the corridor to mess. How could Bryce not want to be with me? I can't believe I straddled him, and he pushed me off. I must be the most unsexy thing he's ever seen. Yes, I wish I hadn't gotten so drunk, but I didn't want to be in my head that night. I was so, so sad when he left... verging on mad.

Charli and Kellie stand by their lockers as I walk by. Normally I'd ignore them, but with Will there, I'm unable to look away. Kellie gushes to Charli, and while overly excited she grabs onto Will and squeezes. Will's face grows a lighter shade of pale and he whips her hands off him.

As I pass, Kellie huffs and says, "What, you're embarrassed by me, Will?"

"What?" Will deflects. "Nah, it's not like that. Just, you know, PDAs... not cool."

"PDAs?" Kellie scowls. "Like we should only touch in private?"

Over my shoulder, Will sheepishly looks around at the passing student body.

Kellie grumbles and throws her hands in the air. "Don't worry, Will, you won't have the embarrassment of this nerd touching you ever again."

"Let's go, Kel," Charli says, as they storm off in the direction of the quad.

I leave Will in my dust and round a corner. Yelling and cheering send a ringing to my ears as a crowd forms a misshapen circle. It has to be a fight. I edge closer as kids race past me to get a glimpse.

"I'm just tellin you what I saw, man," Sean yells over the crowd.

"Stop talking shit about her."

My heart stops.

It's Bryce.

I force myself closer and through a gap I spy Bryce and Sean sizing each other up.

"I'm not making it up," Sean says, laughing. "She's a fucking slut."

Bryce throws a punch and socks Sean in the face. A squeaked whimper flies out of me as my hands rush to catch it. My hands press to my face as Bryce walks towards me.

"What happened at Chloe's?" Bryce asks. His hand pushes on my back to guide me to the wall. "Sean was saying some nasty stuff."

I can't look at him. I can't catch my breath.

"Brit, it's not true, is it?"

My fingers dig into my sides as I stare at my shoes.

"He said you hooked up with Chloe's brother... This is the part where you're spose to tell me it's not true."

I blurt out, "It was only a kiss."

I find his eyes bulging with shock. His mouth hangs open drawing his face out.

"I didn't mean it." I grab his hands and squeeze. "I was drunk. I was way too drunk. He kissed me and I couldn't think."

He flings my hands off and steps away from me.

"Bryce don't," I say following him. "I didn't mean it. I was drunk and it was a stupid mistake."

"So, what?" he says. "When you're drunk, you're going to forget I exist?"

"What? No!"

"I know you wanted me to stay, but you can't just move onto the next guy."

"That's not what happened."

"I thought you understood why I left."

"I did."

"Then why were you with him?"

"It wasn't like that. I barely remember any of that night."

"He said you were in his room... undressed."

Gasps erupt next to us as a bunch of ninth grade girls eavesdrop.

Bryce shakes his head, turning away from me. "I can't do this right now."

I grab his arm. "Don't go. We need to talk."

"Stop it, Brittany." He shakes me off.

Hurt coats his face and I take a step back. He strides down the corridor and vanishes around the corner. My brain malfunctions. I stand in this spot for I don't know how long until autopilot takes me to mess.

As I approach the table, Chloe stops in front of me. "Um, what do you think you're doing?"

"What?"

"You can't sit here."

I squint at her and then around at the table where everyone gawks at me like I'm an invader.

Chloe shoves me and says, "We disassociate with cheaters."

I stumble, finding my balance.

Kimberley stands by Chloe. "Go sit somewhere else."

I point to my chest and stare down Chloe. "You're calling *me* a cheat?"

Chloe snorts and slams her hands onto her hips.

"What about you and Lucas?" It just slipped out. I didn't mean to say it.

Chloe glares at me as Jace kicks out his chair and shouts, "WHAT?"

Kimberley squeezes between me and Chloe. "Yeah, Brittany. What are you on about, you filthy liar?"

It's not even worth it. I pull at my hair as I find Meah at the table. She plays dumb and acts like she doesn't know the signal to get up and leave.

I stamp my foot as my blood boils. I spin and race out of mess. Hiding in the bathroom for the rest of school is the only option.

Did this really happen?

I squirm under my blankets, crawling into a ball on my bed.

That look in Bryce's eyes. *Hurt.* I hurt him. How could I hurt him? How could I be so freakin dumb?

I swear I'm never going to touch alcohol ever again. It was a stupid, stupid mistake.

There's a knock at the door. "Brit?"

I uncover my head as the door opens and Meah creeps in.

"You ok?" Meah shakes a tub of ice-cream. "I brought rocky road."

I reef the covers over my head. "Meah. What are you doing here? Aren't you spose to act like you don't know me?"

The bed shifts as she sits by my legs.

"Chloe is gunning for you. I can't believe you said that in front of Jace. Is it even true? Chloe and Lucas?"

I contort under the sheets. "What does it matter?"

Meah tugs at the bedding. "Brit, come out."

I pull back. "No. No, I can't."

"Fine. I'll just eat the entire tub on my own."

I rub my palms over my eyes and shift up the bed. I pull the covers down and frown at her.

"So, did Bryce break up with you?" Meah asks, handing me a spoon.

I dig into the tub, ignoring the question.

"Brit?"

My eyes well. "Meah... don't."

"What? It's a simple question."

"No. Maybe. No, he didn't. Not exactly." The ice-cream melts on my tongue. "I don't know."

"How come I'm last to know you hooked up with Chloe's brother?"

"Because I was drunk and wanted to believe I hallucinated it."

"You were in his bed?"

I shove the tub at her. My face collapses in my hands. "Meah, I'm so dumb."

"You were complaining about Bryce ditching you all the time. Maybe it's a good thing you got with someone new."

My face screws up. "When did I complain?"

"When you were on one of your many gin, lime and sodas."

I groan. "How could I let Damien kiss me?" The thought of lying next to him makes me shudder.

Meah snorts. "Easy. He's a Benson."

I swipe my eyes dry. "No. I want Bryce."

"The boy rejected sex," Meah says with a mouthful of ice-cream. "Ditch him."

I flop back on the bed. "It's all such a mess. I don't understand why Bryce wanted to leave the bedroom. I have no freakin clue why I was with Damien. So gross. I'm never drinking again."

"*Pfft*. Whatever."

"I'm serious."

"So, how far did you two go?"

"Huh?"

"You and Damien," Meah says, "in his bed."

"We didn't." We did nothing... I shudder again. "I'm positive. Nothing happened."

"Ok, ok." She shoves the ice-cream in my face. "Eat more."

I wince and push it away.

"Cheer up, Brit. We have the Kings Cliff game tomorrow."

"*Ugh*. Chloe wouldn't let me sit at the table in mess, where is she going to make me sit on the bus?"

"She'll be over it by then."

I raise an eyebrow. "Meah, this is Chloe we're talking about."

"Just sit next to Bryce," Meah says. "If you still want him, tell him."

A hint of a smile curls my lips. "You're right."

Meah slides my laptop off the bedside table and scoots up beside me. "How's about an old school '*Project Runway*' binge?"

I plonk my head on her shoulder as she hits play.

"I'll get Travis to drive us to school tomorrow."

I nod. "Deal."

Meah texted this morning with a phony excuse why Travis couldn't pick me up. I can tell by her wording that Chloe got to her. *Geez*, if she keeps up the *cutting-me-out* thing today, it's going to be so awkward during the away game. They can't cut me out during cheers. Maybe I can get back in Chloe's good graces at the game?

And Bryce's.

It can't be over. Can it?

All he said is that he couldn't deal with it *right now*. Maybe we can deal now?

We will have a whole bus trip to work this out.

Charli stayed at Dad's again last night, so I convinced Sophia to drive me to school late. I tossed and turned last night with visions of Chloe and Kimmy waiting for me at the school entrance to throw harassment my way. I want to get to school as soon as the bell for homeroom sounds. Everyone can scatter as I make my way in. We leave on the bus after second period. Two classes. I have to make it through two classes.

Meah is shifty and silent as we use our sewing machines in textiles class.

"Why are you being weird?" I ask.

Her shoulders droop and she blurts out, "We couldn't drive you, ok."

"I don't care about that. You know I have Sophia."

Meah swivels her fabric, tilting her face away from me.

"Meah?"

"What?"

"Why are you giving me the cold shoulder?"

She huffs and whispers, "Chloe said I can't talk to you."

"She knows we're best friends."

"Brit, I can't be in exile with you. We'd never get back in the group. I have to side with Chloe. It's for the both of us."

I don't want to admit I'd do the same thing. "Chloe's not even in this class. We can talk."

Meah keeps her head down. "People will see and, you know, report back. She's tellin everyone not to talk to you."

"What do you mean *everyone?*"

"It's just as it sounds. Everyone."

Meah and I ride out textiles in silence. I have to keep faith she's got my back in this.

My nerves tingle as I leave for English class. Last night I typed and re-typed messages that I never sent to Bryce. I didn't know where to begin. Him not wanting to talk this through stung. We've had a night's sleep since the ugliness in the corridor. Things have to be ok. They have to be.

My heart beats triple-time as he appears at the other end of the corridor. I slow my pace, so we meet at the classroom door.

"Hi," I say, somehow out of breath.

He tenses, gripping his books close to his chest. His skin is pale and his head tilts back as if recoiling from me.

"Can we talk?" I ask.

His lips twist before he answers. "I dunno."

"Bryce, I love you."

He grips his books tighter and his cheeks grow sunken. Is he gonna hurl?

"Maybe after class," he says.

"But, Bryce—"

"Inside students," Mr Palmer says, ushering us inside.

"Bryce," I persist, but Mr Palmer pushes between us.

Bryce hurries to his desk and I trudge to mine.

We are onto Shakespeare now, which may as well be in French as it is just as difficult to understand. Bryce and I tried reading the parts of Petruchio and Katerina at *Shakes,* but resorted to going home and watching *'10 Things I Hate About You'* instead.

I drown out Mr Palmer and keep eyes on Bryce. His forehead rests in his palm most of class. He swirls his pen on a page in random doodles and I want to be inside his head. He said, maybe after class. That *maybe* has to be a mistake. We WILL work this out.

Charli watches Bryce and then pushes back on her chair. She mouths, 'what's going on?'

I roll my eyes and start doodling on my own page.

When the bell sounds for end of class, Bryce is out in a flash. Everyone seems to dawdle out of the class like, for some reason, they can't bear to leave. By the time I'm in the corridor Bryce is long gone.

I know he's gone to the changerooms to grab his gear, but there's still this unpleasant welling in my throat and eyes.

How could he not wait to talk?

I swallow hard and head to the changerooms. When I get there, the giggles and squeaks of chatter between the girls are deafening. I walk the edges to get to my gym bag. As I reach for it I'm barged from the side and slam into the wall.

"Oh, didn't see you there," Kimmy says, skipping away.

I pull myself up, straighten my uniform and rub my arm. I keep my face stony. *Don't give her the satisfaction, Brit.* I leave with my bag as my name gets passed around. Talking about me, not to me.

I head out the west wing where the bus waits in the teachers' carpark. Some of the boys are already out here, and I crane my neck for Bryce. He's not here.

I sit on the steps as more people come out towards the bus. Every part of my body tenses as I wait for him. I smell his cologne, like it's a missing part of me, and stand up.

"Bryce."

He gives me an uncertain look and keeps walking down the steps.

"Bryce."

"Not now."

I scan everyone. I don't particularly want to talk in front of all of them either, but we need to make this better.

I make my way down the steps and try to get near him.

Chloe sidesteps in front of me. "Here ya are, you dirty skank." She tosses something at me. Black material covers my face. I pull it down and it's my dress I wore to her birthday party.

"Found it on my brother's bedroom floor, ya whore," Chloe snaps.

I fold the dress as wolf whistles and laughter surround me. I find Bryce. His mouth hangs open, his eyes almost circular with shock.

He dumps his bag and escapes onto the bus.

My eyes gleam with tears and I move towards the bus.

Chloe slams my chest. "Stay away from him. He can do so much better than you."

I gasp, stumbling backward. The girls move towards the bus and I shamefully crouch to the ground, cramming my dress into my bag.

They all hate me. It's the only thing to makes sense right now.

Ohmigawd. Bryce can't hate me, can he?

A tear drops.

He hates me.

On the bus, Fiona sits next to Meah. I bite my tongue hard. Last I saw they were clawing each other's eyes out. Tayla waves to me and I almost smile, but Chloe calls out to her. Chloe orders Tayla to sit next to Madison.

I don't look for Bryce and the chance he's sitting alone. I sit at the front of the bus.

Alone.

Like the loser I am.

Almost an hour and a half later we are in Kings Cliff. Chloe and Kimberley spent the trip bringing me up in conversation as another word for something disgusting. Like, if you went to the bathroom, you'd drop a Brittany. I put on headphones to act like I wasn't listening. Nothing was playing. I needed to know exactly what was being said about me.

Our first stop is a restaurant to fuel up before the game. I get off the bus first because I'm at the front. Total loser. First I hang back so everyone goes in the restaurant before me, but I figure neither way is ideal. I head inside and a waiter shows me to a long table. I take a seat at one end, hoping everyone else will be at the other. I'm surprised when Will and Naveen sit only a few seats down. Others sit at the opposite end, which gives me time to breathe.

Bryce sits near Will and my heart palpitates.

I'm glad when food arrives. I'm nowhere near hungry, yet I busy myself with eating, nonetheless.

"How come you're not eating?" Naveen asks. He taps the table by Bryce's plate.

Bryce's eyes are closed as he rubs his forehead.

"Hey, man." Will pushes Bryce's plate closer to him. "We got a big game. Eat up."

Bryce groans, opens his eyes and picks up a fork. "Fine."

"You look like a ghost, man," Naveen says.

Bryce ignores him, hurrying to finish his plate.

I refocus on my food, stabbing at my salad.

When I'm almost finished, a screech grabs my attention. It's Bryce backing his chair. He gets up and leaves. My chance. I *need* to talk to him.

I get up to leave and walk as fast as I can so Chloe can't yell at me. In the foyer he disappears into the bathroom. I pace a small section of carpet with my arms folded. I don't know where to begin, but we will be alone.

I'm scared he will be mad I'm waiting for him. What else can I do? I clutch my elbows as he seems to be taking a long time. I creep towards the bathroom but stop dead.

I gulp. I think I hear vomiting.

"Matthews," Ms Harvey calls.

I jump. My cheeks burning.

"Time to get on the bus," she says.

I fan my face and follow her out. I stop by Will and Naveen. Sean walks up to them and asks where Chloe and Jace are.

Naveen sniggers. "Round the corner. Think Chloe's giving Jace a BJ."

"Oh, a Brit Job?" Sean smirks.

Will kicks Sean behind the knee.

Sean drops to the ground. "*Ow.* We got a game, arsehole!"

The grin on Will's face makes me tingle with hope.

Bryce comes out of the restaurant, the back of his hand brushing below his lower lip.

"Shit, BK," Naveen says. "How do you look worse?"

Bryce drops his hand and rolls his eyes.

"Are you—" I say, walking towards Bryce, but Will grabs me and walks me towards the bus. "I was just going to ask if he's ok," I say, wriggling in his arms.

"Sorry, Matty, I'm on strict instructions to not let you near him."

I groan. "You're listening to Chloe, too?"

He shakes his head. "Not Chloe. Him."

My jaw drops. We walk onto the bus and I plonk on the front seat. He wants me kept away from him? He hates me that much?

I swallow whatever leapt from my stomach and sit as rigid as possible. He walks onto the bus, and I can't help it, I clutch his hand.

Bryce shakes me off. "Stop."

He walks past and I feel punched in the gut.

Stop?

Once changed into my cheer uniform, I make my way down to the footy field. One of my skirt pleats keeps blowing out. I fidget with it, trying to smooth it over.

"Why are you feeling up your arse?" Madison asks behind me.

"My skirt's being weird. It's not sitting right."

"Show me." I move my hand. "Brit, its fine. Stop being such a worrywart."

Madison walks on ahead, and I cross my fingers the cheer routines won't be a complete disaster. I mean, she was talking to me, right.

"Isn't this great," Meah says, skipping past me. "I'm still allowed to hang around them. I don't need you anymore."

"Need me?"

She snorts. "*Gawd*, Brit. Ya know what I mean."

Meah skips away and I shake her off. The boys warm up on the field and Ms Harvey gets us to stretch on the sidelines. As I sit and stretch towards my toes, my gaze is on Bryce. His hands are on his thighs as his back straightens in a forward fold. He stands and doesn't seem to have his head in the game.

He's sick.

Maybe he will be benched?

Chloe and Fiona whisper and giggle a metre or two away from me. I move onto my other leg. I couldn't give a shit what those bitches are saying.

During the first half of the game I shake my pompoms, call out cheers, and take my steps in the routines. It's all robotic. I'm worried about Bryce. He's slow. He pants after running. He doesn't go after the ball like he normally does.

Every time one of the girls call out his name, I get mad. They have no idea about him. No one knows him like me. He has to remember that. We can't throw that away.

I threw that away...

But we can get it back.

At half-time I manage to get near Will.

"You guys got to keep the ball away from Bryce."

"What are you talking about?" Will asks.

"He doesn't look right. Like, he's sick. You gotta keep him outta the action."

"He's a halfback. He's not really in the action."

"Please, Will."

Will shrugs. "I can try to keep the ball on Nav's side of the field."

"Thanks."

I turn around to where Bryce sits on the grass, and I fume. Fiona dropped to the ground behind him, rubbing his shoulders. He wriggles away from her touch, but she stays near him. Her childish giggle muffled by cupped hands.

I want to pull every strand of hair out of her head.

I'm so stiff during the second half of the game. It's an effort forcing my wrists to move the pompoms up and down. My breaths are shallow while watching Bryce. He needs to be benched. Should I talk to Mr Felding?

Sean runs the field with the ball. He throws it to Will who passes to Naveen. Naveen dodges some Kings Cliff players, then calls out, "BK!"

My pulse super speeds. The ball propels through the air. Bryce stops, watching, waiting to catch it. He catches and a Kings Cliff player leaps and tackles him to the ground.

A gasp erupts from me.

The Kings Cliff player gets up, but Bryce doesn't. Will and Jace run to his side. Mr Felding marches onto the field with Kings Cliff teachers. They pull the boys back and check on Bryce.

Our squad lunges toward the field, but Ms Harvey stops us.

Bryce is carried off the opposite side and I badly want to see what is happening. Before I know it, Bryce is taken away from the field.

Jace comes off the field with Mr Felding. I toss my pompoms and run to him.

"Jace, what happened? Is he ok?"

Jace squirts water in his mouth from a bottle. He shakes his head. "He didn't look good."

"Is he coming back?"

"They said they were taking him to hospital."

"Oh shit." My body trembles.

Jace pats my arm. "Don't fret. He'll be ok."

Bryce was taken to hospital.

I didn't pay attention, but we won.

He wasn't on the bus to Sanford.

That night I escape to my bedroom after dramatically screaming in the foyer that Bryce was in hospital.

There's a knock at my door and it swings open. I lift my head from my pillow as Charli wanders in. "What do you want?"

"I wanted to check on you," she says.

"To tell me I'm an idiot?"

"No, never. You seemed so upset about Bryce."

"Well, I am. Despite what everyone at school says."

"Brit," she sits on the edge of the bed, "you can't listen to those morons. It's hard, but I had to block them out after what happened between Travis and me."

I reef the blanket over my head. "Do not even try to compare us."

"You remember how I was that night?"

I scrunch the blanket around me, not wanting to listen.

"Maybe you gotta give Bryce time? You both looked equally upset during English."

"What would you know?"

"You and Chloe's brother is just like Travis and GiGi. He'd be hurt right now."

I drop the blanket. "You're calling me a cheat too?"

"No, Brit." She moves up the bed. "If you tell me nothing happened, I'll one hundred percent believe you."

"How do you even know what happened?"

Her shoulders droop. "It's all over school."

Crap. How do I fix this?

Charli's eyes are red-rimmed and her frizzy hair is bigger than usual. "Are you ok? You look like a mess."

She smooths her hair. "I'm fine. So, Bryce is in hospital?"

"I hope he's out by now." I check my phone. "He's not answering any of my texts."

"Concussion, maybe?"

"He hates me."

"He does not hate you."

I push her off the bed. "Don't even try to act like you know our relationship."

She stares at me wide-eyed. She gets up quickly and storms out.

I pant like I've finished a run.

No one knows us, but us. I don't care what anyone says.

24

Charli

Was it four hours of sleep last night? Yeah, I might have gotten four.

My eyes are crusty. The focus pills keep me alert at night, yet I'm haggard in the mornings. Is this what a hangover feels like? I load my mornings with copious amounts of green tea and No-Doz.

I dig my fingers under my neckerchief which is almost choking me. My desert-dry throat needs soothing. My elbows anchor on the breakfast table and I hide my face as the tea cools. Can you pull too many all-nighters? I spend all my free time at school cramming in the library. Is there a point when your brain can't take any more words?

"Charli?" Mum stares at me from the island bench. "You ok?"

I look up at her, my head aching. "Yeah."

She frowns and walks over to me. "Your eyes are all bloodshot."

"Are they?"

"You look like a zombie." Her hands plant on her hips. "You're not doing drugs are you?"

I burst out laughing. "What? That's absurd! How can you even ask that?”

“You have been out of it all week. It’s a reasonable assumption.”

I shake my head, smiling, “No, Mum. I’ve just been studying.”

She looks at me with concern. “Ok then.” She walks back to her coffee.

I slide down in my seat and tap my fingers against the cup. Those focus pills are just vitamins, right?

I find it hard to concentrate during English. I rub my temples, pulling back the skin around my eyes. My vision blurs and I catch only half of what Mr Palmer says. Another distraction is the empty seat beside me. Bryce is still away from school and whispers are becoming loud rumours about where he’s gone and why. I look over to Brittany who has her head down. She still won’t talk to me. Hell, maybe I don’t have time for her either.

I rub the heel of my palms over my eyes until tapping on my desk stops me.

“Charli, can you answer the question?” Mr Palmer asks, standing over me.

“Um, sorry, what?”

“In the final scene of the play which couple seems happier? Can you give reasons for your answer?”

“Oh,” I start, flipping between my pages, “yeah, I have an answer on that. Um, I wrote it down. I usually remember my answers off by heart, um, wait a sec.”

“Charli,” Mr Palmer says softly. “You read the play, yes?”

I nod.

“Then you should have a gut feeling. Remember, everything in this class is subjective. If you can give a reason, you’ve given an answer.”

I swallow and let out a slow breath. I turn to Brittany who’s looking my way. Her face is heavy with sadness. *Which sister is happier?*

"I don't know," I begin, looking down at my copy of '*The Taming of the Shrew*,' "can a woman really be happy if she has to be under a man's thumb? Shakespeare implies Kate and Petruchio leave the party happy, but will Bianca be happier if she counters Lucentio? Or will her life be a constant battle until her will is ultimately broken? I don't know, maybe I can't answer because I don't know what happiness is."

Mr Palmer holds my gaze for a moment before walking on, asking for someone to add to my statement. I catch Brittany's stare again. We look across at each other like reflections in a mirror. Sorrow in her eyes, pangs in my gut. She looks down at her book and I face front. With a sigh, I slide down in my chair waiting for the bell to sound.

At the end of class I pack up and skim my notes. I've no idea what I wrote. Hopefully it's useful when I revise tonight.

"Charli?" Reece says.

I turn from my desk, awkwardly holding my mess of stuff. "Huh?"

"I asked if you were coming round after school. Remember? I got the new '*Dark Ensemble*' game. You and Kellie could come round to play?"

I shake my head before I have an answer. "No, I have so many assignments to start."

"They don't all have to be started on the same day."

"I just want to stay ahead of everything. I want to make everything the very best."

"We never see you any more," his voice is small. "Well, I never see anyone any more. Kellie's always in the lab working on her experiment, and you never tell me where you are."

I step around my desk. "Sorry."

Reece's cups my wrist. "Don't forget about us, ok?"

I'm stunned by his hand on me. He lets go and walks out of the classroom.

I dawdle through the corridor to my locker and chuck everything inside. My headache is overgrown so I walk to mess for a bottle of water.

In the food line I stretch my arms over my head as knots run up my back.

My mind clears. "*Oh, crap.*"

I dart out of the line and out of the mess hall. I'm supposed to be at a yearbook committee meeting. How the frig did I forget that?

It's a fight to find what I need in my locker. I need my notes but I'm wasting so much time. All organisation is chucked out the window, just like my bedroom which is now a constant explosion. I find the correct notebook and haul arse to the library's tech room 1.

"Nice of you to show up, Charlotte." Heather crosses her arms, standing at the head of the table.

Panting, I take a seat and flip through pages, ready to make my points.

Heather walks up to me. Her head lifted high because of her superiority complex. "I don't think we need to hear from you today."

I place my hands flat on the book. "What? Why?"

"You're unreliable. We can't set someone tasks when we don't know whether they will show up."

Everyone gawks at me. They agree?

"I always show up. I do have a lot of responsibilities. Sometimes it's hard to get from one to the other quickly."

"We need people who will make the yearbook a priority."

Dad's voice sounds in my head, "*you've made commitments you have to stick with.*"

"Why are you looking at me like you've decided to kick me out?" I stand, looking Heather square in the eyes. "You don't have that right. I'm a hard worker, and I have a lot of quality ideas."

"Fine." Heather points a finger at me. "One last chance."

I sit down, a wooziness taking over my head. Maybe it's ok they don't wanna hear my ideas today.

I leave the library deflated. My mind has moved onto the next task. Working on my speech for Spanish. I'm really falling behind on verbs.

I walk towards my locker to return my notebook when I spot Tayla ahead.

Light bulb moment.

"Tay. Tayla." I run up to her.

She stops and grins. "Hey Charli. What's up?"

"You speak Spanish, right?"

"*Hablo española bastante bien.*"

My tired eyes squint as her sentence takes too long to process. Bad sign. "Right. I was wondering... Can you help me with my Spanish assignment? I'm really struggling."

"Of course I will." Her arm lassos around me. "What part do you need help on?"

"I need to write a speech on my day at school. Could you write some points on classes, friends and other activities? We can catch up later and go over it. It'd help me out so much. I'm just so behind right now."

She nods. "Easy-peasy. I'll write it during geography."

I drag her into a hug. "Thank you. You're a lifesaver."

"That's what friends are for."

I squirm out of the hug as guilt swells my gut.

"Hey, I'm going down to the footy oval, wanna come?" she asks.

"I was going to do some studying."

Tayla snorts. "Girl, we get enough study in class. Come down and watch the game with me. You used to always sit outside, now I never see ya at lunch."

I shrug and nod. "Ok, I guess I could use some fresh air after being around Heather."

"*Ohmigawd*. Why would you be around her again after how un-fun she made the dance committee?"

I gather my hair to the side and sigh. "Because I want so badly to chair a committee. But no, she took that one away from me too."

"*Geez*, we're only in grade ten. You got a couple more years to do that."

"My dad will want it to happen now."

As we walk across the quad Tayla says, "Parents have gotta check themselves."

Cheering sounds from the oval and I ask what game this is.

"Senior boys. They're playing *West Sanford High*."

I stop dead. "*West Sanford*?"

Tayla stops by me. "Oh, you thinking bout that guy you were seeing?"

"I wouldn't call it *seeing*."

"Don't worry bout him. Wasn't he... kinda geeky?"

My lips curl. "Yeah, I guess you're right."

We find a space by the sidelines and Tayla finds out they are in the middle of the second half.

"Dang, we've missed most of it." She points out to the field. "If anything, I thought you'd be more worried bout seeing him."

I follow her finger out to the field, to Travis running and calling for the ball. My heart *ba-booms* for a reason I'm unclear about. I drop to the ground, so my trembling doesn't become obvious. In every wing of school I've heard gossip about Travis and GiGi hooking up at parties. I had been lucky with not seeing him. Escaping to the library has kept me from breaking.

Tayla sits next to me and I spy the ridiculous cheerleaders. GiGi sashays her way to the front. My fingernails stab my palms. I've never known hate until dealing with her manipulations.

"Have you heard much about Travis and GiGi," I whisper to Tayla.

"From your brother?"

Tayla thinks on the subject. "Not much. I don't think there is a lot to tell. It seems pretty one-sided."

My gut quivers. "Whose side?"

Tayla splutters a laugh. "Hers, obviously."

I exhale quick relief, but it doesn't stop the jealousy. GiGi's the reason everything got screwed up. If she didn't send everyone to Kellie's house, maybe things with Travis wouldn't have ended the way they did. She threw sex into every conversation. Maybe if GiGi hadn't ruined Kellie's game night, Brittany wouldn't be partying so recklessly or mending a broken heart. Maybe if GiGi stayed the hell out of my life, I wouldn't be escaping all of my problems and be in the bad books with my best friends.

The buzzer sounds and the PA says *West Sanford* has won. I can't help looking for him. Travis dawdles off the field, rubbing the sweat off his brow. I focus on his frown.

"What was that?" Mr Watkins throws his hands up in the air at Travis. "You can do a lot better than that sorry display."

Travis rolls his eyes and picks up a bottle of water.

Mr Watkins smacks the bottle out of Travis' hand. "Don't roll your eyes at me. What's the point in putting you through all that training if you're just going to throw it away like that?"

Travis picks up the bottle and slings his bag over his shoulder. "See you at home, Dad."

He's miserable. I want so badly to run to him and tell him to quit. He never truly enjoyed it. But I can't. He didn't want to hear it when we were together. Saying it now would be an epic mistake.

GiGi saunters over to him, leaning in with puckered lips. "Hey Travy."

Travis plants a hand in her face. "Not now, GiGi."

GiGi backs off like a timid child. She joins the cheerleaders, giggling, as Travis walks towards the gym.

#

After school, I find Kellie in one of the labs. "Working hard?"

"Hi. What are you doing here?" she asks, not looking up from her textbook.

"I need a reason to see my best friend?"

"Seems so these days."

I bite inside my cheek. "Sorry, things have just been a bit crazy lately."

She flips a page. "Tell me bout it."

"I know what I'm hiding from... Is this all about Will?"

Kellie looks at me for the first time and I don't like it. Her nostrils flare as she scowls at me.

"Will?" she snaps. "Are you seriously asking me whether I'm working so hard on a project I'm passionate about because some boy can't stop being a jerk?"

"Kel."

"Whatever, Charli. Maybe you're the only one allowed to throw herself into study."

"Don't be like that," my voice warbles. "Anyway, I just came because Reece said you two aren't hanging out."

She tosses the textbook onto the ground. "Well, when is anyone ever going to look out for me?"

"Kel?" I edge closer to her.

"I know I'm being selfish," she whispers. "But can't I have a selfish moment... just once?"

I boost my bravery and stand in front of her. "Of course you can."

Her shoulders droop as her eyes become wet. "Are you back?"

"Back?"

"Normal?"

I smile. "Normal?"

Kellie sighs and sits on a stool. "I really thought Will had my back this time."

"I know."

"He said all the right things. But at school he was TwoFace."

It takes all my might not to say *I told you so.*

Kellie sees right through me. "Don't say it."

We let out uneasy laughter.

"Should we go to Reece's?" Kellie asks.

I grit my teeth, trying to answer. We should, but I really want to work on my assignments. Kellie eyes her workstation.

"Maybe tomorrow," we say at the same time.

"His brothers are coming home this weekend for his birthday," Kellie says. "Maybe we should rock up and surprise him."

I give her an uneasy look. "You wanna give Reece—I repeat, Reece—a surprise party?"

Kellie laughs. "What, you think I'm insane? *No.* We can save him from the extended family invasion at his house. Like, chill at the skatepark, or whatever."

I nod. "We should do that for him. So, we aren't going to tell him?"

"I'll video chat him tonight and see how he's going, then decide."

"Ok. See you tomorrow."

I walk into the living room of Reece's house almost an hour after I was told to be there. The two texts from Kellie got me moving. It was just so hard to leave in the middle of writing my essay.

Reece's brother Jeremy laughs whilst having Reece in a headlock. I go to call out *stop*, but I'm beaten by Kellie.

Kellie reefs the back of Jeremy's collar, and shouts, "Let go of him, would ya!"

Jeremy unleashes Reece and flips around to Kellie. Still hunched, Reece backs away from his brother.

"I say I never hit girls," Jeremy smirks. "Lucky it's just you, Kel."

Kellie tackles Jeremy and hooks her arms around his neck. I turn away and ignore the pair.

I nudge Reece's arm. "Happy birthday."

Reece gives a shy smile. "Thanks."

I hand him a wrapped gift. He taps his fingers on it. "Should I open it now?"

"Sure. If you want."

We flop on a couch together and he picks at the tape on the wrapping paper. "This is from you?"

"Yep." My heartbeat speeds up and I swallow dryly, hoping he will like it.

He pulls away the wrapping and holds up '*Biographia Literaria*' by Samuel Taylor Coleridge. "*Whoah*. Thanks, Charli."

"You're welcome."

He moves like he might hug me. I don't move a muscle, so he doesn't freak. This little voice inside me squeaks, *I hope he hugs me.* Reece looks at the book and flicks through it. I sigh and lay my head against the couch. My eyes beg to fall shut.

"You look buggered," Jeremy says.

I open my eyes to see him and Kellie staring at me.

"What's wrong with you?" Jeremy asks.

I sit up straight. "Nothing is wrong."

Jeremy screws up his face and leaves down the hall. *Geez*, I have not missed him. He's in his first year at *Defence University* now, and he was such a pain at school. One of those boys who has to be the centre of attention and is somehow always involved in a schoolyard fight. However, like their two oldest brothers, he was always protective of Reece. To this day, no one starts trouble with Reece because his brothers' reputations never left *John Thomas High*.

"He is right," Kellie says. "You have black bags under red eyes."

"Stop it, it's not that bad," I say, swiping my eyes. "Just a couple of all-nighters strung together."

"You mean a few more," Kellie says.

"You need to take it easy," Reece says. "You're gonna drive yourself nuts."

I leap off the couch. "C'mon. Let's do somethin."

We head towards the back of the house when my name is called. I duck my head into the kitchen where Steven, Reece's second oldest brother, waves from the bench.

"Steven, hi. It's so great to see you." I walk in and give him a one-armed hug.

"How's the kid I babysat?"

"Yeah, good. How are you?"

"Good, kid." He pats my arm. "You're looking a bit rattled."

"I am?"

Reece's mum peers over Steven's shoulder. "You tired, Charli?"

I nod. "Guess you could say that."

"Is he still on the phone?" Kellie asks, throwing her thumb back at the eldest brother, Eric.

Steven smirks. "When he's not on the phone, he's ignoring us by writing emails."

Kellie jumps up and down, waving. Eric looks up and gives her a lop-sided grin.

Reece's mother picks up a tray of drinks and walks them to the table where Reece's dad, uncle and aunt are sitting. Meah slouches in the corner behind them, constantly texting. I turn my attention back on the table. I haven't seen Travis' parents since before the break up. *Please don't ask me any questions.* And, oh man, Travis isn't here, is he? I glance between Steven and Eric. No, surely if he was, he'd be in this room. I shake off the tremor in my hands.

"So, has Reece actually spent much time with you," I say to Steven.

He nods. "Yeah. Today was all family stuff. We have all promised to stay out of the way tonight." He nudges his head back at his parents. "Some people are embarrassing."

Eric tosses his phone on the bench. "Hey girls. How you been?"

"Great! And you?" Kellie answers over-excitedly. Ever since she was little, Kellie swooned over Eric. This is actually as tame as I've seen her around him.

Eric smooths his thick dark hair. He is so broad now and swimming up the ranks of the navy just like their dad. "Yeah good. Just work, work, work."

"Hey, how's your dad?" Steven asks me. "I heard he's back in town. I'd really like to go around and say hi."

"Yeah, he's ok. He's at *Swan Apartments* in town."

"He was my inspiration for getting into law. Are you still heading that way?"

I nod.

"Careful," Eric says to Steven. "Rob'll be trying to get you into his firm and out of the navy."

"Over my dead body," their father calls from the table.

"I saw that horrible, bratty girl you used to hang out with today on the boardwalk," Steven says to me. "What was her name again? Kimmy?"

"Oh, really," I murmur.

"Wasn't she the one giving you trouble?" Eric says to Kellie.

"*Pah*-lease," Kellie snorts. "I'm tougher than Kimberley Jones."

Eric smirks. "Well, we are in town till tomorrow arvo. Let us know if you need anything."

"Weren't we going to the skatepark?" Reece mutters behind us.

Kellie and I turn to him leaning against the doorframe and say goodbye to his brothers. In ways Reece looks like his brothers, but ultimately, he's the black sheep. Luckily his mother is sensitive to that, even after his dad's disappointment. Reece went through cadet training like his brothers, but it was obviously not for him. His mum introduced him to books at a young age, and Reece's obsession began. The doctors explained it's normal for him to be infatuated with one thing, so Mrs Watkins encouraged Reece to explore the book world to his heart's content.

I tell Kellie and Reece I need the bathroom before we go and make my way up the hall. Jeremy's voice echoes from a room, loud and fast. I stop mid-step when I recognise who he's talking to. I'll never mistake Travis' voice. My hands tremble and my stomach launches to my chest. I look up the hall and gulp. I think I can make it.

On tiptoes, I race as silent as a ghost, and accidentally slam the bathroom door shut.

I splash water on my face after getting a shock at my reflection. I've been avoiding mirrors like sodas thrown by Sean Hastings.

Adrenaline wakes me up, but I'm scared I'll crash at the skatepark. I slip out a focus pill from my pocket and take a slurp from the tap. It's worth it to be awake for Reece. I dry my face and open the door.

"Oh, hey," Travis says in the hallway. He shifts his weight and digs his hands into pockets.

"Hi," I mumble, holding myself up with the doorframe.

His eyes narrow. "You ok?"

"Yeah." I put my head down and try to slink past him.

His hand grazes my jawline as I pass. I shiver and look at him.

"Sorry. You just don't look like yourself."

"I'm fine."

"I hope so."

I swallow as I follow every wave of his chocolatey hair. My gaze slides down his nose until I'm hypnotised by the shine of his bottom lip.

I almost stumble backwards when I look into those dark eyes.

"I have to go."

I don't wait for his response and dash towards the front door. When I meet the others on the front porch, I head straight for my skateboard, so they don't see anything is wrong.

I don't want him in my head. *Charli, stop picturing yourself kissing him.*

Please.

Reece and I skate next to each other, while Kellie cycles. She's always refused to learn to skate. I'm still working on her.

As we approach the skatepark I get a whiff of something. My nose scrunches. Damn, I know what that is. Veronica sits with her legs dangling over the rink, dragging on a joint. Kellie sits by her and takes it from Veronica, and I have to look away. *Don't think about it, Charli. Don't you dare think about it.*

I follow Reece to Simon and Lenny. Lenny is strumming on his guitar, tapping his foot and singing. *Wild thing. You make my heart sing. You make everything, groo-vy.* Tayla is hovering about him, giggling and swinging her hips.

"So, birthday boy," Simon says, "going to try for that three-sixty kickflip tonight?"

Reece plays with the headphones around his neck. "What makes you think I could do it now?"

"You know, a year older and all," Simon teases. "What about you, Charli?"

"I only just nailed one-eighties."

Simon grins, making too much eye contact. I forgot he did that. There was always too much eye contact and sloppy kisses. Why did I even date him? He wasn't even a friend. An acquaintance who had mutual friends. I guess it didn't really matter when I was thirteen going on fourteen.

Tayla squeezes behind the guitar, onto Lenny's lap, and I'm sure I don't need to see any couple action right now. I glide along the rink's edge and then drop down, scuttling across and up the other side. My board and I twist in the air and I race down and manage an ollie.

Reece and Simon join me in the rink. Simon grinds a rail, making it look easier than I ever could.

"Are you going to try the kickflip again?" I ask Reece.

He stares at his board. "It shouldn't be this difficult."

"You're doing fine. Your therapist said you'd be too unco for skateboarding and you showed her."

He backs up a bit. "I'm still slow." He pushes on his board and crouches low. He jumps, pushing down his back foot and manages a variant kickflip.

"Dude, you're gonna get it," Simon cheers. "I know it."

"Don't pressure him," I tell Simon.

"I'm not. I'm encouraging."

Reece shakes his head and slips on his headphones.

Kellie cheers by the edge of the rink, clapping her hands over her head.

I skate over to her. "Gonna give it a go, fraidy-cat?"

Kellie takes another drag and breathes out white smoke. "My lovely, I'm doing A-OK up here."

I skate around the boys, wishing Simon would rack off, when Lenny joins us. It's relief when he takes Simon's attention away. I practice riding low and making air while keeping an eye on Reece. He's so close. I'd love him to nail it on his birthday.

With a deep breath intending to be bravery, I skate up the ramp for bigger air. As I come down, cheers fill the rink. I look about for what I missed. Reece steps off his rolling board and collapses to the cement. He flops on his back and smiles the biggest smile I've ever seen.

I race over to him and lean over his face. "Did you just do it?"

He nods, his giddy grin unshakable.

"Damn," I collapse next to him, "I missed it. Will you do it again?"

"It was a fluke."

"Shuddup." I playfully nudge him.

We laugh silently, lying on the smooth surface of the rink.

A yawn escapes me, and he nudges me. "Stop yawning."

I cover my wide-open mouth. "Sorry."

We laugh again, this time much more audible. I look up at the blanket of twinkling stars, and I'm glad for a night away from textbooks and my laptop screen. I look at Reece. I'm glad for a night next to him.

25

High school has morphed into primary school. The days when I was a friendless loner. Meah kept to her word with shunning me. Classes we share are unbearably awkward. I don't even go into mess hall any more. Without allowing her to ask questions, I've asked Sophia to make lunch for me when she makes Charli's.

Charli is still acting like a goblin and only talking in grunts. Without her looking over my shoulder, I feel eleven-years-old again. When she and Kimberley were best friends and always left me out.

I don't know what was wrong with me back then, but I just couldn't involve myself. It was a higher level of shy. My mouth would clamp shut and I couldn't speak. Kimberley always called me names in front of Charli. I never let Charli in because she didn't stick up for me. We were two halves of one being. You don't do that to your twin. I've never been able to forget that.

The name Kimberley called me the most was cry-baby. Gosh, I cried so much as a kid. Now I never let myself break. I always see it as weakness when Charli pulls the waterworks. She's bunged it on since Dad moved out. Enough is enough.

Although I have broken a few times over Bryce. I haven't seen him in two weeks, and I miss his face so much. He helped me out of my shell. Without him, I wouldn't have gotten in with Chloe. Dance just wasn't enough. My mouth was still ironed shut.

I suck in a sharp breath as I pass Chloe & Co in the corridor.

"Yeah, our poor Brycey," Chloe says as the girls circle around her. My ears prick and my heart races. "I visited him in hospital just before he left. He was so sweet and confided in me. Told me about all the troubles he was having and how hard everything is. It's like he hasn't had anyone dependable in his life before talking to me. But yeah, they've taken him to rehab. He's, like, sick as. Like bulimic or something."

I walk out to the quad acting like I didn't hear Chloe.

That can't be right?

Confided in Chloe?

He won't reply to my texts, but he'll confide in Chloe?

She visited him in hospital? When? Which hospital? Was he back in Sanford?

Gahhh! She makes me so mad.

I sit down on a patch of grass and pull out my unappealing sandwich. I take three bites before I realise how *out-in-the-open* I am. I usually hide in a corner, but I was so frustrated and distracted I plonked. I scan my surroundings and notice Charli with her friends. She watches me and my insides clench. She's like a sad reflection, except she's not the one alone. She nudges her head to signal come over.

I take another bite and get off the grass. I trudge towards the school building. Sitting in the bathroom is better than her pity.

"Brittany!"

My body trembles against my locker the next day at school as Chloe marches towards me. She's going to tear me limb-from-limb.

"How you been?" she asks, grinning.

"Um, ok."

Chloe twirls her platinum hair, not making eye contact. "So, we're going away this weekend. To Damien's uni."

I hold my breath, waiting for her to continue. What is the point of her telling me this? To rub it in? To point out I'm no longer in her group? An opportunity to get close and pull my hair?

Crap. I'm sweating.

She eyes me. "You wanna go?"

I stumble. "Me?"

Chloe scowls. "Like, I don't even want you around after what you said about me, but, like, Damien wants to see you. He won't let me stay unless you come."

"Oh, um, I don't think I can go this weekend."

"I already texted your mum from my mum's phone. So, it's already organised."

"You really want me to go?"

"No, *I* really want to go. You're just the bargaining chip." She crosses her arms. "And the fact you know more than expected makes me want to keep you around." She pops a hip and smirks. "Luckily I was able to squash the filth you said in front of Jace about Lucas. One ballsy move, Brit."

My eye twitches.

"Be ready at eleven Saturday morning for the train, bitch."

Chloe walks away and I can't stop blinking.

In Meah's kitchen I'm frantic. "She's planning to kill me, isn't she?"

"Paranoid?" Meah says, passing me a mug of hot chocolate.

"*Hello?* I've been a total loner for almost three weeks... and now I'm invited on a trip away? It screams slasher film."

Meah giggles, playing with a marshmallow. "So dramatic."

"The fact you are playing this down makes me think you are in on the slashing."

Meah grins. "I'd tell you if I was in on it. You know I couldn't keep something like that a secret."

"This is the first time we've talked in ages."

"You know why I had to do that."

"I'm totally ignored at school, and then Chloe invites me on a trip away, and suddenly you invite me over to your house." If I talk any faster, I'll choke on my words. "I'm not wrong, it's a quick turn around."

Meah takes a slurp of her drink and shrugs. "Chloe needed to let off some steam."

Is Meah trying to say that Chloe vented about me to her?

The doorbell sounds along with banging on the front door. Meah huffs and walks to the front door.

Stomping closes in and Meah calls out, "GiGi, Travis isn't home."

GiGi walks into the kitchen and her eyes bulge at sight of me. She slaps a hand over her chest and breathes out. "Shit. I thought you were the other one." GiGi struts through the kitchen towards the stairs. "I'm gonna surprise Travy, don't tell him."

"Is she over here heaps now?" I ask.

Meah returns to her hot chocolate. "I don't pay much attention. She's so shrill and I've got my own stuff going on."

"It was quick after Charli."

"They were a weird couple anyway. Who cares?"

"No, you're right. I've got bigger things happening as well. My boyfriend dumped me and apparently told all his secrets to Chloe who is now plotting against me."

"The plotting is in your head."

"She called me a 'bargaining chip.' She's at least using me." I bite my lip and squirm in my seat. "She's still pissed about what I said about her and Lucas."

"Can you blame her?" Meah scoffs.

The door from the garage opens and Travis walks through, damp with sweat and pulling out earphones. He refills his water bottle from the kitchen tap and Meah grins deviously at him.

"GiGi's waiting for you in your bedroom."

"What the fuck?" Travis groans, slamming his bottle down.

"She marched her way through the house."

Travis catches my eye and frowns. "Don't tell..."

My face is stony as I stare him down.

"Just please don't tell her," he says and then leaves towards his bedroom.

My lip upturns as a gross taste coats my tongue. "As if."

"So, what rehab do you think Bryce is in?" Meah asks.

I pout. "He's not in rehab. He's not a junky."

"You're still so defensive over him even though he dumped you."

"I didn't mean for what happened to happen. I just wanted to be with him." I sigh. "I still want him. I do not want to see Damien."

"Well, too bad," Meah says, slamming her mug down. "You don't go, none of us go. And I have to go!"

"Have to?"

"I'm in, Brit. I need this trip to keep me in."

Suddenly I'm a puppet being thrashed about as Meah and Chloe hover over me, fighting to take control.

Dad was pissed I wouldn't be spending any time with him this weekend, but he dropped me off at the train station at quarter to eleven anyway.

"Meah, you look so damn *hawt*," Chloe cheers as we take our seats for the hour-long train journey to the city.

Meah blushes and tries to hide her smile. Her trip to the salon last night gave her a balayage with light blonde. Her weight has dropped off, and while I was on the outs Kimmy and Madison took her shopping for a new wardrobe.

"You'll be finding a boyfy this trip," Chloe winks.

Fiona had to stay in Sanford this weekend for her Grandfather's birthday, or as Kimmy called it, the *staying-in-the-will* party. The other girls take four seats that face each other. I take a seat opposite and alone. Thankfully I have a fully charged phone to keep me entertained, or at least *look* entertained. The whispers and giggles make me hate myself and wish Dad had refused to take me to the train station. Hating *him* would be so much easier.

After the train trip from hell, we roll our suitcases towards the university. The grown-up vibes of the tall buildings make me squirm like I shouldn't be here.

"Hey Chlo-Bo." Damien bear hugs Chloe in the dorm hallway.

Chloe squeals in his arms.

The sight of him makes me shiver, like when you see a spider on a wall and you're afraid to look away because it might scurry out of view.

"Hey Damien," Kimberley says, walking past and patting his arm.

"You remember Madi and Meah," Chloe says as I shrink into invisibility.

"Hi Madison," Damien says, waving. He shakes his head at Meah. "Don't think we've met."

Chloe huffs and sits a hand on her hip. "Sure, you have. She's Travis' sister."

"Travis who?"

"Watkins."

"Oh, Jeremy's cousin. Hi."

Meah smiles and I see the annoyance in her eyes from being recognised only by her older brother or cousins.

Damien sees me and smiles. "Oh hey, I wanted to see if you were still alive."

I bite my bottom lip and wave at him. I slink behind Meah to avoid his line of sight. *Geez*, why am I here? Yes, Chloe had murder in her eyes, but I could have taken the easy way out: stayed at Dad's this weekend and then wandered the corridors of school like they're solitary confinement. Social suicide has me so terrified. I'd rather be here, face-to-face with a guy I was in bed with, and have no idea what happened.

Chloe grabs Damien's arm and swings him around. "C'mon, show us around."

"I got you these two rooms," Damien says, stopping by open doors across the hall from each other. "They're empty for the weekend. Sorry they are a bit squishy with three beds jammed in."

Chloe takes Kimmy's hand and races in one room. "Ours!"

Meah, Madison and I dump our bags in the other room.

"We gotta get going," Damien says. "I teed up the guy for the next hour to do your IDs."

"IDs?" I whisper to Meah.

"To get into the clubs," Meah whispers.

Damien takes us on a bus to get two suburbs over. The air smells of public bathroom, the streets gritty with garbage and angry people. Damien opens the door to a tattoo parlour and beckons us to enter. The buzzing is overwhelming and everyone inside gives the impression they're from a biker gang.

"Tattoo anyone?" Madison smirks.

"Should I get Jace's name on my butt?" Chloe jokes.

Kimberley laughs and adds, "You should get Sean, and I should get Jace. Really confuse them."

"No one get a name tattooed on them," Damien yells over the buzzing.

"You're Damien?" a man asks, peering out from a curtain.

"Yep."

"Ok, fall in," he says, retreating into the room.

I follow behind everyone into the back room.

The man drops a shoebox on a table and says, "Check in there if any look like ya. I'd really prefer to not make a new one." He scans us all. "You blonde girls should be fine, but I have limited supply of black and Asian."

"Even when you generalise it that much," Madison replies with thick sarcasm.

The man's face is rigid, and I imagine him hurling us out onto the street.

Kimberley picks up an ID and moves it against the light. "Are these real?"

"They have been acquired," the man replies, "from those who lose their property."

"So, they're stolen?" Madison says.

"As long as they look like you," the man says, reclining and kicking his dirty boots onto the table, "you'll be golden. They will pass any test the bouncers put them through."

As the girls dig into the box, I stand back with a creeping fear taking over. What the hell am I doing here?

"You ok?" Damien says, stepping beside me.

I nod and take a step to the left to create some distance between us.

"Waiting to see what's left over?" he asks.

I clear my throat. "Better than dealing with wayward elbows."

He laughs and steps closer to the girls. "Chlo, howzit goin?"

Chloe shows him an ID. "Does this chick look like me?"

"All you gotta do is match the face. Your hair is obviously fake, so it don't matter if it's a brunette."

Chloe whacks him. "What d'you mean *obviously fake*."

"No one's born with silver hair."

"It's platinum," Kimberley and Meah say at once.

I break out in a laugh. I get glances but I shake it off and walk over to the box. Meah slides an ID in front of me and I pick it up. *Damn, she could be my twin.* I laugh at how dumb the thought was.

A couple of hours later, plastered in makeup and covered in hairspray, we're on our way to the uni bar for a foam party.

I'm strapped into black stilettos and forced into a metallic silver dress by Meah and Madison. I've owned it for a while but was never bold enough to wear it. At least its spring so I won't be freezing my butt off like at the other parties.

"You look bonkers," Kimberley says to me.

"Is that a good or bad thing?"

"Crazy good."

Chloe struts out of the dorm to meet us. Her top is basically a shiny black triangle covering her boobs. Her skirt hangs off her hips and is snug around her thighs.

"*Ohmigawd*," Madison, Meah and I all gasp.

Chloe whips her hair off her shoulders. "We're out of Sanford, right?"

An easiness of giggles floods the group. My shoulders relax and we follow Damien and his friends to the party. Something about not knowing anyone gives me a rush. There will be no rumours roaming around school. No talk of ex-boyfriends.

When we get to the uni bar, Damien and his friends hang back to make sure we all get in. Chloe flicks her ID between her index and middle finger. She doesn't make eye contact with the bouncer. Dripping with attitude. She's let in.

I wait behind the girls. I'm jittery as Meah gets scrutinised. She's in. I fumble with my ID. My fingers shake so much I drop the ID on the ground.

"Oh crap." I lean to pick it up.

"I got it." Damien ducks down to pick up my ID. "Been drinkin already?" he jokes and hands it over to the bouncer.

I get waved through. "Thank you," I whisper to Damien.

He smiles and nods.

The music is pumping. It's dark except for the laser lighting criss-crossing the room. Foam seeps over the dancefloor and up our calves.

"Drinks, girls?" Damien yells over the music.

We all cheer, Madison being the loudest.

A guy, who obviously rolled around in foam, chats up Chloe. She laughs at the soapy guy, puts her hands on her hips and pivots when more guys crowd her. Something under that shirt is pushing everything up. Massive cleavage.

"Hey, how you doing?" a guy hovers over me, smelling of beer and rubbing his hand down my arm.

I flinch and back away. "Ah, I'm fine."

"Hey!" a girl screeches, dragging the guy away by the collar.

Phew.

I hug my sides. Kimberley runs a finger in circles on Damien's friend's chest. I search for Meah.

Meah stands with her hands clasped behind her, swinging gently. I make my way over and grab onto her arm. "Oh *geez*, don't leave me. I'm not ready for this."

She shakes me off her. "Sorry, Brit. I've got plans of my own."

"Huh?"

I find where her eyes have settled. A guy smiles at her over his drink. She's standing here flirting?

He waves her over. Meah dips her hips and saunters over. Who is this girl?

"Drink?" Damien holds a drink out in front of me.

I thank him and take the glass.

"You look unhappy."

I quickly smile. "Do I?"

He smiles back. "Well, not now."

"Some creepy guy just tried to crack on, that's all."

"So, I should stick around to get rid of them?"

I bite my lip. I don't know that I want him so close, but is Chloe's brother better than some random drunk guy? "That'd be nice."

"Dammit," Damien grizzles. "Look at all these douches surrounding my sister. I swear I'm going to knock out the first one that touches her."

"I don't think she'll care if they touch her."

"Yeah, that makes everything more difficult." He takes a sip of his drink. "Maybe you should tell me about yourself to distract me."

"About me? There's really not that much to tell."

"Oh, c'mon. There's gotta be a good reason for Chloe to keep you around. She's popular, but not exactly friendly. How'd you two meet?"

"I've always known her cause of school, and I joined her dance class over the summer."

"Another dancer. That's cool."

"Then she told me to join cheerleading, and we just kept hanging out."

"See, you've already told me so much about you."

"What about you? What are you studying?"

"Advertising. Dad told me I had to do something business related. For my first year at uni, it's been pretty good. Advertising seems a good fit with me. I can get away with adding art classes."

"I don't really get art unless I can see patterns. I guess that's why I like textiles and design."

"Art is subjective. It's up to you how you 'get it.' So, are you going to be a big time fashion designer?"

"I dunno, I guess we will have to see."

"I think you'll make it."

I giggle. "If you say so."

I search the room. Kimberley is now grinding against that guy. My jaw drops seeing Meah dirty dancing with her flirting partner. I can't even see Chloe any more, and Madison is MIA.

"You look worried again," Damien says.

I laugh and lower my gaze. "No, I was just looking around for everyone."

"Don't worry, they'll all be fine. Maybe you should drink up so you relax?"

I tap the glass. He's right. It does numb all my thoughts. It would numb my lingering fear of the girls ditching me at this bar. It would numb my thoughts of Bryce wanting to talk to Chloe more than me. It would numb the burning question of why I woke up next to Damien.

Shirtless Damien.

In his bed.

I take a big mouthful.

Damien's attention returns to the crowd around his sister. "Excuse me for a sec."

He walks over to them. He taps one guy on the shoulder who doesn't react. Damien grabs his shoulder and reefs him backwards. Damien grabs Chloe and pulls her out of the circle.

"*Oi.* What the hell?" Chloe whacks her brother.

My eyes glue to the pair. I almost roll an ankle when Madison tugs on my arm.

"Come dance, girl," Madison hollers over the music, dragging me behind her.

I toss back the rest of my drink and plant the glass on a nearby table.

Madison didn't fully cut me out at school like the others. My hips shimmy in time with hers as I hope dancing doesn't lead to a disaster.

She smiles at me, and my arms follow hers up, pumping to the music. I dip lower and heel-toe my feet, barely seeing my shoes in the foam. I scan the dancefloor and take in all the unfamiliar faces. It'll be ok to relax. I arch my back, roll my stomach and let out a cheer.

Madison grabs my hand and twirls into me. I twirl her out and foam flies up around her. She cheers, throwing her arms up. Madison gasps and pulls on my hand.

I lunge forward. "What?"

Madison points ahead. "*Look.*"

"What the hell?" Meah is making out with her dirty dancing partner. Did they even have time to exchange first names?

"What is actually happening?" Madison hangs off my shoulders and laughs.

"No idea."

Madison let's go off me and two-steps. "You heard from Bryce?"

"Nope. He hates me."

Madison snorts. "He doesn't hate you."

"He does."

"So, you want something like that tonight?" She hurls a thumb in Meah's direction.

"I think I'm good without any more boy dramas."

"It's not drama. Just some fun. That's all boys are good for. Fun."

"I am having fun now."

"No, you lez. You know why you were brought along, right? Damien wants to finish what you two started at Chloe's birthday party."

We're both tapped on the arm. Chloe shouts over the music, "This foam shit is ruining my outfit. We're heading to the clubs."

Chloe wrangles Kimberley, and Madison tries to pull Meah away. Meah throws some choice words and then sucks the lips off her guy.

"C'mon Meah," Kimmy shouts as she and Chloe stride through the foam. "You can find another one of those at the next place."

My eyes take a moment to adjust when we leave the bar. The street lights are harsher than the laser lighting. We take a train into central station.

"Did you like your taste of uni life?" Damien asks, walking beside me as we leave the station.

"Yeah, I could get use to that."

"We're heading to this club called *Spaz*."

"*Spaz?*"

"It's sick. You'll like it."

This time I ace the ID check. The bouncer looks me up and down more than the ID. He waves me straight in.

Chloe, Kimberley and Madison race ahead to the dancefloor. Meah's hands are down the back pockets of her new friend's jeans. Her foam party make-out partner followed us onto the train. She's suctioning his lips off with hers. I avert my eyes and keep walking.

"You're looking worried again," Damien says, walking beside me.

I eye my feet. "Gosh, can you stop watching me?"

"I'm sorry, it's too hard to stop looking at you."

My cheeks flush and I laugh. "What a line."

"Why, thank you."

We stop by a table, just the two of us. I take in his smiling face with a quick breath in and out. "What happened between us?"

"Whaddaya mean?"

"I was in your bed."

"Yes, and you left while I was sleeping. What was up with that?"

"I didn't remember going to bed. I was in my underwear. I was freaked out."

Damien laughs and shakes his head. "So, you really don't remember anything?"

I bite my lip and shake my head.

"You were plastered, and I was trying to help you walk. You were babbling about not wanting to be around everyone, so I took you to my room. I thought you might crash, and I'd leave you alone to sleep. You took your dress off on your own and then fell on my bed. I went to leave you, but these drunken guys were wandering the halls. I was worried they might go in there with you asleep and outta it. I stayed to make sure you were ok and ended up falling asleep."

"*Ohmigawd*, that's so embarrassing. I'm so sorry."

"Don't worry about it. Everyone has those times when they drink a bit too much."

"They always happen to me when it involves your sister."

"Does that mean tonight will be a big one too?"

"I sure hope not."

He takes my hand. "Don't worry, I'll look out for you."

A spark runs up my arm and a flash of kissing him in the cold fills my mind. I shiver and pull my hand away.

"Everything ok."

"Mhmm," I reply.

"You wanna dance?"

Dancing is better than more drinking. "Sure."

Damien groans at the sight of Chloe grinding against a guy. "I always have to be watching that stupid girl. She knows what it's like to be touched by someone and have it get outta hand. Why does she keep putting herself in these situations?"

"What do you mean?"

"Do you mind if we dance close to them so I can keep an eye out?"

"Ok. It's nice you're so protective of her." I eye Chloe and she scowls at me. My lips curl. *You banished me at school.* If you hate seeing this, Chloe, it makes it all the more sweeter.

"I have to be," Damien says. "It's clear none of our other brothers give a damn about her."

Damien takes my hand on the dancefloor and holds it high. He pulls me, spins me out and I can't help squealing. He spins me fast and I land against his chest. His hands press onto my hips and our hearts beat against each others. His face edges towards me and for a moment everything goes blank. His cheek brushes against mine and then his lips tease me. Bryce flashes in my mind.

My eyes rush open. I push against his chest and reef my head back.

"*Whoah*, you ok?" Damien asks.

"Sorry," I pant.

He takes me in his arms. "It's ok, I got you."

His arms run down my body and he cups my bum. My forehead creases. My arms tense around his shoulders. He kisses the nape of my neck and I badly want to relax.

Over his shoulder, Kimberley storms towards me. Once over to us, she whispers in my ear, "We're all heading to the bathroom. C'mon."

I take it's not optional and slip out of Damien's arms. I tell him I'll be back and follow Kimmy to meet with Chloe and Madison.

"Who's that guy you've been grinding with?" Kimberley asks Madison in the bathroom line.

Madison giggles. "Didn't get a name."

Kimberley whacks her arm. "Bad girl."

Chloe moves close to me. Way too close. "You and my brother, huh?"

"Um... Yep."

"Like, maybe that's not a good idea."

"Why?"

She says, low and flat, "You, like, cheat on your boyfriends."

My face scrunches like I've tasted something foul. "I'm not dating him. I'm just having fun."

"Well I don't like it," she hisses.

"*Whoah.*" Madison tries to separate us. "Chloe, chill out."

Chloe places a hand over her heart. "Me chill?"

Madison nudges me. "I told her to have fun."

"My brother?"

"I didn't specify. Technically."

"What's your problem?" I lean over Chloe. "Like you said, you brought me so he could see me again."

"I don't like seeing you together. Go find some random guy to dance with instead. All I needed to do was bring you here. Now stay the hell away from him." Chloe flicks her hands in front of my face and marches out of the line. Kimberley races after her.

I shake my head at Madison. "Well, I don't need the bathroom."

"Me either."

Walking towards the dancefloor, I spy the bar. Chloe's D&M-ing with Damien.

My eyes roll and my attention turns to the dancefloor. "You wanna dance, Madi?"

"Let's find guys who'll buy us more drinks."

"Fine by me. It was fun with Damien for the fact it pissed off Chloe."

"You are one bad bitch, Brittany Matthews."

I couldn't help myself. Once Chloe left Damien's side, I pounced. Before when Damien's lips closed in on me, the guilt soared to breaking point. Bryce was so clearly in my mind. Now my heart shrinks, knowing I don't want Damien, but Chloe is the reason I lost Bryce. If hanging around Damien makes her mad, I'm going to hang around Damien.

We cosy into a booth as he rains compliments on my appearance. I don't want him getting the wrong idea, so I swivel the conversation to Chloe. Has he had enough drinks to spill dirt on her? The Lucas thing wasn't enough to hurt her, but maybe her brother is the vault where all her secrets are kept.

"What was it like growing up with a sister like Chloe?"

He laughs as he slides his drink on the table. "You mean the princess? The golden child who can do no wrong. Or, pardon me, does everything wrong and gets away with it."

I giggle. "Yeah, her."

"She's all right. She's Cheryl's only kid and Dad's only daughter so she gets spoilt."

"Cheryl's only kid? What about you?"

He shakes his head. "Nah, Jarred and I have a different mum to Chloe. Cheryl is Dad's third wife. We call her Mum because ours is outta the picture. That's what Dad does. Cuts people out."

"You never see your real mum?"

"They got divorced when I was six-months-old. I think they got married after she was pregnant with Jarred, so they were only together a bit over three years. Apparently, she was a drug addict. Dad was ashamed of her and cut all ties. I mean, it's all right. Cheryl is really good to us."

"I heard you have older brothers. Do you see them?"

"Nope. Cut out too. They sided with their mum when Dad divorced her. Dad was pissed off and they're effectively dead to him. We have nieces and nephews we have never met. It's their too bad. Dad has loads more money now than he did during his first two marriages."

"I can see where Chloe gets her ruthless streak."

Damien laughs. "That's one way to put it."

"So, you just grew up with Chloe and Jarred? You three must be close."

He shifts in his seat. "Just with Chlo. Jarred does some screwed up stuff."

My gut tenses as I can't bring myself to say *like what?*

"Are you and Chloe close enough that she told you?"

I purse my lips as puzzlement creases my face. Do I really want this vault opened?

"I was so worried he would rock up at her party, even when I told him to stay away. He'd do it just to be a shithead." He takes a long swig of his drink. "He does messed up things to Chloe... like in her bedroom at night."

Revulsion churns my insides and I slide away from him in the booth. My heart knocks like it wants to give up. I grimace and hold my stomach. Damien returns to his drink, staring ahead, and any chance of appearing like a romantic item is obliterated.

The next morning, we roll our suitcases down the dorm hall. My ears hurt from the thumping of last nights' clubs.

I squint at the morning sun. Chloe has dark oversized sunglasses on and her hair up in a messy ponytail. I can tell she has no makeup on and is trying to hide it. It's the most underdone I've ever seen her.

Damien meets us out front, carrying his sister's bags. They hug and Damien tells her to say hello to their parents.

I give him a small wave as we all get ready to go to the train station.

He walks up to me. "Last night was fun."

"Yeah, it was."

"Sorry my sister had a temper-tantrum and we couldn't hang out more. Maybe I can give you a call the next time I'm in Sanford."

"Ah, maybe." I'm pretty sure Chloe is eavesdropping.

"And, remember, you're always welcome here."

He kisses my cheek and I whisper, "Thanks."

I give him a wink and turn to follow the girls. Two holes in my back care of Chloe.

26

It's like wasps are rampaging inside me. At first I was over the moon when Mrs Vandergarten submitted me for the Whitby Prize, but now I'm so queasy. I can't stop fidgeting as I stand by my entry. The sweat under my arms is out of control as my parents smile, wave, and take pictures.

What makes it worse is Brittany was forced to come. I wish she'd gotten her way and stayed home. I doubt she'll remember the photo. She could not have cared less when I brought it up. She probably won't even look at it. She's too busy picking at her nail polish.

"Hello. Hello everyone," Mr Granger, the gallery curator, talks into a microphone on the small stage. "Thank you all for coming."

Everyone moves around the exhibition with champagne or sparkling apple juice in hand and gathers in front.

"Thanks for taking the time to view the photography from our artists," Mr Granger continues. "It's now time to announce the winner and runner ups of the Whitby Prize."

I swipe my damp palms across my hips and curl my toes in my

ankle boots. I bite inside my cheek hard and retell myself I won't place. I can't even take a picture. How could I win? I'm a fraud.

The runners-up take to the stage and I start to relax. *Phew*, I didn't get called.

"And the winning piece for the Whitby Prize, we are proud to announce, is '*Wilderness*' by Charlotte Matthews."

Applause erupts and I rub my ears, working out if I heard him right.

"Charlotte," Mr Granger says, "will you join us on stage?"

My hands and knees quake as I make my way to the stage. Mr Granger hands me a plaque and a cheque while congratulating me. He gestures to the microphone and asks if there's anything I'd like to say.

My mouth is ironed shut. My voice box is cemented, and my eyes are bugging out.

I won?

Mrs Vandergarten joins me on stage to take a photo for the local paper. The flashes jolt me back to reality, and I don't think I smiled once. Mr Granger describes my work into the microphone as Dad and Tara sweep me up in hugs.

"So proud of you, Pumpkin." Dad is elated, kissing the top of my head.

"You worked so hard and it's paid off," Tara cheers.

My heart rate zooms. I look to Dad and am met with overpowering joy. I swiftly turn away. I've worked so hard for that look, and now I can't accept it.

"I'm going to see Mum," I say sheepishly.

Dad gives me another squeeze. "Sure thing, Pumpkin. I say, after this we should go to *Le Petit* for celebratory crème brûlée."

I fake a weak smile. "Sounds great."

Mum and Brittany stand by my photograph as I scuff my boots towards them.

"This is fantastic, Charli," Mum boasts, throwing an arm around me while keeping eyes on the photograph.

"Thanks, Mum." Out the corner of my eye I view Brittany. Her arms are folded, her head tilted, staring at the photo.

"Brit," Mum says, "are you going to say anything to your sister?"

I suck in air as Brittany turns to me. Her face is so stony I can't read her.

"It's good, Charli."

I gulp. "Thanks."

"Our girl did well," Dad says, strolling up behind us.

Mum smiles softly. "Yes, she did."

Tara's shoulders bunch high as she nods to Mum. "Hi Julie."

Mum nods back. "Hi Tara."

I side-glance Brittany, but her attention is on the photograph. Dizziness sends me into a spill and I almost overbalance.

"You ok, Pumpkin?" Mum says, clasping a hand over my forehead.

I back away and tell her yes.

"Maybe it's all this attention," Tara says.

"Julie, we were thinking dessert at *Le Petit*," Dad says. "Will you join us?"

"All of us?" Mum replies. "Together?"

Tara takes a step towards Mum. "I don't have to be there, if you would prefer."

Mum looks at Dad and Tara and then at us. "No. No, it'll be fine. I'm sure we can all be civil for something sweet."

"Perfection," Dad says. "Let's go, shall we?"

I take a step to follow them when Brittany grabs my wrist. "We'll catch up," she says. "I just want to talk to Charli about her photo."

They all give us endearing looks like we are the sweetest twins in the world.

Brittany stares at me as everyone walks away. "Your skin is turning a little grey."

"Grey?"

"Like you're sick or something." She turns to the photograph. "Or like you stole something."

"Brit..."

"It's mine, isn't it?"

My jaw clenches.

"I probably wouldn't have taken any notice, but you've been squirming and looking guilty all night. Why did you use mine? Did yours suck that much?"

"I didn't have time to reshoot." It's all I can think to say.

"You won a prize with my photo."

"I'll give you the money."

"I guess you'd hate if Mum and Dad found out you cheated."

I quiver. "Are you blackmailing me?"

"Cover for me tonight and I'll keep your secret."

"Cover you? For what?"

"I'm going out with my friends."

"Out where?"

"To a pub."

"A pub? Forget it. No way."

She swivels on her heels. "I'd better catch up to Mum and Dad then."

I grab her shoulder and spin her around. "Ok, ok. I'll cover for you. Just, please, don't say anything.

She pats my head. "Deal."

Brittany came home with Mum and me after an awkward outing at *Le Petit*. When I caught up to them chatting in the carpark, I was moments off asking Tara to keep her offer to not come with us. It could be just the four of us. A family occasion we haven't had in years. But their smiling in my direction and the fear Brittany would say something kept me a nervous wreck. I focused on my crème brûlée and have no idea what anyone said for the short time we were there.

Once home, Brittany changed into something way too tight and plastered on a week's worth of makeup. I distracted Mum and Sophia so she could sneak out. Now it's almost two in the morning and she's not home. Every part of me is tense. I strangle a pillow as I sit on my bed, ears pricked for the front door.

Last I checked, Brittany was sitting alone at school. Now they are all friends again? Suddenly Chloe has let Brittany hang around them again? It can't be that simple. The overwhelming feeling that something has gone wrong cloaks my body. What if they ditched her somewhere? What if it's all a cruel prank? My eyes tear at the thought she is lost or hurt somewhere. I need to find her.

I scroll through my phone contacts with a shaky finger. I pause on Preston. We left things on such bad terms, but he has a car. He always wanted to help, although he was so pushy. I don't really want to go down that road.

I scroll further to Shae. Telling her could easily get back to my parents. She's too close to her mum and I don't trust that she has my back.

Before I can think twice, I click call on Travis's name. My hand tremors as I pull the phone to my ear. My stomach twists and I sniff light sobs.

It rings about seven times and I shut my eyes, sure it will ring out.

"Hello?"

The sound of his voice makes me cry.

"Charli? What's wrong?"

I cover my mouth, squeezing into a ball to make the sobbing stop.

"Charli? Are you there?"

I nod even though he can't see me.

I finally croak, "Yes."

"Where are you? Are you ok?"

"It's Brittany," I say and hiccup a sob.

"What's happened?"

The sound of music, laughter and people shouting is in the background. He's at a party.

"Is she there?" I ask with hope.

"No, I haven't seen her. You don't know where she is?"

I sniffle, "At a pub."

"A pub?"

Three throat-scratching cries rush out of me.

"Oh, Charli. Please don't cry. I'll find her for you."

My sobs intensify. "I... I don't know where she is."

"Charli, it's ok. There's not that many places in town. I'll find her."

"Ok."

"D'you want me to come pick you up?"

I shake my head even though he can't see me. "No, I'm going to wait for her."

"Ok. I'll call you back. Please don't be scared."

"Ok."

I drop the phone and stare at the Travis' contact page. A shiver runs down my spine and I hug a pillow.

I drag myself off the bed and slowly pace my bedroom. My hands clasp over my heart and ease washes over me. He's going to help. He helped so fast.

I didn't even ask.

After almost fifteen minutes of sitting cross-legged on the floor and clutching my phone, a creak sounds downstairs. I toss the phone and bolt out of the room. I bound down the stairs and spot Brittany, stumbling as she reefs off her stilettos.

"Brittany," I whisper. "How did you get home?"

She collapses to the tiles to tug off her shoes. I kneel beside her and help with the buckles as she replies, "Taxi."

My heart sinks.

She twirls my hair around her fingers. "Sometimes you're a good sister."

"C'mon, let's go upstairs."

"Everyone says you're such a goody-goody. You really came through."

As I pull her up, I get a strong whiff of alcohol. "*Geez*, Brit, how much did ya drink?"

Her thumb and index finger close in on my face. "Just a little bit."

"Can you walk up the stairs?"

"I'm not a baby."

"You can barely walk straight. Just let me help you."

"You should go out more. It's fun."

"Where did you go?"

"*O'Malley's.*"

"How did you get in?"

"With my ID."

"Like a fake ID? Where did you get that?"

"In Sydney," she slurs.

"When were you in Sydney?"

She rubs her forehead. "I'm dizzy."

"All right, Brit. Time for bed."

Upstairs, Brittany stumbles into her room, zigzagging left to right, and struggling to get her skin-tight top over her bust.

"Hang on, let me help you."

"I'm fine," she mumbles as I pull down the top and unzip the back.

Before she can fight me, I unzip her skirt. She curls up on her bed as I pick up her pyjamas. "You wanna put these on?"

She lazily waves me off.

"I'll get a makeup wipe to clean your face."

Brittany tugs on my arm and says, "Thanks, Sissy."

I blink my watery eyes and squeeze her hand. It's been a long time since she's called me that.

Before going to the bathroom, I walk into my room and get my phone.

> *(Me)* **She's home.**
>
> *(Travis)* **I'm glad to hear it. You want me to come over?**
>
> *(Me)* **No, it's ok.**
>
> *(Travis)* **You sounded so upset. I can come and just talk…**
>
> *(Travis)* **If it'll make you feel better…**
>
> **(Me) IDK**
>
> *(Travis)* **I'm near your place anyway. I'll park outside your house. I'll be there for 10 mins. You come out if you want to talk. If you don't come out by 10 mins…I'll drive away.**
>
> *(Travis)* **All up to you…**

My hands sweat and shake so much I drop the phone. I sit against the doorframe and hold my knees. My mind races with incoherent thoughts. Nothing that helps decide whether I should see him.

I stand up and move to the landing. I creep downstairs and my heart *ba-booms*. I need to see his car outside. I don't know what I'll do, but I just need to know he's there.

Peering out the living room curtains, I squeak at sight of his car. *Ba-boom, ba-boom, ba-boom.* I slide down the wall and clutch my phone over my heart.

I check my phone to see if he's texted again. Nothing.

I poise my thumbs, ready to type. Nothing comes to mind. I drop the phone and peer through the curtain again. I'm beyond dizzy.

I push myself up ready to go outside and instantly fall down again. Images of that night pour into my mind. The glassy look in his eyes, his exploring hands, the way I had to hurt him to make him stop.

The way he didn't listen to me.

Tears roll down my cheeks, the saltiness stains my lips. My nose runs and I sniff gross sounds. I edge towards the foyer and sit against the front door. My heart hurts but I grip the door handle. I sit with my arm up for what feels like forever. I peek at my phone and tense with only two minutes left. I let go of the doorknob.

My hands clasp over my mouth, and my breathing sucks them in, like I'm moments off hyperventilating. I rest my face against the door and release my hands to press against it.

My phone buzzes and I check the message.

(Travis) **It's ok.**

An engine starts up. My tears stream as he drives away. I hate that he might think I don't care. Just a couple more minutes... I might have gone out there...

It felt like an eternity sitting on the foyer tiles. I swipe my face dry and climb the stairs. I get the makeup wipes and walk into Brittany's bedroom. She breathes with heavy sleep sounds. I climb in next to her because I'd hate to be alone right now.

She shifts, flips around to me and whispers, "I'm glad you're back."

I hug her and shrink under the covers. "I need you, Britty."

She gulps loudly and tenses. "He called me that."

"Bryce?"

She sniffles. "I want to keep partying to forget him. But it never goes away." Her arms pull around me. Her heart beats against mine as we miss them both.

Two hearts battling,
In a war of love and loss,
Two beings of one life,
Struggling apart.

I woke this morning to the sounds of Brittany puking in the bathroom. The anxiety while waiting for her to come home last night must have taken its toll as it was the deepest I'd slept in a while. It's midday and she's still green as we pile into Tara's minivan. Mum wasn't too happy about Dad taking us during her weekend, but they seem to have come to a secret agreement.

I'm too busy keeping eyes on Brittany, hoping she keeps in the remaining contents of her stomach, I don't notice we are in The Heights until Tara parks. Out the window is a massive house surrounded by a construction fence.

"Right, everybody out," Dad hollers, sliding open the passenger door.

I squint at the house. When Dad said he *and Tara* wanted to see us, I expected to be going to that shoebox across the tracks. The yard is littered with pavers, paint cans and a giant skip bin. The confused expressions on Nick and Shae calm me down. At least they don't know what's going on either.

Dad opens the fence gate and beckons us to follow. Brittany cuffs my wrist and walks glued beside me. She doesn't want to keel over, but I appreciate the closeness. We follow Dad and Tara around the path to the backyard. They stand on the grass holding hands and grinning ear-to-ear. Shae, Nick, Brittany and I semicircle awkwardly while Alyssa squats on the ground complaining of boredom.

"See that beach down there." Tara points between the trees.

This yard in on the highest point of The Heights. Below, the waves crash navy into turquoise with a wash of white onto golden sand.

"That's where we will be getting married," Dad blurts out, followed with a chuckle.

My throat closes in and I splutter a cough. Brittany's fingers intertwine with mine and she clamps down hard.

"What?" Shae yells.

Tara giggles, swinging Dad's arm. "We're getting married."

"Wow... well, that's great," Nick grins, his eyes unable to hide the surprise. He rocks on his heels and then speeds his courage to hug the pair.

They break away from the hug and Tara moves towards Shae. "Sweetie?"

"You didn't marry Mason," Shae says. "Why are you rushing?"

"Hunny, we're not rushing. When it's right, it's right."

Shae purses her lips and hugs her mother.

Dad walks towards Brittany and me. "Girls?"

My chest rises with my rapid breaths.

"You're getting married?" Brittany murmurs.

Dad nods, smiling.

Brittany flings my hand away and embraces Dad.

I'm frozen.

"Charlotte?" he whispers as he moves away from Brittany. He bends his knees to meet my eyes.

I can't even blink.

He cups my chin. "It's ok."

I look past him to Tara. My eyes sting.

I lost.

I bang my head against his shoulder, and he pulls me into a warm hug.

"So... explain why we're here," Shae says.

Dad eyes Shae, an arm still around me. "You don't like your new home?"

I cough and look up at him. "You bought this place?"

"*We* bought this place," Tara answers for him.

Shae claws at her hair. "I'm prepping for final exams and you want to move?"

Tara jitters with excitement. "Kids, this is where we will live."

"Hang on, what?" Nick says.

"Hunny, we can finally move out of Nanna and Granddad's."

Nick steps away from his mother. "And what will happen to the house?"

"We'll sell it."

"You're selling Granddad's house?"

"We don't need it."

Nick's voice wavers, "How can you say that?"

Tara steps towards Nick, and he takes three steps back. Shae moves between them, wrapping her brother in her arms.

"You're getting married on the beach?" Shae asks.

Tara claps, giddy. "Yes, we can see the spot every day from our new home."

"Not in our church?" Shae fires back.

Tara's smile flips upside-down. "Ah, no."

"The church we go to every Sunday," Shae says, holding her brother tighter. "Our community. You won't make your vows there?"

Tara smiles and walks towards Dad. "Rob's not religious, so we will commit to each other somewhere that means something to both of us."

"It doesn't bother you he doesn't go to church?" Nick asks.

Dad takes Tara's hand. "Your mother and I have had these

discussions. We will never get in the way of each other's beliefs."

Tara unravels her hand from Dad's and asks him to give her a minute with her kids. Dad beckons Brittany and me to follow him into the house.

"It's an old house," Dad says and walks into a massive open living area. Dust cakes the rich, dark timber floors. "We busted the walls open to make it feel bigger. Each of you kids have a bedroom downstairs, and upstairs will be an office for Tara and me, plus our bedroom and ensuite."

Brittany's eyes bug as big as mine. We get to visit Dad in a house instead of an apartment... that'll be nice. He'll be living with another family? Not ours... And, wait, he's...

"You're getting married?" I whimper.

Dad takes my sister and me by the hand. "It's a shock?"

We nod.

"I hope you can understand and get past that this seems fast. Your mum and I have been apart for years. Yes, the divorce may have only been finalised at the end of last year, but we were separated long before. Tara is good for me. We help each other and make each other stronger. Being in a good relationship will only be a good influence on you two. Can you trust in that?"

Tara and her kids join us in the plastic covered, paint fumed living room. With solemn faces, Shae carries Alyssa and Nick stands behind her, it's evident they feel the same as me and my sister. No one has it better in this situation, except, perhaps, our parents.

Tara walks by Dad and says, "The house will still take some time to finish, so we won't be in here until after your exams, Shae."

"And the wedding will be the beginning of summer," Dad adds.

"A ceremony with only family," Tara says. "Then we can all live here and overlook the spot we became a family."

"And, Nick," Dad says, "you can transfer to *John Thomas*."

Colour drains from Nick's face. "Um, we'll see."

I link arms with Brittany and it's a relief when she doesn't nudge me off. Dad and his apparent fiancé stand together, and I shake my head. What is even happening?

27

Brittany

"I'm so exhausted from all the dance practices this week," I complain to Meah as we walk to our lockers. "It's getting as intense as ballet was. I'm so over it."

"Yeah, yeah, whatever," Meah says, flicking her hair and skidding to a stop at her locker.

"Whatever?"

"You keep rubbing dance classes in my face."

"What?"

"You get all this extra time with Chloe and you pretend it's so hard."

I squint at her, shifting my weight.

"I wasn't the one who was kicked out, but I still have to work my butt off to get some attention." She huffs, flicking her hair to the max. "You get this advantage and mock me with it. I got skinny and shit, but you always gotta one-up me."

"I only said I was tired."

353

"*Gawd*, whatever." Meah slams her locker shut and marches down the corridor.

I throw my arms in the air and shake my head. I shouldn't be surprised really. When I said my dad is getting re-married, you know, *earth-shattering* news, all she had to say was, *"Whoah, so you, like, get step-brothers and step-sisters now?"*

I know we were in this for some popularity at any cost, but she could still try to be a friend. It's like she doesn't even see me as a person anymore. I'm competition.

With a huff, I grab a textbook from my locker and leave in the opposite way to Meah. I hug the book as I close in on Kimmy and Madison. Madison is ok, but Kimberley scares me. At any moment she can snap. If Chloe decides to be nice to me, Kimmy follows. I know she doesn't like me... *still* doesn't like me. I grow rigid as steel ready for an attack every time I'm near her.

"What are you looking at, freakshow?" Kimberley yells across the corridor.

I panic, but Kimberley's not looking at me. I follow her gaze and land on my sister.

Charli walks in my direction, attempting an escape from Kimmy's radar.

"Like seeing what washed and brushed hair looks like?" Kimmy cackles. "You sexless dopehead."

Madison eyes me and elbows Kimmy in the ribs. "Cool it."

Kimberley shoves Madison. "What?"

Madison nudges her head towards me. "It's her sister. Zip it."

"Shuddup, Madi," Kimmy hisses. "I can say whatever the hell I want."

Charli zips past me. "Just ignore them."

I get a flash of holding Charli's hand in my bed on Saturday night. "I can't."

Charli stops and frowns at me.

"She can't say that stuff to you."

She smiles, steps in close and whispers, "It was on the tip of my tongue... I so wanted to shout, loud enough for everyone to hear, about the time I'd covered the fact she peed herself in grade four. No way has she forgotten that. But somehow she'd flip it back on me."

"I'll say it."

"It's not worth it, Brit. Forget her."

Humiliating Kimberley in front of everyone would be so satisfying. After all the times she left me out. Every time she made Charli pick her over me. All the times she dissed me in front of Chloe.

I hate how much time I've spent around her this year. I march towards her.

"Brittany." Charli grabs my arm and reefs me back. "Don't."

Kimberley crosses her arms and lets out a slow laugh.

"We haven't forgotten what you were like as a kid," I say.

Kimberley rolls her eyes and turns away from us.

I raise my voice so everyone in the corridor hears. "When everyone called you names, and Charli felt sorry for you."

"Brit," Charli hushes.

Kimberley whips around to us. "You'd better shut your mouth."

I throw my arms up. "Or what?"

Charli yanks my arm down and pulls me back. "We are so going."

"Don't you want to say something to her?" I ask Charli.

Charli frowns at Kimberley. "She's a totally different person to who I knew. I wouldn't know where to start."

Kimberley's eyes dart between Charli and me. Her lips purse almost like she's scared of what we might say.

I shrug and whisper to Charli. "At least she's quiet now."

Charli presses on my back. "C'mon, let's go."

A small smile relaxes my face. I walk by Charli's side, happy she pulled me away from Kimberley.

"I can't believe I was ever friends with her," Charli whispers. She eyes me. "How are you hanging out with her?"

I shake my head. "She's just around."

"You don't need them."

"Don't start with me, Charli."

I turn towards the north wing and dig my hands in my pockets as Charli doesn't follow.

That afternoon I reef my gym bag over my shoulder and trudge from Sophia's car to the dance studio. Getting ready felt like a massive effort. Thank goodness the end of year concert is coming up soon. I need a break from all of this.

A few steps away from the studio door, I stop mid-step and double-take at someone ahead.

Bryce?

He leaves an office building and turns my direction. My bag drops to the ground as we lock eyes.

"You're back?" I manage.

He stops and his hands scrunch in his hair.

I rush to him. "What's happened?"

Dark circles hang beneath his red-rimmed eyes. His chapped lips struggle to form words.

My eyes tear. "When did you get back?"

"My mum," he says, hugging his waist.

Dread sinks me into gravity.

"She's in hospital." His voice cracks. "They put her in a coma."

My balance stumbles. "What does that mean?"

He sniffs and tears roll down his cheeks. "She's dying."

"Bryce." I pull him into my arms. His head falls on my shoulder and his body shakes as his cries become audible.

"It's my fault," he sobs. "I went away, and she got worse."

I hold him close. "No. No, it's not your fault. Don't say that."

"Bryce?" Amy calls behind me. "Bryce, let's get going."

Bryce pulls away, wipes his face and walks away from me. I turn, stunned, as Amy takes him by the hand and leads him to her car. My chest rapidly rises and falls as they drive away.

His mum is dying?

No...

She can't be dying.

I rub my heart. I'm crushed for him.

A plaque on the building he came from reads, *Dr Henry Vernon, Clinical Psychologist.* I shake the eeriness off my shoulders. I walk to my bag and hoist it into the studio.

"Hey Brit," Tiffany says, bouncing in her sneakers during warm up. "We'll begin in two minutes."

I dump my bag and robotically begin stretches. Bryce never leaves my mind. I badly wanted to ask him where he's been, but he was so devastated. I spy Chloe across the room. Does she know? She says she knows everything about him. I will the tears back to their duct as anger curls my fists. I hate the idea of Chloe comforting him.

Tiffany calls us in to begin our opening routine for the concert. I take my mark and assume I'm making my steps. All I can see is Bryce. He was broken. My heart is in pieces.

I slam into the girl on my right when I make a wrong step.

"Ouch, watch it," she grizzles.

"Sorry," I mumble, rubbing my arm.

Tiff gets us to start over, but I still don't focus. I want to be with him. I want to hug him. I want to tell him everything will be ok.

I want to make things better between us.

"*Ohmigawd*, Brittany," Chloe snaps. "What are you even doing?"

I shake out of my thoughts and take in all the eyes on me. A red heat coats my face.

"Brittany, stand up front with me," Tiffany says. I feel like a puppy about to be hit with rolled-up newspaper. "Step alongside me as the rest of the group practices the routine together."

I try to hide the rolling of my eyes. It's not my first day. I don't need to be babied. I just need a break.

The rest of class was unbearably humiliating. Chloe kept her eagle-eyes on me. I really couldn't care less about her opinion any more. It's not important. Seeing Bryce and helping him is what's important.

It's dinner at Dad's tonight. Tara fusses in the kitchen like she has to make a better impression now she will be Mrs Matthews. That news hit me like a freight train. I'm not wrong, it's fast, right? Charli has barely talked to me about it, but she always takes longer to process things than me.

Dad takes a seat at the table and asks Charli and me to put our phones down. It's like my phone in superglued to my hand. I've been staring at the old message chain with Bryce, trying to figure out how to word a new text. The chain is littered with unanswered texts from me after our break up. I close my eyes and slide the phone to the middle of the table.

"So, your birthdays are coming up," Dad says and rubs his hands together. "Sweet sixteen. You kids deserve the best, so we will celebrate in style. How does your first cars sound as a birthday present?"

My heart skips a beat and a smile cracks my face. "You serious?"

"Of course," Dad says. "We'll take a trip to the dealership and you can choose your models."

I get this sick feeling about being happy. It's not right with what Bryce is going through. I scoot my chair back and excuse myself from the table saying, "Thanks, Dad, that's really great."

"Brit?" Charli says.

I keep walking away from the table, clasping my elbows.

"What do you think, Charli?" Dad asks, still upbeat.

"Yeah, Dad, it's fine," Charli rushes. She leaves the table and meets me by the couch. "What's up with you?"

I keep my face from her. "Nothing."

"I hear it in your voice. Something's wrong. What's happened?"

"I want to go home."

Dad moves over. "Sweetheart, what's wrong?"

I hug myself tighter. "I want to go home."

He rubs my back. "You are home."

I flinch from him. "No, I want Mum."

Charli steps in front of me and whispers, "Will you talk to me?"

I avert my eyes.

"Brittany," Dad says, "this is your home, too. Let's talk this out. Do you not want a car?"

I groan furiously. "What? It's nothing to do with a stupid car."

"Dad," Charli says, "maybe give us a minute."

Dad backs off and I slip down to the carpet. Charli sits by me, waiting for me to speak.

"I saw him," I whisper.

"Saw who?"

"Bryce."

"Oh wow, really? He's back?"

I rub my heart and say, "He's back because his mum is in hospital."

"Oh shit. That's horrible."

"Charli, he cried in front of me. He was a wreck."

Charli wraps her arms around me. "I'm sorry. So, you can't stop thinking about him?"

I shake my head as I fight back tears.

"What can I do?" she asks.

"I'm so scared for him, you know. All he's ever thought about is something bad happening at home... and now it has."

"I got you. Tell me how to help and I'll do it."

"Sis, I don't even know how I can help."

28

Charli

(Shae) Hey Charli! It's still so crazy to think our parents will be married. One big family. CRAZY. Maybe we can chat about this? Mum was talking bout getting dresses. Maybe you and Brittany can come shopping with us? What do you think?

(Preston) Heyyy. Hope you ok? Shae told me bout the wedding news. You need a hug? I'm still here for you.

I shove my phone in my pencil case, ignoring all incoming texts. Just in time as Mr Phelps places my marked test on my desk. Fifty-three percent. I blink hard at it. Fifty-three percent?

I flunked?

My heart rate amps up as realisation set in. I'm bad at maths... but this bad? Fucking shit. Dad will flip it.

I'm battered as I scuff my way out of the classroom. My blazer scrapes against the wall as I make my way through the corridor.

"Charli," Travis' voice pulls me out of my haze.

I stop as he walks towards me.

"I know from Meah that Brittany's ok, but are you ok?"

"Ok?"

"After Friday night? You sounded so shaken up."

"Oh, that. That's nothing. It's like life keeps dumping buckets of crap on me every time I think things are clearing up."

He tilts his head to find my eyes. "What's happened?"

My eyes water the moment they make contact with his. I purse my lips and move away from him.

He takes my shoulders and spins me back. "Charli? What's wrong?"

"I can't," I sniffle.

"Can't what?"

"I can't talk about it. I can't talk to you."

He squeezes my shoulders. "Yes you can."

I close my eyes and suck back a sob. *I wish I could.*

A hint of vanilla from his cologne plays at my nostrils and I shake my head. I want to curl up in his arms and share all my problems with him. Like I used to. When it was safe to do so.

I clutch his wrists and remove his hands from me. I open my eyes and walk around him and continue down the corridor.

Part of me wishes he'd stop me again.

I escape out the west wing and hide behind a pillar by the teachers' carpark. I pull out my phone and call Kellie.

"Yo," she answers.

"Where are you?" I ask with a shaky voice.

"At my locker. Shit, what's wrong?"

"I can't be here any more. I can't stand another minute in this school. Will you ditch with me?"

"You not wanting to be here is some deep shit. Where are you?"

"Teachers' carpark. Meet me by delivery dock behind mess hall?"

"I'm on my way."

I end the call and a buzz alert vibrates my phone. **New Text -**

Travis.

My hand trembles as I open the message.

> **(Travis) I get not wanting to talk to me in front of everyone. If you want, there's a 7.30pm screening of a tale of two cities at old cinema. I'll be there if you want to meet up. Up to you...**

I lock my phone before I can think of a response. Before my shaking drops it, I slip the phone in my pocket. I wish everything hadn't changed. That going to the old cinema with him would feel normal and right. But, I guess, if things hadn't been messed up with Dad I'd never have that summer with Travis. What would be worse? Keeping Dad at home with all the screaming matches between him and Mum, and never having the love of Travis...

I know you're leaving,
How can you think it is ok?
I need you
And I don't want you to go.
It's so very tough
Wish you weren't so sad,
I want to make it better
But not an idea how.

Please don't go away,
Be here when I come home.
Let me give you my problems,
And help me with solutions.
Stop yelling
And just be still,
What am I to do without you?
Alone and empty shell.

I hate that I still remember every fucking line. I wrote it the night before Dad officially moved out. Deep down I knew it was coming, but

I hung onto denial like a safety blanket.

Mum was always screaming at him to not give up, not to walk away. I don't know why I didn't check on her more. We wanted the same thing. Dad would stay calm and, with a flat tone, say there was nothing left to save. That it was done.

Our family was done.

He'd say we were all still in this together. That just because the marriage was over, didn't mean the love was gone. But he left for months. He thought of another family before ours.

I think I can delete that poem from my memory.

"So, you failed a test," Kellie says as we cycle into the forest. "Majority of your tests you have aced, so it's not going to affect your grades much."

"Not the point, Kel. You know what my dad's like. School is the only way I can communicate with him."

"Bullshit."

I brake hard. "Excuse me?"

She keeps cycling.

"Kellie."

She brakes and leans her bike against a tree. She huffs as she walks up to me. "School is what you talk about with him instead of dealing with the real issues."

I trigger the kickstand and get off my bike. "I, what?"

"You want him to pat you on the head and tell you you're amazing, like it'll erase everything from the past."

"It's not like that at all."

"I was there, Charli. I heard the way your parents screamed when we were in your bedroom. I was there to pick you up after he moved out. And you think good grades will make everything better?"

I scoop my wayward curls and hold them in a bun as I groan and turn from Kellie.

"I didn't mean to make you mad, but maybe it's good I did. Maybe you need to be angry."

I let go of my hair and turn to her. "What, at you?"

"If it helps."

I groan again and crouch on the ground.

"C'mon," Kellie says, bending down to touch my shoulder. "Let's get to our spot in the row of trees and talk about it."

"About what? How I'm shit at life?"

Kellie *tsks*. "Damn, when'd you get so depressive?"

I stand up and wrap my arms around Kellie's neck. "Ok, you lead."

The sun criss-crosses through the trees as we reach our favourite part of the forest. We sit down on the patchy grass and I fling myself backwards to stare at the sky between the tall trees. My ears prick to the sound of sparks. I lift my head as Kellie lights her joint.

"Where did you get that?"

She taps her blazer. "My pocket."

"You had it at school?"

She takes a puff and smiles. "That's the good thing about being a goody-goody. No one suspects the goody-goody."

I sit up and rub my tired eyes. "Travis asked me to meet him tonight."

"What?"

"I didn't tell you... he helped me on the weekend."

"Helped you?"

Deep breath. "You know the Whitby Prize."

Kellie dips her glasses. "Yeah?"

"Brittany took the photo. My photos sucked. Like, *fail-art-class* bad."

"Wait, Brittany took the photo for you?"

"*Nah-uh*. She took some photos with my camera and Mrs

Vandergarten liked them. She said I'd be a shoo-in if I used them. I knew I wouldn't win with my photo. I didn't really think too much about it... I mean, the editing was all my work."

"Holy shit, Charli!" Kellie says, throwing her arms out wide. "No wonder you're bugging out about failing when you stole somebody else's work."

I bite my lip hard and then say, "And there's more."

Kellie's jaw drops, waiting.

"Tayla wrote a speech for my Spanish class... I intended to rewrite it... at first."

"You used her speech for your assignment? *Geez*, I didn't know when I did your science homework for you I'd send you down a wrong path."

"I didn't have time to write it. You know I was struggling with the class."

"You're pinning this on me because I didn't help you study verbs?"

"No, no, of course not."

"Shit, Charli. Is it really worth impressing your Dad if you are cheating? What's been going on with you?"

My bottom lip quivers. "It's just been hard, you know? I had all these intentions to get perfect marks, then he comes back to town and flips everything upside-down. I could never predict a new family getting in the mix."

Kellie takes my hand. "Of course, you didn't. You've held it together really well. You don't have to be perfect. Be real. The real Charli is pretty freakin awesome."

I break into a smile. "Thanks, Kel."

"Well, I should tell you," she says with a sigh, "I didn't get the Ferguson Award."

"Oh, Kel. After you've worked so hard. I'm so sorry. Are you ok?"

"Thanks, I'm ok. I was sad, but nothing like Rikki."

"What? Did she get it?"

Kellie splutters a laugh. "Nope. Some guy in Tully got it. Rikki went psychotic."

"You're kidding?"

She shakes her head, smirking. "She flipped a table."

Shocked laughter tumbles out of me. "That's insane."

"I know." Kellie grabs my hand, changing pace. "Wait, what did your story have to do with Travis?"

I explain how Brittany recognised her photo and blackmailed me into covering for her going out all night. How I was out of mind scared she was in trouble. How I called him for help.

"Why didn't you call me?"

"Kel, I was a wreck. All I was thinking about was someone with a car... he got in that car before I even had to ask. He was there for me just like he always had been."

A concerned expression takes over Kellie's face.

"Don't give me that look."

"Sorry. I know I shouldn't talk after the whole *Will thing*."

"Forget it. I should have been more sensitive about that."

"Ok, we both need to shuddup," Kellie laughs.

"Anyway, Brit came home on her own, so I let Travis know to stop looking. He texted that he'd be outside my house if I needed to talk. He gave me a ten-minute timer to decide. Kel, I was like seconds off going out there. I can't forget what happened, but my Travis still exists. I don't know what to do."

"Damn, I dunno either. Do you want to be with him?"

"I don't know."

"Do you know what you want at all? You've been pushing yourself for grades when it hasn't come naturally. What do you really want?"

I collapse backwards on the ground. "To be free."

"Excuse me?"

The trees dance in the gentle breeze. "What do you think of me going away for a while?"

"What the hell does that mean?"

I sit up and pull a flyer from my pocket. "This."

Kellie unfolds the paper and grows wide-eyed as she reads it. "Charli, this is epic."

My excitement bubbles. "I know."

The joint twirls in Kellie's fingers. *Fuck it.* I grab it and put it between my lips. I inhale and instantly start coughing.

"Damn, girl. I cudda givin ya instructions if you'd told me you wanted a drag."

I tap my chest as my throat clears. "Spur of the moment decision."

Kellie takes the joint and another wave of guilt crashes over me. I pull out my phone and bring up a page on Google. "I shouldn't have given you a hard time about weed when I've been using these."

Kellie takes my phone, her eyes bulging in her frames as she reads about the focus pills. "What? You've been taking these? How long?"

My body caves in. "A while..."

"Charli, these are amphetamines," Kellie says, dropping the phone. "This is really dangerous. Stop taking them."

"I just wanted to stay up at night." Even I want to slap myself right now.

"You'll get insomnia if you take too much of these."

I sigh and run my fingers through a patch of grass. "I know. I've stopped taking them, but I still can't go to sleep. It's like my body forgot what it means to go to bed. I'm tired all day but wired at night."

"You're going to crash hard. You need to see a doctor." She whips out her phone. "I'll make the appointment for you."

I push her phone down. "I'm sorry I didn't talk to you about this sooner."

Her shoulders droop. "Girl, you should have told me right away.

Promise me you won't keep anything like this a secret again."

I smile and clutch her hands. "I promise."

From the forest I cycle straight to my dad's new office. Fresh from a Kellie pep talk, I got this.

Hopefully.

She was right. Grade ten was the year of the fake Charli.

Dad's receptionist tells me I have to wait in the foyer, but I'm busting. I text him three times that I'm out front and need to talk.

"Tina," my dad's voice sounds through the intercom. "I'm wrapping things up with Mr Birchman. Can you please make my daughter a green tea while she waits?"

I squirm in my seat. Way to say, *stop texting, Charli.*

After an eternity, Dad's voice nears the foyer as he walks his client out.

"This is a surprise," he says, greeting me with a hug.

"Hey Dad." I kiss his cheek.

"What's up, Pumpkin?"

"Can we talk in your office?"

"Sure thing. Follow me." When we get into his office, he shows me to an armchair. "Did you race here after school? It's early for you to get here."

"Kinda... Dad, I don't want a car."

Dad chuckles. "Don't tell me you want a motorbike or something crazy. That's not happening."

"No, I want to go overseas."

"I'm sorry?"

I take out the flyer and steady my hand as I give it to him. "It's an exchange program. In Spain."

Dad takes the flyer, frowning. "You want to go to Spain? Charli, you're prepping for senior studies. I don't see how you could think this is a good idea."

He hands me the flyer, but I push it back, wanting him to read it. "It's an international school. All my grades will count when I get back. I'll start in early January and be back at *John Thomas* ready for term four, when classes really count."

"This is something you really want?"

"I'll learn so much more. And it'll look really good when it comes time to applying to universities."

He nods. "I'll talk it over with your mother."

I bite my bottom lip and dare a smile. "It is what I really want."

"You'd be ok being so far away for almost a year?"

"Don't know if I don't try."

"Is this because Tara and I are getting married?"

I huff and slide down my chair. "No, I'm just thinking of myself for once."

Dad breaks a smile and chuckles. "For once? You're a teenager. Thinking of yourself is the default."

My forehead crinkles, the frown ironclad. I stand and reef the flyer from him. "I'll talk to Mum myself. Forget it."

"Charli. Sit."

"Why?"

"Sit down."

I plonk down and keep eyes on the window overlooking the bay.

"I just want to check you're not running away from your problems," Dad says. "I won't allow that. The wedding will be happening." He points to the flyer. "If you're going to Spain, we will have to set the date before then."

I eye Dad. "If I go to Spain?"

"I can call your mother now and ask if she can join us for this conversation."

I sigh in relief. "Do it."

Dad, Mum and I sit down for dinner. Relaxed and comfortable at *Sal's Pizzeria*. I called Brittany and she agreed to join us. She's been so down since seeing Bryce, I'm glad she's keeping her family close.

We talked about the exchange program and Mum and Dad acted like parents. Like co-parents. That didn't happen when they lived together. The evening neared perfect. Who'd have known getting my parents together took me leaving the country?

Our dinner ran well through '*A Tale of Two Cities.*' I text Travis, hoping he will understand.

(Me) Coming out of darkness, Lighting up my life.

29

Today, I dress in black. A few days ago Bryce texted saying his mum died. It was the hardest I've cried in my life. I texted him every day so he knew I was there. I hate he thinks it's all his fault. She was sick. In no way was this his fault.

The funeral service was as morbid as expected. Mum and Charli sat with me. Once it was over, we made our way to Bryce's family. As we neared the front of the church, Mr Kerry accepted condolences, but Bryce wasn't near him. I spied him trying to be invisible on the other side of the pews. I didn't blame him.

Mr Kerry asked us to their house for the wake. My nerves scatter, though I want to be there if Bryce needs me.

I walk the house with Mum and Charli, and don't see Bryce. I bypass his bedroom and the door is shut. I have no game plan other than to stand by the door, awkwardly.

The door opening startles me. We stare at each other. His face is sunken, his posture drooped. Something familiar sparkles in his eye and

I immediately move towards him. I wrap my arms around him, and he limply latches on. He sighs like he has no energy to cry.

"I need air," he says.

"Oh, ok," I reply, stepping away from him.

He takes my hand. "Will you come outside with me?"

I nod as tingles run up my arm.

I follow Bryce to the backyard, dodging an onslaught of aunts, uncles, and family friends. We sit on a bench in the courtyard, and he says, "Thanks for being here."

"I wouldn't be anywhere else."

Caitlyn walks outside, paper plate in hand. "I got us some cake."

Bryce waves her off. "Thanks, I don't want any."

"Mum said I have to make sure you eat."

Bryce tenses up.

Caitlyn shoves the plate at him. "Eat! Eat!"

"Ok, ok," I say taking the plate from Caitlyn. "You take one Cait, and I'll make sure Bryce has one."

Bryce taps the space beside him and his sister hops on the bench. He shrugs and breaks off a piece of cake. "If I'm force-fed something, cake's not a bad option."

Will, Naveen, Chloe and Jace join us outside.

"How you doing, BK?" Naveen asks, sitting opposite us. Will pats Bryce on the shoulder, mute for the first time in history.

Chloe pinches my dress. "You look pretty today." She smooths over her silky black dress. "I can't believe I found this at Tully mall. I have heaps of little black dresses, but none that say funeral, you know. More like for when we go clubbing."

I roll my eyes. *Just shuddup.*

I rub circles on Bryce's back as he hunches over. Suddenly, he's up and rushing into the house.

"Bryce?" I chase after him.

I follow him around the house and stop by the guest bathroom he escaped into. I press my hands against the door. "Bryce? You ok?"

A garbled gagging noise comes from inside the bathroom. Just like the day at Kings Cliff. And then there's silence in the room. Too much silence.

"Bryce, baby." I knock gently on the door. "It's ok."

The flush sounds and I unclench slightly.

I knock again. "Bryce?"

The latch sounds and the door creaks open. I slip inside and close the door behind me. He's hunched over the basin.

"B." I hold his shoulders and try to stay strong.

"Sorry," he whispers.

"What for? You've done nothing wrong."

"It was just a bit much out there. I haven't seen everyone in weeks. Suddenly they're all at my house."

"Because they care about you and want to support you. That's what friends are for."

"I'm glad you're still here."

I smile but the guilt of where we ended things tornadoes inside me. I blurt out, "I'm sorry about the whole Damien thing."

"Brittany, you don't have to."

"I hate that I did it. It's just that Chloe kept telling me I had to sleep with you, or you'd dump me, and when you didn't—"

He faces me. "She did what?"

"I thought I should listen to her about that stuff."

"How dare she? Our relationship is none of her business. It's only ours."

Our relationship.

"I can't talk about this right now." He wipes his eyes.

I take my hands off him. "Do you want me to go?"

"Um, I'd like it if you stayed." *Ba-boom.* "Maybe just in silence, but maybe if I need to talk.”

“Anything you want.”

“Having you to talk to did make life easier.”

“I feel the same. I hate that it all ended.”

He leans against the vanity and crosses his arms. “We never actually broke up.”

Ba-boom.

Bryce asks me to follow him to his bedroom. He sits on his bed as I wall-hug. Two months ago, I was in here spouting *I-love-you*’s. Now it’s like I don’t belong.

He pats the bed, gesturing for me to sit. *Ba-boom, ba-boom, ba-boom.*

I creep over and sit with him. The silence is raw yet being beside him is comfortable. We dangle our legs over the bed with a distinct gap between our hands. My fingers want to intertwine with his. I scrunch the bed cover instead.

“It was hard being around you,” he breaks the silence.

Slick sweat runs across my chest.

He exhales and slumps over. “I can’t believe my mum is gone.”

A lump clogs my throat. “Oh, Bryce.”

“It was hard living with her, but it’s hard to imagine not seeing her every day.”

The sorrow shifts his eyes a darker shade. “Last thing I ever heard her say was ‘fix him.’”

I jolt in surprise. “Fix him?”

His face collapses in his hands and he nods.

I touch his shoulder. “There’s nothing to fix.”

“They sent me away. They didn’t want to deal with my problems.”

I purse my lips, but I have to ask. “Where did you go?”

“They called it a wellness centre.”

I drop my fidgety hands to my lap. “Like a rehab?”

"Kinda... like a mental health one."

I whisper, "So, Chloe was right."

"Huh?"

"Chloe said she came to see you in the hospital, and you confided in her."

"Confided?" His nose scrunches. "I never saw Chloe."

"Really? She was telling people at school..."

His shoulders droop. "She was spreading rumours about me?"

I focus on the carpet as we fall into silence. His breathing seemingly megaphoned.

"I wanted to tell you so many times," he says.

My gaze stays down so he can take his time.

A shattered sigh puffs out of him and he continues, "Like at the beach or at your house. But I made excuses not to."

"You're sick?"

"They talked me through it at *Kleinwood*. They called it a binge eating disorder... I dunno, I felt useless at home, but I could control what I ate... or didn't eat."

A shiver runs down my body. "I had no idea. I knew things were tough... I wish I could have helped."

He slides a hand over mine. "You did. I was a little better after meeting you. After the move to Sanford the family was happier, so I eased up. Yet things went down with Mum's mood. Having you to talk to helped."

I cup his hands and whisper, "What happened after the football game?"

"When the doctor checked me out, he could tell straight away something was up with me. He told my parents I wasn't looking after myself. I guess I can't blame my dad. His whole focus is my mum. But they didn't ask me what was wrong. They sent me to other people to do that.”

As I squeeze his hand, my eyes run up and down this beautiful boy and I want so much to take his pain away. “I’m so sorry, B.”

“Can you distract me?” he asks. “Tell me something new that’s going on.”

“You sure?”

He wipes under his eyes. “Anything. I don’t want to think about my stuff for a while.”

“Hmm, lemme think. Well, dance rehearsals are driving me nuts. They are non-stop because our end of year concert is coming up.”

“Can I watch?”

Ba-boom. “If you want. Just don’t make me nervous.”

He cracks a smile. “Ok, I’ll hide in the back.”

“And besides that...” Gigantic sigh. “My dad is getting married.”

“What? How did that happen? I’ve only been gone a month, right?”

“It’s happening super fast.”

“*Whoah*.” He intertwines our fingers. “You ok?”

“Yeah, maybe. I mean, my parents will never be back together, and Tara seems to make Dad happy.”

“Is your Dad here?”

“No, just Mum and Charli.”

“They ok with everything?”

“Bout the same.”

“One day I’ll have to meet your dad.”

“If you come to the concert?”

“You’re ok with me going?”

“Yes, if you can.”

He lets go of my hand and slides away from me. “Tell me what happened between you and Chloe’s brother.”

“Nothing, I swear.” Huge breath in. “He started talking to me when I was well over tipsy. He kissed me and next minute I woke up in his bed. He said I fell asleep in there by myself. He only stayed because he thought some drunk guy might go in if I were alone. I swear, I didn't mean to kiss him."

His face is pale. "Don't go near that guy again."

Guilt and sickness swirl inside me. "Ok."

"He kissed you when you were too drunk to know what you were doing." He finds my eyes. "That's not a good guy."

I bite my lip hard. I didn't consider this situation as not being my fault.

"I left that party because my mum was really mad that I picked hanging out with you over sitting by her side," he says. "Her mood was really manic all week. I left because she started having tremors. I'm sorry I didn't explain it to you. I was too in my head about it being my fault."

"Oh, Bryce," my voice grows small as I clutch his hand. "If anything, it's my fault. She hated me."

His hand falls limp in mine. "So, it's all one big mess?"

"I want to be clear, not your fault."

"You were mad at me, I could tell."

"At the time... but with what I know now, it's convincingly not your fault."

"I thought maybe you'd want nothing to do with me."

"As if." I shake off the tension in my shoulders and ask, "What was that before about us not breaking up?"

He fidgets awkwardly, watching his shoes. "Nothing was ever said about us not being together... we just stopped talking. Or, did you think we broke up?"

"I was sure you dumped me. That you hated me."

His face softens. "I don't hate you."

"Maybe you should have? I was pretty selfish."

His hand grips mine. "I can't go from love to hate that quickly."

"Bryce, I love you so much."

He pecks me on the lips before pulling away and whispering, "I can't say it right now. But I don't hate you."

"We don't need to rush anything. I'm sure of that."

"Thanks."

I take in the garbled noises of everyone in the living room and ask, "Is this the first time so many people have been in this house?"

"Yeah, it's weird."

We sit side-by-side, hand-in-hand, in comfortable silence and I'm ready to catch him anytime he needs to fall.

I check my reflection to make sure the false lashes are perfectly glued. Tiffany stands over me, dousing me in hairspray. My forehead is sticky.

"That's enough, Tiff. Stop."

"Ok, ok," Tiffany says, moving onto Chloe who is reapplying hot pink lipstick.

I edge towards the closed curtain and take in the muffled sounds of the audience. I hope my family aren't too close to the front. Just gotta stare into the darkness and not find the faces. Butterflies take over at the thought of Bryce watching me dance. I haven't heard much from him. He hasn't been doing well, so I wouldn't be surprised if he's not here. It'd be ok if he's not here.

"Get ready for places," Tiffany whispers.

Our group takes over the stage. I close my eyes. *Remember, you can't see the faces.* I open my eyes and put on my cheek-hurting stage-smile. The music starts and the curtains draw. We swing our hips with one popped knee as the audience applauds with a few random wolf whistles.

I lift my chin and smile at the shadowy audience. The girls in front shimmy to the side and I stand tall, ready to glide into my solo. I zone out the cheers and focus on my moves. I'm nimble yet strong. Adrenaline inside, goosebumps outside. The placement of my hands is careful and the bounce in my steps agile. Booming claps bring me back to reality as my solo ends.

As we come to a close another group takes over the stage. I can't stop smiling. Totally pumped for the next routines, even though I was cast out of other solos.

"Sweetheart, you did so well," Mum cheers, as I meet her after the concert. She gives me the best hug.

"Thanks, Mum."

"You were really good, Brit," Charli says. It's obvious she's eager to hug me, so I nod and let her.

Over Charli's shoulder I spy Dad, Tara and her kids. I'm glad they're hanging back, Mum deserves that respect.

Our friends rush to circle Chloe. I crane my neck for signs of Bryce. He's not with them. I thought it'd be too much for him. It's ok.

I ignore the group and go to Dad and the new family. Dad looks different somehow. Like, I don't know him. He seems at ease... and happy. Maybe this is the real him? Maybe the uptight nag is dead?

Tara swoops me into a hug, telling me I'm amazing and marvellous. I hug her back. If she can make me like my dad and make it easy to be around him, I'm happy she's now in my life.

I run into Dad's arms. "Thanks for being here."

He holds me close and I listen to the tempo of his heart. "Of course, Sweetheart. Wouldn't miss it for the world."

Nick and Shae congratulate me on my performance. Shae makes a move like she might hug me, but I don't embrace either of them. I don't know them. They will be part of my life. I thank them for being here. Baby steps.

We make our way out of the performance centre. I follow Mum to the car and hear my name called. I pivot in every direction, recognising the voice instantly. I spot him and rush towards him.

"Sorry, I wanted to come earlier," Bryce says flatly. "I tried to get ready, but—"

"Oh, don't worry," I interrupt. "I didn't think I'd see you at all."

"Sorry."

"No, it's fine. Honestly. It's been a horrendous week for you."

"I caught the end of your show though." He tries a smile. "It was really great watching you. Made me forget what was going on with me for a while."

I smile softly. "I'm glad."

"Oh, Brycey," Chloe squeaks, sidling up to us and linking arms with Bryce. "You came. I'm so glad you could make it."

Bryce's face grows sour and he pulls away from her. "Yeah. Can you give us a minute?"

Chloe nudges her head for me to scram.

I fold my arms. "No, you."

Chloe's eyebrows raise. "Huh?"

Bryce frees his arm. "Can you leave Brit and me to talk, Chloe?"

Her mouth hangs open, her eyes wide and stunned.

"Now," I push.

She shines a beauty-queen smile. "Sure, Bryce, anything for you. But you should know something before I leave. Brittany hooked up with my brother again while you were away."

His mouth falls open and he blinks rapidly.

"I did not!" I snap at Chloe.

She folds her arms and leans in. "Um, yes you did. Your hands were all over each other, amongst other things."

"Get out of my face, Chloe!" I yell.

Charli rushes to my side and shoves Chloe.

Chloe pushes Charli back. "What the hell, you skank."

I put an arm in front of Charli. "Stop."

Chloe touches Bryce's shoulder. "You don't need this. We can get outta here."

He eyes her. "You need to leave."

She squints. "With you?"

He shakes his head slowly. "No."

Chloe purses her lips and backs away. When she's gone, I repeat, "She's lying. That didn't happen."

Charli fidgets in place and whispers, "Everything ok?"

"Give us a minute, Charli." I pull Bryce to the side and start again. "I did see him again and he did try to kiss me. I didn't let him. I didn't tell you because it was nothing to tell."

He rubs his head and groans. "I can't listen to any more of this."

"Aw shit, I'm sorry."

He drops his hands. "No, all these bullshit rumours. Can they just stop?" He holds onto my arms. "I just wanted to see you. I just wanted to be happy."

I bite hard on my lip. All I want is for him to be happy.

"She's such a bitch," he whispers.

"Not news."

He puffs out a laugh which takes me by surprise.

"Is that a smile?"

His smile grows bigger. "I forgot how funny you are. Thanks for all the random texts this week. Sorry that I didn't reply much. I did like them."

I wipe my brow. "*Phew.* I was scared I was annoying."

"No, it was good. You are a true friend."

"I'm happy being just that. After everything, I'm so happy we can still talk, even if you can't respond right away."

Bryce looks past me and asks, "Is that your dad?"

I turn. "Sure is. With his fiancé and her kids. You still want to meet him?"

He nods and squeezes my hand as we walk over to them.

"Dad, this is my friend, Bryce."

Dad cocks an eyebrow and smiles at us. "The friend, huh." He extends his hand to Bryce. "Nice to meet you."

Bryce shakes Dad's hand. "You too, Mr Matthews."

Tara giggles, rubbing Dad's shoulder and her bright eyes take me in. Everything might be ok.

30

Charli

"Here's the transcript you need for your exchange paperwork," Mr Palmer says, handing me a piece of paper after English class.

"Thank you, Sir."

"We'll miss you around here."

"I'll miss this place too. But I'll be back."

Mr Palmer pats my shoulder. "Take care of yourself, Charlotte."

I leave the classroom with Reece to meet Kellie for lunch.

"Just let me explain," Will huffs, standing by Kellie at her locker.

Kellie folds her arms, tensely looking away from him.

"I didn't want you to get hurt again," Will persists.

Reece whispers to me, "What's happening?"

"Something dumb," I reply and march towards the pair.

"Charli, it's ok," Kellie says.

I grab onto her arm. "Come with us."

"Chazzy, give us a minute, would ya," Will says.

I scoff. "As if."

Kellie wriggles from my grip and says to Will. "Will, leave it be. You're obviously embarrassed to be seen around me."

"No, that's not it," he rushes. "Ok, ok, I may have had one dumb thought like that and freaked. Honestly, I didn't want anyone to give you crap... like before."

Kellie frowns. "I'm a big girl."

"I know, I know. You can handle yourself. I just feel like a dirtbag about all the stuff that happened to you before. How can I make it up to you?"

"By being reliable," she replies. "Stop listening to all the gossip and make your own friggin decisions. Or do I have to hold your hand through life?"

He blushes and scratches his head. "I wouldn't mind that."

Kellie laughs, shaking her head. "You are such a dickhead."

Will grins at her. "C'mon, that's what attracts you to me."

"*Pa-ha!* Whatever ya reckon."

I slam my hands over my eyes. "Not this again."

Will squeezes me in a bear hug. "You know you love me, Chazzy."

"Good lord, please let me go."

He lets me go and softly says to Kellie, "I promise to be better."

Smile lines crinkle around Kellie's eyes and she rubs Wills arm. "We can give this thing a go."

Will's throws his fists in the air. "YES."

Kellie giggles. "Goofball."

Will kisses Kellie's cheek and then asks me, "Did I hear right? Are you leaving on a jet plane?"

"Correct. Passport, visa and accommodation are all taken care of."

"How dare you leave us for a whole year," Kellie pouts.

"It's not a whole year, it's only nine months."

"*Only.*"

"There's always video chat."

Kellie attacks me with a hug. "I'm gonna miss you so much!"

As my bones creak, I can't help grinning. "I'm not leaving this second, but I miss you already."

I walk into the kitchen to a hurrah of *happy birthdays*. Mum and Sophia rush me with hugs and kisses. It's all a bit much at eight o'clock on a Saturday morning, but at least I'm back to getting sleep at night.

"Is your sister up?" Mum asks, overly excited.

"It's still early," I reply. "She will probably come down around midday."

"It's your sweet sixteen," Mum gushes. "She needs to be up."

"Come now, Ms Matthews," Sophia says. "Let the girl sleep."

Mum chuckles to herself. "Brittany was first born and is always last one out of bed."

Sophia passes me an already-brewed cup of tea and I thank her with a massive smile. I sit in the breakfast nook as Mum considers going on a bakery run. I sip my tea as she weighs the merits of croissants over danishes. She ultimately decides on both and promises to be back quickly.

When I put down my empty cup, Brittany shocks me by walking into the kitchen. "You're up?"

"Happy birthday to you too, dear sister," she mocks.

I slide out of the nook and we meet in a hug. "Happy birthday, Brit."

"Happy birthday, Sweetheart," Sophia says, kissing Brittany's cheek. "We thought we wouldn't see you until midday."

"*Geez*, it is my birthday. I'm too excited to stay asleep."

Sophia walks behind the island bench. "Well, now my timing is all off. Give me a minute to make your cuppa."

Brit and I sit opposite each other in the nook. "Where's Mum," she asks.

"Gone to the bakery," I reply. "She'll flip it she wasn't here when you got up."

Brit grins and shrugs. "She'll just have to buy me more presents to make up for it."

When Sophia places a mug in front of Brittany, she leans down low and curves her arms around us. "Happy birthday, angels. I'm so glad I've been able to see you two grow up."

Brittany leans into Sophia. "We're glad you're here too."

"Do you miss home?" I ask, rubbing a circle on Sophia's back.

"Of course," she replies. "But someone in the family had to come to Australia and send money home."

"Why didn't you bring your kids with you?" Brittany asks.

"We can't afford that," Sophia says, hugging us and then standing up straight. "Besides, they are being looked after now because I live here with you."

"Oh man," I say. "I was sad when Dad left for six months. How many years has it been since you've seen your kids?"

"Almost three," Sophia says. "It's no bother, you two will be out of the house soon, and I won't be needed here anymore."

Sophia walks to the other side of the kitchen. The shine in Brittany's eyes and the twist to her lips shows she feels the same way I do. We're sad for Sophia and her kids, but life in this house would be so hard without her.

We wait until Mum returns to exchange gifts. Amongst the crumbly bakery treats, I slide a small, wrapped box across to Brittany. "I hope you like it."

She tears through the wrapping and reveals the felt box. She pushes it open and my heart patters from her smile. She holds up an earring by her earlobe and gushes about how beautiful they are.

"I thought because they don't dangle you could wear them to school without the teachers going berserk," I say, as light flickers off the art-deco style crystal earrings.

Brittany launches over the table and pulls me into a hug. "Thanks, Sissy."

I fan my face, blushing as she lets me go.

Brittany hands me a similar box. "Think we had the same store in mind."

I smile as I run a finger along the tape. It'd be too funny to find a pair of the same earrings in here. I open the box to a sterling silver pendant on a chain.

"Some reason I was adamant about getting you jewellery," Brittany says, "but you're so hard to buy for. I was clueless until you decided to go overseas. It's a Saint Christopher pendant. He keeps travellers safe."

"Oh Brittany," Mum says. "That's so thoughtful."

I rub my chest. "Brit, I love it."

"I'm glad."

I squeeze her hand and thank her.

"I still can't believe you're up and leaving like this," Brit says.

"I know. I'm so nervous-excited."

Brittany laughs. "I'd be crapping myself."

"It won't be the same around here without you, Charli," Sophia says.

Mum wipes a tear from under her eye. "I don't know how I will let you on that plane."

I pat my eyes dry and joke, "Well, you'd better."

Mum has always had this thing about giving us matching birthday presents. It's not like Brittany and I ever try to be matching throughout the year, but it's her thing. We open matching beaded bracelets, luxury bath products, and then what Mum called 'the big gift.' One big box that Brittany and I have to open together.

"A shared gift?" Brittany wrinkles her nose before opening.

"C'mon, it'll be fun," Mum enthuses.

We tear open each side and lift off the lid. Inside are tickets, bikinis, sunglasses, fake tan and a dozen palm tree figurines.

I scan a ticket. "Fiji?"

"Yes! A trip for the three of us," Mum says.

"That's awesome," Brittany cheers.

Mum squeezes my shoulder. "I bought them before I knew about Spain. I've had the travel agent move the dates."

Brittany scoffs. "We have to wait until she gets back?"

Mum shakes her head. "No. Charli leaves January second. There's plenty of time between when school ends and then."

I slink in my chair, smiling. "That's exactly what I need."

Mum claps her hands together. "I'm so glad you girls are excited."

I eye Sophia in the corner. "Mum... when we go to Fiji, can we send Sophia to the Philippines to visit her family?"

Brittany gasps excitedly. "Yes, can we?"

"Oh, no, Ms Matthews," Sophia says, waving her hands. "I have plenty of tidying up around here to do."

Mum looks at Brittany and me, to Sophia, and then back to us. She relaxes and smiles at Sophia. "Ten days with your family will be a better way to spend Christmas."

Sophia's eyes water and her anime smile lights up the room. "Thank you. Thank you very much."

Dad arrives at the house at midday, riding up in a Ferrari-red Beetle Brittany picked out. Mum does the biggest eye roll when Dad toots the horn. Brittany is hysterical. Squeaking and squawking and jumping up and down.

Dad urges Brittany to get in the driver's seat and Mum reminds her she doesn't have her Learner's yet. Giddy Brittany stays in the car as Dad meets me on the front porch.

We sit on the step and he says, "I'm not exactly thrilled with the thought of you on the other side of the planet. Let's call it Scared Dad Syndrome." He throws an arm around my shoulders. "I know you'll do us proud. Keep those grades up and send me heaps of photos."

I lean into him. "I will."

The house grew louder with Kellie's arrival. She gave me a new e-reader to take away with me and then proceeded to crush my bones with her *hugs*. "You can't leave me, you just can't."

She is a stark comparison to Bryce who sits quietly by Brittany. He smiles while watching Kellie though. I'm glad he's doing better. I was taken aback when he arrived and kissed Brittany on the cheek. Are they back together? If so, that was super quick, but maybe I don't have all the details.

"I got you this," he says to Brittany.

Brittany's grin lights up the room as she pulls out a crystal pendant from its box.

"That's gorgeous," I say.

Brittany clutches her heart. "I love it, thank you."

They hug and I'm still trying to piece together their relationship.

"So, big party tonight?" Kellie says.

"*Ugh,* yes," I reply. "Mum still has it in her head we need joint birthday parties."

"Shuddup, it'll be fun," Brittany says.

"Whatever."

Kellie moves over to Brittany to examine the new necklace around her neck, and Bryce says to me, "I hear you're leaving for Spain."

I jitter. "Yes, I can't believe it."

"You'll be fine. You'll come home speaking fluent Spanish."

"That'd be nice after my trashy year in Spanish class."

"Make sure you send us a postcard," Bryce says.

"Ok," I say, nudging towards my sister, "make sure you take care of this one while I'm gone."

Bryce smiles at Brittany. "Not a problem."

I've never felt more uncomfortable in my own home. Brittany is loving the swarms of people taking over our living room, but this is my nightmare. How in the world did Mum think this would be a good idea?

Kellie stands by me, even when Will tries to steal her away. Like, c'mon dude. It's my birthday. People keep stopping by me, saying 'happy birthday' and giving me awkward hugs. My shudder-o-metre is about to crack.

"It's nice how many people are acknowledging you," Kellie says. "Not just Brit."

"Yeah sure. It'd be just as polite to not touch me."

Kellie laughs at me and I notice her holding hands with Will. "Man, just go. It's fine, you two can canoodle in the corner."

"Charli, no," Kellie says, dropping Will's hand. "I'm sticking with you."

"I'm fine, really." I eye Will. "He's about to burst."

"Thanks, Charli," Will says and rushes Kellie away.

The only thing my birthday is missing is Reece. He's been at the naval base for something to do with Eric. I decide waiting on the front steps to his house would be a level up from the party and push my way through to the front door to escape.

"I can't go in there, it's my ex's place."

My gaze runs up the front path and the air is smacked out of me. Travis hangs by his car and his friends walk towards my house. *Just get to Reece's, just get to Reece's.* I barrel forward with my head down.

"I wasn't going to go in or anything," Travis says as I turn towards Reece's house.

I stop and keep my back to him.

"Happy birthday."

My tongue is dry and sticks to the roof of my mouth as I pinch the bridge of my nose.

"I wasn't going to go inside, but I was hoping to see you." Something clunks so I look over my shoulder. He's put something wrapped on the car bonnet.

"What is that?"

"It's for you."

"Why... Why did you buy me something?" I stammer.

He folds his arms, staring at it. "Actually, I got it when we were still together. Before I screwed everything up."

My face is as stony as I can keep it. "You cudda returned it."

"No, I couldn't. When you see it, you'll see how it's made for you."

My eyes are drawn to the gift. I gnaw the inside my cheek as my feet sink into the cement path.

He puts his hand on the gift. "It's ok. You can open it."

I look away. "I dunno."

"Charli, I don't think I can say it enough," he says stepping towards me. "I am truly sorry."

I'm paralysed as he stands in front of me.

"You deserved better and all I was thinking about was sex. Everyone was in my ear and I got obsessed. I know it's not an excuse. Nothing has been good since losing you." He takes my hands. "You're the only person I've ever confided in. Everything is worthless if I don't have you."

I shut my eyes, so my welling tears won't run. A flash of GiGi appears in my mind. I open my eyes and reef my hands away. "You were with GiGi."

He rubs a hand over his face. "I know... it just sorta happened."

My eyebrows raise at him.

"She was just kinda there and then always there."

"You replaced me. Quickly."

"I'm sorry. I'm sorry about her being a bitch. Especially at the formal. We weren't going together then. She told people we were, and I'm sorry she made you think we were, straight after our relationship... She was spreading rumours and I was hoping you weren't listening."

"I've heard things about the two of you."

"Things just kinda spiralled after a party."

"So the rumours were true?"

"Eventually." Shame draws his face. "It wasn't worth it. I wish I was never with her."

My voice cracks, "But you were."

"It was only about sex, and I can tell you now, sex means nothing to me. I'm completely ashamed I was so caught up with it, and I'm sorry my actions scared you." His eyes gleam with tears. "I can't believe I tried to force you into something. I'll never do it again."

I hold myself and nod. Part of me wants to thank him for acknowledging his actions, but I'm too overwhelmed to talk.

His hands slide down my arms. "No one has mattered to me like you do. I still love you."

I croak a sob and stare at his shoes as a tear rolls down my cheek.

"Charli?"

"I'm sorry I didn't make it to the cinema. I would have but..."

"Don't mention it. I shouldn't have asked."

His hands creep by my fingers and I latch onto him. Our fingers intertwine and for a moment its six months ago.

"You wanna open your present?"

Without answering, we move to the car. My hands shake as I peel away the paper, revealing a bark-covered book.

"It's a journal," he says. "For your poetry."

I run my fingers over the indentations. "It's stunning." I open the book to rich, cream paper and notice something inscribed on the first page. I recognise a quote from '*An Affair to Remember*' and shut the book before reading more. "I can't do this."

"Huh?"

"Travis, we can't pick up where we left off."

"I know but..."

"I'm going to Spain on exchange." Surprise takes him back a step. "And you're going off to uni next year. It's too much to even think about us being us again."

"We can still text or call," he offers. "Like, just friends."

I shake my head. "I'm going because I need a fresh start. This year has been one massive punch in the gut. It's been really hard without you. Every time something happened I just wanted to talk to you about it. To lay in your arms. To feel safe. Now I need to try something new. On my own. I have to stop trying to please someone else."

He steps close to me and brushes back my hair. "It's gonna be really hard not being in the same town as you."

I nod and his face inches closer to mine. I close my eyes as his lips press on mine. Relief coats my body. For a moment everything feels right, and then I pull away.

"I have to go," I whisper.

He points to the house. "Isn't this your party?"

I shake my head. "Bye, Travis."

He hands me the journal. I take it, hugging it to my chest and keep walking towards Reece's house.

At the gate, I break into a run and rush to his front door, banging furiously.

No answer.

I race around to the back of the house, hoping a sliding door is open. On the deck, Reece kicks back reading a book with his golden retriever, Sammy, by his feet.

He sees me, lowers the book and sits up straight. "I swear I was coming to the party." His eyes form slits. "You look scared?"

I march towards him, holding the book out in front.

"What's that?"

I plonk down beside him. "Travis just gave it to me."

"What? What was he doing there?"

I huff and rub my temples. "It doesn't even matter. I walked away from him."

"He wanted to get back together?"

My eyes water and I nod my head.

"What are you going to do with this?" he asks, tapping the journal. "Throw it in the bin."

I hug it again. "No."

"Why not?"

I clear my throat. "It's pretty."

"You keep it and you'll be holding onto him."

"Since when do you know about relationships?"

He gets up and walks to the house. "Since when don't I know you? Wait here." Reece pats his thigh, signalling for Sammy to follow him inside.

Reece returns with a long, thin, crudely wrapped gift.

I gasp and stand up. "I know what that is."

He hands it to me, and I tear at the paper quicker than any other gift. I am holding the skateboard I had my eye on. "Dude! I love it. Let's test it out."

"You don't want to go back to your party?"

I toss a thumb back at my house. "*That* is not my party. Let's go to the skatepark."

"I'll text Kellie."

"No just us. She's, ah, tied up."

"*Eww*, Will?"

I laugh and beckon him to follow me to the road.

My skateboard glides along the tar like a dream. I thank Reece again as he boards beside me.

The skateboard feels different in the rink, but it hasn't magically improved my skills. Reece and I are silent as we board, which is welcomed after the bombardment of noise at my house.

Reece and I sit on the edge of the rink, dangling our legs in the air. "It's going to be weird without you," he says. "You're part of my routine now."

"I'm going to be sad to leave you."

"I'll miss you."

"I'll miss you, too.

Being by his side is comfortable. It's easy. It's exactly the kind of relationship I should have more of in my life. He plants his hand beside me and I rest mine on top. He looks at me, and before he questions, I push my lips on his.

Reece reefs his head back and I open my eyes to a revolted expression.

"Oh, uh, I'm," I stammer, "I'm sorry."

He shuffles away from me and says, "Maybe I should get Kellie."

I sink my chin into my hands. What the hell am I doing?

Reece walks away from the rink, texting on his phone and I feel lower than low. Am I just trying to push Travis out of my head? Some small part of me hopes Reece could be a better version of Travis... but that doesn't mean I can ruin what I have with Reece.

I gnaw inside my cheek.

I need out of this town.

31

Brittany

"Nice car, Brittany," Madison says.

I place a hand on my popped hip and flick my hair Chloe-style. "Yeah, my dad does all right with the b'day presents."

Fiona picks up the pendant on my necklace. "Is this from Bryce?"

"Yes. Isn't it beautiful? A crystal heart."

"It's gorgeous. I love all the colours that reflect with the light."

"Is he here?" Madison asks, peering around the room.

"Yeah, he's here. Just out getting some air."

Fiona rolls her eyes. "He's not doing that again, is he?"

I clear my throat. "It's cool. I know what's going on with him."

Madison nudges me. "I thought you'd be glued to his hip, now that you're back together."

"Don't worry yourself, girls. We're good. Excuse me while I greet more guests."

My dorky smile won't rub off as people keep throwing attention at me. I'm finally the star.

"Happy birthday, Matty!" Will shouts, pulling me into a bear hug.

I giggle even though he's cutting off air. "Thanks, Will."

He lets me go and Kellie appears by his side. "Hey, have you seen Charli?"

"No, I haven't."

Kellie furiously types on her phone. "I just checked her bedroom and the backyard and she's not here. D'you think she's gone down to the beach?"

"I really don't—"

"Ah, Reece is with her." She pats Will's arms. "I've gotta go."

"What?" He yelps. "Party's just gettin started."

Kellie shrugs, walking away. "Have fun."

As Kellie leaves through the front door, Meah pushes her way in.

"Happy birthday," she cheers, holding out a gift.

"Thanks," I say, balancing the box in my arms. What the hell did she get me? I awkwardly fumble my way to the gift table as she makes her way into the party.

"Sorry I'm late," Meah says, playing with her slightly blonder hair. "I was hanging with Chloe and time just flew by."

"Oh, that's cool," I say as my heart shrinks. "Have fun?"

"Yeah," Meah says, scanning the party. "She's on her way. Jace started pawing at her so I took my cue." She turns to me with an exaggerated smile. "So, I could see my bestie on her birthday."

She leans in to smooch my cheek and I try to stop wincing.

"So glad you're here," I say with my stage smile. *Bestie?* Kellie was here for Charli all day, and Meah rocks up well after the party has begun.

"Chloe said she'll be here soon," Meah says, walking further into the party.

"Great." She'll only steal my spotlight when she gets here.

I move from the table and gasp as I run into someone.

"Sorry, Britty," Bryce says, standing me upright.

I giggle, taking his hands. "That's ok. Are you having a good time?"

He nods, but his closed-mouth smile tells another story. I note the still open front door and lead him outside. We sit on the front porch step and watch the new influx of guests. I get a lot of side-hugs and *happy birthdays*. Bryce shies away beside me so I persuade everyone to move inside.

"We should join your party," he offers.

"No, it's cool. I don't mind sitting out here." I fidget. I don't want to say it, but I should. "You know, if you're not comfortable being here you can go home."

"No," he replies much more animated. "No, I want to be here. Really. It's just..."

"What?"

"I notice how people are looking at me now."

"No one thinks badly of you."

"They look at me like I'm weird."

"They don't know what's going on with you. They just make up stories."

"I hate that."

I sigh. "I hate that."

He grabs onto my hand and stands up. "It's your birthday party, and dammit, I'm gonna dance with the birthday girl."

A smile lifts my face. I stand and go inside with him. Sean has messed with the music so EDM fills the living room instead of my bubbly pop, but I can make this work. Bryce holds my waist and I blush, draping my arms around his neck. Like magic, we fall into our rhythm of slow dancing to fast songs.

He glances around the room, so I run a hand through his hair and gently swing him to face me. Smile lines crinkle below his eyes. Our foreheads rest together and even though the room is noisy, I listen to his faint breaths like it's the only music I need to hear.

"Happy birthday, beautiful," he whispers.

I whisper, "Thank you."

His hands push further up my sides and tingles rush down my spine. I edge closer to him and his shoulders shake. *Ba-boom.*

"Hey birthday girl!" Chloe shouts in my ear and Bryce and I jolt apart.

"Err, hi."

She wraps me in a hug and plants a kiss on my cheek. "Having fun?"

"Of course." My heart is in my throat and it's pounding in my ears.

Jace gives me a one-armed hug and then moves onto Bryce with a, "Sup?"

"You look super cute, Brit," Chloe says. "Don't be mad at me for being late, like, I'm totally here now to save your party."

"Save it?"

She pinches my cheek like I'm a child. "Don't worry, hun, you don't have to thank me."

Did she hang with Meah purely to spite me? My brain can't even imagine the two of them one-on-one.

She releases me and waggles her hips further into the living room, which erupts with *hey Chloe*. I dig my shoes into the carpet and grit my teeth as she takes over my party. I could use the ammunition Damien gave me. Spread something nasty about her. But she covered the Lucas thing so quickly... and what would it say about me? Plus, Bryce hates rumours. I'd be as bad as Chloe is in his eyes.

Nervous energy bubbles inside me from being so close to him moments earlier. I turn to the boys and take a step back when it's only Jace. Jace passes me to follow his girlfriend while I scan the room. I walk through the foyer and into the kitchen, relieved to find Bryce by the island bench with Sophia.

"Sorry," Bryce says, holding up a cup. "Needed some water."

"You need to stop apologising," I say, walking over to them.

"How's the party going, gorgeous?" Sophia asks.

"Great. I think Charli left though."

Sophia shakes her head, holding onto laughter. "Your mother can't see that you two are growing up. She always wants you to be her baby girls in matching party dresses. I'm surprised Charli stayed as long as she did."

"True." I suggest to Bryce, "Wanna go to the beach?"

He throws a thumb back at the living room. "What about your party?"

"I don't care about it."

Bryce follows me out of the house, but I pivot. "Can you wait one sec? I'll be right back."

"Sure."

I move quickly so no one at the party sees me. I move down the corridor and knock on the door of Mum's study. I had asked her to be out of the house for my party, and it didn't go down well. She promised to hide away in here.

I open the door and sneak in as Mum says, "What's up, Sweetheart?"

I scuff towards her and put on a sad face. "Um, Mum, there's stuff going on at the party I don't like."

Mum rips her glasses off and gets into protective mode. "What's going on?"

"Some people brought alcohol and I'm not really comfortable being around it."

Mum stands, fuming. "I'll kick those kids out."

I stop her and say, "Charli left because she didn't like it either. I think we'd both be happier if the party was over. Can you do something to kick them all out?"

She frowns and rubs my arms. "Ok, if that's what you really want. I'm sorry you're not enjoying your party."

I lean into her. "It's ok. It has been fun, and I still had a great birthday. I'm going down to the beach with Bryce, ok?"

"Ok, Sweetheart." She lifts my chin and smiles. "You're such a good girl."

Ok, the guilt is overflowing, but it's my birthday and I should be able to spend it with the people I want. Popularity means nothing compared to what I have with Bryce. I'm outta the house in a flash and Bryce and I make it to the sand. I grabbed a throw rug from the deck we sit on together, and I tell him what I told my mum.

"*Whoah*, you sabotaged your own party?"

"I'd rather spend time with you where we're both comfortable."

"What if everyone is pissed at you?"

"No, Mum won't say I said anything." My eyes bug. "*Geez*, she'd better not."

Bryce lets out a breathy laugh and I lean into him, resting my head on his shoulder.

"I wasn't always completely comfortable on the beach, you know," he says. "I like being down here and watching the waves crash, but the thought of having to take my shirt off freaked me out."

I lift my head and move away from him in case I'm making him uncomfortable.

"I didn't want anyone to say anything." His arms cross his stomach. "I just think I look too skinny."

"Still?"

"I'm working on it."

"We've all got stuff like that," I try. "It's scary for me to get down to a bikini."

"Uh, you have a good body," he replies, playfully nudging me.

I laugh and hope the swirling sea breeze will cool me down.

"Thanks for hanging out with me today," I say. "It's meant a lot."

"You're too special to me to miss this." He pulls me into his arms and kisses my forehead.

"I would have understood if this was too much."

"You already have. You kicked everyone out of your house."

Nervousness ripples through my body and I hold him tight. "I love you."

His face nuzzles by mine. "I love you too."

32

Charli

We stayed overnight at Dad's apartment so we could get ready here this morning. I couldn't bear to look at Mum. She says she's ok, yet the sadness in her eyes talks louder. I've repeated to myself countless times it's nearing two years since Dad moved into his apartment. Everything still seems so sudden.

It took me by surprise when Brittany accepted Shae's offer to go dress shopping. I can't even remember the last time we shopped together and then we go shopping with our future step-mum and step-sister. Brittany spent the trip asking Tara and Shae *getting-to-know-you* questions while I spent the time trying to keep my brain from imploding. Made worse by Shae trying to talk up Preston. *Ugh.* Can't everyone understand I'm leaving the country for a reason? I don't want to keep going over this stuff. I don't care that she tried to play wingman after he spotted me in the bookstore. I want a clean slate.

Thank goodness it's a family-only wedding.

Brittany and I walk into the living room in our matching lilac cocktail dresses. My cheeks hurt from smiling when she agreed to buy the same dress. She was snappy with me this morning when she did my makeup. Apparently, I was fidgeting too much and my eyes were too fluttery. When I pointed out her nerves, she went easier on me.

"Gosh, girls, you look breathtaking," Dad swoons, his hand resting over his heart.

Brittany hands Dad her phone. "Can you take a picture of us? Mum would love how matching we are."

"Sure, Sweetheart."

We curve our arms around each other. Brittany fixes a wayward curl of mine and I smile at her matching side-swept curls. Dad calls *cheese*, and we cuddle in.

"You look really handsome, Dad," I say as Brittany collects her phone.

Dad fumbles with his tie and smooths down his waistcoat. "I look good without the jacket?"

"*Pah*-lease," Brittany says, fixing Dad's tie. "It's a beach wedding. If anything, you're still overdressed."

"Are you nervous?" I ask him, rubbing my feeble stomach.

"Immensely," he says, grinning. He takes our hands. "Everything will be ok with my best girls by my side. Know that you two are still number one in my heart and your happiness is my number one priority."

My throat tightens and I blink back the welling in my eyes. I rush in to hug him and Brittany moves in on the other side.

The buzzer breaks up our group hug. Dad moves over to answer the call and Gran's voice calls out, "Do I have to climb all the way up there or are you going to come down here and meet me?"

Dad laughs, shaking his head. "It's ok, Mum. We're ready. We'll be right down."

Gran does her usual thing of retelling the hardships of leaving her house during the short drive to the ceremony location. My heart bangs against my chest as we park, and I glimpse the altar draped in silk and flowers.

Dad helps Gran out of the car and across the sand. She complains, again, about the unsuitable location. My heart slows as Dad keeps smiling. Nothing will disturb his good mood. He's happy. No, he's blissful.

The celebrant shakes Dad's hand and gives him a playful pep talk. Gran sits on a fold-out chair while Brittany and I stand by Dad's side. I tremble as the tide roars and waves smash, eyes peeled to the carpark for them to arrive.

"It's ok," Brittany whispers, rubbing my arm.

I swallow hard and force a smile. Dad's smile hasn't shifted. *Just be happy, Charli. Just be happy, too.*

A car rounds the carpark and stops. I'm two seconds off fainting. I clutch Brittany's hand to keep me upright. She whispers, "It's ok," again and I try to believe her.

Alyssa walks towards us first. Her white dress balloons around her as she carries a small wicker basket. As she nears, she tosses rose petals onto the sand and we *awe*.

Shae follows, her arms linked with who I guess is her grandmother. Lastly, Nick is arm-and-arm with his mother who is stunning in an ivory and lace, boho-style gown. A slit by her left leg drapes the dress effortlessly to the sand. Pearls glisten from Tara's ears and neckline. The wildflowers in her bouquet sprawl above her hands. My shaking settles as they walk towards us. My dad wipes away a tear. I smile, I'm genuinely glad he's found a woman who makes him this happy.

Tara stands by Dad and her kids smile and wave. The celebrant begins the ceremony and I'm mesmerised by the light in Tara's shining eyes.

"I, Robert Michael Matthews, take you, Tara Lynn Cooper, to be my lawfully wedded wife. To have and to hold, from this day forward.

For better, for worse. For richer, for poorer. In sickness and in health. Until death parts us."

I see stars as Tara repeats the vows. Brittany takes my hand again and I squeeze, letting her know I'm ok.

"Tara and Robert, you have expressed your love to one another through the commitment and promises you have made. It is with this in mind that I pronounce you husband and wife."

I breathe again after *the first kiss*. Dad and *his new wife*. It happened. I check Brittany's ok and she's smiling. So, it really is ok?

Dad pulls us into a hug. "Can you believe it, girls?"

"Congrats, Dad," Brittany says.

"I'm happy for you," I say.

"Thanks, my angels."

He lets us go and we get a view of Tara hugging her kids. We all meet at the altar and the celebrant gathers us for a *family photo*.

The snap is taken, and Shae moves towards me, arms wide. "Hi Sis."

We hug and I reply, "Let's ease into that."

"It was a beautiful wedding," she says.

I nod. "Yeah, it was."

Tara closes in on me. "Hi darling, I'm so happy you're here." She hugs me and ropes Brittany in at the same time. "I'm so happy you girls are coming into our family."

"You look exquisite," Brittany says.

"Congratulations," I add.

We move on to a restaurant Dad has booked out for our party of nine.

"Why'd you have to be twin girls," Nick says across the table. "I already have two sisters. I don't need more ganging up on me."

Brittany giggles beside me. "Maybe you can bribe us to be on your side. I take chocolates and lots of them."

"Are you guys already plotting?" Shae asks.

"Mind your own business," Nick jokes.

Shae plays with her food and says, "I can't believe we'll be moving into that big house."

"Well, you won't really be there," Nick replies. "You're going off to uni."

"I know. It's still weird to be coming back to a new home."

"We'll only be there part of the time," I say, glancing at Brittany. "If that."

"It'll be nicer than that apartment," Brittany adds.

The clinking of glasses stops our conversation. Dad stands at the head of the table, holding a champagne flute high.

"I'm so delighted to see all your faces at the table," Dad begins. "That we can bring two families together and that we have the support of our loving kids. All of you are so wonderful and you light up our days. I want to especially thank my magnificent daughters, who look stunning today and are my whole reason for being. I love you two more than you can imagine. Thank you for being here today."

I pat my eyes dry and blow Dad a kiss. Everyone raises a glass to toast the newlyweds.

> **(Me)** Can you meet me at the boardwalk?
>
> **(Kellie)** Sure. Now?
>
> **(Me)** 10 mins.

I clear my plate and whisper to Brittany that I'm leaving.

"What?"

"I'm meeting Kellie."

"Now? You have to stay for the cake."

"I can't."

I get up and move around to Dad and Tara. I kiss their cheeks, looping my arms around them. "I'm going to go."

"What?" they ask at once.

"I have a bit of a headache." I rub my temples for show. "It's been a really nice day."

They stand and thank me again for being here. After too many hugs, I wriggle myself away, calling out a group goodbye to everyone else.

"How was it?" Kellie asks when I join her on the boardwalk.

"Rough."

"Did you speak up at that part where they ask for objections?"

"First of all, they didn't have that part, and second of all I wouldn't have objected."

"In front of everyone."

I huff and hunch over the railing. "At all, at this point. He looked so damned happy. He's happy, Kel."

She throws an arm over my shoulders and hunches with me. "Isn't that a good thing?"

"I guess."

"Him being happy is a good thing. He'll be happier around you and Brit and you won't have to compete for his attention. He married Tara, now he doesn't have to share time between you. You'll visit him and she'll already be there, so he'll be like, over her."

I snort. "Is that how you see it?"

"I think everything will be ok, Charli."

"I won't have to worry. I get to leave soon." Kellie punches my arm. "*OW*. What was that for?"

"Reminding me you're leaving me. How can you do this to me?"

I grin, fixing the drooping glasses on her face. "I'll be back before you know it."

"It won't be the same around here without you."

"It won't be the same going to school without you. I'll text you every day."

"Ya better." Kellie squeezes her arms around me. "Talked to Reece lately?"

I slide along the railing. "I've texted him."

"What was the deal on your birthday? I can't believe you kissed him. When I caught up with you two there was so much distance and more silence than usual."

"Has Reece talked to you about it?"

"No. It's Reece."

I rub my palms over my eyes. "Man, I don't know why I did it."

"Are you into him?"

I sigh at my feet. "He doesn't treat me like other boys do. Like, as bad as they do. Something hopeful flickered in me. It was dumb."

"Did it happen because of Travis?"

My jaw clenches and I hold onto to the rail. Part of me knows it's more than that, but I push away the thought. "I stuffed up and now Reece won't talk to me."

"You just freaked him out. He'll come around."

"We barely made eye contact before... but now at school it has felt so much worse."

"I'll talk to him. Keep trying with him before you leave for Spain."

"No, I will. I will." I fidget in place and whisper, "Are you packing anything?"

"Huh?"

"Like, something to puff on?"

"Ex-squeeze-me? Did Miss High-And-Mighty actually cross to the dark side?"

"It's a yes or no question."

She laughs. "Yes, of course. Let's head to the sand."

#

"No crazy parties," Dad says as we stand before the border control at the airport. "Keep your head down and your grades up."

"Please, Dad. I left my own sweet sixteen, as if I'm gonna party."

He rests his forehead against mine. "I know, Pumpkin, I'm just going to miss you like crazy."

I kiss his cheek. "Me too."

"Send us lots of photos," Tara says beside us.

"I'll try."

She clasps her hands together and talks to the ceiling. "It's just so exciting you get this opportunity. Make the most of it, Charli."

"Thanks, I will."

"I love you, Charlotte," Dad says, eyes welling.

"Love you too."

I move towards Mum who is a ball of tears. She grabs me and sobs, "I can't believe you're leaving, my gorgeous girl. It doesn't seem real."

"It is, Mum. I'm getting on that plane."

"I'm so glad we got that time in Fiji, even if it was all lounging by the pool while drinks were brought to us. I needed all the extra time I could get."

"I'm not dying, Mum. I'll be back in a couple of months."

"*Months*. That's the hardest part. I'm not ready for you to be away from home that long."

"Get ready," Brittany says behind me.

I leave Mum's arms and drag Brittany in with us.

"You're going to Spain!" Brittany cheers. "That's so freakin exciting."

"See, now that's the enthusiasm I need," I say, grinning.

"I'm crazy jealous," Brit says, "but I don't have your guts. You're so brave, Charlotte Jane."

411

"Thanks, Sis. It'll be weird to be apart from you."

"Super weird. Your crap music won't be blaring from the room next door."

"Um, try your room has the crap music."

We laugh as she pulls me in a tight hug. "I'll miss you and I love you."

I take in the sweet scent of her shampoo and smile. "I love you too."

Here grows the vine,
Up and up the line.
It swerves and jerks,
As it strives to rise
Inch, by inch, by inch.

Company only the shadow that lurks,
The top it hazily spies
Inch, by inch, by inch.

Tumbling off a step,
Courage it must be kept.
Wind and hail it may distress,
But from dark clouds a new bud can bloom
Inch, by inch, by inch.

Appearing as an entwined mess,
Surrendering from growth should not be so soon
Inch, by inch, by inch.

The ladder hard to grasp,
Time begins to lapse.
Its fragile form,
Vulnerable, immature
Inch, by inch, by inch.

Little journey seems far from norm,
But any weakness can find cure
Inch, by inch, by inch.

Here grows the vine,
Up and up the line.
Existence just starting,
So much ahead, yet so short
Inch, by inch, by inch.

On so many paths, darting,
Many hazards to be taught.
And if this all, or just a pinch,
Is taken in, at just an inch,
Life would still, be far from a cinch.

To be continued...

THANK YOU FOR READING

Don't miss the companion story **In Fiji** that follows the twins' vacation for their sweet sixteen. *Rumour has it*, there is a cute British boy, cliff jumping, waterfalls, and sisters swapping identities!

To continue with the **In It Together** Series:

#2 – In The Haze

#3 – In It Together

#4 – In The Beats

And many more to come!

Other books by Emily Bourne are the **Happily After When** Series, look out for the following books:

#1- JAZZ

#2 - ARIA

#3 - CARA

And many more to come!

CONNECT WITH THE AUTHOR

Visit author **Emily Bourne** in the following places:

Website: www.emilybourne.net
Instagram: @iemilybourne
Twitter: @iemilybourne
Facebook Page: Author Emily Bourne
YouTube: Emily Bourne